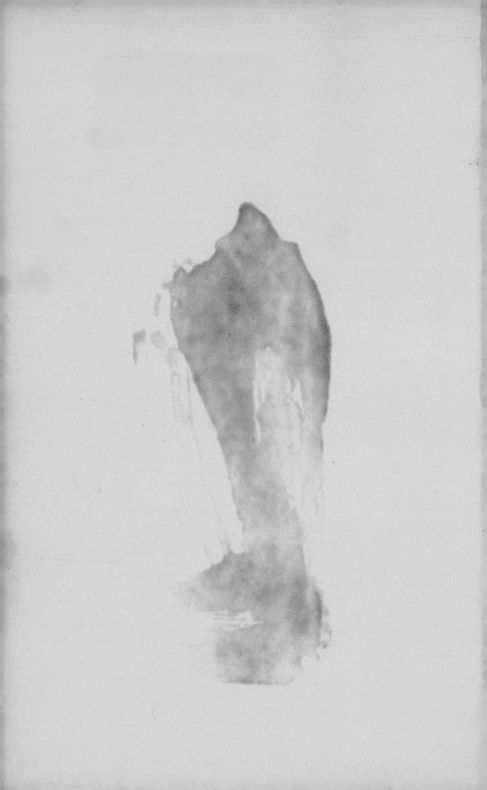

THREE-
CORNERED
COVER

GEORGE MARTON & CHRISTOPHER FELIX

THREE-CORNERED COVER

HOLT, RINEHART AND WINSTON

NEW YORK   CHICAGO   SAN FRANCISCO

Published simultaneously in Canada by Holt, Rinehart
and Winston of Canada, Limited.

ISBN: 0-03-001371-2
Library of Congress Catalog Card Number: 72-78114
First Edition
Printed in the United States of America

THREE-CORNERED COVER

International
Herald Tribune

Published with *The New York Times* and *The Washington Post*

Paris 1972

NICE, Apr. 14 (AP)—French police reported the death near here last night of Otto Miller, the American music publisher in Paris. . . .

The Naked and the Nude

By PHOEBE HORSEY

CANNES, Apr. 15— . . . The speaker, smiling beatifically at His Serene Highness, said there was nothing to worry about: "This little girl hasn't forgotten a thing. . . ." . . . At that point the police hauled him away. . . . He was identified as Otto Miller, an American music publisher in Paris. . . .

1

MILAN, Apr. 21 (Reuter's)—Italian police today reported the death in a mysterious shooting here this morning of Otto Miller, an American music publisher in Paris. . . .

PARIS, May 15 (NYT)— . . . "Otto Miller," Mr. Dowling stated, without revealing the source of the funds, "has recently attracted considerable international capital." . . .

A RARE DAY. A rare, blue-skied, Paris April day. One of those four days each year, Peter observed to himself as he approached the reception desk of the Hotel San-Regis, when they can take the pictures for color postcards of Paris. The clerk looked up at the thick, sandy hair, the rangy figure, and the blue eyes in a longish face with its curious mixture of animality and distinction. "Good afternoon, Mr. Dowling," he said. "Quel beau temps!"

Peter nodded and handed over his passport. "Unusual," he said.

The clerk smiled his regret at the unwelcome truth, made a notation, and handed back Peter's passport. "Mr. Miller's office has been calling you since yesterday," he said.

Peter raised his eyebrows in surprise. "If you'll get me the number I'll take it in my room," he said. He rode up in the little paneled box which served as an elevator, and was shown by the bellboy to his door. He glanced about the luxuriously furnished room in recognition. The one with the red marble bathroom, he said to himself in approbation, then sat down on the bed and picked up the ringing telephone.

"Miller Enterprises," said a woman's voice.

Peter asked for Miss Goodman. "This is your New York lawyer," he said, when she answered. "What's the fuss?"

Helen Goodman's smile was almost audible over the telephone. "Where have you been?" she asked.

"I told Otto I might be tied up in Madrid an extra day on my way here. And I was," he answered.

"Spanish girls tie me in knots too," Helen Goodman retorted with some asperity. Her tone became businesslike. "Mr. Satori is here from Munich. Otto was hoping you would get here in time to dine with them yesterday or lunch today. But they're still in there talking. I'll put you through."

Otto Miller's deep voice, slightly accented, came through the telephone. Peter said warmly, "This is Juji, the Great Khan's favorite son. How are you, Genghis?"

"I'll be better after a few days at Eze," Miller answered with an air of complaint that didn't hide his affection. "I'm taking off tomorrow. Meanwhile, I wanted you to meet Alexander Satori. In case you have to protect me from him if our Bavarian Jazz Festival turns into a Woodstock. Or worse. But you're too late. He has to leave here in a few minutes. How about dinner tonight anyway?"

"That's what I'm in town for," Peter answered.

"Good. I'll pick you up at seven at the San-Regis," said Miller, and rang off.

Peter put down the telephone and lay back on the bed. Otto he liked. Otto's legal problems were another thing. What had Dean Acheson said about the law? "It has the worst features of medical practice with none of the recompenses. It doesn't relieve pain, and it doesn't help a person to live or die. The only way to accept the practice of the law is to be so busy that one doesn't think about it." Well, there's more than one way to be busy, thank God. He picked up the telephone and asked for the same number.

In his office, Otto Miller, looking very much as Genghis Khan would have looked had the Khan been tall and, at fifty-five, clean shaven as well as bald, returned his attention to the younger man sitting across from him. Alexander Satori, small and slight, dark, of a singular smoothness of skin, looked coldly at his host. "So you will try to fill that last one-hour spot, Otto, giving us twenty-four in all." The tone was courteous, but a wisp of querulousness hung in the air.

4

"I think Eva Kanday's the answer," Otto said. "I'll look into it."

A trace of sarcasm flitted across Satori's features and was gone. "I remind you," he said, pointing a finger, "we can't afford 'a Woodstock. Or worse.' "

Otto Miller stood up. "We'll do all right, Sandy. I'm certain," he said jovially.

As he rose Satori's face assumed a less severe expression. "I'm sure you're right, Otto. You have been for many a year now."

Miller beamed at the compliment. He looked down at the little man and placed a hand on his shoulder. "As at Schattenwald," he said.

Satori smiled. "Always nostalgic," he commented.

The good humor seemed to bring Satori out of himself. "Speaking of nostalgia, Otto," he said. His voice was cordial, persuasive. "When you were in the O.S.S." He paused and added, "In Unit 37. There was a man named Forbath with you. Lazlo Forbath. Do you know what ever became of him?"

His hand unmoved from Satori's shoulder, his smile unchanged, Otto Miller said, vaguely, "No idea. No idea at all."

Satori nodded, seemingly preoccupied, and made his way to the outer door. "You'll come to Munich next week, then, direct from Eze, and we'll look over the ground." Still smiling, Miller nodded in reply.

"Good-bye, Mr. Satori." Helen Goodman smiled from behind her typewriter at the disappearing figure. She rose to join Miller, but he shook his head and re-entered his office. The door shut behind him. Helen Goodman shrugged and sat down again at her desk.

Her gaze wandered to the window. From beyond the small terrace came a persistent growl, regularly alternating in pitch as the traffic on the Champs-Elysées below changed direction in reluctant accord with the stoplights. She looked at the blue sky and sighed with pleasure. It would be a nice night. She turned in her chair and stretched her legs out before her.

She ran her hands along her skirt and to her knees. Quite good, she concluded. She pressed her hands to her waist and frowned a bit. Masseuse at seven thirty. She glanced down at her blouse. At forty, she reflected, the advantages of small breasts were at last becoming evident. She shifted in her chair. The evening would begin late. But it would be good. Friendly. Uncluttered. And, yes, reassuring.

The telephone buzzed. Otto Miller said, "Get me the American Embassy, Helen. The Ambassador's office."

OTTO MILLER swung the Jaguar around the Grand Palais, and stopped at the light on the cours la Reine. The engine died. He cursed, started it again, and turned right with the light.

Peter said quietly, "I don't think much of the arrangement with Satori. For you, I mean."

Otto answered less quietly. "What else could I do? I put him in business, and he's simply done better than I have. He's providing the place for this jazz festival, and in fact taking most of the risk. It's my big chance to recoup. Even with the arrangement as it is, if the thing works, I'll have no more worries. And that's why I have to do this one. Hell," he said grimly, "if I were to die now my creditors would take everything and all my people would be out on the street."

The car sped along the cours Albert Premier, and edged over into the tunnel under the place de l'Alma. Peter thought they both looked cadaverish in the yellow light. "Now," Otto continued, "we can talk about that later, at dinner. For the moment we're going to the Residence. I have to talk to the Ambassador, and he didn't have time this afternoon, and I won't have time tomorrow morning before I leave. So he kindly invited us both for drinks."

"I didn't know you were chummy with the Ambassador," said Peter, "but I can't think of anything more welcome at the moment than a drink, so I'll be glad to accept one from him."

Otto parked on the steep hill below the Residence wall, and they climbed up to the avenue d'Iéna. As they entered the small driveway at number 2, Peter saw a dozen people preceding them. "I forgot to mention," said Otto, "he also asked two hundred and fifty other people. It's one of his regular receptions."

"Perfect setting for a quiet talk," Peter observed.

Otto shrugged. "He said he'd find a moment to see us alone. I want you with me when I talk with him."

"As your friend or your lawyer?"

"Both."

They passed through the doorway, which Peter noted was larger, and more hotel-like, than that of his hotel. Three or four young men stood in the middle of the vast, high-ceilinged hall. One detached himself, came up to them, and politely asked their names. Rapidly, he ushered them to the right, into a small, sparsely furnished, and paneled room. A short line of people, each group or couple accompanied by a young man, waited their turn to approach the tall, slender couple standing at the center of the room. Whitney D. V. Ballard, millionaire Virginian, Intelligence on Eisenhower's staff in London during the war, a brief stint in the C.I.A. in the late forties, in and out of government under Democratic and Republican Presidents, now for the third time an ambassador, and his wife Lillian were receiving in the name of the United States of America.

Peter was always curious at meeting the grandees of the republic. Did the man make the public image, or was he uneasily, sometimes frantically, trying to catch up with it? He had seen both—but mostly the latter. Peter watched his host and hostess responding to the wave of visible self-satisfaction which began when the guests caught sight of them, rose in each bosom as it progressed along the line, and crested in the greetings and handshakes in front of them. He knew that Whitney Ballard, gray-haired, erect, and smiling, was in his

7

early sixties, and that Lillian, his auburn-haired and elegant second wife, was a good twenty-five years younger, but there was no discernible difference in the vitality emanating from them.

The voice at his side said, not loudly, but very distinctly, "Mr. Ambassador, Mr. Miller and Mr. Dowling."

Peter saw Otto bow slightly, saying only, "Mr. Ambassador," and heard Whitney Ballard's "Mr. Miller. A pleasure," in reply. Cordial, but no more than any of his other greetings. So they aren't so chummy after all.

As Otto lowered his head to kiss Lillian Ballard's hand, Peter greeted the Ambassador. "Very kind of you to have asked me, Mr. Ambassador."

He saw that the Ambassador's look was much more direct and forceful than he had thought from a distance. His handshake showed he was not skimping. "We're delighted to have you, Mr. Dowling."

After greeting Lillian Ballard, who had smiled warmly and said, "It was very good of you to come, Mr. Dowling," as if she meant it, Peter found himself in the next doorway with the waiting Otto and an unprepossessing but pleasant woman, who said, "Now, Mr. Dowling, I'm sure you want a drink," and led the way to the bar. Peter nodded to himself. Very good indeed. They passed a name along not merely unobtrusively, but also efficiently: in four lightning passes no one had called him Dow—or Darling.

The large white and gold room was packed. Aged but ramrod-erect Frenchmen with the inevitable rosette in the buttonhole cackled volubly. Despite the obvious efforts made by all the ladies present, there was a striking shortage of attractive women. After about a half-hour Peter saw Lillian Ballard streak across the room with long, hurried strides, concluded she was certainly the most attractive woman in her own house, and then listened to the distinctive buzz in the noisy room as word was passed about that she was pregnant again and suffering constantly this time from nausea. Peter mentally bowed again to the Ambassador and his wife.

The young man who had escorted them to the Ambassador suddenly appeared and signaled to Otto and Peter. Excusing themselves, the two began to work their way through the crowd. The door of the small room off the entrance where they had originally been received was now closed, but the young man opened it and showed them inside. The Ambassador was alone. He motioned them to a couch, told the young man to put his head in in five minutes, sat down in a chair across from them, and lit a cigarette. Peter saw that he smoked consciously, for enjoyment. "Contrary to public opinion, this is not the most enjoyable side of diplomacy," said the Ambassador, "but it is a necessary one. I hope at least you could get near the bar." He seemed thoroughly relaxed. "What can I do for you, Otto?"

"I wouldn't bother you personally with this, Whitney," Otto began, "but it concerns your promise to me in 1944." The Ambassador nodded. So they *are* chummy, thought Peter. The Ambassador nodded again, and Peter realized he was the subject of the second nod. His presence was being questioned.

Otto smiled. "Peter is an old friend, besides being my lawyer. You will recall that in 1951, during the Korean War, although you were no longer with the C.I.A., I asked you privately to do what you could for a young friend of mine who wanted to serve in the Agency." Again the Ambassador nodded. "That was Peter."

Peter looked at Otto in astonishment.

"He spent over five years in the Agency," Otto went on. "He's secure. In the circumstances which I'll describe to you, I wanted someone close to me in on this too. You can never tell." Whitney Ballard remained silent.

"The arrangement was," Otto continued, "that those who served in Unit 37 would never be publicly identified, no matter how many years passed. Unit 37 would never be men-

9

tioned in any context. Above all, if there was any kind of slip on this, the work we did would never be identified—or admitted." Whitney Ballard nodded again. "Now there has been a slip—and one that identifies me with Unit 37."

The Ambassador frowned. The young man put his head inside the door. The Ambassador looked up at him. "Roger Heston's out there. Tell him to join us here. Discreetly." The young man disappeared. "Hold the rest until Heston gets here," the Ambassador said to Otto. "He's the chief of station."

He looked directly at Peter. "Why did you leave the Agency, Mr. Dowling?" he asked quietly.

The direct question, Peter thought. Power hath its privileges. "I did my stint, Mr. Ambassador," he said politely, but firmly.

Whitney Ballard looked at him steadily. "Some are still doing theirs," he said.

Peter thought for a minute. "Hemingway once wrote," he said to the Ambassador's inquiring eyes, " 'If you serve time for society, democracy, and the other things quite young, and, declining any further enlistment make yourself responsible only to yourself, you exchange the pleasant, comforting stench of comrades for something you can never feel in any other way than by yourself.' In short, it wasn't my dish," he concluded.

The Ambassador nodded. "Some of us keep hoping one can have both," he said mildly.

The door opened and then closed behind a man of about fifty, somewhat overweight, and looking, behind his glasses, like a prosperous mutual fund salesman. It was evident that he took pleasure in being summoned. The Ambassador performed the introductions and waved him to a seat. "Roger, you recall Unit 37 during the war?"

"Yes, sir. The only less-than-battalion-size, autonomous operational unit with a two-digit identifying number." He beamed, and the Ambassador flicked his eyelids. "Among

10

other things," Heston added, and clapped an attentive, serious look over the beam.

"Mr. Miller, here, for your private information only, was the chief of Unit 37. Mr. Dowling is his lawyer, from New York, and was formerly with the Agency." Heston's expression passed rapidly with the explanation from pleased surprise to unease. "You know that Unit 37 and its personnel were never under any circumstances to be mentioned," the Ambassador went on. "Mr. Miller believes that he has been compromised. Go on, Otto."

Otto waved his hand deprecatingly. "I don't attach too much importance to this," he said, "but still, I'd feel much better if things were tightened up. Particularly since the leak comes from Germany." The Ambassador raised his eyebrows.

"I have a partner in Germany, in Munich," Otto went on. "His name is Alexander Satori. He is Hungarian—Satori Sandor is the Magyar version of his name—and came out after the Revolution in 1956, with the rest of the refugees. He was twenty-six then. His father had been my father's partner, between the wars. He got in touch with me. I set him up in business and he has done very well. Very well, indeed," said Otto, a bit ruefully.

"This afternoon, in a conversation," he went on, "he not only mentioned the O.S.S., but he also specifically said 'Unit 37,' and he knew that I had been in it. In fact, that's why he mentioned it." Otto looked from the Ambassador to Heston. "If there is to be a leak," he said, "the last place it should be is Germany."

Heston shifted in his seat. The Ambassador spoke. "As you know, Otto, I was unable to get the files of Unit 37 destroyed at the end of the war. They went to the Pentagon. When I was Ambassador in Germany, in the Eisenhower Administration, I brought the subject up with Ike one time, and asked him to have them destroyed. He sent me a note later saying they had been transferred to the C.I.A., and that Allen absolutely guaranteed their secrecy." He looked at Heston.

11

"Obviously," said Heston, shifting again in his seat, "I know nothing about Satori. But after Allen left the Agency, the files of Unit 37 were pulled out—" he looked at the floor, and then resumed, "and they were used in some of our advanced training courses. Not that we thought of undertaking the same kind of thing," he added hastily, and then smiled at Otto, "but as an example of how operations ought to be conducted. But all those files were sterilized. Perfectly sterilized, I assure you."

Otto looked at him with what appeared to be sympathy. "That brings me to my next point," he said. "Obviously, Satori is your man. I certainly have no objection to that. He's a good man. But I want you to clamp down on him, and tell him to keep his secrets better. I'll never admit to him that I was in Unit 37, and he should never mention it. It's my life," he finished dourly.

The Ambassador turned to Heston, Peter thought with just a trace of coldness. "Roger, look into this and let me have word as soon as you can."

"Certainly, Mr. Ambassador." Heston gave a reassuring smile to Otto. "We'll straighten your man out, don't worry."

Otto rose. "Thank you, Whitney. We won't keep you any longer from your guests."

The Ambassador also rose, but seemed in no hurry. "So you're off to Eze tomorrow, Otto?"

Otto nodded.

The Ambassador shook his hand. "You always do things well, Otto. I still hope to see your house down there."

Otto bowed. "Yours whenever you want it, Whitney."

Affably, the Ambassador turned to Peter, "What is your firm in New York, Mr. Dowling?"

"Hammer, Rutledge, and Barry."

"Oh, yes. Give my best regards to Paul." The Ambassador extended his hand.

Of course, thought Peter. Paul Hammer, former governor, a near-presidential candidate twenty years ago, *the* senior

partner. The grandees of the republic all know each other.
"I shall, Mr. Ambassador."

Whitney Ballard maintained his grip on Peter's hand. "I
don't ask you to forget this conversation, Mr. Dowling." The
courteous voice was even in tone. "I do warn you of the consequences of repeating it. Anywhere. Anytime."

PETER LOOKED ABOUT him at the single mahogany pillar, the brass rails behind the benches, the mirrors, and in
them, the reflections of the florid designs of the painted glass
panels in the outer room, and of a strikingly pretty girl sitting at a table to his left. She glanced up into the mirror,
caught his eye, and coolly turned back to her companion. He
finished his coffee.

"You're right," he said to Otto. "The girls haven't deterio-
rated at all. But I must have. They don't respond to me the
way they used to. The coffee, I might add, is almost as bad as
in New York."

Otto drained the last drop from his *sérieux*, the great gob-
let of beer which distinguished the house, and reached for
the check. "The coffee is better than it was, but the proprietor still doesn't believe in espresso after meals. You are also
probably better than you were. The problem is that at your
age the girls respond differently. You're at the turning
point." He grinned at Peter. "Forty next year? No more just
looking at them and striking a fire. From here on you have to
reach them with the mind rather than the eye. The intellec-
tual approach. The way to young girls' hearts, for more senior citizens, is through their ears. It takes a little longer, but
it's just as sure. And the fire is sometimes even more
warming." He counted out the change and rose ponderously
from the table. "Alternatively, of course, you can make a fortune. Then the word gets around. Seems to work better than
looks or brains."

Peter laughed and followed Otto out the narrow passage by the service counter. They crossed the boulevard Saint-Germain, walked past the massed heads at the Flore, and into the ambling crowd in the rue Saint-Benoît. Otto unlocked the car and they got in. He pressed the starter. It ground on and on, whining in its labor. He turned the key off, waited a moment, and then tried again. This time the engine caught. "Very temperamental machine," he said. "To the San-Regis?"

"Yes, thanks, Otto," answered Peter. "Your machine's almost as temperamental as you are."

"So what does that mean?" Otto, turning left into the rue de l'Université, glanced over his right arm at Peter.

"I mean, for the twenty years or more I've known you, you've kept up that story about being in the Signal Corps in the war, and all these years you've kept the secret that you used your connections to help me get into the C.I.A. Thanks, by the way, although I'm not convinced you did me a favor. But now, after all that, you suddenly drag me into this affair tonight. I don't get it."

Otto looked at him disdainfully. "I trust Whitney," he said. "He was my chief in those days. But you saw the situation tonight. He's protection, but not complete protection. He has much larger fish to fry these days. And there is less immediate power at the top than you might think. You saw he had to call the Agency man in and turn it over to him, in effect. He has to stay somewhat in channels too. And you know the Agency. They give their word, but then the people change, and things change, and so does their word. They let those files out, 'sterilized' or not. In short, I don't trust them, Whitney's a busy man, and I do trust you."

"Thanks, Otto," said Peter, "but I don't think Whitney Ballard does."

"Why the hell should he? He doesn't know you. The important thing is that I do. Anyway, the whole thing doesn't amount to much, really. Satori's just feeling self-important. Common agent defect. A slap on the wrist will straighten it

14

all out." After a pause Otto said, "If he hasn't gabbed to the Germans—to the wrong Germans, that is."

Peter thought for a minute. "With all that trust you still don't want to tell me what it was that Unit 37 did?"

"No," Otto said, curtly. He pulled the car around the edge of the place François Premier, into the rue Jean-Goujon, and stopped before the San-Regis. Peter reached for the handle of the door. Otto leaned back and rested his hand gently on Peter's shoulder. "On second thought," he said softly, "perhaps you should know. In case something happens."

Peter watched his friend. There was a long silence, as Otto stared absently down the empty street. Then he turned to Peter. His voice was matter-of-fact. "Our mission was murder," he said.

Peter thought for a moment before he spoke. "As your lawyer," he said, "I note a contradiction in terms. Murder is unauthorized killing. A mission is something authorized. *Ergo* . . ."

"That's what we thought at the time," Otto said. He smiled faintly. "Also, the cause was good. We seldom touched the Wehrmacht. Our targets were the Nazi administrators in occupied Europe. The bullies and the sadists. The exile governments in London, through the Resistance movements, knew what was going on, and when things in a particular area got too bad the case was turned over to us. But we learned from the Heydrich affair, in Czechoslovakia. That cost several thousand lives, in reprisals. So our job was to create accidents. Or pin the murder on another German. Whatever our solution, rule number one was that the death not be attributed to the local population, or Resistance."

Otto turned and looked down the street, then back at Peter. His expression now was grim. "We did quite well," he said. "We had some very imaginative people. But you can see why some Germans—the wrong ones—even today wouldn't feel bound by your legal distinction. In fact, had they won, no one could have made that legal distinction."

Peter nodded. "Thanks for telling me. I agree. Prudence is a better defense than legal niceties." He looked steadily at Otto. "You can count on me. For both."

Otto smiled broadly. He clapped Peter on the shoulder. "I know it. That's why I told you. When will you be through again?" he asked. "You can't miss the Bavarian festival, in any event. Come see Otto Miller make a million. Then I'll show you how to catch the girls' eyes," he added, his good humor returned.

"Maybe I'll catch you in Munich next week, Otto," Peter replied. "I have to go to London tomorrow, check into the office there, and go out to the country for the weekend. Then I have some business in Zurich. And, with this late spring, I hoped to work in some skiing. But early next week I'll be going to Munich too." He shook his head, then laughed. "I'm trying to make a million myself."

"Oh?" said Otto. The engine sputtered and died. He turned off the ignition.

Peter put his hand to the door handle, then dropped it. "It's an odd case," he said. "It seems an old gentleman in California died some months ago, intestate, and with no known relatives in America. Originally, he was Hungarian. Went to California many years ago, and made a respectable sum in real estate. Then in recent years, in his old age, he became a bit absent-minded, and a bit of a recluse. When he died he didn't really know all that he had. His holdings now turn out to be worth no less than 30 million dollars."

Otto turned to the street and gave a smart, almost military salute.

Peter looked past him. "Someone you know?" he asked.

Otto shook his head. "I salute automatically for all sums in excess of ten million dollars," he said.

Peter grinned and continued. "The Los Angeles lawyers have had no luck finding the heirs. Actually, they got in touch with me—not with my firm—because one of their partners happens to know that when I was with the Agency, in Germany, I was working on Hungarian affairs. I'll leave it to you to guess how the partner knew that. Anyway, they figure I can find the missing heirs—although the State of California won't be overjoyed if I do. So I'm going to Munich to see if I can't get someone in the Intelligence Center there to give me a possible lead or two. I got a Hungarian visa in New York, just in case I find a lead to track down in the old country itself. If I succeed, the fee will be enormous. Hammer and company will have no choice but to make me a partner."

Otto put a hand on Peter's shoulder. "You're going too fast, and in the wrong direction," he said. "Are you sure the old gentleman's name wasn't Miller? Or rather, Müller? As we used to be? In the old country?"

Peter smiled. "Be nice if it was. I'd double my fee for you. No, the name was Forbath. Emery Forbath. Originally from near Veszprem."

Otto's hand fell to the seat. He stared at Peter.

Peter looked at him in surprise. "Don't tell me you knew him?"

"No," said Otto. "But that was the name Sandy was asking about this afternoon when he brought up Unit 37."

"What do you mean, 'asking about'?"

"He asked me if I knew the whereabouts of a man named Forbath who served in Unit 37."

"*Did* a man named Forbath serve with you in Unit 37?"

"Yes," said Otto, "but he's not your man. It wasn't his real name. He'd changed it years before from Bakony. Oddly enough, he's in real estate now himself. That is to say, he's a colonel in the Israeli Army."

Despite himself, Peter smiled. "What did you tell Satori about him?"

Otto drew himself erect. "Told him I had no idea. No idea at all."

The two men were silent, but finally Otto spoke. "I don't know. Too complicated to figure out tonight. I'll take it for a coincidence for the time being. After all, it's a very common Hungarian name. Thanks again, Peter."

They shook hands and Peter got out of the car. Otto leaned over. "Check with Satori's office when you get to Munich. I'll probably be there." He grinned and waved. "Schattenwald," he said.

Peter smiled at Otto's farewell, his way of wishing well by evoking the name of a favorite summer haunt of his childhood, in the eternal, futile hope of regaining its joys. "Maybe I'll glimpse it this trip," Peter said, and shut the door.

Thoughtfully, he watched the car pull away, and then entered the hotel. At the top of the steps he paused. The hall was empty and silent. With a rattle the concierge handed him his key. Peter shook his head, still in thought.

After a minute he said, "No, thank you. Would you call me a taxi?"

"AH, LOVELY." Helen Goodman rolled over onto her stomach. The light from her bedside lamps shone on her buttocks, printing a crescent of shadow between them. She buried her face in the pillow, breathed deeply, and then raised her head.

"You'll have to give them up one of these days," she said.

There was a noncommittal hum from the bathroom, and the sound of running water and splashing.

She rolled over onto her back and stretched her legs. Raising them slightly, she pointed her toes. The muscles of her belly tightened on either side of her navel, and she exhaled. The water stopped running in the bathroom.

"So will I," she said pensively.

There was another hum from the bathroom.

"I'm serious," she said.

"About what?" came the muffled reply.

She turned her head to the bathroom door. "About these friendly matings," she said. "You're going to have to get married one of these days."

18

She put her hands to her breasts and rubbed them gently. "Your physical charm isn't going to last forever. You have at most five more years. Then you better find someone you can live with. Because by then the little girls won't be looking at you anymore."

There was a stir from the bathroom. "They've already stopped."

"You see?" She sat up straight on the bed, still holding her breasts. "You'd better take my advice."

Peter Dowling emerged from the bathroom, stuffing his shirt into his trousers. "And you?" he asked.

"I'm already looking," she said. "There's Alexander Satori. He's small, but with what he has I can overlook that." She laughed. "If only I could overlook *him*."

Peter smiled. "I don't know him, but I don't recommend him. What makes you think he's available for your private social security plan?" He stooped to knot his tie before the mirror on her dressing table.

Helen grimaced. "Nothing. He's all business."

Peter turned from the mirror and sat down on the bed beside her. She lay back and stretched her arms above her head. Her breasts flattened, and disappeared. He leaned down and kissed the slight indentation of her sternum.

She fastened her arms around his neck. "Ah, Peter," she murmured. "You're a delight. A distant delight."

He rose, took his jacket from the chair, and put it on. "Back to the San-Regis in time to be waked up," he grinned. From the doorway he blew her a kiss. "Good morning," he said.

"A BLOODY BICYCLE could make better music than this."

The Jaguar coughed and sputtered in reply. Otto Miller pushed the accelerator to the floor. The motor answered with a long-drawn, rebarbative sigh, and was silent. There was a loud squawk behind. Otto started, then pulled the wheel to the right. A two-horsepower Citroën loped past, its occupants glaring at him, its engine giving hurried voice to their indignation. Cars whipped past him in regular succession and without pause, the air eddies buffeting his windows. The Esterel, Otto observed to himself, is no place to break down.

The engine caught and the car gathered speed, rolling beneath a great sign, "Sortie Cannes 2000 m." Again, the Jaguar coughed, sputtered, and slowed. Otto looked at his watch. Calvi. Anything will be better than this heartless concrete strip. He eased into the exit lane and swung sharp right onto the access road. The car coasted downhill, past the villas set in luxuriant gardens amid great trees, then past the massed apartment houses.

Otto emerged from the underpass beneath the coastal railroad and stopped at a red light. He looked curiously at the traffic. It was heavy, but there was something missing. It lacked body. No trucks. Damn, he thought, it's a local holiday. The light turned green. He shot to the far side of the intersection, turned his wheels sharp left, and stopped abruptly, conforming to the French style which makes of a left turn a sort of automotive diphthong: a U-turn followed by a right turn. Again the light changed. He completed his turns, and pushed the accelerator to the floor to cover the remaining hundred yards to where a sign proclaimed "Garage J. Calvi—Spécialiste—Voitures Etrangères." Again the long wheeze from the motor. Mush.

The advantage of a holiday, he thought as he coasted with dead engine to the curb, is that you can park. He got out of the car and rapidly walked the hundred yards to Calvi's. A handwritten sign, taped to the wide doors, informed his kind clients that Monsieur Calvi's establishment was closed, exceptionally, "jeudi le 13 avril." Otto pounded on the door. Then he noticed the night bell. The very label gave promise of at least a watchman. He rang, and then rang again.

A small door set in the larger doors opened a trifle. A bald head, surmounting a seamed, benign face appeared. A great smile brought Otto's cheekbones into even greater prominence. "Joseph!" He spread his arms in greeting. *"Ami!"*

Calvi smiled back at him. "Monsieur Miller, I believe. You are welcome to intrude on my holiday. I am spending it at work on my accounts." His face expressed utter distaste, then brightened again. "You are looking for a game of pétanque?" he asked hopefully.

"Another time," said Miller. "Right now I'm trying to get to Nice airport. I have to be there at eight. Without fail. I did Paris to Vienne yesterday. No trouble. But today that machine—" he pointed down the street to the Jaguar—"has broken down nineteen times. The last time right where you see it. I throw myself on your mercy."

Calvi frowned at him. "Always the American rush. I have no mechanics today. Here I am, an entrepreneur, an employer, and you wish to put me back to being a mechanic." He shook his head, but accompanied Miller down the street. "Otto, my friend," Calvi said, "you have not only the American, but the Parisian, pace. You should slow down a bit. More pétanque. Those young girl singers are pushing you too hard." He looked wryly at Miller. "Or perhaps you are pushing them too hard?"

Otto Miller looked up at the fiery sky. "Your reproach, my dear Joseph, might be acceptable from another source," he said. "But having followed your career for twenty years now, I for one know of too many ladies on this coast who can testify—even if, for the sake of discretion, they won't—that it is not only with the steel balls of pétanque that you are a champion." Calvi tossed his head back and with his tongue gave the single click of the Mediterranean negative. Then he lifted the hood of the Jaguar and grinned at the engine.

After about ten minutes of expert but futile manipulations he went to the trunk and banged forcefully on the fuel pump, apparently also futilely. "It is not in this car that you will be at the airport at eight," he said. "It is now seven. I can change your fuel pump in a few minutes, but even that won't bring gasoline to the engine. I'll also have to disassem-

21

ble the carburetors. Two hours." Miller's jaw tightened; he looked more like the Great Khan than ever.

"Without being indiscreet, where are you going after the airport?" asked Calvi.

"To my house, at Eze."

"And you would rather not come back here after the airport?"

"Much rather not," said Otto, briefly.

Calvi smiled. "She doesn't want to be seen in Cannes?" Otto looked at him impassively and said nothing.

"Very well," said Calvi. "You take my car. I'll bring the Jaguar up to Eze when I've finished. Leave the keys and papers to my car in your mailbox at the house, and I'll leave yours in exchange." He smiled again. "That way I can drop over and see a sick friend in Menton afterwards."

"Many thanks, Joseph." Otto clapped him on the shoulder, then took his bags from the Jaguar, and the two walked back to the garage. With some difficulty Otto installed himself in Calvi's Renault 8. His big frame filled the front of the car. "Come up to the house on Sunday and we'll have a game," he said, "but not before Sunday. Come to think of it, I better call you first."

Calvi nodded. "Okay," he said, with the special tweak that only a Frenchman can give the word, "but if it lasts till Sunday you won't be fit even for pétanque."

Otto shut the door and started out of the garage. He managed to extrude his head from the window as he did so. "Your sick friend in Menton," he said, "she doesn't want to be seen in Cannes?"

A FLASH OF TUMBLING blonde hair, of gleaming teeth, of pale honey-colored mink, and of a white dress beneath, passed through the customs gate. Onlookers for whom airports have replaced the afternoon promenade as the place to catch a glimpse of their dreams stared at the girl with por-

22

cine satisfaction as she rushed up to the tall, rather ferocious-appearing man waiting majestically at one side.

"*Aahht-*toe!" She beamed at him.

"Eva." He smiled broadly, his eyes looking deeply into hers, and bent to kiss her hand. He took her suitcase with one hand, her arm with the other, moved her to the door, and guided her across to the parking lot and the Renault 8.

"What is *this?*" she said in manifest disapproval.

"The Jaguar broke down," Otto answered. "A friend is fixing it and loaned me this. He'll bring my car up to the house later." Mollified, Eva got into the car. A luscious piece, a bit of a whore, and a great deal of fun, thought Otto with genuine affection. He leaned in and kissed her, pressing hard against her as her mouth opened in quick response.

He shut the door, went around and climbed in behind the wheel. The two of them took all available space, and Otto found his right elbow resting on mink. "We will both roast to death in your coat," he said.

"Mink comes off so easily," she retorted.

"New?" he asked.

"*I* bought it," she answered proudly.

"Herr Doktor Roessli," Otto said. "He no longer gives you gifts?"

Eva shrugged. "I didn't marry him for gifts," she answered. "Swiss functionaries aren't big givers. But they are security." She looked at him mischievously.

"What did you tell him about this trip?" asked Otto, his eyes on the road and the newly lit necklace of lights stretching to the mountains at the end of the bay.

"A recording session," she said simply. "Until Saturday afternoon. He knows French technicians don't work on Sunday." Pétanque for Sunday it is, Otto said to himself.

He slowed in the traffic flowing between the threadbare palm trees and speculated for an instant on the anomaly of speaking Hungarian on a French avenue called the promenade des Anglais. "What other horrible news do you have for me?"

"Not horrible," she replied, a little dreamily. "Just that you'll disapprove."

He swung out around the chateau of Nice, on its bluff, and, descending into the port, left the placid, enveloping sea behind. "It has to be pretty horrible for that."

"I was in Budapest last week."

He looked quickly at her, his eyebrows raised in astonishment. "How in God's name did *that* happen?"

"It was Gunter's idea. He said he'd never seen my country, and he thought as my husband he should. It's all very easy. Practically anyone can go there. Besides, I'm a Swiss citizen now, so there was no danger."

He plunged into the traffic at the end of the port. Sixteen years since she had left, tramping out with two hundred thousand other refugees. Otto had eventually come across her singing in a Vienna cabaret. And now she had gone back. It was more than thirty years since he himself had left. (She was three then; he dismissed the thought.) And he had never gone back. Why seek warmth in the ashes of a fire if you have the wood to build a new one?

"Well, how was it?"

"So poor," she said. There was a pause, and then she continued. "It was poor when I left, but at least it was noble. Now, it's still poor, and anything but noble."

They began to climb in the night to the Moyenne Corniche. Beneath them the sea was visible only by supposition —the dark mass beyond the sparkling lights. To their left they could only suspect the great mountain rising even more darkly.

"The people?"

"They're either apathetic or greedy," she said. Greedy— perhaps, he thought. Understandable enough. But apathetic they had never been. He sighed.

"Could you find your old friends?"

She too sighed. "You know I have no family left. Almost everyone I knew either left or was buried in 1956. All except my oldest friend. Maria Kodaly. She's still there, and I saw a lot of her."

"Any relation to Zoltan?" Otto had always admired the composer. Not only for his great music, but also as a man. At the height of the Stalinist period they had asked him, thinking they had him well in hand, to comment on the latest Moscow policy directive for the "People's Choirs Movement." "One mustn't sing falsely," he had rejoined. And then, in his seventies, he had married a young woman and spent his last years in a whirlwind of concerts, teaching, composing, love, and acclaim.

"I wish to God she were," said Eva. "No, she's from a medical family. That's the trouble. Her father and mother were doctors, her grandfather was a famous professor of medicine, and so she wanted to become a doctor. That's why she wouldn't leave in 1956," Eva added in evident irritation. They rolled onto the Corniche itself, the lights at the bottom of the more than thousand feet of cliff to their right no longer visible. The car's headlights and those of approaching cars illuminated the tan and pale yellow rocks and the occasional guard rail. In the darkness Eva continued talking.

"We were brought up together," she went on. "She was like a younger sister for me. In 1956 she was still only a student intern. I pleaded with her to leave with me, but she said she had to stay and help, there were so many wounded short of care. It broke my heart then to leave her, and it broke my heart now to see her. She's beautiful; she's intelligent."

"You must give me her address and telephone number," Otto interrupted.

"Isn't your list long enough already?" Eva retorted. "You can get it from Gunter. He was very taken with her. He even got rid of me once to have lunch alone with her. Anyway, there she is, stuck. Now she *is* a doctor, and they'll never let her out, not even for a vacation."

"Does she want out?" asked Otto, familiar for years with such stories.

"That's the worst part. I don't think she does. She's sunk in that morass like all the rest of them." Eva was silent for a moment. "You don't know anyone going to Budapest soon, do you?" she asked. "I want to send some cosmetics to Maria."

Otto steered carefully around a sharp curve, feeling Eva's softness against him. "As a matter of fact, yes," he answered. "Peter Dowling, a good friend—and my New York lawyer— may be going. I'll let you know if he does." He glanced at Eva, her face and hair seeming to glow next to him. "Don't tell me they don't even have cosmetics in Budapest now. How in heaven's name did you get along?" he asked with a grin.

She ignored his taunt in her shrill explosion. "Cosmetics? Do you know I went into the best—what do I mean? The *only*—parfumerie in town, and I asked for some face cream. I told the salesgirl exactly what kind of cream I wanted. She looked at me as though I had come in with sled dogs from Antarctica. 'We have *a* cream,' she said. '*A* cream.' And then she said, 'It's Polish.' 'Polish?' I said. 'I want face cream, not sour cream.' Then the salesgirl was insulted. Finally, she tried to be sympathetic, and that was worse. 'Too bad you weren't here last week,' she said to me. 'It was East German then.' " Eva's voice vibrated with outrage.

Otto laid a finger on her nose. "You're spoiled by the West," he said, and then added, "for which we are all thankful." A kilometer farther on, he turned right off the road, ran up a steep incline, and brought the car to a halt in the municipal parking lot of Eze.

Each carrying a bag, they climbed the paving stones of a narrow street, the fortress and church looming high on their right. Soon they began a steep descent. Most of the houses lining the street were shuttered and silent; it was too early for the summer residents. From an occasional shutter a blue light and snatches of booming dialogue bespoke the hold of television on the year-round residents.

They continued down, weaving between houses only a few

feet apart, then through a long archway, and down a flight of steps until they found themselves before a wooden gate. Otto opened a mailbox to the side of the gate, and put in the keys and papers of the car. Taking out his own keys, he opened the gate. They passed through into a small, graveled courtyard.

Otto opened the front door and they passed through a small vestibule into a living room which, together with the two small bedrooms at either end, made up the entire width of the house. He switched on a lamp, then went to the far side of the room and opened the wide sliding glass doors. At one side he pressed a button and on the terrace beyond the doors a rectangle of brilliant turquoise water shone in the dark night.

They stepped outside and walked around the end of the pool to the iron balustrade ringing the terrace. Spread in a great arc before them was a string of lights stretching from Cap-Ferrat on their right to Cap-d'Ail on the left. They looked down. Through twelve hundred feet of empty darkness directly below them were visible the lights of Eze-bord-de-Mer. Linking them with both ends of the arc, and moving in what seemed from such a height a stately, but infinitesimal, procession, were the pinpoint lights of cars on the coastal road. Beyond Cap-Ferrat was the glow of Villefranche and Nice, but to the left there was only the darkness of the great bluff rising from Cap-d'Ail and shutting off Monte Carlo. They were suspended between sea and sky.

The air was warm and still. Otto drew her to him and slipped her coat from her shoulders. "You're right," he said, "it does come off easily." She nestled in his arms. He lowered his mouth to her ear and murmured, "Swim?"

She nodded silently, and joined her hands and elbows in front of her. She arched her back. "Unzip me," she said.

WHITNEY BALLARD ROSE from his desk in a corner of the high, paneled office. The scarlet carpet, running from one end to the other of the room, glowed up at him. As he always did, he blinked. Blinds the visited, he thought, as well as the visitors. He went to the center window and looked out at the place de la Concorde, a plain of grays in the dusk, and across to the National Assembly. How "national" are assemblies these days? Someone had told him recently that the Métro station there was still called "Chambre des Députés."

He heard the door of his secretary's office open, and he turned around. Beaming, Roger Heston marched in, followed by a tall, thin, brown-haired man, with a small mouth and thick eyeglasses. The Ambassador let them cover the distance to him, and then said, "Good evening, Roger. Sorry I couldn't see you earlier."

"Of course, Mr. Ambassador," answered Heston. "It's about the matter of that leak on Unit 37." The Ambassador sat down with his back to the windows and motioned them to the black leather couch. Heston gestured to his companion. "This is Ross Trumbull, Mr. Ambassador. He's in charge of C.E. I was able to get hold of Ross Thursday night, after we spoke at the Residence, but he took off yesterday for Munich and only got back this afternoon. I think he can explain the matter to you."

Trumbull spoke evenly, but in a rather high-pitched voice. "I'm happy to be able to say that this matter is not as serious as Mr. Miller apparently made out, Mr. Ambassador. Satori had come across the Unit 37 name in an advanced training course he was given. I have no indication that he actually knew Miller was chief of the unit. But he has known Miller for many years. Is very fond of him, in fact. He was just teasing Miller, because he himself had never believed the story Miller puts out that he was in the Signal Corps during the war. In short, it was a joke that hit the mark, quite by accident."

The Ambassador looked at Roger Heston. "I thought you said those files were sterilized, Roger."

Heston looked at the floor, and then back at the Ambassador. Smiling, he spread his palms before him. "I was told they were, Mr. Ambassador. I think probably the Unit 37 name was used in another, historical course, rather than in the operations course based on the files, and Satori may have been able to put the two together."

"As would any nincompoop in that case," said the Ambassador. "Go ahead, Mr. Trumbull."

"I beg your pardon, sir?"

"What is the rest of the story?"

"Why, I believe that's all, Mr. Ambassador."

Whitney Ballard stirred slightly in his chair. "What is the source of your information about what Satori thought and said?"

Trumbull was silent for a moment. Then he smiled briefly, a smile at once self-deprecating and pleased. "I am," he said. "I've just seen him in Munich. Naturally, I reprimanded him severely, and I'm sure there'll be no further difficulty on this score."

"How is it that the counter-espionage officer in Paris is seeing Satori in Munich?"

A pause, and then, "My field of operations is rather wider than just France, sir, and Satori is within it." The small mouth closed and remained shut.

Whitney Ballard turned to Heston. "Roger?"

Heston assumed a serious expression and turned to Trumbull. "Ross, if the Ambassador states his desire to know, you're required to tell him."

Trumbull's eyes moved from Heston to the Ambassador. His face was expressionless, but he spoke as though uncovering a jewel. "This man Satori, Mr. Ambassador, is a part of our most important penetration operation. I can, of course, give you further details if you require them, but I don't imagine you will want them."

The Ambassador studied him for a full minute, and then he turned to Heston. "This was not in the briefing I was given at Langley."

Heston looked unhappy, then brightened. "I think I can explain that, sir. You see, this is not, strictly speaking, a French operation. It really has nothing to do with France. I'm sure it was left out for that reason."

The Ambassador, by now slouched deep in his chair, lifted an eyebrow. In a voice that sounded just a trifle bored, he said, "But it's being run from my Embassy. I gather by Mr. Trumbull?"

"Yes, sir," said Heston. He rubbed his chin; again he brightened. "But Trumbull here is not operationally on my T.O. Only administratively. You know how it is with C.E. They're autonomous. Actually *I* didn't even know about the operation until Ross told me this afternoon. In fact, he hasn't told me any more than he's now told you—and I'm not really entitled to know that much."

Ross Trumbull remained silent, snug in his autonomy decreed by Washington. Who watches the watchers, Whitney Ballard thought. "Yes, I know how it is with C.E." he said, noncommittally. He added, "One aspect of this, of course, is that Mr. Trumbull is holding a blank check signed by you and me, Roger."

Ross Trumbull leaned forward. "This operation was set up this way, Mr. Ambassador, because of its very great potential," he pronounced the word "great" with heavy significance, "and because it's extremely sensitive. We didn't want the slightest suspicion of his American connections attaching to Satori. Therefore I run the operation from here, rather than having him in contact with our people in Germany, which would double the risk of it becoming known." Now he spoke with cool assurance. "In this present matter, I imagine we may count on Mr. Miller to keep his new-found knowl-

30

edge to himself. And I can assure you, of course, that Mr. Miller is in no danger: Satori can be counted upon not to make a slip with any Germans. A much more serious problem, from my point of view, is this lawyer, Dowling. I understand he was present at the conversation at the Residence the other evening." Trumbull shrugged. "We've had a lot of trouble with these people who come in for a few years, then say they're disappointed, and get out. Was the decision really their own? Or does someone hope that in a few years, if a real crisis comes along, we'll call them back in? I don't say that's the case with Dowling, but we have to think of it. I've asked for his file, and I may run a check on him."

"Not a bad idea," said the Ambassador. He rose. "It's been my experience, Mr. Trumbull, for whatever it's worth to you, that it's the holder of a blank check who is in the really difficult position. Not the signers. The holder has to judge exactly what to fill it in for. Too little, and he's filled with regrets about what might have been. Too much, and the check bounces. My credit—and Roger's—is good. Up to a point. Good evening, gentlemen."

Heston smiled appreciatively. After a moment, Trumbull followed suit. Then the two headed towards the door. The Ambassador looked out the window. A carpet of lights stretched across the place de la Concorde. As the two men reached the door, he turned back. "There is one detail, Mr. Trumbull, that I wish to know."

"Sir?"

"Just whom are you penetrating with this operation?"

The Ambassador watched the struggle between professional reticence and personal pride on Trumbull's face, and the final victory of pride. "Why, the K.G.B., sir," he said, his soft voice a sop to reticence.

"Not the Kremlin?"

"For our purposes they're the same."

Whitney Ballard raised his eyebrows. His voice expressed curiosity. "Do you really think so?"

"SCHATTENWALD," said Otto Miller. He lay on the couch, his head in Eva's lap, one hand toying idly beneath her terrycloth robe.

"Shadow Wood," she translated. She reached her hand inside his robe and stroked his chest. "What does it mean?"

"An earlier heaven," he answered.

She giggled. "You certainly wouldn't know it from the name."

Otto grunted. "You have too cinematic a sense of names," he grumbled. "They know better in the theater. Shakespeare covered the subject. In Romeo and Juliet: 'a rose by any other name' etcetera."

In the silence that followed he deduced that she was thinking. He waited for her question.

"Otto?"

"Hmm?" He could hear her phrasing the question. What she didn't know was that he wanted her to ask it.

"When are we going to make another record of mine?"

Well put. He decided he might as well be brutal. His idea meant effort on her part, but even if she didn't make the effort she still couldn't ruin anything for him. Not with twenty-three other acts in a field covered with thousands. Not thousands. Hundreds of thousands.

"Look," he said. He waved his hand in the air to fix her attention. "I like your voice. The Swiss burghers like your voice. Everyone likes your voice. Your earlier records did reasonably well, but that was six years ago. Now you need a springboard. Something new to launch you. Your St. Gotthard Bar in Zurich is a happy compromise between being the wife of a Swiss banking functionary and continuing to sing. It's distinguished. It's refined. Very comfortable. A springboard it's not."

He judged the weight of her silence. Attentive, not resentful. So far so good.

"You need something more contemporary, a place or an occasion which will have meaning to the kids. They're the only ones who buy records in the millions, or even hundreds of thousands, for that matter. And for them the Danube isn't blue—Hungarian folksongs, Roumanian doinas, and Viennese schmaltz are not what they're doing this year. Nor last year. Nor the year before that. For the kids the big musical rivers are the Mersey and the Missouri, not to mention the Brahmaputra."

"I'd love to really let loose sometime, do something new," Eva said pensively.

"If you can do it, I think I may have just the place, and the occasion."

"Where? When?" She was the excited little girl, hoping for her present.

"*Télé-Nuit,*" said the announcer on the television set across from them.

"Shush," said Otto. "After this."

"Drink or drive, you must decide," said the announcer.

"Mmm," answered Otto.

"Again, a holiday here on the Côte d'Azur brings us a tragic toll," the announcer went on. "Four dead, eighteen injured in accidents in the Département du Var, five dead, seventeen injured in the Alpes-Maritimes."

"Imbeciles," said Otto. Eva tugged gently at the hair on his chest.

"A particularly vicious tragedy on Route Nationale 564, the Moyenne Corniche, tonight took the life of the American music publisher Otto Miller. Since 1946, Mr. Miller directed his enterprises from Paris. Witnesses of the accident say that Mr. Miller was in fact killed by a driver who must have been drinking, and, in an imprudent attempt to pass Mr. Miller, forced him from the road."

Otto whipped his head around for a full view of the screen just in time to see a badly lit scene of smoking wreckage.

"Mr. Miller's car broke through the guard rail and fell nearly two hundred meters from the Corniche before catching fire," the voice went on. "The machine, a Jaguar, and its occupant were totally burned. Police were able to identify the remains by checking the registration according to a license plate which, fortunately, could still be read." In the garish half-light of the image Otto saw a gendarme scrambling from rock to rock, stooping to pick something off the ground, straightening, stooping again. Just before the image faded he approached an officer and handed him a sheaf of untidy papers. "The car responsible for the accident," the announcer concluded grimly, "was stolen. It has been found abandoned in Monte Carlo. Police are searching for the thief. Mr. Miller was one of the organizers and backers of the Bavarian Jazz Festival, scheduled for next month."

Otto leaped to his feet and switched off the lights of the swimming pool. With a quick gesture, he shut the glass doors and drew the curtains. Eva watched him with her mouth agape. "Quick," he said to her, "for God's sake, quick! Dress! Pack your bag!"

He dashed to the kitchen, hastily rinsing and replacing the dishes they had used, and putting the pans back in place. Eva stood at the door. "Eva!" He spoke harshly to her over his shoulder. "Dress! Pack!" He saw the shock on her face. More softly, he said, "Believe me, if we're not out of here in a few minutes, I may really be dead." When she still stood there, speechless, he added, "Neither of us would like that." Quietly and quickly she ran to the bedroom, slipping off her bathrobe as she went.

Otto checked the living room to see that all was in order, and then went into the bedroom. Eva was just pulling on her dress. He reached over and zipped it up. Hastily, he dressed himself except for his shoes. He grabbed their wet towels from the bathroom, threw them into his suitcase, and closed it. He handed Eva her suitcase, and took his own in one hand, his shoes in the other. He switched off the lights and led her to the door. They stepped out into the black night and silence.

Otto closed the door without a click, opened and closed the gate, and reached into the mailbox. He looked at the keys and papers of the Renault as though they confirmed his worst fears. Soundlessly, they set off up the narrow street.

At the parking lot he glanced at the road below. It was empty. "You can put your shoes on now," he said to her, and slipped on his own. He threw the bags in the car, started the engine, and switched on the lights. He looked around the parking lot. The same cars that had been there before. He swung out of the parking lot and down to the main road. He drove across it and entered a narrow road on the opposite side which climbed up the mountainside into the blackness.

At the top he came out onto the Corniche Supérieure and turned right, towards Menton and the Italian border. With a barely perceptible sigh of relief he turned to Eva. "I can't explain all this to you," he said, "but tonight someone pushed my car off the road thinking I was in it. They must continue to think they were successful. Otherwise they'll do it again, only they'll make sure the next time."

Eva nodded. Her eyes were big, and he saw that she was frightened. So much the better, he thought. "Therefore," he spoke very slowly, "you must let no one know that you saw me tonight."

"I can't, anyway," she reminded him.

"That's true." He remembered. Also so much the better. "We're going to Menton now," he went on. "We'll leave this car there. You take a taxi. Spend the night in Nice. Then call your husband tomorrow and tell him the recording session was canceled. You can say someone was in an accident. Say I was, if it rings truer. Then take the plane back to Zurich."

At Menton he left the car on a side street near the beach, with the keys and papers inside. No use depriving Calvi's estate of it. They walked inland one block and found a taxi. Otto put her bag in and kissed her.

She looked up at him. "It's a springboard all right, but not exactly what came to my mind when you spoke of one," she said.

"You'll have the one I spoke of, whether or not I get out of this. It's that Bavarian Jazz Festival you heard mentioned. May thirteenth. You're on for one hour. Three hundred thousand kids in a field. Work on it, but say nothing. To no one. I'll get word to you before then."

"If you're not out of this, I don't want it," she said, and got into the car.

He watched the taxi disappear along the coastal road. Come to think of it, that last remark of hers was most unprofessional. He lifted his bag and walked to the railroad station. "Next train for Ventimiglia?" he asked the ticket-seller, barely visible behind thick, yellowed plastic.

Muffled, the answer filtered through. "Ten minutes." Otto bought his ticket and went to the waiting room.

LILLIAN BALLARD LOOKED down at her negligee in some bewilderment. "Thank you for the compliment, darling, but I'm not wearing green. I'm in pink," she said.

"That's what you think," her husband answered. "I wish you'd stay in bed in the morning until this passes."

She shrugged: "The pills do help." She sipped her coffee with distaste.

"Indeed?" he rejoined. "As nearly as I can see they suppress it a bit in the morning so that you can be violently sick later in the day." He turned a page of the *Herald Tribune* and glanced down it.

"Is something wrong, Whitney?"

Motionless, the Ambassador continued looking at his paper. At last he looked up. "During the war Admiral King's aide-de-camp customarily breakfasted with him, arriving at table with the night's messages," he said reflectively. "One morning the Admiral opened the messages and read them, and his aide asked the question you've just asked. The messages said that during the night we had lost four cruisers to the Japanese. That was all the cruisers we then had. Admiral King laid the messages face down on the table and said, 'Later. There's no use spoiling two breakfasts.' " She recognized the signs of his anger. "That's my policy this morning," he concluded.

He rose from the table, leaned over, and kissed his wife. "Call Miss Fox, will you, and tell her I've left for the Embassy, and that I want to see Mr. Heston and Mr. Trumbull in my office in fifteen minutes."

She smiled up at him. "Tell me about it later, then, at lunch. When I'm pinker."

He paused. "I may not be here for lunch. I'll let you know."

The silence in the Ambassador's office stretched out. Whitney Ballard and the two men seated across his desk from him blinked occasionally in the glow from the scarlet carpet, but otherwise there was no movement. Roger Heston's initial beam had been replaced by a worried look, Ross Trumbull was even more watchful than when he had come in, but both maintained their respectful attitude. How is it possible that they don't know, Whitney Ballard asked himself.

Finally, he spoke. "Have you gentlemen seen the paper this morning?"

"Not yet," volunteered Heston. "My press man distributes the digest a little later, after the morning staff meeting." The Ambassador made a mental note: I must remind Lil to let me have a supply of those anti-nausea pills for here in the office.

"Uh, which one, sir?" asked Trumbull. Ah, yes, the cleverer of the two. The Ambassador ignored the question.

"Otto Miller is dead," he said.

The consternation of both was genuine enough. Heston, the Ambassador observed, was simultaneously shocked, sympathetic (of course: he knew my affection for Otto), and indignant. Trumbull was more controlled, but plainly disturbed. He is calculating the effect on *his* operation, the Ambassador reflected: perhaps natural enough in his position. In a cold voice Whitney Ballard recounted the news.

After a silence, during which Heston looked thoughtful, Trumbull spoke up. "We can sort this out. If it was an accident, there is no problem. If it wasn't, the question is who is responsible. I can vouch for Satori not having leaked anything which would have drawn Miller to the attention of people who would want to revenge themselves."

The Ambassador interrupted. "In your trade vouching for anyone is rare. How can you vouch for Satori in this case?"

Trumbull flushed slightly. "Because I was with him from Wednesday morning until Thursday afternoon. The time after I left him was not sufficient for him to have leaked word about Miller, and for this to result." He looked just a trifle disdainful. "It was not even sufficient, if we want to go to extreme hypotheses, for Satori to have arranged Miller's death himself."

The Ambassador nodded. "Go on."

"I can't say the same thing for Peter Dowling," Trumbull continued. "We don't know who he's been talking to these past three days. Furthermore, although I haven't got his file yet, I do have an interim report that's interesting. I don't say the two things are connected, but Dowling applied for and received a Hungarian visa before he left the States. We have no idea what his business in Hungary, if any, might be." Whitney Ballard recognized Trumbull's professional pleasure in information secretly gained, without the subject's knowledge. Again the question came to him: who watches the watchers?

"No doubt that's of interest in your special line of work," said the Ambassador, "but the significance of foul play in the case of Otto Miller would be German, not Hungarian— or even Russian. As you know, I don't agree with the subsurface fear of a Nazi danger in Germany. It doesn't fit the facts. And certainly not the present German government. The young rioters in the German universities certainly have strong affinities with fascism, but they are certainly not adherents of the old Nazi party or ideology. They even think they're leftists. But, at the same time, if any genuine ex-Nazis are still active enough to revenge themselves on Otto Miller, we want to know it."

Trumbull nodded noncommittally. Heston appeared bored by the speculation. "Most tragic," he said somewhat absently.

"Yes," said the Ambassador, "and we're not going to leave it there."

Roger Heston raised his eyebrows. Quietly, carefully, Whitney Ballard gave his orders. Roger Heston looked startled, then he swallowed. However quietly the Ambassador had spoken, his tone brooked no opposition. "Very well, sir. I'll get to work on that right away. We'll certainly work something out by Monday."

Whitney Ballard looked at him for just a moment. "No, Roger, that won't do," he said. "You have access to all the special facilities, including air transport, that you need. And I need that done successfully by tomorrow." He thought for a moment, and then added, "In time, let us say, for your press man's digest."

In the stone and marble hall outside the Ambassador's office, Ross Trumbull spoke in an undertone: "So now we play cops and robbers?"

Roger Heston shrugged and answered with similar discretion. "Like I told you, being an Ambassador is entirely a glandular matter."

Inside the Ambassador's office Whitney Ballard said to his secretary, "I want to speak to a Mr. Caxton Burroughs. He's secretary of the Voyagers' Club. If he's not at the Club yet, leave word for him to call me when he gets there. Don't disturb him at home."

It was eleven thirty when a weary voice came over the Ambassador's telephone. "Caxton Burroughs here, Mr. Ambassador. You left word for me to call you?"

"Yes, Burroughs, how are you?"

Puzzlement sounded in the weary voice. "Why, fine, thank you, and yourself?"

"As well as can be expected, thank you," said Whitney Ballard. A smile played about his mouth. "You know, Burroughs, in the time I've been here, I still haven't seen the inside of that Club of yours."

There was a silence at the end of the line, then mild irritation replaced the puzzlement in the voice. "Well, you *are* an ex-officio member, Mr. Ambassador."

"Why, that's very kind of you."

"Not at all, sir. It's customary." The voice now was wary.

"No, I mean very kind of you to invite me to lunch today," said Whitney Ballard.

He waited while Caxton Burroughs indulged in a lengthy, exploratory coughing fit. Finally the voice, touched this time with resignation, said, "The pleasure will certainly be mine, Mr. Ambassador."

"Thank you very much," said Whitney Ballard. "I'll be there at one o'clock."

"PETER," Lorna Vernon had said as she sat up in bed and reached down into the ice bucket for an eye-opener of champagne, gasping as a drop of ice water fell between her breasts, "I do wish you would spend an entire night here. It would be so restful, instead of having you dashing through the cold streets to your hotel in the dawn."

Peter had laughed. His last laugh of the day. "And what would the servants say?" Peter had inquired, as he pulled his tie into place.

"But, my dear," Lorna had remonstrated, "they're paid to keep quiet." And then as Peter kissed her good-bye, she had said, "Ah, Peter, you're a delight. A distant delight." And Peter had frowned in the shock of recognition.

If only that had been the sole shock of the day. But there had been the morning paper at the hotel, with his breakfast. And the real shock. Otto dead. It was impossible. And the doubly horrible suspicion that it was not an accident. Poor Helen. She had been overwhelmed by the cruelty of an inane accident, and he was unable to tell her that if he could be sure it was an accident that alone would be some solace. Was it or wasn't it an accident? He was bound to Otto to answer that question. But he couldn't begin to find the answer until he could get out of London, and that damn meeting this afternoon was unavoidable. And after that the first thing was to see Whitney Ballard. Then get to Eze and see about the arrangements. And whatever he could find out there.

Peter glanced out the window of the tower in the City where his firm had their London offices. The blue backdrop looked icy cold. The telephone rang and he picked it up. Helen Goodman's voice sounded low and distant. "Satori called from Munich," she said. "He was very upset, naturally. I told him you would be going to Eze, to make the arrangements, and that as executor of Otto's estate you'd be in touch with him next week. He said he'd await your call." Her voice broke.

"What about the Ambassador?" Peter asked stiffly.

Helen Goodman sniffled. "I left your message asking if you could see him either at the Embassy or the Residence any time from six on this evening," she said, "and his secretary just rang back to say she was very sorry but the Ambassador has to go out of town this afternoon and won't be back until Monday."

"What?" Peter's consternation was tinged with a quick surge of anger.

"That's what she said," Helen responded weakly.

Peter clenched his fist. "Okay," he said deliberately. "I'll take the nine o'clock flight from here tomorrow morning. Put me on a connecting flight to Nice, and meet me at Orly.

Bring along the extra keys to the house, and a copy of my power-of-attorney." He thought for a second. "And reserve me a car at the Nice Airport."

Helen repeated his instructions, and then Peter rang off, his anger fueled by the additional burden that he could be of so little help to her. So the Ambassador is backing out, he said to himself. Well, in that case, we'll just tackle this without the Ambassador.

EIGHT MEN FILED OUT of the bathroom with gold fixtures where, for just the right mixture of opulence and privacy, they had been accommodated for lunch. Two rooms farther along, in, what had presumably been an expansive boudoir in the old mansion of the Voyagers' Club, the members at the common table pushed back their chairs. "Excellent cheese, Caxton," said a French member.

A tall, slender man rose. "You'll excuse me, gentlemen," said the president of the American Chamber of Commerce in Paris. He smiled towards the head of the table. "I don't know how Caxton managed it, Mr. Ambassador, but it's an honor for us to have you. I hope we can see you here more often."

"Hear, hear," said an English member, and raised his glass.

Whitney Ballard acknowledged the salute with a nod. "Thank you, Charlie," he said to the tall man. He turned to the rest of the table. "Thank you, gentlemen. I am glad Mr. Burroughs was so persuasive. I hope he will be so again, but, as you know, I am not my own master."

The members rose. Caxton Burroughs, slight, sharp-nosed, with scanty blond hair, and seemingly utterly fatigued, said, "Shall we take our coffee in the library, Mr. Ambassador?"

Burroughs signalled to the waiter and he and Whitney Ballard went to a far corner of the library. They settled in the deep leather armchairs and watched the waiter approach.

"Remarkably ornate. Splendid thing that you've been able to preserve it all," said the Ambassador, looking at the carved paneling, the swirling columns, and the painted ceiling outlined in heavy gilt molding. The elderly waiter set down the coffee and two cognacs and silently padded away.

Caxton Burroughs leaned forward. "Was it an accident?" he asked.

The Ambassador sipped his coffee. "I don't know. That's what I want you to find out."

Burroughs gazed at the wall. He downed his coffee in rapid sips and reached for his cognac.

Whitney Ballard said, "You realize, don't you, that if it wasn't an accident, the rest of you from the unit may also be in danger?"

Burroughs swirled his cognac gently in his mouth and then swallowed. "I'm not objecting," he said, "I'm thinking. After all, you do have the entire Agency at your disposal."

The Ambassador looked at him steadily. "You've been out of it too long. I don't have the *entire* Agency at my disposal. Just the part of it that's here. I already have them on it. After a fashion. But *they're* the people responsible for the original leak."

"Of course," said Burroughs, wearily. He sank lower in his chair.

"I need someone to watch the watchers," said Whitney Ballard.

Again Burroughs took a swallow of cognac. "I'm not objecting," he said. "One can't do these things alone, you know."

"I assumed you could get the others."

"I can get one this afternoon," said Burroughs, leaning his head back and staring at the ceiling. "Another in two or three days. He has to come from a long way. There'll be expenses."

"They'll be covered," said the Ambassador, wryly.

For the first time Burroughs smiled more than merely politely. "Slush fund?" he asked.

The Ambassador tasted his cognac. "If it was an accident, I'll be out of pocket. If it wasn't, I fully expect to be reimbursed."

"And if it wasn't an accident we'll also need some equipment," Burroughs said.

"Maybe we can draw on the government for that," said the Ambassador.

"Automatics, so long as they're not forty-fives," said Burroughs. "Too bulky. Three. No, make it four. A hundred rounds each for a start."

"The captain of the Marine Guard will deliver them this afternoon. In civilian clothes, of course," said the Ambassador.

"Of course," Burroughs said. He held his empty cognac glass to the light, and put it down regretfully. With a sigh he took out a cigarette and lit it. "And what makes you think it might not have been an accident?"

Whitney Ballard leaned forward. "There are two things wrong here. Or rather, two people who could have done the wrong thing," he began.

Fifteen minutes later Caxton Burroughs stood at the door of the Voyagers' Club. "We do hope you'll take advantage of your ex-officio membership, Mr. Ambassador," he said to the departing figure as the doorman saluted.

THE MUFFLED ROAR of the engines rose to a whine, then to a shriek, and then turned into a noiseless vibration as the plane climbed steeply. For the twentieth time in twenty-four hours Peter went back over his last dinner with Otto. Now there was the funeral to arrange. And then the problem of what was left of his assets. Peter chewed his lip as he wondered whether Otto's description of his financial status the other night would turn out to be accurate. Well, that would wait until next week. He checked the power-of-attorney

44

Helen had brought to him at Orly, the reservation for a car at the Nice Airport, and felt for the keys to the house in his pocket. At least the house would bring a tidy sum.

He opened the *Herald Tribune* Helen had also provided. The American Ambassador to France, the paper informed its readers, would be the guest speaker at a luncheon Saturday, April 15, of the Comité France-Amerique. Peter put down his paper and looked out the window. That was today. So much for the Ambassador's "trip out of town." He recognized the technique of a grandee of the republic. Plainly, Peter himself was under suspicion, and Whitney Ballard would be of no help to him. It remained to be seen how much of a hindrance he would be.

Peter turned the pages of the paper mechanically, his eyes running rapidly down the columns. On page 4 they skipped over a photo, then stopped abruptly as his brain registered the familiar bald head. His eyes flicked upward and back to the photo. Two French gendarmes were dragging a struggling figure through a doorway. The figure was a man in dinner jacket. Except for a cheek turned towards the camera as he apparently shouted something, the man was visible only from the rear. Still, there would be no mistake. It was Otto Miller.

Peter's eyes dropped to the caption. *"Lèse-Majesté,"* it said. "Otto Miller being removed on princely orders from Cannes Casino." His eyes leaped to the adjoining column:

The Naked and the Nude

Received Differently at

Cannes Casino

By PHOEBE HORSEY

CANNES, Apr. 15—Last night's gala fashion show and ball at the Palm Beach Casino to launch the Côte-d'Azur Mode, presided over by Their Serene Highnesses, seemed to demonstrate that nudity is in—

but nakedness is out. An audience which included a sparkling contingent of the *tout-Paris,* in thankful refuge from the frozen northern spring, warmly applauded the new nude look as it was displayed by a series of ravishing haute-couture models. Nakedness, however—or rather an announcement of it—aroused the ire of the Prince, and the perpetrator was ejected from the hall.

Following the fashion show one of the guests appeared on the stage and took possession of the microphone. Calling for silence for an important announcement, he brought a gasp from those present with the declaration that "our beloved Princess has consented to return to films." Her first new feature, he claimed, would be his own production of " 'Lady Chatterley's Lover,' in color and full detail." Lady Chatterley would be played by the Princess—the phrase he used was "naked as a gooney-bird." The speaker, smiling beatifically at His Serene Highness, said there was nothing to worry about: "The first rushes were terrific. This little girl hasn't forgotten a thing about how and where to act." With a roar, the Prince called for guards and himself headed at a gallop for the stage. "Mellors," the man shouted above the pandemonium, "will be played by Mick Jagger." At that point the police hauled him away. French police said the man would be charged with "lèse-majesté for insulting a foreign head of state."

He was identified as Otto Miller, an American music publisher in Paris. It seems he was erroneously reported killed in an automobile accident a day earlier, but as "Teddy" Benvenuto, heir to the Italian soap fortune, and the delight of this year's hostesses, was heard to remark, "He might as well be dead now." . . .

Peter looked at the paper in consternation. Stark, raving drunk. Otto must have been stark, raving drunk. But to be that he had to be alive. Otto was alive. Peter dropped the paper in his lap and started to rise. Just in time he remembered the baggage rack overhead and dropped back into his seat. He looked about him. The other passengers were as unconcerned with his staggering discovery as they had been with his sorrow when he boarded. Peter laughed aloud, reopened the paper, and read the account of Otto's misbehavior through from beginning to end.

Why in God's name hadn't Otto telephoned Helen yesterday to set everyone's mind at rest? Obviously, he hadn't heard the reports of his own death. Peter leaned against the back of his seat. I'll make him pay dearly for this, he thought; I'll go straight there without telephoning, he decided, and walk in on him. The more embarrassing the situation for him the better. No matter who he's with, he can damn well put me up for the weekend.

Peter parked the rented Peugeot in the parking lot of Eze. The noon sun beat down on his head. The first thing I will have is a swim, he thought. He trudged up the road to the crest and began the descent through the narrow streets of the village. From occasional houses came the sounds of voices at the midday meal; the rest were shuttered and the street deserted. Peter passed into the shadow of the long archway and out again into the sunshine. He loped down the flight of steps and pushed at the gate. It swung open.

He passed into the small courtyard and came up to the front door. It stood slightly ajar. He must have a hangover this morning, thought Peter; he is seldom as negligent as this. He pushed the door open quietly and stepped into the vestibule. Through the shadow of the living room he could see out to the sunlit terrace and the endless backdrop of blue sea and sky beyond. A deckchair faced the swimming pool. Projecting above its back Peter saw Otto's bald head.

He crept forward. It won't do to frighten him too much, he thought, but certainly enough to repay him for these last twenty-four hours. He paused in the doorway. Suddenly he couldn't breathe and he felt himself falling backwards. He reached to his throat with his hands and tried to tear away the arm that gripped him. A sharp jerk on his throat, his feet slipped as he was dragged back into the living room, and he fell on his back. He heard the scuffle of feet on the terrace and a large bald man in swimming trunks landed on his knees beside him and pinioned his arms. It was not Otto.

Peter looked up beyond the bald man and saw a vaguely familiar face looking down at him. From the man's left hand a revolver pointed at him. Peter heard steps behind his head and raised his eyes. Even from the floor, and at the odd angle, there was no mistaking Roger Heston. He too had a revolver in one hand, but it dangled idly as he regarded Peter.

The bald man let go of Peter's arms and frisked him. He looked up at the vaguely familiar face and shook his head. Now Peter remembered. The face had grown pudgy since, but he had last seen it at training school. There he went under the name of Wyant, but there was no knowing his real name. Nor did it matter. Obviously, the Agency was taking a hand in Otto's affairs. Deliberately, Peter regarded the three men about him.

"Not quite what we expected," said Roger Heston, "but still it's something." Wyant looked puzzled, but kept his revolver aimed at Peter. Peter continued to lie on the floor, motionless.

"You may as well get up, Dowling," said Heston.

Peter glanced backward at Heston and shook his head. "Tell Wyant there, or whatever his name is, to put his cannon away." Heston waved his hand at Wyant, and the hand holding the revolver dropped to Wyant's side.

Peter sat up, and then rose to his feet. He looked out across the terrace, then turned, walked to an armchair, and sat down. "Where's Otto?" he asked Heston.

Roger Heston sat down on a couch. The bald man went and shut the front door. Peter heard the lock catch. Then the bald man returned and he and Wyant sat on another couch.

All three regarded Peter silently. Wyant and the bald man remained expressionless—Peter recognized the training—but Heston, he thought, looked as though he were holding four aces.

"We thought you might be able to enlighten us a bit on that," said Heston.

"Well, let's put it this way," said Peter. "What the hell are you doing here?"

Heston smiled. "No, no. Not that way," he said. "That's my question to you."

"That's easy," said Peter. "I am Otto Miller's lawyer, as you well know. I hold his power-of-attorney. I am also his good friend, as you also know. Further, I am the executor of his estate. On the report that he had been killed I came here to make arrangements for his burial, and to look after his affairs. In the plane I read that the report of his death was an error, and that he was very much alive. Had the door not been open I would have entered here with the keys to the house, which I am entitled to have—and have." He jingled the keys in his hand. "Instead of which I find the door open and three trespassers, who assault me. Also I don't find Otto Miller. The explanations, obviously, are due from you, not from me. First, where is Otto?"

Heston sighed and looked at his watch. He rose and went into the bedroom, shutting the door after him. Peter heard the muted sound of dialing, and then, not clearly enough to distinguish the words, the sound of Heston talking. After four or five minutes, during which the bald man hovered about Peter's chair, Heston emerged from the bedroom. He nodded to Wyant and went to the desk in the corner of the room. He returned to Peter and laid a dozen battered sheets of paper in his lap. Peter looked down. They were all the same. At the top of the page was the skull and crossbones insignia of the Totenkopf Hussars. Across the middle of the page was scrawled, in dark but broken lettering, "Unit 37." Superimposed on the lettering, so that its arms traversed the broken spaces, was a swastika. Peter looked at Heston. "A number of these were found by the French police scattered down the cliff where Miller's car went over," Heston said.

"So where is Otto?" Peter asked blankly.

Wyant pointed to the bald man standing beside Peter's chair. "That's Otto Miller," he said with a laugh. "Fresh from last night's triumph at the Palm Beach Casino. We thought he performed quite well."

Peter felt the stab of loss again. The bastards. "That's a lousy joke," he said.

"It's not a joke at all," said Heston. "You've been in the business, if only for a short time," he added with a trace of scorn. "You ought to be able to recognize the purpose." He scowled. "I may add, it was not an easy thing to pull off."

Peter looked at the sheets of paper. "I find these hard to believe," he said. "It's awfully childish."

Heston shrugged. "I can tell you *we* certainly didn't print them. *Or* distribute them."

Peter was silent for a moment. The bald man sat down. Heston looked somewhat absent-minded. "It would be helpful if you'd tell us where you've been and who you talked to since Tuesday night," he said matter-of-factly.

We might as well finish with this once and for all, thought Peter. "I dined with Otto Miller Tuesday night," he said. "Wednesday morning I went to London on business. I came from London here, changing planes at Orly, this morning. Everyone I talked to in London was either a banker or a lawyer, either a hero of the last war or a potential hero of the next one, and there certainly wasn't a Nazi among them. More importantly, I did not discuss Otto Miller with anyone."

Heston looked at Wyant. The pudgy face leaned forward. "Did you by any chance talk with someone after you had dinner with Otto Miller Tuesday night?"

"No," answered Peter.

"You mean you were just walking the streets from near midnight to five o'clock in the morning?"

Peter stared at Wyant. "You people mess around much too much in private lives," he said. "So you bribed the concierge of my hotel, or got the French police to talk to him for you. No matter. My answer stands. It's 'No' for the original purpose of your question."

Wyant's lip curled. "Chivalry, I suppose?"

"Knock it off, Wyant," said Peter. He rose. The bald man stood up. Peter turned to Heston. "Do you happen to know where the body is?" he asked.

Heston stood and looked at him in surprise. "What for?"

"I've told you," said Peter. "I'm here to make the arrangements."

Heston shook his head. "I'm afraid that won't be possible."

"And why not?" Peter felt his jaw tightening.

"The French authorities," Heston said. "They'll tell you they have a report Otto Miller is still alive, and the body is therefore not yet identified."

"Oh, for God's sake," said Peter. "That's carrying your clowning too far."

"Not far enough," said Heston. "As a matter of fact, I have a request for you from the Ambassador, on just that subject."

Peter raised his eyebrows. "He's out of town this weekend, isn't he?" he said sarcastically. "Don't tell me he's in on this gag too."

Heston spoke with a mixture of reticence and confidence. "I'm in touch with him." He nodded towards the bedroom. "Just spoke to him, in fact. He knows you're here."

"That obviously doesn't make my problems any easier," Peter retorted.

Heston ignored him and went on, this time in a conciliatory tone. "It could. The Ambassador conceived the idea himself. On the sound premise that if Miller's death was not an accident, and if it is announced publicly that Miller is alive, the assassins will try again. Then we'll know what we're dealing with. Obviously, he wants this operation to go on for another forty-eight hours, at least." Operation, thought Peter bitterly. The neutral word that covers all kinds of idiocy; why do they have to be so pompous? "But we have a little problem," Heston continued. "One the Ambassador hopes you will help us on."

Peter looked at Heston noncommittally. Typical, he thought. First they assault you, then they ask you to do them a favor. "Miller's office in Paris, his secretary," he said, "has been calling here since ten thirty this morning. We just tell her Miller is out, and will be back later. The Ambassador wants you to call her and tell her Miller's okay, and keep her calmed down for a few days."

"I can't do that," Peter said, "and then have to break the truth to her, for a second time, a few days from now."

"That's understandable," said Heston. "But if she knew the facts I'm sure she'd want us to lay hands on the murderers." Peter glanced in surprise at Heston. He was capable of thinking straight after all. Poor Helen.

"All right," said Peter. Heston pointed to the telephone in the bedroom.

Peter went in and sat on the bed. Heston and the two others stood in the doorway and watched him. "Dial sixteen, then one, then the Paris number," Heston said.

Without looking at him Peter dialed. There was the receding, interminable beep of French long-distance calls, seeming to count off each kilometer of the intervening distance, and finally Helen's voice, gay, even a bit silly. "Peter!" she cried. "What wonderful news! Where is Otto?"

Peter swallowed and endeavored to match her tone. "He's recovering from a very bad hangover. He's gone down to Monte Carlo for a few hours," he said.

Helen's voice took on an acerbic note. "I hope he realizes what hangovers he's given *us*," she said. "Will he want to talk to me later?"

Peter grimaced. "No," he said. "There are guests here, and he said to tell you he'll call you next week. Tuesday or Wednesday. Before he goes to Munich."

"Good," said Helen. "Actually, Peter, what I was calling

about was that there is a telegram for you here. It was at the office when I got back from the airport. You want me to open it and read it to you?"

Peter looked at the floor. "Yes."

There was the sound of tearing paper, and then Helen's voice in the earpiece said, "It's from Portofino. You know, in Italy. The message is, quote: 'As I said you have to do it intellectually now stop try Albergo Nazionale here for start,' " she read. Her voice turned cool. "Unquote. It's signed 'G. Kahn.' "

Peter pressed the telephone hard against his ear and turned his head away from the door to avoid meeting the eyes of the watchers in the doorway. "Is that G for Genevieve?" said Helen bitingly.

Peter repressed a smile. "No. Ginger," he said.

"Ginger Kahn. Sounds like a new toothpaste. Have a good time, lover boy," said Helen.

"Thanks," said Peter. He put the receiver back in its cradle.

The three were watching him. Careful of the face, thought Peter. He rose from the bed. As though in disgust, he said, "Okay. You have your few days to play." He pushed through them to the living room and turned to the front door.

"The Ambassador would want me to thank you," said Heston, pompously.

"Really?" said Peter. "He can try it when he gets back to town from his weekend in the country." He unlocked the front door and opened it. "And after that you can clear out of here so that I can sell this house. Meanwhile, try not to dirty the swimming pool too much." He stepped out into the courtyard, shut the door, and began to climb back up the steps to the village. Restraining himself, he moved slowly, almost wearily.

The three inside the house settled themselves in the living room. Wyant looked in truculent astonishment at Heston. Angrily, he said, "That's a bad apple if I've ever seen one. And you saw how he crept in here when he thought it was

Miller sitting out by the pool. Are you going to let the bastard wander off without a tail?"

Heston shrugged and leaned back in his chair. "Apparently," he said. "That's what the Ambassador just now told me to do with him."

"VERY GOOD, Herr von Satori." It gave the severe, middle-aged secretary pleasure to know that she worked for someone of noble family. She had never quite understood the matter of the Hungarian "untitled nobility," but Herr von Satori had been quite insistent that the German version of his name include the "von." And he was obviously so refined, and so gifted, particularly for one so young. She took the papers from his desk and moved soundlessly over the deep carpet to the door. There her customary rigidity gave way to a slight bow, and a small tight smile. "Good evening, sir. And I wish you a pleasant day tomorrow."

Alexander Satori gestured with his hand in her direction, then swept it back over his head to smooth his dark hair. "Thank you, Frau Graebner."

He swiveled in his high-backed leather chair and looked out the window into the courtyard. In the twilight a truck bearing the legend "Melodie Verlag—München" painted on the side was receiving a special Saturday afternoon loading. The bell of the church in the Theatinerstrasse tolled five o'clock. Although the church was only a few yards behind the wall of Satori's office, the bell's deep ring came through the soundproofing as no more than a distant vibration. Satori rose from his chair. With a glance he checked the wall of built-in sound reproduction equipment to be certain all was switched off, then walked to the far end of the room and entered a small bathroom. Having washed his hands, combed his hair, and satisfied himself in the mirror that all was in order, he crossed to a door leading directly into the hall and stepped outside. The door locked automatically behind him.

Two floors below, he emerged into the courtyard, turned right, and passed through an archway into Briennerstrasse. In the long, arbored loop of the adjoining Maximiliansplatz he hailed a taxi. "To the Hauptbahnhof," he said. The driver began a conversation, but Satori listened to him in silence, and the driver ended by grumbling to himself. At the station Satori disappeared inside. Five minutes later he emerged by a farther entrance into the heavy crowds, walked along Bayerstrasse to the Karlsplatz, where he again hailed a taxi. This time he got out at the corner of Beethovenstrasse and the wide Kaiser-Ludwig-Platz. He walked the whole length of the square at an easy pace, and finally, almost as though in doubt, turned into Haydnstrasse. At number 2 he paused in the entrance and rang the bell beside a card which read, "Heinrich Pfalz." He leaned against the door as the lock buzzed open. One flight up and to the left he rang a single time. The door opened almost immediately. Without a word, Satori stepped inside.

A tall, thin, brown-haired man, small-mouthed and wearing thick eyeglasses, was standing behind the door. He removed a large cigar from his mouth with his left hand and shook hands with Satori. He grinned. "I was watching. No one behind you, Sandy."

Satori smiled in reply. "If there was he's probably still caught in the rush at the Main Station," he said. "How are you, Ross?"

Ross Trumbull shook his head. "Come in and have a drink and I'll tell you." Satori followed him into the living room. The apartment was sparsely furnished. It had the air of a temporary refuge used by a number of different migratory birds. Drab and bare, it just escaped being unkempt: a safe house is rarely a happy house. Trumbull poured two whiskies, passed one to Satori, and sat down on a brown, stained couch. With his collar open, his cigar, and his somewhat tousled appearance, Trumbull fit into the surroundings.

Satori, immaculate and a bit too well-tailored, looked out

of place; a parakeet in a pawnshop. He was nevertheless entirely at his ease. "What's the latest trouble?" he asked.

Behind his thick glasses the expression of Trumbull's eyes was unreadable. He looked owlishly at Satori, who had learned to read his moods by his voice. "Otto Miller," Trumbull said in a rather high-pitched tone.

Satori laughed. "Happily, that's no longer a trouble," he said. "He's alive. Don't you read the papers?" He laughed again. "Not only alive, but made a complete ass of himself last night."

Ross Trumbull shook his head. "That's a brainwave of Ambassador Ballard's."

Satori looked puzzled. Trumbull knocked the ashes of his cigar off into a standing ashtray which reeled drunkenly when touched. "The Ambassador ordered Heston to lay on that farce," he said. "It wasn't Miller, but a stand-in for him. The Ambassador seemed to think the trick will uncover the killers. Amateurish, to put it mildly."

Satori looked shocked. "You mean Miller *is* dead?"

"No doubt about it," said Trumbull. "What's more, the French police found some leaflets with Nazi insignia at the site of the accident."

Satori grimaced. "This is terrible," he said in a low voice. He stared at the floor. "You can imagine my relief when I read that he was alive. And now we're back where we were yesterday morning. I can't tell you how horrible this news is for me." He was silent, and then went on, his voice breaking slightly. "I owed Otto a great deal. We were very old friends, you know. When I was a small child our families used to go to the same resort in Austria, in the Alps, every summer. Schattenwald it was called. Otto was older than I was, but he took so much time to play with me, and teach me things. As you might say, he was my hero then. And now he's gone. And just when we have a promising venture coming up that could have done a great deal for his finances. They're very shaky, you know." He took a sip of whiskey and shook his head.

"Obviously, the Ambassador was inclined to suspect you, after Otto coming to see him last Tuesday night, as I told you," Trumbull began.

Satori looked up quickly and interrupted. "Look, as I told you, that was an idle joke. It was perhaps even a little bit silly of me. But the fact is that I didn't even know Otto was in that Unit 37—as you can check by looking up the records of those courses—but I was sure he hadn't spent the war in the Signal Corps. I thought we were friends enough so that I could tease him." He sighed. "If the American Ambassador to France wants to suspect me of bringing about the death, even inadvertently, of my best friend, there's nothing I can do about it." He was silent for a full minute, and then he looked thoughtfully at Trumbull. "We may as well be frank, Ross," he said. "Perhaps it would be better if I withdrew from our work."

Trumbull chewed violently on his cigar, then removed it from his mouth and waved it at Satori. "There's one thing I can tell you, Sandy, and that is that it's not the American Ambassador to France who's running *this* operation. *I* am." He drew again on his cigar. "Hell, I know you didn't leak anything about Miller. I know you didn't know anything about him: they didn't give you the names of the members of Unit 37 in that course, and I told the Ambassador that. What's more, I told him that the obvious source of the leak is that lawyer friend of Miller's, Peter Dowling. And now he's down on the Riviera, too. Under the excuse that he's Miller's lawyer."

Satori said nothing, but raised his eyebrows in inquiry. "I found out just before I came here this afternoon," Trumbull continued, "that Dowling showed up at Eze this morning. Heston and company gave him a bit of a rough time, but then Heston checked with the Ambassador—like the gutless wonder he is—and the Ambassador told him to let Dowling in on the act, get him to cooperate, mind you, and then send him on his way without even having him tailed."

Satori looked sympathetically at Trumbull. "That doesn't make much sense to me."

Trumbull smiled sarcastically. "Ambassadorial sense, maybe. Anyway, I foxed him on that one. I had one of my people down there, without even Heston knowing about it. He checked with me, and I told him to keep close to Dowling until further notice. And just to show you my hunch was right, Dowling, instead of going back to Paris, which any normal lawyer would do who was seeing about the affairs of a dead client with a Paris office, checked into the Negresco in Nice. Dancing on the grave, I call it."

Satori nodded. "Odd, at any rate."

Trumbull gestured with his cigar. "Well, it's a problem, but not our main one. And not what I'm here for today, anyway. When's your next appointment with Pegov?"

Satori looked attentively at Trumbull. "Tonight," he said.

"Good," said Trumbull. "Here's our real problem. We want you to keep him from coming over as long as possible. The stuff you've been bringing us from him is sensational. Washington is, as you know, more than satisfied with it." Satori nodded modestly. "We want to keep it coming," Trumbull continued. "Obviously, we'll honor our promise to take care of him at the appropriate time. You've got to reassure him on that. But you've also got to talk him into staying where he is as long as he can. You think you can handle that?"

Satori thought for a moment. "Obviously, I'll try," he said. "Certainly, you could handle it with a great deal more authority and finesse, but I've told you how wary he is of a direct contact yet. That being the case, I don't think it's a matter of his coming over next week. But he's been indicating all along that things have been getting very difficult for him. You know very well that he can't carry this on indefinitely. The Penkovskiy example is very much on his mind. It may be that in about a month he'll have to come over. But I'll do my best."

"Good," said Trumbull. "Incidentally, the Chinese material is very good. About fits with our estimates. The Middle East stuff is a little thin. And we really do need more on East Germany. Not the kind of material the West Germans are flooding us with. We know how many screwdrivers the East Germans are making every day. We want to know who they're screwing with them." Trumbull appeared greatly tickled by his own joke.

Satori laughed with him. "I'll tell him," he said. He looked at his watch, finished his whiskey, and stood up. "Will you stay until tomorrow?" he asked.

Trumbull rose. "No, I'm going back tonight. I want to stay close to this situation around Dowling for the moment. But if you've got anything important for me, give the usual call here and I'll be up in a couple of hours." He accompanied Satori to the door. In an undertone filled with amusement, he said, "Hasn't the K.G.B. promoted you lately? Still just a lieutenant-colonel?"

Satori looked up at him. "Still just a Podpolkovnik," he answered. He smiled. "I don't really think I want to go any higher than that."

BY ELEVEN O'CLOCK of any evening Der Nackte Ritter Club in Munich's Schwabing district is an exploding box of sound; on Saturday, by the same hour, the noise is indistinguishable from that of a wind tunnel testing a new jet engine. Alexander Satori made his way into this holocaust with unruffled calm. Through a seething crowd of students—African, Asian, and European, of all nationalities—of older gawkers and sympathizers, of heads alternately bushy, lank-haired, merely fluffy, or sleek, and of bodies draped, hung, clothed, or barely covered, in every conceivable cloth, he pushed tenaciously towards the bar. There the barman caught sight of him and nodded his head deferentially. In a moment he had cleared a place for him, and Satori ordered a whiskey. Professionally, he eyed rather than listened to the musicians, as they worked their way through a screaming, chanting, gyrating number, the heavy German words dropping like stones in the din.

Satori finished his whiskey and ordered another. Apparently deep in thought, he faced sideways to the bar and inserted his hand in his jacket. He ran his fingers up his tie to the knot and then back down. He glanced about him. A girl with frizzy black hair, eyelids heavily painted in bright green, stepped forward from the crowd about the bar. A dozen chains hung about her neck to her waist, over a purple satin shirtdress open to her navel. As she moved her shoulders her shirt swung open from side to side, showing her breasts almost to the nipples, which were in any case evident through the satin, and the chains caressed her bare skin. A provocative smile on her lips, she twisted her way towards Satori through the crowd. He saw that her skirt did not quite cover her bottom, so that there were occasional glimpses of taut white beneath. He winked at her, and she smiled back.

"May I get past you to put my glass down here?" she asked Satori. Her open smile displayed a delicate and moist pink tongue between gleaming white teeth. She was as tall as Satori, so that he looked directly into her eyes.

He stepped aside to allow her to reach the bar. "I would be very pleased if you put yourself down here as well," he answered.

She flounced her tiny skirt in the air, and her white-clad bottom onto the bar stool. She joined her hands between her thighs. "You are a musician?" she asked.

He looked at her with amusement. "Only in a small way," he said. Her eyes clouded with uncertainty. Satori advanced and whispered in her ear, "I am a music publisher."

She smiled as though reassured. "Perhaps you know my favorite song, then?"

Instead of asking her which it was, Satori softly recited two lines of a song. The girl leaned her head forward to catch them. When he had finished, she picked up where he had left off, and completed the verse. "Very good," said Satori.

"My name is Helga," she said, laughingly.

Satori signaled the barman for two more drinks. "Dance, Helga?" he asked.

She wet her lips and nodded. Her knees, glistening in nylon, dropped and her bottom slid from the stool. Taking her by the hand Satori opened a path to the dance floor. It was as crowded as the bar, but here, instead of standing and talking, the crowd swayed, turned, and rocked in seeming private and unspoken ecstasy. Helga began to move her feet in small and repetitive steps, her arms moving in accompaniment, and the chains swinging across her breasts with the beat. Her mouth was open, the full lower lip protruding expectantly, as though awaiting a drop of honey. Her eyes were fixed on Satori's.

The movements of Satori's feet and arms made a mirror image of Helga's, but his torso remained more rigid and inclined slightly backward. His expression was one of deliberate unconcern. From beneath lowered lids he looked steadily into her eyes. Her breasts jiggling beneath the satin, Helga's shoulders and hips seemed to take on a rhythm of their own. Satori dropped his eyes to a point just above the center of the hem of her tiny skirt. Below it her angled thighs scissored in time with the music. Her eyes dropped to Satori's fly, and fastened there as her body moved ever more rapidly. Satori continued to stare just above the hem of her skirt. Slowly, her hips jerking backward and forward, she turned her back to him. There was a ripple of white beneath the purple. Satori smiled. She swung around again and faced him, her shoulders and hips still pumping to their own distinct rhythm. Gradually, Satori raised his eyes to her navel, to the chains swinging between her jiggling breasts, to her throat, to her open mouth, and then to her eyes. She smiled triumphantly. The music stopped. Laughing, she fell forward and pressed herself against him.

One against the other, they pushed back to the bar. Helga took a swallow of her drink appreciatively. Satori began the kind of intimate banter which marks an accord already reached; she responded with the provocative sallies which signify that, if the accord has been reached, it has still to be fulfilled. When the barman came to refill their glasses Satori glanced at his watch. "Ready?" he asked her. She nodded. Satori shook his head to the barman and signed the bill on the bar. The barman bowed slightly, his smile conveying discreetly his admiration of Herr von Satori's prowess.

Satori paused at the cloakroom, but Helga kept straight on. "No coat?" he asked.

She looked back. "I'm hot," she said teasingly.

They made their way up and out into the cold air, and walked briskly until they came to a dull black Karmann Ghia. Helga took the keys from her bag and unlocked it. She pulled out a simple black wool coat and put it on. Then she slipped behind the steering wheel. Satori slid in beside her.

She drove confidently and expertly. She turned onto the Leopoldstrasse, and headed towards the center of town.

"Student?" asked Satori.

She shook her head. "Painter."

They rode on in silence. At the Residenz she turned left. The old palace stared somberly across the street lights to the Hofgarten in darkness opposite. Helga drove on and into the Liebigstrasse. Before a massive, drab apartment house, which looked like a neglected fortification, she parked the car. As they got out she locked it.

Cautioning silence with her fingers to her lips, she led the way through the entrance into a bare, grimy lobby. The elevator was small and battered, its wooden walls scarred with carvings and graffiti. At the third floor they got out and walked along the hallway through a cold, weak light towards the front of the building. At an unmarked door Helga took out a chain of keys and opened it. The light disclosed a narrow corridor running parallel to the hallway outside. At various intervals along the length of the corridor doorways in the facing wall marked the rooms of the apartment, lined up one after the other in solemn inspection of the street in front. Or so Satori assumed, for all the doors were closed.

Helga stopped before the second door. Taking another key from her chain she unlocked it, switched on the light, and showed Satori into the room. It was a comfortably furnished study, containing a desk, several armchairs and bookcases, a large armoire, and in a corner near the door, a wide couch decorated with multicolored cushions. The desk stood before the window, which was hidden by heavy curtains. On either side of the desk doors gave onto the adjoining rooms. It could have been a psychiatrist's office. "Wait here," said Helga. She went out and shut the door. Satori observed that its inner side was padded to deaden noise. He heard the lock turn.

Satori contemplated the couch for a moment, and then sat down in one of the armchairs facing the desk. There was not a sound audible in the apartment. Calmly, he waited.

At the end of five minutes the lock of the door to the left of the desk turned, and the door swung open. A man only slightly larger than Satori stepped into the room. He was in his late fifties, dressed conservatively in a dark blue double-breasted suit which could not conceal his paunch. His graying hair was swept back from a broad forehead. A slight cast in his right eye made his gaze curiously searching, rather then penetrating. From a bulbous nose deep furrows ran down either cheek, framing a thin mouth. Fastidiously, he closed the door behind him, then advanced to Satori and extended his hand. "Aleksandr Pavlovich," he said in a musical voice. His smile was formal.

Satori had risen when he entered. He shook the hand offered him, and smiled warmly. "Lazar Matveyich!" he exclaimed, abbreviating the patronymic familiarly. "You are looking well."

In the manner of a confirmed hypochondriac, Lazar Matveyevich Pegov frowned and waved his hand as though to dismiss the good news. His mouth set in an expression of severity he motioned Satori to sit down. Seating himself in the other armchair before the desk, he adjusted it so as to face Satori. "Sorry to keep you waiting," he said, "but I cannot afford the slipshod methods of your American friends. They are working in friendly territory. I am working in hostile territory."

"Of course, Lazar Matveyich," Satori answered.

Pegov frowned again. He lit an American cigarette and hastily expelled the smoke. "No doubt one of the most unpleasant features of foreign duty is foreign cigarettes," he observed. His eyes shifting nervously, he watched Satori in silence. At last he spoke. "Trumbull has bungled it."

A faint smile played around Satori's mouth. He shook his head. "It only looks that way," he said.

"Ah?" Pegov's expression was one of polite disbelief. "And how do you reach that conclusion?"

"Because you correctly foresaw the course of events, Lazar Matveyich," Satori replied earnestly. "You will recall that you chose Otto Miller precisely because of his old connection with the American Ambassador Ballard. And it worked out exactly as you foresaw. The Ambassador suspected something, even before he knew about the leaflets. He ordered his C.I.A. people to create a false Otto Miller, in the hopes this would uncover those responsible. The man involved in Friday night's scandal was not Miller, but a C.I.A. man playing his part. The C.I.A. is presently occupying Miller's house at Eze as a trap." He laughed. "They hope."

Pegov nodded as though in agreement, but then he added, in the tone of a schoolmaster, "And?"

Satori raised his eyebrows. "I had this from Trumbull today," he answered.

Pegov nodded again. "All this may or may not be," he said. Then, softly, he said, "You have forgotten the control."

Satori looked at him questioningly. Pegov leaned forward and spoke deliberately. "As you know—or should have known—we have been controlling this operation. It is essential that Russ Trumbull be implicated in the murder of Otto

64

Miller. But our man in the French police there has given us some interesting material. It seems that on Thursday night one Joseph Calvi disappeared. He has not been found since. But his car was discovered, abandoned, in Menton on Friday. Calvi, you will be interested to know, was a friend of Miller. What is more important, he ran a garage in Cannes which specialized in repairing foreign makes of automobiles. Jaguar among them. Our man is convinced, because of this and because of the size of the remains, which were much too small for Miller, that the body in Miller's Jaguar was Calvi. This suggests they had exchanged cars, and that Miller, possibly on learning of the accident, escaped in Calvi's car, leaving it in Menton. What we don't know is why Miller should have become frightened. In any event, it is sufficient that Trumbull bungled."

Satori regarded Pegov steadily. Then he shook his head. "No, Lazar Matveyich. You underestimate Trumbull. I told him that when I last saw Miller, on Tuesday, he was extremely apprehensive. Most unlike himself. I don't know why. Perhaps his conscience, as they call it. And Trumbull has taken all this into account. One fly was caught in the Ambassador's trap at Eze. It was Miller's lawyer, and his very close friend. An American from New York named Peter Dowling. If there was a mistake on Thursday night, Trumbull is convinced Dowling will lead him to Miller. Unknown to the Ambassador or the C.I.A. he has a man trailing Dowling now. He's at the Negresco in Nice at this moment."

Pegov's eyes crinkled as he permitted himself a smile. "Was that your idea or his?" he asked.

"His, of course."

"It may be that he is learning from you, as you have learned from me," said Pegov. "You are convinced that Trumbull is genuine, I take it?"

"There is no question about it," Satori answered promptly. "My mission during all these years since I was sent out to the West, Lazar Matveyich, has been to penetrate the C.I.A. I think you have reason to be satisfied with my work?"

Pegov eyed him benignly. "You have reason to be aware of our satisfaction."

"You know better than I do the caliber of the C.I.A. people, Lazar Matveyich," Satori went on. "In all these years the only one I have come across whose political motivation and professional qualifications were up to our standards is Trumbull. And I remind you it was he who initiated the effort to get in touch with us. In short, he has a correct political viewpoint."

"All that is true, but it is not enough. One can never be too careful with *Zapadniki*," he said, using the Russian word for Westerners, "no matter who they are. It is not only that they are sly and tricky. We know they would all sell their grandmothers if the price were right. But more than that, they are inherently confused. It is not possible for a Zapadnik to see the situation correctly in all its aspects. There are too many relics of the past buried in them, and they have no awareness of the struggle that must be waged to root out the past. Particularly not of the length of the struggle."

He lit another cigarette, exhaled, and coughed. "Of course," he continued, "Trumbull's material has been very useful to us. No complaint there. But you understand that a Zapadnik who comes over to us out of, if you will, simple idealism, is not necessarily a good risk. I've seen them in Moscow. They go to pieces, if they weren't already in pieces when they arrived. Then they begin to sulk, and finally we have to dispose of them."

He contemplated the ceiling for a moment, then went on. "In Trumbull's case there is the special problem that he is more useful to us where he is than if he were to come over to us. It is your job to make him understand that. If he is in danger, we will of course honor our commitments to him. We take care of our people. That is known the world over. I need only remind you of Abel, Blake, Lonsdale, the Krogers, and the many others."

He looked at his cigarette in distaste and put it out. "But there is another problem which is not peculiar to Trumbull.

66

It concerns, as I said, all Zapadniki. Whoever they are, their private motives and reasoning are weak reeds. That is why we must have a hold on Trumbull. One that, if he hits a difficult moment, will reinforce his will. One on whose force *we* can depend. That, as you know, is why we have insisted that Trumbull dispose of Miller. The disposal of Miller was not a test of Trumbull, Aleksandr Pavlovich. It was a steel chain forged by Trumbull himself binding him to us."

"Of course, Lazar Matveyich."

Pegov rose and went to the armoire. He opened it and removed a bottle of vodka and two glasses. He set them on the desk and, without asking Satori, poured for both of them. Pegov tossed his off in a gulp, and then belched. He sighed, waited in silence while Satori gulped his, and then poured another round.

"Naturally, I have explained the Miller question to him in terms of its political significance," Satori said. "That is to say," he added delicately, "its *international* political significance."

Pegov nodded in agreement. "And right you were. It is necessary to indicate convincingly to the Americans that they are wrong in their German policy. The fact that a band of Nazi adventurers are set on avenging certain wartime losses, even at this late date, *and* are able to do so, will not affect the American ruling circles. But it will arouse progressive opinion against them." He tossed off his vodka and poured another. "Of course, you and I know that, as far as the objective situation is concerned, it is of no importance that the band of Nazi adventurers are in fact some people working for Ross Trumbull. With things the way they are in Germany today, it could perfectly well happen without our little assistance to history."

"Of course, Lazar Matveyich."

Pegov frowned. "You understand the problem in all its ramifications, Aleksandr Pavlovich. The Chinese are nothing but a primitive mass. We will hold them off with a wall, with a desert, of flame. Ah, but the Germans. That is another story. That is more delicate. The affair of Miller will spread about. It will weigh with those comrades in the Politburo who are weakening our stance in the West to take care of the Chinese. And even worse, are pretending the German Social Democrats—the original fascists, I tell you—can be treated with reasonably. A treaty with Brandt! Such idiocy!" He settled into a glowering silence.

"What of the rest?" Satori asked finally. Pegov looked at him vaguely. "Unit 37," Satori added.

"We've found another one. Caxton Burroughs," said Pegov moodily. "Sounds like a petty bourgeois section of London, but he's another American. Lives in Paris. I'd rather have the next episode somewhere else, however. It would spread the noise about better."

Satori looked at his hands. "You haven't found Forbath yet?"

Pegov waved his own hands. "No. The man seems to have disappeared. We've checked a number who it turns out have died since the war, but he was not among them." He stared at the vodka bottle, and finally poured himself a glass. "But we'll find him. We always find them."

"Of course, Lazar Matveyich."

Pegov sat in silence for several minutes. Finally, he swallowed his vodka and rose. Satori stood up. Pegov tilted his head back slightly and looked down his nose at Satori. "We will first see whether Trumbull bungled this one," he said. Satori nodded. "As you see," Pegov continued, "you have a new contact. Two-two, nine-nine, two-one. Her telephone. You have it?"

"Satori nodded again. "Two-two, nine-nine, two-one," he repeated.

"As usual," Pegov went on, "nothing on the telephone but sweet nothings and rendezvous." Again Satori nodded.

Pegov shook Satori's hand, said "Aleksandr Pavlovich," somewhat stiffly, and disappeared through the door by which he had entered, shut it, and locked it. After a minute a key turned in the door by which Satori had entered and Helga swung it open. She was wearing her black coat. Satori passed through the doorway and went to the front door. He waited while she locked the door of the room he had just left and then unlocked the front door. Then he stepped out into the hallway. Helga left the key, a half-dozen other keys dangling from its chain, in the inner side of the lock and shut the door from the outside. As they waited for the elevator Satori heard the lock turn.

On the way down in the elevator Satori said, "I should know where your apartment is. Just in case."

She spoke barely audibly. "Yes, the comrade Doctor told me you should. It's directly overhead on the floor above. Number 42."

Satori looked at her frizzy black hair. "Your own is showing," he said to her sharply.

She looked to see where his eyes were directed and then lifted her hands and tucked a blond wisp in under the wig. She shrugged. "It's not a disguise," she said. "It's supposed to attract men like flies." Her tone was ironic.

Satori's was disdainful as he answered. "You mean it's supposed to act like honey," he said, "or to attract men who are like flies?"

In the car he said, "Drop me at the Bayerischer Hof. I keep an apartment there."

She nodded. "I know."

She drove to the Maximilianstrasse and then turned right. It had rained, and the cobblestones and baroque facades were a glistening black. At the Opera she turned right up Residenzstrasse, swung around down Theatinerstrasse, and then turned into Maffeistrasse. The doorman at the Bayerischer Hof opened the door of the car and raised his cap. "Goodnight, liebchen," said Satori. "And thanks." He kissed her warmly on the mouth.

"Mmmm," said Helga, audibly, and gave him a big smile which also took in the doorman. Satori stepped out and acknowledged the doorman's greeting with a nod.

As the glass door closed behind him Satori heard the car

drive off. He went to the stairway by the bar and descended to the nightclub. He entered and stood for a minute in the darkness. To his left, still another level below, were the tables and the dancefloor. Spotlights shone on the blaring orchestra, and revolving lights bathed the dancers in changing colors. To his right the bar offered a wall of golden light in the surrounding darkness. He went over and ordered a whiskey. When it came he took it and strolled away to a large square pillar. He leaned against it and watched the dancing below him.

A tall, heavy man, massive without being corpulent, in his middle fifties, with an expression that combined sadness and resentment, stepped from the bar and joined Satori. In a jovial voice that carried over the music, he said, "Pleasant evening, Sandor?"

Satori looked up in surprise, and said, "Ah, Horst. The usual, the usual." Satori moved around the pillar to the side away from the bar. He beckoned with his head to the tall man, who lowered his.

"Get word to Begovic immediately," Satori said in a steely voice. "There's an American lawyer at the Negresco in Nice. Name is Peter Dowling. He's Miller's friend. It seems Begovic got the wrong man and Miller has fled. Dowling should lead him to Miller. Dowling is already tailed by a C.I.A. man. Tell Begovic to get rid of the tail and take it up himself. Remind him if he fails this time his file goes to the police."

Horst nodded. Softly, he asked, "Always as Trumbull?"

Satori looked up at him coldly. "He doesn't know you by any other name, does he?"

IN THE ORANGE ROOM which had comprised his world for more than fifty hours, Otto Miller sat at a small table and stared glumly into what he could see of the evening. On a weekend one could never tell who might drop by Portofino.

70

For the moment it was better to stay indoors, but this couldn't be done indefinitely. Perhaps it had not been a wise choice. What was taking Peter so long? Had he believed that weird newspaper story of his whereabouts? No, he surely would have the telegram by now. Otto sighed. Give him twenty-four more hours. He leaned back in his chair just as there was a knock at the door.

Warily, he rose and walked to the door, "Chi è là?" he asked.

"Permesso, signore?" a woman's voice answered. There was a steady, faintly perceptible vibration of glass against cutlery. Otto opened the door.

A tray, spread with dishes, a glass, and a bottle of wine, appeared, then olive-skinned upper arms, then black hair framing an eagerly friendly face. "Il suo pranzo, signore," the maid smiled. Otto closed the door after her. As though dispensing bounty, but without a wasted motion, she laid out his dinner on the table. Otto seated himself. Appreciatively, he regarded his meal.

"Lèi ha fame?" she asked. Otto looked up at her. This was the seventh meal she had served him, and he had come to count on her friendly interruptions to his solitude. Neither young nor old, she exuded both concern for him and a private vivacity. Her dark hair tumbled in disorder, and her face, made almost pretty by her animation, was flushed.

"Gran fame," Otto answered, looking steadily into her eyes.

Her eyes on his, a responsive smile on her lips, she reached for the wine bottle with her left hand and pushed it into her skirt, between her thighs. With her right hand she inserted and turned the corkscrew, rhythmically. After a half-dozen turns she pulled on the handle. There was a squeak, followed by a soft pop, and with an air of satisfaction she took her eyes from his and leaned over him to pour his wine. On an impulse Otto reached around and squeezed her buttock firmly in his hand.

She squealed, but Otto noted that she had paused before

71

she did so. "Cattivo," she murmured reproachfully, but she was still smiling. Her face became even more flushed. Otto left his hand where it was. She looked at him and laughed. "Non la dominica mai," she said teasingly.

Otto laughed in reply. "Never on Sunday": a bounteous promise for all the others days of the week—as well as a challenge for Sunday itself. He started to say, "In four hours it will be Monday, but he was cut short by a penetrating buzz in his room. He jumped involuntarily, then looked in astonishment at the telephone on the wall.

"Il telefono, signore," she said gently, as Otto sat rooted to his chair. He gestured to her to answer it. She took the receiver down and spoke into it. Otto rose and approached her, his expression worried. She handed him the telephone with a shrug. "E per lèi, signore."

Otto shook his head. "Chi chiama?" he whispered.

She repeated the question into the receiver, then turned to Otto. "Un signore Giugi," she said.

Otto looked puzzled. Then he frowned. Finally, he shook his finger negatively. "Di' che io no sono là," he said softly. But before she could say he wasn't there Otto clapped his hand to his forehead, cried "Momento!" and grabbed the telephone from her.

"Juji!" he shouted into the receiver. "The Great Khan's favorite son! Where are you, my boy?"

"In Genoa," Peter's voice answered in his ear. "I seem to have a lot of trouble getting through your secretaries."

"That's because of the morbid interest you take in them," Otto retorted.

The maid backed out the door. "Più tarde, signore," she whispered.

Absently, Otto waved his hand. "Man lives not in a hotel room alone," he added to Peter.

"On the contrary," Peter said drily, "that seems about the only place I can be alone. I've been followed all the way here."

"How's that?" asked Otto anxiously.

"I can't tell you now," answered Peter, "but in the circumstances it would be foolish for me to come there."

Otto thought for a moment. "Any suggestions?" he asked. "I don't know this coast well."

"I spent a couple of holidays around here when I was stationed in Munich," Peter answered. "Do you know San Fruttuoso?"

"No."

"It's a small bay out around the point and to the west from Portofino," said Peter. "There's a trail over the mountain from Portofino, but that takes a couple of hours. By boat you can do it in less than a half-hour. Hire a speedboat tomorrow, drive it yourself, and go to San Fruttuoso. Be there by noon and wait for me in the restaurant. There's only one. I'll be coming from another direction. Okay?"

"Right," said Otto.

"Just in case, have your bag packed and your bill paid at Portofino before you come," Peter added. "And one final thing."

"Yes?"

"Moor your boat so it's facing out to sea, and leave your blowers running. Hasta mañana."

"This is Italy. You've wandered into Spain," Otto observed.

"The way things are going here that's not a bad idea," said Peter, and hung up.

Ten minutes later Otto remembered his cooling dinner. Two hours later, when the maid knocked at his door, ostensibly for the tray, he was already, ostensibly, asleep.

THE SMALL PORT of Camogli, at the western base of the Portofino peninsula, is made up of tall houses rising like early intimations of the skyscraper. They form a semicircular backdrop of many hues to the port and little beach, with pine and olive groves soaring up the steep slopes on either side. Paradise Gulf, the people of the region call it. And as Peter locked his car and walked down to the port, he conceded that in circumstances other than his own, it might well be.

He made his way around the port. At the single dock offering boats for hire, three Riva speedboats lay rolling gently in the dark green water. One was a twin-engined craft, almost twenty-six feet long. The other two were smaller, each about twenty feet long, one equipped with a V-8 engine. Their deep varnish gave off mirrorlike reflections in the sunlight, their sleek V-hulls and shining chrome outward and convincing evidence of the Italian's efficiency in design and superb craftsmanship when it comes to the sea. "All in running order?" Peter asked the owner.

"All three," he answered proudly.

"Good," said Peter. "I'll take all three."

Cupidity broadened the boatman's smile. Then doubt shrank it. "How, all three?" he asked. "You are only one person." Peter explained that he would take the twin-engined boat, and pay for the other two for the time he was gone. The owner frowned his disapproval. "No, signore," he said righteously. "You deprive others of their pleasure."

In other words, thought Peter, business is good; he knows he can hire them out to others, perhaps for more in the end. He decided to take refuge behind the confusion of language. "You do not understand," he said to the boatman. "I hire the other two for my friends. They will be along shortly to join me."

The boatman beamed. His hands spread expansively. "Of course, signore," he agreed. "How will I know them?"

Peter improvised quickly. "They will ask for me. Signor Dowling." Those thugs following me can probably do that, too, he thought. "It will be two men," he continued, "with three women and three children. You know," he held his palm flat a couple of feet above the dock, "small children."

The owner nodded amiably. "Si, si. Very good." Peter

74

showed his passport, signed the necessary papers for the insurance, and paid for all three boats. Then he went back to the quay and had an espresso in a cafe. He looked about as he sipped it. No sign of the three who had followed him the day before. He returned, not too hurriedly, to the dock. The owner cast him off, and Peter threaded his way out of the small port, breathing deeply of the heavy mixture of pine, salt, and fish. As he glided past the breakwater he looked back. All was calm in Camogli.

Beyond the breakwater Peter pushed the throttles as far forward as they would go. The motors roared and the boat leaped forward and up. The sun beat on his forehead as the air, now lightened of harbor-enclosed pungency, rushed past him. The sleek hull raced through the almost somnolent Ligurian Sea, past the looming cliffs of the Peninsula. He rounded the southern tip and headed east. Offshore the sea was calm, rippled only by an occasional breeze, but a deep ground swell washed up against the cliffs with a sudden crash, the waves hammering against the wild, jumbled rocks, and the spume sliding away from them in boiling currents.

He glanced out to sea. About five hundred yards off the coast a mottled shadow lay motionless on the glaring water. Peter smiled. Now, as years before, when he had last been here, the Italian Coast Guard's cutters plied their frustrating trade: policing something over 5,000 miles of coastline, almost all of it seemingly designed by the Lord as a smugglers' heaven. He turned back to the monumental, forbidding cliffs. Ahead, a break in their solid wall signaled his destination.

Peter pulled back on the throttles as he turned into the V-shaped bay of San Fruttuoso. The boat's bow dropped into the water. On all sides densely forested slopes descended abruptly to the rocks at the water's edge. In a cove at the end of the bay there was a small arc of beach. Behind it, a half-dozen old stone buildings formed a solid bulwark. The one on the right, Peter knew, was the remnant of a tenth-century monastery. Inside, in an ancient cloister, were tombs of the

Dorias. Behind the monastery rose the Romanesque steeple and cupola of the church. On the left, at the opposite end of the beach, was a great outcropping of rock. At its base was a concrete landing platform; from it, steps carved out of the rock ran up to an arched entrance in the nearest building. On the top floor of the next house, its windows overlooking the bay, was the restuarant. The only access to the church and cloister behind San Fruttuoso's seaward face led up from the arched entrance and through the restaurant.

He headed the boat for the right side of the bay. Except for a couple of sturdy fishing boats drawn up on the beach itself, the half-dozen small boats in the bay were all anchored just off it. Among those in the water was an empty speedboat. Nearby, a boatman in a dory rested on his oars. Peter pulled his throttles back to idling. The boat glided over the clear, blue-green water, its light-shot depts bespeaking a cool, sensual haven. Despite himself, Peter stared down into the water. From below, the upturned face of San Fruttuoso's Christ of the Depths, moored on the seabed, looked up at him.

He looked back up. The boatman in the dory was hailing him, and pointing to the speedboat already moored. Peter glided alongside. He understood not a word of the stream of Genoese dialect which the boatman addressed to him, but he gathered from the gestures that he was expected, that he should anchor alongside the other speedboat, and that the boatman would row him to the beach. Peter maneuvered his boat into position alongside the other, anchored, put out his fenders, and cut the ignition. In the ensuing silence the high-pitched hum of the other boat's blowers was audible. Peter switched on his own, and clambered into the dory.

In silence the boatman rowed him to the beach, and gestured to the arched entrance at the far end. Peter jumped onto the stony beach and walked rapidly to a flight of stone steps, leading up into the archway, where they joined the steps and ramp coming from the dock. He mounted the steps and entered into darkness. He followed the damp stairway upward, then a twisting passageway, and emerged into the restaurant. At a far table, overlooking the water, Otto Miller sat with a glass of wine before him.

As Peter approached, Otto rose. "You made it, Juji," he said warmly.

Beneath the cheerfulness Peter detected the note of strain. "The last time I was here I was in much prettier company," he answered with a smile. He clasped his friend on the arm and the two of them sat down. "I don't know how long we have," Peter said quickly. "If we have to run for it, I want you to do only one thing. Head for Portofino, as fast as you can. From there beat it even faster to another hideout. I'll take care of the rest. Even if we're not disturbed here, you better leave Portofino, now that I've brought the goons this close."

Otto scowled. "You mean you haven't shaken them?"

"As of this morning I may have," said Peter, "but the traffic was so thick coming out from Genoa, I could have missed them. There were three speedboats for hire in Camogli, where I came from. The other two are slower than the one I came in, but I took the precaution of hiring them all. However, there's a regular boat service along this coast, or they might even settle on hiring a dory with an outboard. All they need is one sight of you to know where you are." He signaled the waiter for an espresso. "Now, how did you get here?" he asked Otto.

Otto quickly described his trip to Eze: the breakdown, the exchange of cars with Calvi, and the television announcement of his death. He made no mention of Eva Roessli. When he was finished, he looked at Peter in puzzlement and asked, "But what was the comedy last Friday night in Cannes?"

Peter shook his head in disapproval. He summarized for Otto his voyage from London to Nice, Whitney Ballard's refusal to see him, and, with patent chagrin, his reception at Eze. Otto looked more and more discomfited, but said nothing. "It was when I was speaking with Helen," Peter went

77

on, "that she read me your telegram. Even if the line were tapped it meant nothing to the C.I.A. boys. However, when I left I went to Nice and spent the night at the Negresco, as though killing time. Up to Saturday night I could have sworn I was being followed by a single. A young, sort of foppish type. Could have been an American. But Sunday morning his place was taken by the three who have been with me since.

"I did everything to lose them. No luck. I didn't come along the coast road from Nice. I went inland, over the Tenda Pass to Cuneo, as though I was sightseeing. They managed to hang on all the way. This morning, too."

Otto bit his lip. "You saw the Nazi leaflets, you say?"

"Yes, I saw them," Peter retorted, "and I slipped one away. Heston doesn't know all the tricks." He reached in his jacket and pulled out a small, thick piece of paper. He unfolded it carefully and laid it before Otto. "Frankly," he said, "I don't think it's for real. The real Nazis, survivors or successors, go by other names today. The someone who pushed Calvi off the road knew your movements intimately—in advance. But they didn't know them well enough to know when something unexpected, like your car breaking down, happened. And now they still know enough so that, after that gratuitous bit of creative theater by the Ambassador, they follow me to get to you."

Otto grimaced. "I see Whitney's point in staging the comedy," he said, "and if I were dead it would be a valid one." He frowned. "But for the moment I'm alive, so the point is reversed and he's only put me in more danger."

"It's a somewhat complicated problem," Peter said drily. "you're dead for the right people and alive for the wrong ones."

Otto nodded. "At least Whitney Ballard has to be told I am alive."

"And if he won't see me?"

"He probably will," Otto answered. "He asked you to do him a favor and you did it. In politics that gives you the

78

right to at least an audience. The real problem is whether he'll believe you. Got some paper?"

Peter reached in his jacket, took out a notebook, tore out a piece of paper and handed it to Otto. Otto took up the waiter's pencil lying on the table and scribbled a note. "If he won't see you," he said, "deliver this in an envelope marked personal to the Embassy." Peter picked up the note and the leaflet, folded them both, and put them in his wallet.

"Now," said Otto forcefully, "there's another problem. The Bavarian Jazz Festival has got to go on. Financially, it's my only hope. That means you'll have to let Helen and Satori in on the fact that I'm alive too."

Peter leaned back and stared in disbelief at Otto. "Not on your life!" he said. "First of all, you're confused about whether you're alive or not. Helen thinks you are. The problem with her is to explain your absence. You can't be in touch with her, either. Someone is sure to be watching your office, and her, if not tapping the lines. As for Satori, I don't know what he thinks. I'll find out, though. And play it by ear from there. If he thinks you're alive, I have your power-of-attorney. If he thinks you're dead, I'm your executor. And that's not all. I'm going to take a good look at your Munich associate. For my money, that's where the trouble lies."

Otto leaned forward as though to argue. "No argument," said Peter.

Otto shrugged. "If you insist," he said.

"I do," answered Peter.

"In that case," Otto continued, "there's one gap left in the Bavarian program. I want it filled by a singer named Eva Kanday. She sings now at the St. Gotthard Bar in Zurich. You better go there and talk to her about it. She has a very jealous husband, a Swiss banker named Gunter Roessli. She sings in the evenings, from nine to eleven."

"Does she know anything about this proposition, or do I approach her cold?" asked Peter.

Otto smiled. "No one approaches Eva Kanday cold," he said, "or if they do they don't stay cold long. And she knows about it. In fact," he added, "I was talking to her about it last Thursday night at Eze when I learned I was dead."

Peter looked at him in astonishment. He started to say something, but a motion on the water caught his eye. From the direction of Camogli a launch had turned into the bay and was approaching the landing platform. The launch slowed, seemed to drift, and then bumped gently against the dock. A gangway was put over and a horde of passengers began to debark. They were plainly tourists—some expectant, some skeptical, some weary, others delighted, others with vacant stares, but all waited in uncertainty for their guide to take charge. With a gesture worthy of a cavalry commander summoning his troop to attack, he placed himself at their head and waved his arms at the steps leading up to the archway and the restaurant.

As they milled about on the dock, and then filed upward, Peter scanned their faces. He was about to sigh with relief when Otto grasped his arm and pointed to the bay. A speedboat had come about the western headland and was heading to shore. Peter started, then stared. The boat raced the length of the bay. As it approached the anchorage it slowed. As the bow settled into the water Peter recognized the three heads. "It's them," he said quickly to Otto.

Otto blanched. "So much for your hiring all the speedboats in Camogli," he growled. "This couldn't have happened under Mussolini," he added in disgust.

Peter watched the passengers from the launch filing upward. They began to stream into the restaurant. The occupants of the speedboat nodded to each other in silent recognition of Peter's boat. They gave way as the launch made a cumbersome turn and headed back down the bay. Then they glided slowly forward to the beach. The same young, round-faced man who had been driving the day before was at the wheel. He beached the craft. From above, Peter and Otto watched in silence. Around them, the tourists milled in babbling confusion, filing through the restaurant to the church and cloister behind.

A dark-complexioned man, his face still expressionless, rose from the speedboat, stepped over the windshield onto the bow, and dropped to the beach. He was followed by an older man, with deeply furrowed cheeks and a grizzled head. They glanced about and spoke to a fisherman lounging nearby. Then they nodded and headed across the beach for the archway. "Come on," Peter murmured.

INSIDE THE CHURCH, Peter and Otto stood with their backs to the side wall. In front of them, stretching around to the door, were the serried ranks of the sightseers, attentive to the guide's explanation. "Duck," Peter said to Otto. "You're too tall." Both of them bent their knees and slid down the wall. Peter kept himself at a height where he could peer through the ranks before him at the doorway. "When they don't find us in the restuarant, they'll come here," he whispered to Otto. The guide's voice rolled on. A shadow fell across the doorway. The guide paused, then beckoned impatiently for those standing there to enter. Peter watched the grizzled head and his expressionless companion enter. They took their places at the edge of the crowd, apparently listening to the guide. Peter watched the two heads turn slowly and examine all the faces in the crowd. He pulled Otto farther down with him.

There was the sound of footsteps. Peter raised his head just enough for a glance. The two men were no longer there. He listened. Through the guide's monotonous accents he could hear the footsteps mounting the nearby stairs. "They've gone to the cloister," he whispered to Otto. "When this crowd goes on up that stairway, it'll block them up there. We make a dash for it through the restaurant and down to the dock. If we can get that boatman to row us to the boats quickly enough, you hightail it. I'll hold them off. How will I know where you are?"

"I'll let Eva Kanday know," Otto answered in a whisper. "She *has* to keep it a secret."

The guide finished his discourse, and dispiritedly gestured to the doorway. He led the way out and up the stairs to the left, to the cloister. "Okay, let's go," said Peter. Brusquely, he pushed his way through the crowd and out the doorway, through resentful mutters.

Peter burst out into the piazza and headed at a run for the restaurant. A glance to the left confirmed that the stairway to the cloister was blocked. With Otto at his heels he raced up the steps, into and through the restaurant. Another glance as he passed the windows showed the young, round-faced man lolling in the speedboat, his back to the archway. Peter and Otto descended the dark staircase and emerged into the sunshine on the rocks. Now moving at a normal walking pace they descended the steps to the dock. The driver of the speedboat still had his back to them. Wordlessly, Otto beckoned to the boatman. Slowly, idly, he pulled on his oars and brought the dory to the dock.

Peter and Otto stepped in, making no response to the boatman's stream of dialect. The boatman shrugged, and bent again to his oars. Silently, the dory glided across the bay. The young man in the speedboat, his back to the bay, continued to regard the houses of San Fruttuoso. The boatman brought them alongside Peter's boat. As Peter handed the boatman a banknote, Otto stepped onto Peter's boat, and then across to his own. There was the sound of footsteps on the hulls of the two boats. Peter vaulted into his, just as the young man turned his head.

The young man pivoted in his seat, stared for a second, then reached over and switched on his ignition. His horn blasted out a long cry, blaring across the small beach and echoing off the houses. In tandem, Peter and Otto flipped off their blowers, switched on their ignitions, and pressed the starters. Both motors caught. Peter leaped forward onto his bow, stepped over to Otto's, and hauled in Otto's anchor. He looked up to see the grizzled man and his expressionless companion break out of the archway at a dead run, and streak across the beach to their boat. Over the sound of his own and Otto's motors, Peter heard the roar of the third. "Swing wide out to sea," Peter shouted to Otto. "I need room."

He leaped back and into his own boat. Otto pushed his throttles forward and his boat surged ahead. Peter followed. A hundred yards out he veered to starboard and idled his engines. Swiftly, he hauled in his fenders and watched as Otto, hunched over the wheel, his bow already high out of the water, sped down the bay. He swept straight out to sea, starting a wide arc to the east, towards Portofino, his wake a white streak in the blue-green sea.

Peter pretended to be having trouble with his controls. An angry roar to his left signaled that their pursuers were in full chase. Peter glanced over at their boat. The three men ignored him. They headed out to sea at full speed, straight after Otto. Peter nodded to himself and opened his throttles to about three-quarters speed. The boat leaped forward. Peter, his eyes on the two boats ahead, swept wide to the seaward side of Otto's pursuers. A quick glance at the cliffs and he saw they were gaining on Otto: they had the V-8 engine. He opened his throttles to full. Quickly he pulled even with them. Before he could pull ahead of them, he veered slightly to port, and began to close in on them. He calculated the angle and the speed, and then slowed slightly, so as not to pass harmlessly across their bows.

The young, round-faced man was at the wheel. Peter saw him look nervously to starboard as the distance closed. Peter kept on his course. The gray-haired man shook his fist menacingly at him, and waved him off. Peter turned the wheel slightly so that his bow aimed directly at theirs and then increased his speed. By now the two boats were only about ten yards apart and closing swiftly. Peter saw the pilot push his throttle, but it was already at full. The distance closed to less than three yards. The round-faced man pulled hard to port on his wheel and the boat went into a tight, counter-clockwise turn.

Peter swallowed his taste of triumph, and followed in a wider circle to port around the other boat. The cliffs swept past him, a brown and yellow haze. Otto's pursuers came out of their turn and headed in a more seaward arc to the east. Peter straightened his wheel and followed astern. He looked down the coast. The maneuver had gained Otto perhaps five hundred yards. Peter saw that the pilot of the other boat was trying to avoid being caught between Peter and the cliffs again. So much the better, he thought. The next one will cost him more.

Again Peter opened his throttle to full. Quickly he pulled even with the other boat. This time they were running to starboard, with nothing but the open sea beyond them. As Peter began to overtake them he slowed slightly, pulled his wheel to starboard, and then held to a collision course. Again the round-faced man held to his course, and again, as the two bows, racing in the air, approached each other, Peter pushed forward on his throttles. The sudden leap forward startled the other pilot in spite of himself, and he pulled his wheel hard to starboard. His boat turned in a tight, clockwise circle.

Peter ran out to seaward, then slowed and, swinging his wheel to port, made a wide, counterclockwise turn. As he came about he saw that he was almost even with the Portofino church. Again he swallowed his satisfaction as he saw Otto disappear around the lighthouse farther to the east. Now we need time for him to get the hell out of here, he said to himself. He glanced to the west. The other boat was coming out of its turn and was beginning to head on a diagonal course for the lighthouse. The two boats were now some four hundred yards apart. This will be tricky, Peter thought. He pushed his throttles forward and held his wheel so that his course was 90 degrees to that of the other boat. Straight ahead loomed the cliffs of the peninsula. I have to swing him around and still leave room for myself to turn before the cliffs, Peter observed to himself.

As the angle closed he calculated with his eye. Yes, if the

other boat veered off when he should there would be room for his turn afterwards. But if he, Peter, flinched by as much as a second, and the turn was delayed, it meant the rocks. There was always the possibility, of course, that neither of them would flinch.

Peter set his wheel so that he would cut right across the bow of the other boat. Quickly, the angle closed. The round-faced young man eyed him nervously, but gripped his wheel firmly. The other two occupants of the boat gesticulated wildly at Peter. The bows shot towards each other. At the last minute the young man jammed his wheel to port. As they turned away Peter saw the guns in the hands of the other two.

Peter dropped to the floor of the cockpit. He heard the zip of the bullets, and then the shattering of his windshield. Crouched in the cockpit, Peter shoved the gear levers into neutral with his elbow. The engines shrieked and the hull shook so that his teeth chattered. With his right hand, Peter reached up, pulled back on the throttles, and switched off the ignition. Still hurtling forward, the bow of the boat dropped back into the water with a loud splash.

A sudden lurch threw Peter forward against the bulkhead. There was a rending of wood, a scraping of metal, and a sharp hissing of steam, as seawater touched the hot engines. The boat bounced, listed to starboard, and then righted itself, rocking in its own wake. The bow began to rise. Peter looked down. Already there were six inches of water in the cockpit. He glanced skyward. The tops of the cliffs towered above him.

"FLANK SPEED!" the captain of the cutter shouted into the speaking tube. Repeating the order aloud, the lieutenant rang it on the engine-room telegraph. The converted torpedo-boat, which had been gradually approaching the maneuvering speedboats, sprang into life and leaped forward. Six hundred yards separated it from the two boats. The one with Otto's pursuers aboard came out of its last counter-clockwise turn and headed for the lighthouse. The captain pointed to where Peter's boat was foundering. The helmsman swung the wheel to port. "Run by," said the captain. He raised his binoculars back to his eyes.

The small bridge was crowded. Besides the helmsman, the ship's officers, and a sailor holding a rifle with telescopic sights at port arms, there was a colonel of Carabinieri, a slight, sharp-nosed civilian with scanty blond hair, wearing a tweed suit, and still another civilian, a stocky, middle-aged figure with black, unruly hair, who was wearing a turtleneck sweater much too large for him, coming well down over baggy trousers hanging atop tennis shoes. The colonel and the civilian in tweeds had binoculars to their eyes, and were studying Peter's predicament. The more untidy civilian was holding a spyglass, which was trained on Otto's pursuers.

The cutter rapidly approached Peter, just as his boat sank beneath him, and he pushed off into the water from the disappearing hulk. "Dowling is all right," said the civilian in tweeds. "He hit a submerged rock about ten yards off the cliffs. Lucky for him. Throw him a lifebuoy for the time being." Without lowering his spyglass the other civilian repeated the information in rapid Italian, hardly accented. The captain pointed to the speedboat just nearing the lighthouse. The helmsman pulled the wheel slightly to starboard. The lieutenant leaned over the bridge and shouted an order below. The cutter raced by about fifteen yards distant from Peter. As it did so, a lifebuoy sailed off the afterdeck and landed in the water near him.

The cutter swept on and closed rapidly on the speedboat, now beginning to turn around the lighthouse and enter the gulf. The civilian in the turtleneck sweater lowered his spyglass and extended an arm. The sailor holding the rifle stepped forward and put it in his outstretched hand. The civilian smiled somewhat diffidently. "Permesso, capitano?" he asked.

"Prègo! Prègo!" the captain said rapidly, without lowering

his binoculars. Bracing his left arm on the windbreak, the civilian, his hair hanging down over his forehead, took aim.

He fired. Just off the lighthouse there was a sudden sheet of flame, followed by a great billow of smoke. Bits of debris soared out of the smoke and fell with little splashes in the water.

The civilian stepped back and put the rifle down to his side, a sheepish expression on his face. "Oh, I say," he murmured in disgust. The captain and the colonel turned to him and saluted. He looked in some awkwardness at his clothes, and then, his eyes twinkling in his round, weatherbeaten face, he saluted smartly back. Running his hand over his hair, he turned to the civilian in the tweed suit, whose normally weary air was now broken by a sardonic grin.

"Shocking," the black-haired man said. "Bugger must have neglected to run his blowers today. Very dangerous when there are sparks about."

Peter felt waterlogged in his clothes, but otherwise not too uncomfortable. His elbows on the lifebuoy, he kicked with his feet easily and steadily, to propel himself out from the rocks. It was not exactly midsummer swimming, but the sun was hot on his face. He had seen the explosion off the lighthouse, and he now watched as the cutter hovered at the scene. A dinghy had been put out, but the cutter's hull blocked Peter's view. After about ten minutes the cutter came slowly about and headed towards him. Still leaning on the lifebuoy, Peter swam out to meet it. As the cutter came abreast of him it hove to and Peter signaled to the lieutenant on deck to drop a ladder. Rope and wood clattered down the side of the hull. Peter reached up and pulled himself out of the water. Dripping, he swung over the railing and dropped onto the deck.

The lieutenant was smiling broadly. "Va bène?" he asked, with more amusement than concern.

"Sì, sì," answered Peter.

The lieutenant took him by the arm and showed him into

a small wardroom. Leather-covered benches ran along the bulkheads, surrounding a table. The lieutenant pointed to Peter's clothes. Peter emptied his pockets on the table and then took off his clothes. The lieutenant shouted to someone on deck, and a sailor appeared with a faded navy blue terry-cloth robe. Peter put it on and the sailor took away his clothes. The lieutenant nodded pleasantly and disappeared after the sailor.

Peter sat down and looked at the cliffs he had so narrowly missed. From the portholes and doorway behind him sunlight streamed into the little cabin. Peter reached onto the table and spread his passport open to dry. Very gingerly, he extracted his money, traveler's checks, and driver's license from his wallet and spread them on the table in the patches of sunlight. As he did so, the sunlight moved. Peter glanced up and saw that the ship was under weigh again and coming about. He got up and moved to the bench to starboard of the table, so that the land was again in his view. He watched as the cliffs slid past and the lighthouse appeared, and then remained stationary as the ship swung about it. We're heading into Portofino, he said to himself; at least Otto has made his getaway by now.

He reached again into his wallet and pulled out credit cards, identification and membership cards of various sorts, and dried the plastic rectangles on his bathrobe. Lastly, he carefully withdrew a folded piece of paper. It peeled off in small bits, like wet crumbs, at the touch of his fingers. As he tried to refold it, it disintegrated along the creases, the soggy remnants resting in his hand. Otto's writing was barely visible. "Goddamn," Peter swore softly.

"Not irreparable, I hope." The voice came from behind Peter's left shoulder. He looked up and saw a balding, sharp-nosed man in tweeds. The man was smiling amiably down at Peter. "You're all right, I take it?" he said. Peter acknowledged that he was. The man sat down next to him, still smiling in very friendly fashion. "That's what we figured," he said. "So we continued with the main business at hand."

Peter waited, but the man just sat there, his manner rather weary, but his pale blue eyes twinkling. Peter slid the useless remnants of Otto's note to the Ambassador into the pocket of the robe.

"What was the explosion?" he asked.

Without taking his eyes from Peter's the man laughed shortly. There was a tinge of the diabolical in the echo of his laugh, but his amusement seemed genuine enough. "Why, that was the main business at hand," he said. "Two of them sank like stones, one more or less floated. The gray-haired one. We picked him up. Not in the best of shape, but he'll live. He's back in sick bay. There'll be a police ambulance here"—he nodded at the houses and quays of Portofino coming into sight—"to take him to hospital. Seems to be a Yugoslav refugee, resident in France. His papers are in the name of Ivo Begovic. Mean anything to you?"

Peter shook his head. "Not a thing," he answered. He watched the houses and quays come slowly to a halt. There was a splash and the rattle of anchor chain. "You speak remarkable English for an Italian police officer," he said blandly to the man in tweeds.

The man frowned. "I *am* sorry," he said. His tone conveyed both self-reproach and apology convincingly. "My name is Caxton Burroughs. I'm an American and I'm not a police officer of any kind. I'm a friend of Otto Miller."

"Really?" said Peter. His tone expressed both acknowledgment and disbelief.

Burroughs laughed. Before he could say anything more a shadow fell across the cabin. Peter looked up to see a round, weather-beaten face, unruly black hair falling over the forehead, and a turtleneck sweater that looked like a small cassock. The new arrival beamed at Peter. "Congratulations!" he cried, his voice slightly cracked, but unmistakably sincere. He reached over and shook Peter's hand warmly. "A really dazzling performance, if you don't mind my saying so." He gave what might be mistaken for a schoolboy's giggle, and then went on enthusiastically. "In effect, you crossed his T

89

three times in a single engagement. Never been done before that I know of. At least not since the advent of steam. Wonderful to see." He stood beaming at Peter.

Burroughs, smiling, said, "And this is Lord Killitoe."

If true, thought Peter, this is not the C.I.A. David Viscount Killitoe, hero of the British Special Boat Service in the evacuation of the Peloponnesus and Crete, a former minister, a post he gave up out of evident distaste for public life, and the owner of several thriving English shipping and manufacturing firms, might be a dyed-in-the-wool Anglo-Irish eccentric, but an agent of the C.I.A. he certainly was not.

Killitoe's good will was infectious. Peter smiled back at him, inclined his head slightly, and said, "From you that is high praise indeed." Politely, he added, "We missed you at last Friday's meeting. The bankers really couldn't come to a decision in your absence."

Killitoe looked surprised for an instant, then cried out, "But of course! You're *that* Dowling!" He smiled at Peter mischievously. "You're lucky I wasn't there," he said. "Had I been, I would have told you outright to peddle your offer elsewhere. It was ridiculously low. Grenville was surely more polite with you than I would have been."

Peter nodded his head again. Grenville had been the banker representing Lord Killitoe's interest at the meeting he had had in London on Friday to push a takeover bid for New York clients; Peter was well aware that the bid was indeed too low.

Again there was a slight giggle. "And I would have been there," Killitoe went on, "except that Caxton here summoned me away on urgent business in mid-afternoon." That too rang true. Peter recalled that Killitoe had been scheduled to be at the meeting, and that Grenville, as though announcing a death in the family, had deferentially informed the others that "the Viscount" had been called out of town that very afternoon on "urgent business."

"So glad I came, too, Dowling," said Killitoe, still with a mischievous twinkle in his eye. "So much better to meet you here than in those grim offices in London Wall. Third floor, fourth conference room to the right, stenographer Miss Wells, wears her skirt about an inch below the navel?" Killitoe giggled again. Peter nodded; Miss Wells was indeed the star attraction of that particular set of London solicitors' offices. This Killitoe was obviously genuine. Peter glanced at Burroughs, who was listening to the conversation with vast amusement.

"Feel better now?" Burroughs asked him, a smile playing around his lips. "You still don't know *me,* of course," he said before Peter could answer, "but then you'd never heard of Unit 37 until last Tuesday night, either."

Another shadow filled the doorway. Startled, Peter looked up hastily. It was a colonel of Carabinieri. He spoke rapidly to Killitoe in Italian. Killitoe listened and then turned to Burroughs. "He says Begovic has been taken off to hospital. Under guard, of course. Otto took a taxi for Rapallo immediately after he landed. The driver's already returned. He left Otto at the railroad station. The colonel asks whether they should send out an order to pick him up, or just an alert, from the ship."

Burroughs looked thoughtfully at Killitoe. "It's your show, Caxton," said the Englishman.

Burroughs turned to Peter. "I think we'll let Mr. Dowling decide that. After all, he's been in more recent touch with Otto than we have."

"Leave him alone," said Peter.

Burroughs looked at Peter thoughtfully. After a long silence he said, "No doubt you're right. But I suggest your prescription apply to you as well." Peter looked up at Burroughs inquiringly. "After all," Burroughs observed a trifle acidly, "they traced Otto and almost got him just by shadowing you. We must assume there are others where this Begovic came from. I think we should avoid a repeat of today's performance." Peter acknowledged the point by a nod, and Burroughs gave an affirmative sign to Killitoe.

The Englishman spoke to the colonel: his manner was exquisitely polite, but there was no mistaking that he gave an order, and Peter's Italian was just sufficient to know that it was the order he himself had given. The colonel saluted, and then said something, apparently in explanation. Killitoe shrugged. "He says if we change our minds they can always find him within an hour or two after he checks into any hotel in Italy." Peter recalled that once, on vacation here from his C.I.A. job in Munich, he had deliberately left no address, but through the Italian police they had found him in exactly two and a half hours. He sighed; the colonel's was no idle boast.

Burroughs rose and said to Killitoe, "David, would you ask the colonel to place a priority call for me on the radio-telephone. I'll come with him." The colonel listened to Killitoe's translation, and responded with a quick affirmative nod. "By the time I get back Jake should be here," Burroughs went on to Killitoe. "It's been a good half-hour since we sent him that message."

Burroughs and the colonel were replaced in the cabin by a sailor carrying Peter's clothes, dry and perfectly pressed. While he changed back into them Killitoe stepped out on deck and waved to someone on the quay. Peter looked out a porthole and saw a square-set figure dismounting from a motorcycle and waving back. Peter thought a minute and then transferred the scraps of Otto's note from the robe to his jacket. Scooping the rest of his still slightly damp belongings into his pockets, he stepped out on deck. "Jake?" he asked.

Killitoe laughed with boyish glee. "Right," he said. "We gave him the motorcycle duty today. I had it all day yesterday. That was a bone-breaking route you took to Genoa. *And* I almost froze on the Tenda Pass." He looked across the water at the man called Jake. "I only hope his arse is as sore as mine was last night, but there's not a chance. Genoa to Camogli this morning, and now Camogli here. A short spin. Not a chance," he concluded with a mischevious glance at Peter.

Peter stared at the harbor of Portofino. Well named, he thought to himself. The bay stretched out in a dog's leg, the open end protected from the predominant winds. He turned to Killitoe. "Look," he said, "I agree it's more pleasant meeting here than in London. You'll admit the circumstances are nevertheless a bit odd?"

Killitoe looked at him blankly. "Do you think so?" he asked.

"For one thing, you seem to have the Italian Coast Guard and Carabinieri at your beck and call. For another, I gather you must have followed me yesterday on a motorcycle. And for another, when I got into trouble this morning, there you were on the spot, ready to rescue me." Killitoe appeared to be listening gravely. "I don't mean that I'm at all ungrateful," Peter added.

Killitoe's face broke into a wide smile. "Amazing, isn't it?" He relished the thought for a moment, then added, "We'll let Caxton tell you about it. If he's ready to. It's his show, you know."

Peter regarded Killitoe thoughtfully. "His show, or the C.I.A.'s?"

Killitoe stepped back a pace and looked down his nose at Peter with disdain. He snorted. "Sir!" he said. He leaned back against the rail next to Peter and said sternly, "Properly speaking, you should be thrown back into the water for that."

Quickly his face changed expression, and he smiled affably. "I will tell you one thing, though," he said. "I greatly appreciated your view of Otto. You know, even years ago I used to think of him to myself as Genghis Khan." Peter looked at him steadily. "But you made one mistake, Juji," Killitoe said earnestly. Peter raised his eyebrows. Killitoe leaned towards him and spoke confidentially. "Juji was the favorite son of the Great Khan, as Otto said. But the poor chap died before his father. A bad omen for you. You should always take those things into account."

Peter leaned back and laughed. "And, by God, you tap the telephones, too," he said.

Killitoe laughed with him. "Amazing, isn't it?" he answered.

Burroughs came along the deck and joined them. "I see our man in Camogli has arrived," he said, looking at a dinghy heading from shore for the cutter. The dinghy bumped against the side and a square-set man with close-cropped, wiry, brown hair, a strong, square chin, and penetrating eyes climbed onto deck near them. For a moment Peter thought his eyes must be blue, but then he saw that the effect was merely the result of the contrast between his eyes and his very dark skin. He had a suntan that Peter guessed took year-round attention to maintain. Either that or he was a farmer in a southern climate. "This is, uh, Mr. Forman," said Burroughs to Peter, with the faint smile still playing about his lips. Forman nodded and shook hands with Peter. Burroughs gestured idly to Peter, and explained to Forman, "This is Mr. Dowling, who turned out to be the hero of the morning."

"Ah?" said Forman. He was more grave in manner than the other two, and his face gave away nothing of what he was thinking. "What happened?" he asked Burroughs as the four of them went back into the ship's cabin and ranged themselves around the table. With what appeared to be private enjoyment Burroughs recounted the events of the morning up to Peter's sinking. "Otto?" asked Forman anxiously.

"He got away. Clean. Thanks to Dowling," rejoined Burroughs. "But just to make sure we went into action ourselves. David, here," he grinned at Killitoe, "blew the other three out of the water with one shot."

Killitoe frowned and looked out a porthole. Forman looked at Killitoe. Burroughs laughed gleefully. "An accident, you understand," he said. "David was aiming to disable the rudder post. Instead he hit the, ah, petrol tank."

Forman smiled. "Tut, tut, David," he said. "Perhaps I should give you some lessons?" Peter listened carefully. Forman spoke as one who had used English a great deal, even with perfect familiarity, but whose native language it was not; there was just a hint of an unidentifiable accent.

Killitoe scowled at the speaker. "I hope you have a really sore arse, Jake."

Forman laughed a short, deep laugh. "Not at all. I enjoyed the ride. I must have a harder one than you have."

It all might be a goddamn yachting party, Peter thought to himself. A yachting party on an armed cutter. And, Killitoe or no Killitoe, it's not really clear whether I'm a guest or a prisoner.

Forman looked at Peter. "What's Otto running from?"

Peter was thoughtful for a moment, and then answered, "If it weren't for Lord Killitoe here, whom I know if only by name, I might be inclined to say he was running from all of you."

Forman smiled. He glanced at Burroughs. Burroughs smiled faintly. "Your unspoken question is legitimate," he said to Peter. "We are all friends of Otto, however, and, shall I say, his former associates. You heard of the organization last Tuesday night." Three possibilities, thought Peter. Either they have that from Heston, or from the Ambassador, or, much less likely, from Otto. "If there are in fact some Nazi survivors who are trying at this late date to take revenge on those of us who were in that organization, we obviously have no intention of letting Otto be their victim. Nor do we intend to become victims ourselves."

"You know that some Nazi leaflets were found at the spot where Otto's car went over the cliff? A swastika superimposed on the words 'Unit 37'?" Peter asked. The three stiffened perceptibly. So they didn't know that, thought Peter: they're not Heston's men. He decided to hold his counsel on the "Nazi leaflets."

"How did you know that?" asked Burroughs quietly.

"The C.I.A. men in Otto's house at Eze showed them to me," said Peter.

"Ah, yes," Burroughs said noncommittally.

It was Forman who broke the silence. "Who was in Otto's car last Thursday night?"

"A garageman, an old friend, who had repaired it," answered Peter.

Forman looked at him steadily. "So when he heard the report of his own death he took off?" Peter nodded.

"Was he alone?" asked Forman blandly.

Peter hesitated. Otto had said he had spoken with Eva Kanday last Thursday night. It could have been by telephone. "So far as I know," Peter answered.

"Doesn't sound like Otto," commented Forman. "Where has he gone to now?"

"I don't know," Peter answered with evident frankness.

"When will you know?" asked Killitoe, in a friendly, but firm, manner.

"I have no idea," said Peter.

"What are your plans now, Mr. Dowling?" asked Burroughs calmly.

Ah, so I am in a position to have them, thought Peter. "I'm going to Paris," he said. But God knows how I'll get to the Ambassador to tell him to call off Heston, he added to himself.

"I'll make you a proposition," said Burroughs. His perpetual faint smile was gone, and he spoke without a trace of the weariness that seemed always to surround him. "Quite frankly, we had two suspects. One of them was you. However, now that we've been, shall we say, close to you for two days, and after your performance of saving Otto this morning, you're off the list of suspects. Now, if you will consent to have us accompany you to Paris, I guarantee to you that within twenty-four hours—I would hope sooner—all the unanswered questions about us that are worrying you will be answered. To your complete satisfaction. For the moment I'm not at liberty to say more."

Peter looked at Killitoe. "I support that," said the Viscount. "Besides, it will be much more comfortable in your car than on that motorcycle," he added with a pleasant smile. In short, thought Peter, they'll follow me anyway.

He glanced at Forman. The stolid face looked calmly at him. "You don't know me, so it doesn't matter whether I support it or not," said Forman, "but I do. I might also suggest that from your point of view you're better off knowing where we are and what we're doing, until you're satisfied about us, than otherwise."

"And vice versa?" said Peter.

"No," Forman answered. "Caxton has said we're satisfied about you. But we do want to keep in touch with you, so to speak."

Peter nodded to indicate that the statement was obvious. But Forman's reasoning was also right, he reflected. Better to know what they were doing than not. In addition, besides saving him this morning, they had known since the night before of Otto's whereabouts, as Killitoe's reference to their telephone conversation showed, and had done him no harm. "Fair enough," he said to Burroughs.

"In that case," said Burroughs, rising and addressing himself to Killitoe, "will you lay on a helicopter from Genoa to the Nice airport with your Italian friends, David. We'll catch a plane from there. We'll leave Mr. Dowling's car and Jake's motorcycle with the Carabinieri. They'll turn them in at Genoa. And we'll run around to Genoa on the ship. It's faster than driving." As an afterthought, he added, "And a car at the dock in Genoa, so we can go up to the Excelsior and get our things." My God, Peter thought, I'm already under Burroughs's orders; I begin to smell the "pleasant, comforting stench of comrades."

OTTO MILLER sat in a café in Milan's Piazza Beccaria, behind the Duomo. He ordered his fifth espresso. The lesson of

Portofino was clear. In a small village like that it was too easy to discover him, and once discovered, he was as exposed as though he were ten feet tall. But in Milan he could become invisible. If only he could find the place. Not a hotel. In any hotel he would be instantly registered with the police. And registration with the police, until he knew who was bent on destroying him, meant the possibility of a leak. He was in a vicious circle. The only alternative was to stay as a guest with friends. But that involved explanations, talk, and even more possibilities of leaks. What he needed was a friend who didn't know his friends.

Otto looked out into the twilight and pondered his problem. As his eye strayed around the little piazza, he saw a man nod to a girl standing on the corner. She returned his nod, and the two crossed the piazza and entered a small hotel. Otto snapped his fingers, tossed down his espresso, paid, and left the café.

Avoiding the Galleria, where much of that Milan he did not wish to see would surely be strolling or sitting, talking and looking, he crossed the Corso and made his way by back streets to the Piazza della Scala. Out of sheer habit he glanced respectfully at the unimposing facade of opera's holiest shrine, and went on into the Via Manzoni. He turned left at the second sidestreet and paused outside a doorway marked in bronze letters, "Bar." Otto peered inside. A few couples sat at tables. About halfway down the bar itself a woman sat on a barstool. Otto studied her back. She was dressed in a pale blue transparent blouse, through which her bra was visible, and a tight-fitting green skirt. Her hair, blonder at the ends and darker on top, hung to her shoulders in a long wave.

Quietly, Otto opened the door and walked straight to the bar. He sat down on the stool to the left of the blond, leaned over, and murmured in her ear, "Ciao, cara."

The woman turned to Otto. Her eyebrows rose in astonishment, and her smile changed from one of polite mirth to distinct pleasure. "Che sorprésa!" she said, her eyes fixed on

Otto's. She stirred slightly on her stool, as though to make room for Otto closer to her.

Otto smiled at her blandly. She was in her late thirties, and Otto saw that her eye shadow did not quite successfully hide tiny creases appearing at the corners of her eyes. Still, she was a handsome woman: a long, aquiline nose, almond-shaped eyes and prominent cheekbones, and a mouth saved from being too thin by a full lower lip, gave her a classically Byzantine look. She carried the opulent curves of her breasts and hips in a manner to suggest that their sole purpose was to render pleasure to men and to their owner. Otto acknowledged to himself that the effect was successful, even forceful. His memory reminded him that it was also more than a mere facade. "Sorry I'm a bit late, Cristina," he said.

She smiled at his remark. "Let me see," she mused, "that would be about six years late, no?"

"The traverse of a desert," he replied. Again she smiled. The barman stood before them. "A bottle of champagne," Otto said.

Her eyes lit up. "And you are in a good mood, I see."

"I was not until I saw you," said Otto truthfully. She seemed to take his remark at face value and drew closer to him. Otto raised his glass, touched hers, and they drank.

"And what brings you to Milan, Otto?" she asked with negligent curiosity.

"You," he answered, taking a certain pleasure in the fact that the reply, if not true four hours ago, had since become so. She laughed.

He refilled their glasses. "Then you are rich," she said.

Otto shrugged and looked at her. "I can pay the rent," he said.

"It's gone up," she said to him meaningfully.

"So has everything," rejoined Otto.

When they had disposed of another half-bottle Otto asked, "Do we need a taxi?"

She shook her head and dropped off the stool. While Otto counted out the money the barman handed Cristina her bag from behind the bar. They went out the door by which Otto had entered, and Cristina pointed to a bronze-colored Porsche a few feet from the entrance. The chic Italians buy German cars, the chic Germans buy French cars, and the chic French buy Italian cars; what is good for the automobile industry may in the end be good for Europe, Otto reflected.

They stopped by the Piazza Beccaria to pick up Otto's suitcase, and then Cristina drove on past the Public Gardens, towards the Station, and entered the Via San Gregorio. She parked and they went into a modern block of flats at number 81. The elevator took them to the third floor. The card on apartment 39 said simply, "C. Laggi." With a certain pride, Cristina showed Otto her flat.

A vestibule ran parallel to the hallway outside. Opposite the front door was the living room, with a small kitchen giving off it. At one end of the vestibule was a bathroom; at the other a good-sized bedroom, with an enormous bed covered in pink silk. Otto saw with some relief that the furnishings were not the kind of bargain modern one could expect in the circumstances: Cristina's bedroom was hung and upholstered in that style which the eighteenth century decreed as the voluptuousness required for a nest of love, with pink silk lampshades, a thick carpet, and, against the wall by the bed, a large wardrobe mirror.

Proclaiming his admiration, Otto returned to the living room. From Cristina's bedroom came the sound of her shoes falling to the floor. Otto glanced around the rather sparsely furnished living room. A couch, two chairs, a coffee table, two standing lamps. No telephone extension: the only telephone was in Cristina's bedroom. Inconvenient, but not fatal. Otto rubbed his chin reflectively; he could have done a great deal worse.

From the doorway of her bedroom Cristina spoke. "Alorra?" Otto turned. She was wearing a closely cut yellow silk chemise, plunging in front, tight across her belly and hips, obviously made for her. Through the silk Otto could see the dark circles of her nipples. No doubt about it, he thought, Italian women do have the best- and sexiest-looking underwear. He went to where she was standing. She leaned against him. The scent of her body was strong and rich, compounded of warmth and wine, silk and perfume, and the secreted heady odors of a woman who wants to make love. Otto breathed deeply. She took him by the hand and led him to the bed. He lay down and she began to undress him.

As she slid his shirt from his shoulders Otto said, "This might be a long stay."

Cristina laid his shirt on a chair, came back, and sat down alongside him. She slid her hands over his chest and back. "No problem," she said, "as long as you can pay the rent."

THE *PATRON* of the Saint Esprit opened the door of the private dining room, the one with its own entrance in the sidestreet, and put his head inside. "Vous désirez quelque chose, mon capitaine?" he asked.

Caxton Burroughs looked up at the bulbous red nose and the massive paunch protruding beyond the edge of the door. He smiled. "Thank you, no, Henri. It was an excellent dinner. My friends are doing very well with your superb calvados." The *patron* saluted and closed the door. Burroughs shook his head. "During the war he was thin," he said wonderingly.

Peter Dowling took a sip of his calvados, which in truth was superb, and looked at Burroughs. "We've moved so quickly, I haven't had a chance to ask one question—of the fair number—that's worrying me."

Burroughs looked suddenly suspicious. "And what might that be?" he asked warily.

"What's your hold on the Italian government?" Peter asked with a smile.

Burroughs laughed loudly. He pointed to Killitoe. Killitoe waved a hand deprecatingly. "I have some Italian relatives," he said shortly.

Again Burroughs laughed. "And most of them aren't allowed in the country," he mocked.

Killitoe shrugged. "All too true, unfortunately," he said. "My grandmother was Italian. Actually, she was an illegitimate daughter of Victor Emmanuel II. He was the first king of Italy and the Italians are very sentimental about their unification. After all, it was only a hundred years ago. During the coming century they may even go from being united to being unified."

Forman looked up from the table. "I've heard that story before. Even if true, it's only part of the real story," he said to Peter. "David was in Italy during the war, while the Germans were still there. He did some remarkable things in the region we were in earlier today. All the prefects in the north swear by him, and half the government in Rome."

"And what if Otto hadn't gone to Italy?" Peter asked.

Burroughs's eyes looked up at Peter wearily from beneath his wispy brows. "We have other connections," he said.

At that moment the door opened. All four men looked up. Whitney Ballard stood in the doorway.

The Ambassador advanced with a welcoming smile to Killitoe. "David, very good of you indeed to take time off for this," he said.

"I wouldn't have it any other way, Whitney," said Killitoe.

The Ambassador extended a hand to Forman. "Good to see you, Jake. How are things going?"

"We shall overcome," replied Forman quietly. Peter transferred his surprise from Whitney Ballard to Forman. At the Nice airport Forman had produced an American passport, but still the phrase rang strangely on his lips.

"I hope so," said the Ambassador. "I'd like to talk with you about it another time."

Whitney Ballard turned to Peter and put out his hand. "Mr. Dowling, I owe you a profound apology. I misjudged you. The mistake may have been natural in the circumstances, but it was poor judgment. I trust you will pardon me."

Peter shook the Ambassador's hand. "It wasn't a long-lasting mistake, Mr. Ambassador. And this seems a good time and place to bury it."

The Ambassador pulled a chair out from the table and sat down, motioning the others to do likewise. Burroughs looked at Peter. "Everything answered to your satisfaction?" he asked.

"The circumstances are certainly propitious, but I don't have the answers yet," Peter replied.

Burroughs turned to the Ambassador. "Whitney, in accordance with your instructions, I haven't explained the situation yet to Dowling." He glanced at Peter. "Peter, if I may?" Peter nodded. "However," Caxton went on to the Ambassador, "after I spoke with you on the telephone from the ship at lunchtime today, I promised Peter a satisfactory explanation within twenty-four hours." With a slight smile, he added, "We have another twelve hours to go."

Whitney Ballard leaned on the table and addressed Peter. "I'll call you Peter, too, if I may. This is an underground association, so to speak, so let's not give away our family names." He smiled at Jake, and continued. "Peter, I'm very happy to learn that Otto is alive, and I'm very grateful to you for saving his life this morning. As Heston told you, I had him mount that operation at Eze to see what it might turn up. It turned you up, and you in turn turned up Otto. All to the good, so far. But Otto is plainly still in danger, and will be until we get to the bottom of this. On getting the report of Otto's death I asked Caxton to help me. He and David and Jake are all wartime associates, and friends, of Otto. As you no doubt realize, they too may be in danger if this threat to Otto is what it appears to be. They are therefore working with me, for Otto and for themselves. We in this room, I must add, are the only ones who know this."

"No C.I.A.?" said Peter.

"No C.I.A.," said the Ambassador firmly. "Since Otto himself has confided in you, obviously with good instinct, I hope we may have your assistance as well."

"Naturally," said Peter. "I might add," he went on, "that Otto gave me a note today addressed to you, asking *you* to help *me*. It disintegrated in the water, but I see it's no longer necessary."

"It's not," said Whitney Ballard. He turned to Burroughs. "So where are we now, Caxton?"

Burroughs replied, "David and I telephoned earlier to the Italian police in Genoa. The man called Begovic has talked, but he told them only that he was hired to kill Otto by someone named Ross Trumbull. The address he has for him is number 2 Haydnstrasse, Munich. He has no telephone for him. So far it seems to be fitting with the Nazi leaflets."

Whitney Ballard frowned at Caxton, and was silent for a moment. "Not particularly," he said. "For one thing, Heston informs me analysis shows those leaflets were printed in East Germany." He paused, then continued, "For another, Ross Trumbull is a member of my staff."

An astonished silence descended on the room. Forman broke it. "What kind of a member of your staff, Whitney?"

Again the Ambassador was silent for a moment, as though weighing a decision. Then he spoke. "This has become more complicated than I anticipated. We were agreed that the only two people who could have leaked secret information about Otto which would result in danger to him were Peter —whom we know did not leak it—and Otto's German associate, born Hungarian as I understand it, Alexander Satori. You will recall that it was Satori who aroused Otto's fears in the first place by mentioning Unit 37 to him. Accordingly, I had my C.I.A. people look into the question of Satori. The results of the inquiry were brought to me by Heston, and by his C.E. man, who swore to Satori's bona fides. Satori is, in fact, a C.I.A. penetration agent. Into the K.G.B. The man who informed me of this, the C.E. man on my staff who vouched for Satori, and who is the case officer for him, is named Ross Trumbull."

Killitoe whistled. Forman looked impassive. Burroughs studied the table. Peter watched the Ambassador; he was tempted to suggest to Whitney Ballard not to turn the matter over to the C.I.A., even though, or particularly now that, one of his men was involved, but he kept silent. Don't tell the boss how to run his shop. At least, not on the first day.

It was the Ambassador who finally broke the silence. "Any suggestions?" he asked.

Peter spoke up. "It has been my feeling all along, Mr. Ambassador—uh, Whitney—that Satori is at the bottom of this, although I haven't the least idea how or why. I frankly don't take much stock in the Nazi coloring surrounding the thing up to now; it doesn't seem plausible to me. Now, as Otto's lawyer, I have authority to handle his affairs. Personally, I'm obliged to, because Otto asked me to. In particular, he wants a big jazz festival that he and Satori have planned for next month to go on. It means a great deal to him financially. This gives me my cover to take a good look at Mr. Satori. I suggest I do so. I assume Satori thinks Otto is alive after the Eze operation, and I will simply tell him that Otto is on a Mediterranean cruise with English friends."

"That's good, and I agree," said the Ambassador, "but it still leaves us with the problem of Trumbull."

"Obviously, the two must be linked," said Peter.

"No doubt," said the Ambassador. "But we can't leave Trumbull running around loose in the circumstances. And I fear that if I call in the C.I.A. it will only complicate the risks for Otto."

Burroughs leaned forward. "I suggest, Whitney, that we divide the honors in this case. Let Peter go after Satori. I'll take on Trumbull. David can help both of us, and we'll use Jake as communications base. I will, of course, need a look at Trumbull, and the Embassy files on him."

The Ambassador reflected. Finally he clapped his hands and rose. "Good. We'll do it that way. Miss Fox will arrange what you need at the Embassy. But don't go around there too much. I'll be back in town in time for lunch Wednesday, and in the office in the afternoon."

He turned to Peter. "There's one final item, Peter, to which it is my guess you have the key, being the last one among us to have seen Otto. Where is he, and how will we ensure his security?"

The only thing to do is to face up to it, Peter thought. "I don't yet know where he is, Whitney," he said. "I *have* arranged with him to find out, through a channel he believes is secure. I suggest that when I do, as a matter of elementary security, I keep it to myself. It's the only way we can know for certain, if something goes wrong, where the leak was. And I don't plan to leak it."

Whitney Ballard regarded him glacially, penetratingly. Peter stared back at him calmly. The Ambassador's expression relaxed at last, and he smiled. "When I was a child," he said, "my father once played a game with me. He said, 'I know a secret.' He made a tally on a piece of paper. 'I'm going to tell it to you.' With that he made another tally. Then he said, 'I'm going to tell someone else, too,' and made another tally. 'How many people besides myself know the secret now?' he asked, and turned the paper around so I could see it. I counted the tallies and said, 'Three!' He shook his head and pointed to the three lines. 'One hundred and eleven,' he said. I'll accept your proposition, Peter."

"I THINK I'M PREGNANT." Alexander Satori listened to Helga's voice coming through the telephone. It was coarse and juvenile, but provocative, suggesting those randy teen-aged girls who hang about popular male musicians.

"You must have made a mistake," said Satori.

"Seriously, I want to see you," she said. "From Saturday night to Tuesday is a long time."

Satori looked out his office window into the courtyard. "Much too long," he said. "This afternoon?"

"I'll pick you up in the Maximiliansplatz at three," she said. "Unless you want to take me to lunch?"

"I want to," Satori answered, "but I'm tied up. See you at three."

Punctually at three the dirty black Karmann Ghia appeared in the heavy traffic flowing up the Maximiliansplatz towards the Briennerstrasse and stopped before the light at the corner. Satori got in. Helga, her black frizzy hair and heavy green eye makeup set off by a bright orange sweater and skirt, pantomimed a gay greeting to her lover until they were past the Residenz. Then she settled into her customary, somewhat distant, air of efficiency. As they entered the elevator in the Liebigstrasse building a man hastened through the lobby and stepped in after them, breathless with apologies and thanks. Helga greeted him smilingly, and again became effusive towards Satori. This time they got out at the fourth floor, the other occupant squeezing himself to one side and tipping his hat.

Coolly, Helga walked down the grimy hall to the front of the building. She opened a door and led the way into a one-room apartment. The left wall of the room was completely taken up by built-in lockers and closets, running from wall to ceiling. The rest of the room was in utter disorder: dresses, pants, and bits of apparel were strewn all over the unmade bed, brassieres, panties, stockings, and petticoats festooned the two chairs and a coffee table, and the floor was littered with boots, shoes, and mules. Helga took no notice of it all. Instead, she went to the bedside table and switched a radio on, then off, then on again. She sat down on the bed and regarded the radio. Satori watched her silently. After a long wait he saw a tiny orange light on the radio panel flash twice, making a brief click in the hum of the radio each time.

Helga rose and went to the corner closet nearest the window. She unlocked it, opened the door, reached up inside, and pressed a button. Satori stepped up behind her in time to see a trapdoor rising noiselessly from the floor of the closet. From behind a panel in the wall opposite the door of the closet a shining metal ladder slid silently down into the room below. Helga moved back and gestured to Satori to use the ladder.

Satori dropped down the rungs and recognized the office where he had previously seen Pegov. The Russian was standing with his back to the curtained window, watching Satori's descent. His expression was severe, but a certain pride in the mechanism was visible. Satori bowed slightly to Pegov, greeted him, and then, pointing to the ladder, said, "I don't know how you risk these things, Lazar Matveyich."

Pegov raised his eyebrows. "Risk?" he asked. "What risk?" Apparently at a touch from Helga above the ladder disappeared back up into the ceiling and the trapdoor was replaced. Satori looked at the ceiling, which was divided into squares of soundproofing. The joints of the trapdoor were invisible. "All the same," Satori said. "An inspection by the owner. Or, workmen talk."

Pegov shrugged. "We own the building. It is therefore we who make any inspections for the owner. And we import our own workmen. As always. Good Soviet workmen. *They* do not talk."

Satori smiled self-deprecatingly. "Of course, Lazar Matveyich. I should have known." He seated himself.

Pegov remained standing. He was obviously preparing himself for what was to follow. He frowned. The cast in his right eye turned a no more than ordinarily severe expression into a glare. His thin mouth was drawn tight, and his somewhat fleshy chin took on a pugnacious look. Satori regarded him with outward calm, an attentive, respectful look on his face.

"I have some information for you," said Pegov gruffly. He paused to allow the tension to mount.

"Our man in the French police at Nice," he said portentously, "informs us that the victim of the Moyenne Corniche last Thursday was definitely one Joseph Calvi." He stared at Satori, who said nothing.

"This means, of course," Pegov went on as though reading a lesson, "that Otto Miller is still alive."

Calmly, Satori nodded and replied, "Yes. We had foreseen that possibility, as I reported to you last time."

Pegov frowned again. His voice took on a milder tone. Satori leaned slightly forward, as though alerted to danger.

"He also informs us that yesterday afternoon, shortly after four o'clock, a helicopter of the Italian Carabinieri arrived at Nice airport on a specially cleared flight from Genoa," Pegov continued. "It discharged four passengers. They left by plane immediately for Paris."

Satori listened to the now-smooth voice attentively, but remained silent.

"The passengers were three Americans and one Englishman," Pegov recited. "One of the Americans was Caxton Burroughs. I have already told you he was a member of Unit 37." Satori watched Pegov closely. "The Englishman was a nobleman. A former minister of the English queen. A monarcho-fascist, himself a relative of the Italian royal family." Pegov sneered. "David, *Graf* Killitoe. He also was in Unit 37." Satori's eyebrows lifted slightly. "The second American was one Jacob Forman. We do not yet know who he is. We are making inquiries, but we assume he is C.I.A." Satori remained attentive, but impassive. "The third American was Peter Dowling. This is the lawyer and friend of Miller you said Trumbull had under surveillance. Our records show he is C.I.A. When he was last on their regular roster, in 1956, he was here in Munich," Pegov concluded.

Satori pursed his lips thoughtfully. "That doesn't necessarily mean he's a C.I.A. man today," he said.

"Don't talk rubbish!" Pegov barked. "It is obvious what has happened. Miller, somehow alerted—we still don't know how—has gone into hiding, and has managed to summon his former group to help him. They in turn must have enlisted the help of the C.I.A. . . ."

109

"If that is so," interrupted Satori, "what were they doing in Italy?"

Pegov raised his chin and stared down his nose at the younger man. "I assume Trumbull can clear the matter up for us," he said. "In the meantime I can inform you that on the same helicopter which brought the four persons I have mentioned, there was an Italian colonel of Carabinieri. He came to ask the French police for their dossier on a man named Ivo Begovic, who has been arrested in Italy—at Portofino—for assault with a deadly weapon. Begovic himself is wounded and in hospital. The Italian colonel did not say who it was that he had assaulted. But you will recall that Ivo Begovic is a Yugoslav war criminal—one of Pavelic's terrorists—whom we indicated to you some time ago could be used for certain kinds of work. Under proper control, of course."

Satori stared steadily and calmly at Pegov. "Of course, Lazar Matveyich. He was being used by Trumbull, at my suggestion, in the Miller case."

"I guessed as much," said Pegov coldly. "You of course see the rest?"

Satori looked at him questioningly.

Pegov spoke with exasperation. "You are not very quick today, Alexandr Pavlovich. The Italian also did not say who had wounded Begovic. But it is perfectly obvious that it is the four who came from Genoa with him. Begovic must have been on the track of Miller—or thought he was, perhaps lured by the C.I.A. man Dowling—and they stepped in. These are assassins, Aleksandr Pavlovich! That was their role in the war: to arrange for the assassination of Hitlerite officials all over Europe, but in such a manner as to look like accidental, or even natural, death."

Pegov scowled and his voice dropped. "There is no doubt whatsoever that when at last we had defeated the Germans, these hyenas were immediately loosed against us by the fascist Zapadniki. Shcherbakov dead in 1945, Zhdanov in 1948. Those Jewish doctors who were so foolishly released in the panic after Iosif Vissarionovich's death were *their* instruments. No doubt about it. The Zionist links of Unit 37 were clear. Miller, the chief, is a Jew. Forbath is, or was, a Jew." Satori started to say something and checked himself. "So you see," Pegov concluded, "instead of carrying out the operation confided to him, Trumbull has stirred up a hornet's nest."

Satori appeared to reflect on this for a few minutes. Then he shook his head. "No, Lazar Matveyich. It is true that the operation has not gone entirely according to plan. The objective of establishing evidence which will convince both the American ruling circles, and, ah, some misguided comrades, of unrepentant Nazi influence in West Germany has not yet been achieved. But other things have. If, for example, Begovic talks to the Italian police he can do nothing other than give away Trumbull. It may be that this will endanger Trumbull, but your aim of getting a grip on him has been substantially met. Further, you have been having trouble locating other members of Unit 37. You have been unable to find Forbath, is that not so?"

Pegov nodded. Satori blinked rapidly, and then spread his hands. "But now you have two additional members of Unit 37 brought right into our sights, so to speak. Burroughs and the English lord. They have entered the arena of their own free wills. They can fulfill the other objectives of the operation as well as Miller. Particularly if they lose their lives in some organized effort to protect Miller."

Pegov answered stiffly, "I do not have the authority to extend the operation to them."

"But you can request it, Lazar Matveyich," Satori said reasonably. "And there is no question of the weight your own recommendation will carry," he added more forcefully.

"True," answered Pegov. "True." He looked thoughtfully at Satori. "There must have been a leak to Miller," he mused. "If only I knew where it was." He turned and looked out the window for some time, then turned back to Satori. "Very well, I shall ask for authority to substitute targets of opportunity. In the meantime, you should give me a report from Trumbull as soon as possible."

Satori rose and bowed slightly. "Of course, Lazar Matveyich."

Pegov walked to his desk and reached underneath. Noiselessly the square in the corner of the ceiling opened and the ladder appeared. Pegov gestured to it. Satori grasped it with his hands and put a foot on the bottom rung.

"By the way, Aleksandr Pavlovich," said Pegov. Satori turned and glanced at him. "I want you to present Helga to Trumbull at the earliest possible opportunity."

Satori's foot dropped from the ladder. "But I have told you, Lazar Matveyich, Trumbull refuses any contact with us except with me. That is, until he can be brought directly to you," he added. "I fear introducing anyone else into the connection will cause complications."

Pegov smiled amiably. "Of course, Aleksandr Pavlovich. But you will not introduce her as one of us. Just as an attractive friend. Helga will know how to handle it. You understand?"

Satori regarded him impassively. "Of course, Lazar Matveyich," he said.

Satori climbed the ladder and stepped out into Helga's room. She reached behind him and pressed the button which raised the ladder and shut the trapdoor, and then locked the closet. Satori looked about him with disdain at the disorder. Irritably, he said, "I see if we are ever to get to know each other better it will have to be somewhere else. There isn't even room for mice to copulate here."

"I don't copulate with mice," Helga said. With a flick of her behind she led the way out.

FRAU GRAEBNER followed Satori into his office. "A Mr. Peter Dowling called while you were out. From Mr. Miller's office in Paris. He said it is urgent. Shall I call him back now, sir?" she asked primly.

The cloud of irritation which hung over Satori's small,

sharp features vanished. He looked at Frau Graebner with surprise, and seated himself at his desk. Satori studied its surface and then looked up. "Yes," he said. "Yes. Do that."

When Satori's phone buzzed his answering voice was the soul of affability. "Yes, Mr. Dowling. So sorry we couldn't meet last week, but I had to get back to Munich."

"Well, we should get together now," Peter Dowling's voice came through the earpiece. "You know that Otto has had a rather upsetting time these past few days."

"He certainly gave us all a bad scare," said Satori cordially.

"Indeed he did," said Peter. "As a matter of fact, he's pretty much exhausted anyway, and he's taken off with some English friends on their yacht."

"Oh, really?" said Satori. "Where from?"

"Monte Carlo," answered Peter. "Why?"

Satori nodded his head and smiled. "I just wondered. He often goes cruising with some friends who keep their boat on the Italian side. Those French port charges have gone up astronomically."

"Probably it was the same ones," said Peter, "but they were berthed in Monte Carlo for a few days. The limits on British travel allowances have been lifted, you know. In any event, I had a visit with Otto before he left," Peter went on. "He's extremely anxious that your joint project for the jazz festival in Bavaria go on as scheduled. As you may know, I have his power-of-attorney, and he's asked me to work with you. There are one or two ideas I'd like to talk over with you. I was thinking of coming to Munich tomorrow. Will that be convenient for you?"

"Tomorrow? Just a second. Let me look at my calendar," said Satori. He wheeled in his chair and looked out at the courtyard. He hummed and then was silent.

"I'm leaving for Zurich in a half-hour, and I'll be coming to Munich from there on the Swissair flight that gets in at five ten tomorrow afternoon," said Peter. "Perhaps we could have dinner?"

Satori leaned back in his chair. "From Zurich, you say? Wait, perhaps we can get together there. Let me see." He paused. "Where will you be staying in Zurich?"

"The Baur-au-Lac," said Peter.

"No. No, on second thought, I can't," said Satori regretfully. "I do have to go to Zurich, but I see it has to be later in the week. Come ahead to Munich. It will be a pleasure to see you. I'll have my car pick you up at the airport, and then I insist you be my guest for dinner."

"Very good," said Peter. "See you tomorrow evening."

"Right," said Satori. He hung up and pressed the buzzer for Frau Graebner.

"Yes, sir?" she answered on the telephone.

"Ask Mr. Krieger to come in, please. Right away," said Satori. He rose nervously from his desk and went to the sound equipment on the wall. He switched it on and a tape of a popular rock group began to play. Satori turned the volume up.

The door to his office opened. A large man, wearing the same expression of mixed sadness and resentment that he had worn in the nightclub of the Bayerischer Hof, entered and shut the door. Satori turned and spoke to him, still standing before the blaring loudspeakers.

"Begovic is in the hands of the Italian police, Horst," he said. "Something has gone wrong, but it will take me a day or two to piece the story together. Pegov is annoyed and nosey, but I've calmed him down, I think, for the moment. Meanwhile, I think Miller has brought the C.I.A. into this. We know that's not fatal, but it can complicate things with Trumbull. Their first move is to send that lawyer, Peter Dowling, here to Munich. Ostensibly he's coming to deal with me on Miller's behalf about the jazz festival. He's going to Zurich this evening, and arriving here tomorrow afternoon on the Swissair flight from Zurich that gets in at five ten. He must be delayed until I can sort things out. Twenty-four hours at least. Forty-eight would be better. Can you do it?"

Krieger lowered his heavy head in thought. At last he raised it. Obviously his thought amused him. "If you can arrange things at the Budapest end, yes," he said.

Satori looked at him in mystification. Then his face cleared. "Ah, of course. Good idea. Yes, I'll fix that."

He dismissed Krieger with a wave of the hand and went to the telephone. He made two calls, one in Munich which involved him in dinner, and the other to Zurich, which involved him in nothing but left him pleasantly reassured. He had scarcely put down the telephone when Frau Graebner buzzed. Satori lifted it again with a gesture of irritation. "Herr Pfalz is waiting on line 2," she said.

Satori flipped the switch. "Yes," he said.

"Pfalz here," said a voice in slightly accented German. "I thought you would like to know that your last two releases were second and fourth in our sales last week. That fourth is second category." Satori calculated quickly. Today, Tuesday, plus two is Thursday, took care of the first ordinal number. Four plus two for the second ordinal number meant six o'clock, and "second category" meant evening. Trumbull on Thursday at six. Too close.

"Thank you," said Satori, "but are you sure your figures are right? Elsewhere that one in second place is sweeping the field." That would bring Trumbull in the following day.

"Well, I'll re-check our figures and let you know," came the answer.

"Thank you," said Satori. "I'll be curious to see how they come out. Don't hesitate to call me at home."

When Peter Dowling had finished talking with Satori he put down the telephone and looked for some time out the window of Otto Miller's office at the buildings across the Champs-Elysées. "It's possible he won that round," he said reflectively.

Helen Goodman sat in a chair opposite, purporting to be businesslike. "I didn't know you were in battle with him," she said.

"The real question is whether he knows," answered Peter enigmatically. "Come on. We'll go down to the Marignan for a coffee. Jake should be there by now. Then I'll have to dash for the airport."

On the way down in the elevator Helen observed caustically, "It's a hell of a time for Otto to go off on a Mediterranean cruise. He must be getting ga-ga."

"Why not?" Peter answered. "If he has us and his friends to take over for him?"

"I don't know," said Helen. "There's a lot here I don't understand. Otto takes to the high seas at a critical moment, you take over his affairs, you tell me I'm also to take orders from a Mr. Forman, an old friend of Otto's whom I've never heard of, and I'm to take him and other strange men into my flat and let them use the telephone. There's a lot of taking going on here, and it seems to be me who's doing most of the giving."

Peter smiled down at her. "Don't kid me. You do both to perfection."

She looked up at him with both aggravation and pleasure visible in her face. "That's different," she said. "Then I understand what I'm doing."

They walked out into the street and turned into the adjoining café. At a table against the far wall Peter spotted Jake, tanned and composed. He introduced him to Helen and the three seated themselves. Peter glanced at his watch. "I don't even have time for a coffee," he said. "Jake, I'm dining with Satori tomorrow night. I'll meet David at the Vier Jahreszeiten before. I've told Helen we'll be keeping in touch through the telephone at her apartment." He grinned at Helen. "She's agreed, even if she seems surly." He rose to go.

"Very kind of Miss Goodman," said Jake, also smiling at her.

Helen turned around and looked up at Peter. "I was only surly before I saw Mr. Forman," she said. She waved her hand at Peter in dismissal. Airily, she added, "Have a good time with Ginger."

THROUGHOUT THE LENGTH of the parabola between Orly and Kloten airports Peter was absorbed in the puzzle of persons he had never seen. Sandor Satori, a refugee from the Hungarian Revolution at age twenty-six, was a C.I.A. agent whose mission was to penetrate the K.G.B. His case officer was Ross Trumbull, who it seemed had tried to arrange the murder of Otto Miller forty-eight hours after Satori had alarmed Otto by revealing that he knew details only a professional could know about Otto's wartime O.S.S. service. It was possible Satori had this information from the Russians; as a double agent Satori had a foot in both the American and Russian services. The question therefore was: where did Satori's real allegiance lie? There were other questions. Were there any direct relations between Trumbull and his Russian counterpart—whoever he was? Or were both the Russian and the American working blindly, with Satori the only one of the trio to see clearly in all directions? The eternal problem with double agents: for whom was Satori really working—the Russians or the Americans?

Leave that problem in abeyance, Peter thought. Start now with what we know. Someone has tried to kill Otto Miller. The first attempt apparently was intended to give the impression of an act of Nazi vengeance for Otto's work in Unit 37. It turns out, however, that it was Trumbull, an American C.I.A. officer, who hired someone to do it. Peter judged it unlikely that Trumbull was some kind of Nazi crackpot; he had never come across out-and-out psychotics in the C.I.A. Or at least none who were permitted to continue in their official functions. Why, then, would Trumbull want Miller killed? Was his motive his alone? Very doubtful. Did it spring from

117

his relationship with Satori? If so, why might Satori want Otto dead? Surely not because he owed him a great deal. Or was the third side of the triangle, the Russian, also involved? If so, why?

Absent-mindedly, Peter passed through the Swiss police and customs, and the international bustle, at Kloten and took a taxi into town. His taxi was crossing the Quai Bridge in heavy traffic before he was roused to consciousness of Zurich itself. He looked out at the lake, and then turned to the Limmat, flowing between its walls of green stone surmounted by the solid squares of the buildings lining the quays. Peter blinked at the reflection of the late afternoon sunlight on the river, and was reminded of the two other Swiss cities whose topography was so similar to that of Zurich. Ah, but the differences that are so apparent when one moves beyond topography, he reflected. Lucerne—dark, wooded, Catholic, and seeming somehow older, and more quintessentially Swiss, than the other two. Geneva—comfortable, nineteenth-century in its appointments, traditional in its internationalism, its head still a trifle turned from the mixture of Calvin, Voltaire, and Woodrow Wilson *in absentia*. And Zurich—rich, dynamic, and proud, its Swabian virtues and vices muted beneath a cosmopolitan display tempered by a sober, northern Protestantism: Switzerland's shining bridgehead in the twentieth century.

Peter's taxi rolled through the Bürkli Platz into Talstrasse and turned sharp left into the driveway of the Baur-au-Lac. The familiar entrance hall assured Peter that he was indeed in Zurich.

Peter showered, changed to a dark blue suit, and went down to the Grill Room. He was hard put to find a place at the bar: around the U-shaped podium financial victories were being arranged or celebrated, and defeats analyzed and mourned, in a babble of languages—with nasal American English as prevalent as the slurred Schwyzerdütsch. He estimated the average size of the bank accounts in the room at five million Swiss francs each. "Nine to eleven," Otto had said. By the time Peter found a place at the bar, had two whiskies, a third while he waited for a table in the oak-paneled room, and then his dinner, it was getting on towards ten o'clock. He paused at the bar on the way out the Talstrasse entrance.

"The St. Gotthard Bar?" he asked the bartender.

"Fortunagasse," came the reply. "Almost at the Lindenhof."

After a half-dozen blocks of the luxurious and abundantly stocked shop windows of the Bahnhofstrasse Peter turned right into the old quarter, where a few ancient houses still remained. One such stood in the Fortunagasse, an ornately sculpted, corbelled window jutting out from the upper storeys, and an intricate wrought-iron sign hanging over the entrance beneath. To one side a brass nameplate, lighted from above, announced this to be the St. Gotthard Bar. Peter entered into a large hallway. If the outside of the ancient building had been meticulously preserved for several centuries, the inside, while retaining the richly carved and polished woodwork of the original, had also added all the refinements and luxuries of which the twentieth century was capable. Indirect lighting set off the coffered ceilings; a checkered black-and-white marble floor in the hallways, a deep-pile carpeting on a regal staircase sweeping up to the next floor gave an air of indestructible elegance. A majordomo approached Peter. "Dinner, sir? The bar?"

"Actually, I came to hear Miss Kanday," said Peter.

The man bowed. "Very good, sir. The Danube Room." He led Peter past a couple who had just entered and up the staircase. Part way down a wide corridor he ushered Peter into what appeared to be a much more than ordinarily comfortable clubroom. On silk-upholstered couches before low coffee tables, or in armchairs around marquetry tables, each with its silver candelabra, the burghers of Zurich and their ladies sat scattered about the room. At one end, on a dais, accompanied by a pianist and a violinist, Eva Kanday was singing a melancholy Hungarian song. Peter settled himself in a chair by the wall, ordered a cognac, and listened.

Peter found her singing agreeable: Eva Kanday's voice had a throaty quality which she shared with the great torchsingers of the past. But the sight of her, in her clinging apricot chiffon dress, with her radiant blonde hair, and her intriguing presence, was more striking than the sound. Her evident desire to please, her intimate indentification with her audience, and her vibrant sexuality, seemed to captivate the women as well as the men. Peter looked about the room. Eva's singing did not inhibit conversation, but neither did the subdued talk about the room impinge on her singing. It's not the new generation's thing, thought Peter, but it's very comfortable.

As eleven o'clock approached, Peter ordered champagne, then gave the waiter his card, and asked him to give it to Miss Kanday when she was finished singing. At eleven Peter joined the applause as Eva Kanday took her bows and disappeared through a door behind the dais. In about ten minutes she came out again and made her way down the room, greeting people at their tables, her teeth flashing as she smiled and laughed with them. When she came abreast of Peter's table she looked at him and he rose. Her smile, Peter saw, was pure show business; it was appealing enough, even so, but Peter saw that behind it Eva Kanday was worried about something.

He bowed and shook her hand. "I'm Peter Dowling," he said. "I'm a friend of Otto."

Eva, still wearing her professional smile, answered urgently, "Look, I want to talk to you, but my husband is here tonight. It's impossible. Where are you staying?"

Peter smiled in return, as though congratulating her on her performance, and said, "At the Baur-au-Lac."

"Oh, my God," she said. "I can't come there. I'll bump into everyone I know—or that my husband knows. Change your hotel. Go to the Franziskaner. One Niederdorfstrasse.

Across the river. I'll come to your room at three tomorrow afternoon."

Peter gestured as though to describe his pleasure at her singing. "Better make it two," he said. "My plane leaves at four."

She smiled as though receiving a compliment. Her answering "At two," would scarcely have been distinguishable to a lip-reader from "Thank you," and with it she was gone.

Refraining with some effort from watching her progress, Peter addressed himself to his champagne. When he had finished he departed in leisurely fashion, proffering a vague bow in the direction of where Eva sat with her husband. Peter noted a rather heavy-set man with pretensions to a specifically urban kind of good looks. He was reminded of the man's New York equivalents—the men-about-town who studiously foster the outward appearances of dynamic youth, alert to the new and seemingly ever on the rise. But Gunter Roessli, Peter thought, seemed to bear a notably vulpine look.

PETER'S APPOINTMENT at the Bahnhofstrasse fortress of the Union Bank of Switzerland was for ten o'clock. By nine he had breakfasted and checked out of the Baur-au-Lac, and by nine twenty he was installed in a fourth-floor room of the Hotel Franziskaner. The room, although under the eaves, was large, its furnishings plain but solid, and both were scrubbed spotless. The window overlooked a small cobblestoned square harboring an ornate fountain. The passersby were of another world from the Bahnhofstrasse just across the river: here the University and the Polytechnicum were only a couple of blocks away, and the Central Library but one; this was the student quarter and was inhabited by the local version of Bohemianism. It was still Zurich, but of quite another sort.

Peter walked back across the Limmat to the other Zurich and exactly at ten entered the Union Bank of Switzerland. He was shown into a conference room where two officers of the bank, and a member of the bank's legal staff, awaited him. Correct, thought Peter; the atmosphere, to use that favorite Middle European adjective, is correct.

"It is very good of you to stop by Zurich to see us, Mr. Dowling," the older of the two bankers began. "We thought it best to take up the Kaplan case, which your firm has presented to us, in person, rather than by correspondence." He paused, and cleared his throat. "We indicated, in our last letter, that there are complications. There is, of course, no question of your firm's good will in this matter." He ventured what passed in Zurich banking circles for a smile. "We are all well acquainted with Governor Hammer and his, ah, distinguished reputation." Peter stirred slightly in his seat. "But the fact is," the banker continued, "the Kaplan papers were presented to us in due form two years ago, and the funds in question, amounting, with accumulated interest, to some six hundred thousand Swiss francs, were withdrawn from our bank at that time by—" he looked down at the papers before him—"Miss Vera Kaplan herself."

I should have known, thought Peter. Respectful references to the senior partner usually preface either a request for a handout or very bad news. "In person?" he asked.

"In person," said the younger banker. "You understand, Mr. Dowling," he went on, "these funds, deposited in our bank in 1938 by Miss Kaplan's grandfather, came under the supervision of the National Bank Commission on Unclaimed Assets." Ah, well, thought Peter, there has to be some kind of euphemism for the torture and massacre of millions of Jews and for the ticklish problem of what to do with their property confided to Swiss banks; still, "Unclaimed Assets" seemed especially euphemistic. "The Commission requires," the younger man continued, "not only the customary documentation, but the appearance in person of the claimant to the funds, with the necessary personal proof of identity."

"And when exactly was this?" Peter asked.

The older banker looked again at his papers. "September 1968," he answered.

"Remarkable," Peter observed. "Vera Kaplan is bedridden as a result of an automobile accident in New York in 1965. She can't even travel from her home in the Bronx to our offices in Manhattan."

The bank's lawyer raised his eyebrows. "There is obviously a confusion of identities here. The name is certainly a common one. But we would not be able to release the funds to other than the qualified claimant. As you know, the existence of these unclaimed assets, or rather, the identity of the depositors and of the specific accounts involved, is information which is closely guarded by us, in accordance with Swiss law. If we handled the matter otherwise, not only would there be hundreds of claimants for each account, but the accounts themselves would never have survived. The depositors' governments would have confiscated them. Yesterday it was the German government which sought these accounts, and the world thought us right to refuse them. Today it is the Russians, and the world still thinks us right to refuse them. Your own government is only a step from demanding all its citizens' accounts with us."

The older banker frowned, and the lawyer visibly contained himself. "So, as I say," he went on, "in the banks themselves only a handful of officers know of the existence of these accounts. Outside the banks, the information is kept strictly secret in the National Bank Commission. The claimant must therefore have knowledge of the deposits from his or her own sources. I do not say that your Miss Kaplan is engaged in fraud, but the circumstances suggest that she may have heard of these funds after their release to the legal heir. Perhaps she is even a relative. In that case, of course, the matter does not concern the Union Bank of Switzerland, but is a civil matter between the claimants. Our release of the funds was duly authorized by the National Bank Commission on the presentation of convincing proof."

Peter watched the lawyer settle back comfortably in his chair. "Quite," he said. "Except that, as the papers we have filed with you make plain, Vera Kaplan became aware of the existence of these funds, and of her legal right to them, in 1965. As the file makes clear, Miss Kaplan's grandfather, and her parents, all perished during the war. Miss Kaplan herself, then an infant, was saved at Ravensbruck by fellow inmates after the gassing of the rest of her family. The family was Lithuanian, but no one was about to send the child, an orphan, back to Russian-occupied Lithuania after the war. Through the American Jewish organizations distant cousins were located in New York, and they took her in and raised her."

Peter looked steadily at the Swiss lawyer. "Neither Miss Kaplan nor her New York relatives," he said, "had any knowledge of the deposit by her grandfather in your bank. But in 1963 another cousin, then the only living person to have knowledge of the deposit, escaped from the Soviet Union, by small boat, to Sweden. He began a search for his relatives. It took two years, but he finally located them in New York. He himself died shortly thereafter, but it was he who informed Miss Kaplan of the action of her grandfather, and of the existence of these funds. He insisted he had informed no one else. We then took up the case, and it took us until the end of 1969 to assemble the necessary proofs, which we submitted to you. The question therefore really is—" Peter nodded to the lawyer—"not how our client became aware of the existence of these funds, but on what proofs did you release the money to this other Miss Kaplan?"

The Swiss lawyer made a gesture of impatience. "We complied with all the requirements of Swiss law, which in these cases are very strict." He reached over to the file of papers before the older banker, riffled through them, withdrew a paper from near the top, and handed it across the table to Peter. "As you see," he said.

It was a long memorandum, in German, detailing the Swiss laws and regulations dealing with unclaimed assets, listing the compliance of one Vera Kaplan, resident in Buenos Aires, with these requirements, and concluding with the statement that "the Commission on Unclaimed Assets of the Swiss National Bank therefore authorizes the Union Bank of Switzerland, 45 Bahnhofstrasse, Zurich, to release the funds deposited with it in November 1938, by Isaac Kaplan, then of Kaunas, Lithuania, since deceased, and held in Blocked Account No. 7487/331, to the claimant, said Vera Kaplan, of whom the deceased made mention as a possible heir at the time of making the deposit, on submission by Miss Kaplan of the required proof of identity." Peter read through the document carefully. After the final paragraph his eye dropped by habit to the signature beneath. He blinked. Zurich was turning out to be a small town after all.

He extended the document to the Swiss lawyer. "What is the role in these cases of the Secretary of the National Bank Commission, the signer of the document?" He glanced at the paper again and then handed it to the lawyer. "In this case Dr. Gunter Roessli?"

The older banker smiled. "Purely secretarial," he said. "The Commission takes the decision. The Secretary is only head of the Secretariat, and custodian of the Commission's files. He merely informs us of the Commission's decisions. A functionary." He smiled a bit more broadly. "No, Mr. Dowling, Dr. Roessli is not the proper subject for any action you may have in mind." Too bad, thought Peter; I might have rendered Otto a useful service there.

"In fact," the banker went on, "we don't see that you can have any action in mind in the circumstances." Peter listened; despite his words, the banker's tone was much more conciliatory than the lawyer's. "However, while reserving our position, we naturally, having regard for Governor Hammer's eminence, are prepared to cooperate with your firm if you wish to look further into the matter." The Swiss lawyer looked discomfited. Odd, thought Peter, one had to admit that, notwithstanding the faults popularly imputed to them, bankers are often more flexible than lawyers, and—at least internationally—more cooperative. They obviously are also more susceptible, certainly in the present instance, to political "eminence."

"Naturally," said Peter. "We would of course like to examine the records and documentation presented by this other Miss Kaplan. Perhaps you could send them to our London office? I'll send them a cable now to expect them, and give my people instructions. I shall be traveling myself, but I'll be in touch with the London office."

The banker nodded. "I'm afraid they will have to be photocopies," he said, "unless you wish to examine the originals here?"

Peter shook his head. "Let's start with the photocopies. If necessary I'll come back with experts to look at the originals."

He rose to leave, and then paused. "One other thing, though. You say the money was withdrawn from your bank in September 1968. Can you tell me where the money was transferred to?"

Now it was the banker's turn to shake his head. "I'm afraid everything is quite in order there. On Miss Kaplan's written instructions, the funds were transferred to the lawyer who initiated her case, and represented her throughout." He glanced again at the file. "Dr. Hans Pfeundner, of Munich. Dr. Pfeundner is well—and favorably—known to us. We have quite a few dealings with him on such matters. I believe he also represents a large number of claimants before the German courts for compensation of Jewish losses." Peter nodded. The fact remains, he said to himself, that Dr. Pfeundner, however well regarded, has made off with some $160,000 belonging to one of my clients.

A TAXI ROLLED down the hill opposite, its tires slapping the cobblestones, and glided slowly past the fountain, across

126

the square and into Niederdorfstrasse, out of Peter's sight. That had better be her, he said to himself as he turned from the window, or I shall have to cancel my Munich flight; I can't leave here without knowing Otto's whereabouts. He listened for the sound of the elevator door down the hall. It sighed, hissed, and then thudded discreetly closed. There was the rapid succession of a woman's footsteps, followed by a knock on his door.

Peter opened it. Otto's words came to his mind: "No one approaches Eva Kanday cold, or if they do they don't stay cold long." It was not only that she was perfectly turned out, from each beguiling wave of her shining blond hair to her bronze-colored patent leather shoes: she was one of the rare entertainers Peter had ever seen whose smile and features were as radiant in the day as at night. "Come in," he said. "I was getting worried."

Eva's smile took on a tinge of skepticism. "About me?" she asked.

"About my plane," Peter said with a grin.

She acknowledged the correction with a nod, then undid her coat and threw it, her handbag, and a package she was carrying, on the bed. She turned to him. "Otto called me at the St. Gotthard Bar last night," she said evenly.

Peter watched her for a split second. She certainly wasn't overplaying. But was she underplaying?

"How is he?" he asked.

She shrugged. "He sounded all right."

"More important," Peter said. "Where is he?"

Eva nodded and reached down for her handbag. "He said I was to tell you and no one else." She rummaged in her bag and produced a tiny address book. "He is staying with friends. Or perhaps it's *a* friend. In Milan." She looked in the book and seemed amused. "He didn't give me the friend's first name. Just the initial. C. Laggi. Eighty-one Via San Gregorio, apartment 39, telephone, six-four-seven, oh-three-three. Please only telephone in case of emergency, and then preferably only between noon and one o'clock." Peter repeated the details in his head until he knew they were lodged in his memory. Eva laughed. "Do you think the 'C' stands for Carlo?" she asked.

Peter smiled. "No," he said. "Cristoforo, as in Columbus. What else did he say?"

"He spoke very highly of you," she said. "Look," her face became serious, "I don't care if it's 'C' for Carlotta, or Cristina, or whatever, so long as he's safe. What is going on with Otto?"

"If I knew," said Peter, "I wouldn't have to come to Zurich to find out where he is."

"But is he really in danger? After rushing me out of Eze he couldn't get rid of me quickly enough," she said reproachfully.

"Yes, he's in danger," Peter replied. "But so long as only you and I know where he is," he added, "the danger's under control. I can't tell you more, because at this point I don't really know much more." In fact, he thought, the less said on the subject for the moment, the better.

She sighed. "Clear it up soon, will you?"

Peter looked at her and grinned. "As soon as possible." He looked at his watch. "Which means the sooner I get going the better." She nodded gravely. "How do I reach you if I have to?" Peter asked. "At the very least I'll probably have something to tell you in the next few days about the Bavarian Jazz Festival."

"You can always get me at the St. Gotthard Bar between eight and nine in the evening," she answered. "I'm there an hour before I go on. My home telephone isn't a good idea. My husband probably has some kind of recording machine on it. He's violently jealous," she added matter-of-factly.

She gave him the number of the bar and reached down for her coat. Peter helped her with it. Then she picked up the package she had been carrying and turned to face Peter. For a moment she became coquettish. "Will you do me a favor?" she asked.

She offered the package to him. "Otto told me you were

going to Budapest. Would you terribly mind taking this to a very dear friend of mine? It's only cosmetics, but they're unobtainable there."

"Is *her* husband jealous too?" asked Peter with a smile.

"No," said Eva, with a toss of her head. "She's smart. She's not married."

"There's only one trouble," Peter went on. "I have no idea when I will get to Budapest. I may not even go there this trip. It depends on a number of things—not the least of them our friend Otto."

"Take it," said Eva, handing him the package. "If you go, fine. If you don't, they're no great loss to me. I'll send her some others."

Peter took the package. "Who is she and how do I find her?" he asked.

"Maria Kodaly, Viragarok ut 37, Budapest II," said Eva. Peter jotted it down. "It's in Buda. She's lucky to live there still. Her home telephone is six-six-three, five-six-seven. You can get her in the evenings. She's a doctor, and works in a research laboratory; it would be difficult for you to get her at work—and probably make difficulties for her."

Peter shrugged. "All right." Hungarians were forever asking people to carry "little packages" across frontiers for them, and this one was not too large; besides, Peter suspected that Eva Kanday would not be an easy person to say "No" to.

He put the package in his suitcase and turned to the door. "Do you want to go first?" he asked.

She smiled and took his arm, pressing close to him. "Of course not," she retorted. "We'll go down together. I'm at home here."

By the time Peter had paid his bill the taxi summoned by the desk had arrived. Eva watched him throw his bag in the cab. "Good-bye," said Peter. "I'll call you. About the festival."

Eva frowned. "You didn't tell me where I can reach *you,*" she said.

"I'll be at the Vier Jahreszeiten in Munich," he answered.

Peter shut the door and the taxi drove off. He looked back through the rear window. She was a pretty sight, standing on the sidewalk, but she looked starkly alone.

At Kloten Peter checked in, bought a paper, made his way to the departure gate, and took his place in line. The controls were strict, and the line moved slowly. Out of curiosity Peter offered to wager himself on whether the figure in front of him was male or female. The hair, falling in a pageboy bob to the shoulders, gave no clue. The beads visible around the back of the collar were no help. The right hand, carrying a large musician's case, for whatever slight clue it might have offered, was so covered with fringe as to be invisible. The loose, shapeless buckskin jacket, the bell-bottomed trousers, and the sandals could belong to either sex. The languid, shuffling gait as the line moved slowly forward was common to both male and female in certain circles. Peter sniffed. The odor was also unisex. Trust your instinct, said Peter to himself. From your reaction of distaste it must be a boy. If it were a girl you'd find reason to sympathize.

The line reached the police control. The figure ahead of Peter handed over a passport and received it back stamped. But then a Swiss policeman standing by the line gestured to the figure to open the case. The figure lifted the case onto the railing. From where Peter stood, hand outstretched with passport, a stubbled chin came into view beneath the overhanging bangs. Ah, thought Peter. Always trust to instinct.

The boy blandly opened the large black case. The policeman peered in, and so, perforce, did Peter. A mandolin, polished and peaceful, lay snuggled on the blue velvet lining. As the boy stood there with a sullen, yet patient, air, implying his habituation to persecution at every turn, Peter caught the policeman's eye and smiled. The policeman kept his grim expression. No joking with the Swiss on this, Peter noted. And they were right, he thought; better the precautions than the piracy or the bomb.

Peter had been among the last to arrive; as he walked rapidly across the tarmac, outdistancing the mandolin player,

Peter saw that he would not have much of a choice of seats. Indeed, when he stepped into the Caravelle from the tail stairway, the seats at the rear, permitting the quickest exit at Munich, were all filled. He went forward, passing a number of vacant seats in the middle, and dropped into the right front window seat. A fair exchange. He would be the last out at Munich, but at least he would have had room for his legs on the flight.

Peter settled himself in his seat and opened his *Neue Zürcher Zeitung*. Zurich bankers may have given away Vera Kaplan's money, but their city unquestionably produced, with the possible exception of Paris's *Le Monde,* the world's best newspaper. He was on the verge of enjoying it when he became aware of a shadow on his left. He looked up. It was the mandolin player. As though Peter did not exist, he dropped into the adjoining seat, his black case between his legs.

Peter shrugged inwardly and returned to his paper. In the silence before the engines started he became aware of the muted but insidious and steady smacking sound of his traveling companion's gum-chewing. Peter glanced at him. The face was a striking combination of twentieth-century frustrations and resentments stamped on paleolithic features. The eyes were deeply recessed, and surmounted by bulging lobes on which, surprisingly, the eyebrows were sparse. This lack was compensated by the hair line which, it was evident even with the bangs, began no more than an inch above the eyebrows. The nose was wide and flattened, and both upper and lower jaws seemed equally prominent, as though designed to rend flesh from bone on the run, rather than at table.

Peter went back to his paper. Fifteen minutes later the glint of light reflected from a flat surface caused him to look out the window. Beneath was the Lake of Constance. To the south, the narrow valley of the Rhine bored its way up to the barrier of the Rhaetian Alps. Just the other side of their crest, only seventy-five miles beyond the jagged, snowy summits that marked Peter's horizon, lay Milan. Who might

131

"C. Laggi" be? Peter smiled as he recalled the Italian colonel's remark, as translated by Killitoe: "They can always find him within an hour or two after he checks into any hotel in Italy." So Otto, quite simply, had not checked into a hotel. Ten to one "C. Laggi" is a female, and an attractive one at that.

To the distant hum of the engines Peter's mind wandered. Was Otto never lonely, with his rapidly changing harem? How about you yourself, Peter? Well, yes. There were times. And they were becoming more frequent. Helen was right. The time was fast approaching . . . Peter's seat shook and an elbow jostled his left arm.

He looked over at the next seat. The mandolin player had leaned forward and was opening his musician's case. Carefully, he extracted the mandolin, shut the case, and kicked it against the bulkhead. He pushed the button to make his seat recline, cradled the mandolin, and began to play. Peter looked at him in disbelief. The boy began to sing, eyeing Peter with a look compounded of defiance and self-satisfaction. Not only was his strumming monotonous, but his singing was equally so, a kind of whining recital, and off-key at that. It was apparently a cowboy's lament—in German. Oh, no, thought Peter. Not all the way to Munich. While he wondered whether to ring for the stewardess, or open the emergency exit, he caught sight out of the corner of his eye of the stewardess coming down the aisle. Her baby, Peter decided, and leaned back in his seat.

The stewardess was pretty, and unfazed. Politely, she leaned over the musician and said, in German, "I'm very sorry, sir, but it is not allowed to play musical instruments while in flight." The mandolin player strummed a few more bars, then stopped. He seemed to consider the message. Then, scowling, he sat up straight. "Thank you, sir," the stewardess smiled. "It's just that it might disturb the other passengers." Peter admired her tactful stress on "might."

"Goddamn Swiss!" The mandolin player's lips puckered as though to cry, but his eyes glared in rage at the stewardess.

"Zionists! Imperialists!" He raised the mandolin high in the air with both hands. The stewardess recoiled. The boy brought the mandolin down onto his knees with all his force.

The neck of the instrument broke off, the strings snapped, and the thin wood of the body of the mandolin splintered, the remains tumbling to the floor. At the same time there was the clang of heavy metal, and two simultaneous thuds on the carpeted floor of the cabin.

Peter looked to where the noise came from and saw two automatic pistols lying on the floor amid the litter of the mandolin. He made a lunge. As he reached forward and down he was halted by a stunning blow on his chin.

The musician followed through with his left hook and Peter's head snapped back against the oval frame of the window.

Instantly the boy had the two pistols in his hands. He leaped out of his seat into the aisle behind the wide-eyed stewardess, blocking her escape to the rear. Peter shook his head to clear it. The boy aimed one gun at the girl, the other at Peter. "Don't move," he said to Peter. He jabbed the girl with the other gun. He nodded at the door to the cockpit. "Go ahead," he said. "It's for an Arab Palestine," he added, with a crooked smile. The stewardess opened the door and passed through. Quickly the boy slipped in behind her. Peter felt the vibration of running footsteps. The door to the cockpit shut and he heard the lock turn.

Peter shook his head again. A heavy-set man dressed in civilian clothes, but with a revolver in his hand, came to a stop before the cockpit door. He tried the handle but it remained shut. "Verdammt!" he said.

Peter looked at the man and then aft. In the tail of the aircraft the other stewardess and the steward stood with their mouths agape. Between them and Peter, over the tops of the seats, row after row of frightened eyes stared forward. Peter felt his chin. "Goddammit!" he said.

WHITNEY BALLARD looked out from his office at the trees lining the Champs-Elysées, apparently deep in thought. Not even the entrance of Heston and Trumbull seemed to interrupt his concentration. After a few moments Roger Heston coughed. "Good afternoon, Mr. Ambassador," he said cheerily. Whitney Ballard turned and looked at the two men in surprise.

"Oh," he said. "Oh, yes, gentlemen. Sit down, won't you?" He gestured to the couch and seated himself in the armchair. After a long silence, during which he seemed much preoccupied, the Ambassador finally smiled politely. "What can I do for you two gentlemen this afternoon?" he asked affably.

Ross Trumbull looked through his thick glasses at the Ambassador. His lips moved as though to break into a smile, but he said nothing. Roger Heston looked embarrassed. "Why, you asked to see us, Mr. Ambassador," he answered uneasily.

Whitney Ballard looked at him blankly for a moment, and then a broad smile spread over his features. "Of course, of course," he said. He shook his head briefly. "But of course." His voice became hearty. "So how is the operation at Eze, Roger?"

Heston recovered his aplomb. "I still have my men there, Mr. Ambassador. I was waiting for your instructions. There have been no further visitors to the house since Dowling, last Saturday. There is, however, one development of note that suggests we might as well call the whole thing off. The French police have informed us that the man who died in the crash of Miller's car was not Miller. It was a garageman from Cannes, named Joseph Calvi."

The Ambassador looked at Heston in surprise. "Well, that *is* a development!" He appeared bewildered. "Yes, indeed. And very good news, too." He waved his hands deprecatingly. "I mean for Miller, of course. Regrettable about Mr. Kelly. Who was *he?*"

"Calvi, Mr. Ambassador," said Heston patiently. "Joseph Calvi. A garageman from Cannes. Specialized in repairing foreign cars. Probably he was delivering Mr. Miller's car to Eze."

"I see," said Whitney Ballard. "So where is Otto Miller?"

Heston gestured helplessly. "We have no idea. We've been keeping a watch on his office here, and we've asked the French to plug in on the telephones. The only person of interest who's shown up there is, again, Peter Dowling. And he telephoned to Ross's man Satori, in Munich, on some business for Miller, and told him Miller has gone on a Mediterranean cruise."

The Ambassador nodded his head in apparent satisfaction. "Well, that seems to wind it up, then."

"I wouldn't say so, Mr. Ambassador," Trumbull broke in. His high-pitched voice, although tinged with irony, bespoke an inner agitation. "This man Dowling, in my estimation, is dangerous. He certainly is a danger to my principal operation. The one with Satori, I mean. Dowling suspects Satori is working for us, after what, uh, Miller revealed to him last week at the Residence. This could be very bad if, as I suspect, Dowling is working for the other side."

The Ambassador's eyelids fluttered. He closed them. "What makes you think he is, Mr. Trumbull?" he asked.

Trumbull frowned at the apparently dozing man to whom he was supposed to be speaking, and shot a quick look at Heston. "Dowling learned that Miller was in Unit 37 in the war," he said, making an effort to open the Ambassador's eyes with the force of his statements. "Forty-eight hours after that, there was an apparent attempt on Miller's life. Since then, no one has seen Miller. All we have is Dowling's word, which he is spreading around, that Miller is on a yacht somewhere.

"The only person to show up at Eze after Roger successfully baited that trap was Dowling. According to Wyant, who was there, Dowling was in fact sneaking up on the man he thought was Miller. He was told at Eze that Miller was not alive. So then he disappears. I've, uh, picked up some information that he went to the Hotel Negresco in Nice. One of my men happened to be at the desk there when he registered. But from there he vanished, only to show up in Paris seventy-two hours later, saying that Miller has gone on a cruise." By now Trumbull was speaking excitedly. "His next move is then to go to Munich to see Satori, on the pretext of talking about Miller's business. Or so the French wiretap people tell us. Which puts my operation in serious danger. You will recall," he concluded on a triumphant note, "that our lab people have told us those Nazi leaflets on the Corniche came from East Germany. Dowling is going to Budapest. In this business, Budapest and East Berlin are the same town."

His eyes still closed, Whitney Ballard said, "So what do you propose, Mr. Trumbull?"

"Unfortunately, Mr. Ambassador," Trumbull said pointedly, "I was unable to warn Satori before he sees Dowling in Munich. Tonight, that is. I propose alerting our station in Munich to keep a close eye on Dowling, with full information to us. I'm, ah, a little short of people at the moment."

The Ambassador opened his eyes and looked at Trumbull. "If Dowling is going to be seeing Satori won't it compromise Satori to have your people hanging around? You told me last week you run this operation from here to avoid Satori's American connections being known to, among others, the Germans. But your people in Germany would presumably have to inform the Germans of their actions on German territory, and the reasons for it."

Trumbull frowned. "Well, I don't know about that. After all, Dowling is one of our citizens."

"Exactly," said the Ambassador, "and I don't know that the C.I.A. is entitled to mount operations against American citizens."

Trumbull's mouth dropped open with surprise. "There are no legal limitations on what we can do abroad," he said flatly.

"There are if I say so," replied the Ambassador quietly. After a significant pause, he went on. "Tell me, Trumbull, why don't you work it the other way around? As I understand it, you're running a penetration into the K.G.B. Why don't you get Satori to find out for you whether Dowling is working for the other side?"

Trumbull frowned and hesitated.

The Ambassador leaned forward, his enthusiasm evident. "Why, it should be easy," he said. "Who is Satori in touch with—directly, I mean—among the Russians?"

Trumbull appeared uncomfortable. "The Russian Resident in Munich," he said stiffly.

"Ah?" said the Ambassador. "Who's that?"

Trumbull stirred in his seat. "He's a very high-ranking K.G.B. officer."

"So much the better!" cried the Ambassador. He turned to Heston. "You see it, don't you, Roger?" The chief of station looked a trifle baffled, but nodded as though in full accord.

"You're obviously doing a first-rate job, Trumbull," said the Ambassador, leaning back in his chair. "With these connections you're surely getting a great deal of valuable information. A great service to our national security. Who is the Russian Resident in Munich?" He smiled reminiscently. "I wouldn't be surprised if I know him. Or rather," he laughed apologetically, "know of him." He leaned forward, towards Trumbull, smiling expectantly.

Trumbull swallowed once or twice. He looked at Heston, who continued to look attentively at the Ambassador. "Well, I don't know, Mr. Ambassador—"

"You don't know?" Whitney Ballard's smile disappeared.

"No, I know," said Trumbull. "I just don't know if I really ought to give out that information, Mr. Ambassador."

Whitney Ballard's face clouded. "To whom, Mr. Trumbull?" he asked coldly.

Again Trumbull swallowed. "His name is Lazar Matveye-vich Pegov," he said. Hastily, he added, "But that is top secret information. He's really working for us now, through Satori, and we expect him to come over to us one of these days. The slightest leak, of course, would mean the whole operation blown and his end."

The Ambassador ignored Trumbull's cautionary remarks. He looked upward as he searched his memory, and then his face broke into a triumphant smile. "Of course!" he said. "Pegov. He's the one who was running that operation in Holland in 1949 and '50. By God, yes! And he got away from us that time. He was posing as a Swiss building-materials importer, and we found the stuff he bought under his cover was being sold to the Marshall Plan boys at quadruple the price. Of course, Pegov. Always makes a profit on his operations. What's his cover this time?"

Trumbull's thin lips tightened, but he answered, "A psychiatrist. A refugee psychiatrist from Silesia."

"I'll bet his patients are paying through the nose. And God knows for what," observed the Ambassador. Again he exhibited enthusiasm. "And you're in touch with him through Satori?"

"Yes, sir."

"Why, then it's easy," the Ambassador said. Suddenly a look of uncertainty came over his face. "But wait a minute. Where do you meet Satori?"

Trumbull stiffened visibly. "I have a safe house in Munich. An apartment. Satori comes there. With due precautions, of course."

"Of course," said the Ambassador. "But where does Satori see Pegov?"

"Usually in the area around the National Museum," said Trumbull, defensively.

"Ah, yes. Over by the river," said the Ambassador. "Now, your safe house is where?"

Trumbull scowled. "Mr. Ambassador, I really don't know whether . . ."

"You don't know?" Again the Ambassador's face clouded. "But what is this?"

Trumbull licked his lips and looked at Heston. Heston looked at the floor.

"It's extremely sensitive information, Mr. Ambassador," Trumbull began.

"Goddammit!" Whitney Ballard shouted. He slammed his fist down on the table before him and glowered at Trumbull.

"I'm an extremely sensitive Ambassador, Trumbull," he said, his face red with anger, "and if my sensitivity is touched in just the wrong way I can be on the telephone to Washington in roughly one minute. What is that address?"

Trumbull, who had recoiled at the Ambassador's outburst, tightened his mouth and stared at the Ambassador with cold fury. "Two Haydnstrasse," he said.

The Ambassador leaned back in his chair and appeared to be giving his temper time to cool. "Let's see now," he said mildly. "That's on the other side of town, over by the Theresienwiese, isn't it?"

Trumbull nodded.

"Well, that's not too close," said the Ambassador pleasantly. His eyes oscillated vaguely between Heston and Trumbull. "You should be able to ask Satori to find out from Pegov about Dowling without running any risk. Don't you agree?"

Heston and Trumbull exchanged quick glances. "Yes, sir," said Trumbull. Heston nodded vigorously.

Whitney Ballard rose. "Then I think it's all clear, gentlemen. Roger, you will call off the operation at Eze. Mr. Trumbull, you will check on Dowling through your, ah, Russian connections. Thank you very much indeed, gentlemen." He addressed a somewhat absent-minded smile to both of them, and then stifled a yawn.

"Yes, sir. Good afternoon, Mr. Ambassador," said Heston, as he followed Trumbull out.

In the marble hallway outside the Ambassador's office Ross

139

Trumbull's mouth was clamped in fury as he strode to the elevator with Roger Heston.

"The old fart!" Trumbull said explosively.

Heston shrugged. "What do you expect? He's getting along, you know. It was obviously his ga-ga afternoon. I certainly have seldom heard less sense from him."

"You can afford to be philosophical," retorted Trumbull. "But he's just blown the mechanics of *my* whole damn operation in Munich. If not the operation itself. Now I've got to re-do the whole thing. What's a safe house worth that some ga-ga old coot knows about? Zero. And that's what I've got to start all over from now—practically zero." The elevator door opened, and Trumbull stepped in ahead of Heston. "Goddammit!" he said.

In the Ambassador's office Caxton Burroughs was just climbing out from the well of the Ambassador's desk and brushing scarlet lint from his otherwise impeccable suit. "You must do something about this carpet, Whitney," he said. "It's dazzling." Burroughs shielded his eyes from the scarlet glow.

"The Department," said the Ambassador, "has refused me the money for a less dazzling carpet. Now, Caxton, do you have everything you need to know?" The Ambassador's expression was one of mixed amusement and irritation.

"Habitual stinginess combined with bad taste characterize the Department," Burroughs answered. "And thank you, yes. A splendidly devious performance, Whitney. Besides the nuts and bolts of Trumbull's Munich caper, I got a good look at him, and by your insisting that he be here today, we've stopped him from leaving town until we're in a position in Munich to take care of him. David and Peter arrive there this evening. Having had a look at Trumbull now, I'll go along there tomorrow morning."

The Ambassador nodded. "I agree about the Department. As for deviousness," he said, looking with some exasperation at Burroughs, "how, Caxton, do you ever stand all those straightforward problems at the Voyagers' Club?"

140

"What makes you think a tri-national men's club is straightforward?" Burroughs retorted coolly.

THE BURLY SWISSAIR GUARD in civilian clothes dropped into the seat next to Peter. "Are you hurt?" he asked.

Peter rubbed his chin and then stroked the back of his neck. "No," he said. "Humiliated, but that's the least of our troubles now. What took you so long?"

The Swiss kept his revolver in his hand, and shook his head. "The other stewardess was blocking the aisle with the cigarette cart. Probably he waited until he saw her begin her rounds. I couldn't see him until it was too late."

Peter shrugged. "You couldn't have fired anyway." He glanced out the window. "Not at this altitude."

The Swiss regarded him coolly. "It depends on the angle," he said. Peter raised his eyebrows, then decided on silence: never argue with a Swiss about shooting; likely as not he's spent a good part of every Sunday of his life since he was eight or ten years old on the practice range.

"The real question is where we go now," said Peter. He had no sooner spoken than the plane banked slightly to the right. When the mandolin player had taken over, the plane had been over the Allgäu, in southern Germany, heading east-north-east straight to Munich. Peter guessed their course was now east-south-east.

The guard looked out the window. "He's heading into Austria. It doesn't mean anything. It just gets him away from German fighter planes for the moment."

"Meine Damen und Herren." The Swiss captain's voice came over the loudspeaker, tense, but under control. It filled the passenger cabin like that of an eagerly awaited preacher in a hushed church. "I am obliged to obey the orders of a passenger here in the cockpit with me now, who is armed.

141

He assures me that if his orders are obeyed, no harm will befall anyone on the aircraft. Please remain calm. I do not yet know our destination." The loudspeaker clicked, and there was silence. It seemed to blanket the faraway noise of the engines; Peter could feel the fear and tension rolling over him from behind. The passengers were not calm; they were paralyzed. Far in the rear Peter heard a sound like sobbing.

The plane had been climbing since its change of course. Now, it banked again, this time to the left. The Swiss leaned across Peter and looked down. Quickly, he dashed to the other side of the plane, looked out, and came back for another glance out the window next to Peter. "He's heading east," the guard said. "We've left Kitzbühl behind on the left, and that's the Salzach below. From here he can fly into the Enns River valley, and from there he has a choice of all Eastern Europe without having to cross Germany or Italy." He chewed his lip and looked at Peter reflectively. "For a start, that is."

Peter watched the landscape unfolding below. The plane made frequent minor changes of course, but so far as Peter could tell, the general direction remained the same. Gradually, the snow-capped peaks fell away farther and farther to the south. The deep Alpine gorges gave way to more rounded summits and less precipitous valleys. They in turn were replaced by land no more than gently rolling. Then broad, flat areas of rich farming land began to appear. *"Meine Damen und Herren."* Peter unclenched his fists and listened to the captain's voice. He was certainly keeping up a good show. "We will be landing in Budapest in twenty minutes."

Peter sat bolt upright. Well, I'll be damned, he said to himself. At any other time but tonight this would have been a welcome detour. The thought crossed his mind that Eva Kanday was a determined woman: if she wanted a package delivered she saw to it that it was delivered. But what happens at Budapest? Perhaps we land only for refueling; from Zurich to Budapest is more than twice the distance from Zurich to Munich. Or perhaps the mandolin player gets off and we go on back to Munich, making me late but at least letting me meet David Killitoe. An object flashed by outside the window. Peter looked in time to see a Mig circling off to the south in preparation for another pass. Somewhere down below us, thought Peter, is a very nervous Russian or Hungarian officer, suspicious that this whole affair is a trick of some kind.

A range of hills passed beneath the plane, stretching off to the southwest. The Bakony Mountains, Peter guessed; what a way to see for the first time a land he had studied so carefully. The "No Smoking" sign lit up. The Mig hovered watchfully in the distance. The plane had been losing altitude for some time; now there was a slight shudder as the flaps were lowered. At the same moment Peter saw the great, broad, muddy river below, reaching out to the horizon on the south. Here they called it the Duna: only faraway French and English and Americans insisted on Danube. The plane banked sharply to the left, swooped low, and there was the reassuring jar of the wheels on the runway. Again there was the captain's voice. "This is Ferihegy airport. Remain seated with your seat belts fastened until further notice."

The Caravelle ground to a halt, turned about, and taxied back along the runway to an access strip. About two hundred yards off the runway it came to a stop. In the lowering twilight Peter could see only concrete and turf. We're well quarantined, he thought; if we blow up the damage will be minimal. Except from our point of view. He looked again and saw that a firetruck had drawn up on the grass to the rear of the airplane, at a respectful distance. The plane's engines were suddenly switched off. In the ensuing silence the sound of shots in the cockpit crackled like so many snapping nerves. The guard leaped to his feet, his gun trained on the door to the cockpit.

In the rear of the plane a woman screamed, and a man groaned. Peter looked hastily at the nearest emergency exit, one row behind him. With a nervous eye on the cockpit door

143

the steward and stewardess went along the aisle trying to calm the passengers. Peter glanced forward through the window. This time he could see that there were several armed soldiers standing about the nose of the plane. Green cap bands. Frontier Guards, dressed to look as much like their Russian models as possible. At least *they* seemed in good humor; they grinned and shook their heads as though at a good joke. Then, still grinning, they crowded forward about the plane and were lost to Peter's sight.

A deathly stillness settled on the passengers' cabin, broken only by the sound of voices and of dull thuds from the cockpit. There were footsteps, the lock turned, and then the door opened. The guard thrust his gun forward, but withdrew it as the captain stepped through, followed by the stewardess who had gone forward with the gunman. They wore expressions of immense relief. There was a buzz in the cabin and the captain raised his hands for silence. "Those shots you may have heard," he said, "hit no one. Our unwelcome guest decided to destroy the plane's instrument panel. He succeeded, and he has now been taken into custody by the Hungarian authorities. This aircraft will be unable to fly until it is repaired, so we are asking Zurich to send a replacement to take you all on to Munich. Unfortunately, that cannot be until tomorrow morning at the earliest. There will be a bus here shortly to take you all to a hotel for the night. We apologize for this incident. Thank you for your patience."

A voice from the rear intoned, "We're happy to be alive, captain. Thank *you*."

The captain smiled and turned to the stewardess behind him. She pointed to Peter. The captain leaned down. "Are you all right?"

Peter waved his hand in a gesture of dismissal. "Perfectly. He had a good left hook, but I still have my teeth."

The captain looked at him speculatively. "I didn't know about it until after the Hungarians took him into custody, when the stewardess told me he'd hit you. You want me to add assault to the charges?"

Peter shook his head. "No," he answered. "If the rest of his Afternoon of a Faun isn't enough for the Hungarians to prosecute him, they certainly won't just for a poke on my jaw." The last thing I need at this moment, inside or outside of Hungary, thought Peter, is publicity. "Forget it," he said to the captain. "But there is one thing I'd like to know." The captain nodded questioningly. "What was all that good humor among the Hungarian guards?" Peter asked.

The captain grinned. "After he shot up the instrument panel and then leaped out and surrendered, I leaned out and told the Hungarians that I hoped they weren't going to be too hard on the lad. 'Send him back to us,' I said, 'as salami.'"

PETER LOOKED out the window across the Danube. He recognized the steep bluff on the Buda side, its near end crowned by the somber black shell of the Royal Palace, as the Vár. Beyond the ruins of the Palace a floodlit lacy spire pierced the night sky: the Coronation Church. Beyond the spire the squat, round towers and massive walls of the Fisherman's Bastion, also floodlit, jutted over the edge of the bluff. Beneath the near end of the Vár the Chain Bridge stretched its low sweep across the river, its lights reflected in the water below. Bismarck found Budapest more lovely than Vienna, and Peter agreed with him.

He turned and looked at the room. A dozen years ago an American hotel in Budapest would have been inconceivable; perhaps we're making some progress in overcoming animosities and fear after all. The thought failed to assuage what Peter recognized as a sense of unease. He sat down in a bright blue modern armchair. Something was nagging at him. What was it? Not the hijacking, unsettling as that had

145

been. Then the look of surprise on the police officer's face at the airport when he presented his passport for stamping came back to him. That was it. "But you already have a Hungarian visa!" he had said, in a mixture of reproach and curiosity. Then he had scribbled busily. Nothing more. Except that all the other passengers had been divided between the Gellert and Royal hotels; only Peter and the Swissair crew had been brought here to The Intercontinental. After a moment's thought he decided there was nothing he could do about that. But he did have to get word to Killitoe in Munich. A long-distance call to Lord Killitoe, passing through both Hungarian and German official eavesdroppers, was out of the question. He looked at his watch. Eight thirty. Otto's office was closed by now, but it seemed to him wiser not to draw attention, in the circumstances, to Helen, or to Jake, by calling her apartment from Budapest. An innocuous telegram to the office was the only solution. Helen would only get it in the morning, but meanwhile the news was surely on the radio.

His eyes wandered about the room. What does one do one's first night in Budapest, when one has nothing to do? His suitcase caught his eye, and he remembered. Well, we may as well get *that* out of the way now. He reached for the telephone, after glancing at his address book. The operator's English, serviceable if a bit thick, was encouraging. "Could I have six-six-three, five-six-seven, please?" he said slowly and distinctly. By God, I forgot to ask Eva if she speaks English. What is she? A doctor? May as well try it. The woman's voice that answered greeted him with a lilt that Peter recognized as national, not individual.

"May I speak to Miss . . ." Peter corrected himself, "to Dr. Kodaly, please."

Her surprise was almost audible. The voice dropped a tone or two as she answered, warily, in English, "This is Dr. Kodaly."

With Peter's explanation that Eva Kanday had asked him

146

to call her, her voice lightened. "That is very good of you," she said. "How is Eva?"

"She seemed very well this afternoon. She gave me a package for you." Peter wondered whether it would be polite to leave it at the desk for her and suggest that she pick it up at her convenience.

"You move very quickly." Her English was fluent, and Peter found the light, musical accent agreeable.

"Actually, I wasn't coming to Budapest. I was on my way to Munich," he began.

There was evident mystification at the other end of the line. "But you *are* calling from Budapest, aren't you?"

Peter laughed. "Yes. My plane was hijacked."

The mystification at the other end deepened. There was a pause, and then, with an almost contrite air, she asked, "What is a high jack?"

Let that be a lesson to you, thought Peter. Use words that people who don't read American newspaper headlines will understand. "A passenger took over the aircraft with a gun— two guns, to be exact—and forced the pilot to fly here instead of Munich."

There was a long silence. Finally she said, "I don't understand." Peter began to explain again, but she interrupted him. "No, I understand the facts," she said. "It's the reasoning I don't understand."

Peter laughed at both the thought and the phrasing. "You *are* a doctor?" he asked. "Not a lawyer?"

She laughed in response, as though she had read his mind. "I *am* a doctor. You must be a lawyer, from your question."

"I am, but I didn't mean to sound like one," he answered.

She let that drop. "I hope no one was hurt," she said. "Are you all right?"

Oddly, and for the first time in the last four hours, the question seemed welcome to Peter. Before he thought what he was saying, he had answered, "No. I need urgent medical attention."

147

Her answer was quick and without levity. "You are joking, I hope."

"Yes," said Peter. "But I do need attention. I'm very hungry. The only solution is for you to have dinner with me."

The pause was neither too long nor too short. "It's not the *only* solution," she observed, "but it sounds like a good one."

"Agreed, then," said Peter. "What time can I pick you up?"

"Where are you staying?"

"The Intercontinental."

"I'll pick *you* up. In a half-hour or so," she said. "I haven't seen the inside of the hotel yet."

"Good. We can have a drink in the bar on the roof." Peter searched for the word, the Hungarian greeting and farewell between friends. He found it. *"Szervusz,"* he said.

"Ah?" Her laughter was gentle, but she used another Hungarian expression, unknown to Peter, for her good-bye.

Peter showered and changed in leisurely fashion, took Eva Kanday's package, and went down to the desk. He wrote out a telegram to Helen Goodman, addressed to the office. "Plane hijacked stop Inform Munich will arrive when transport available." She and Jake would understand that meant both David and Satori; Budapest was certainly not the place to mention Satori openly. He handed the telegram to the clerk, who read it unabashedly. The clerk nodded his approval. Peter swallowed his annoyance, and handed the clerk some German marks, asking for Hungarian forints. Handing him his change, the clerk gestured across the lobby. "You have a guest," he said. "We called your room, but you had already left to come down." Peter glanced in surprise at the clock behind the desk; forty-five minutes had passed. After a quick glare at the clerk he turned and strode rapidly to where Maria Kodaly sat waiting.

She rose as he approached. Very handsome indeed, Peter observed. A thick mass of tawny hair with golden highlights, cut short. Green eyes, offset by whites so clear as to have a

148

bluish cast, and a smooth, bronzed complexion. High, prominent cheekbones. Wide nostrils underneath a nose more thin than full, its tip turned upward in what must have been tomboyish pugnacity on the child, but had become a graceful curve on the grown woman. She was wearing a silk jersey print. She moved easily, with an air of repose. Her rounded lips, glistening slightly, parted in a welcoming smile.

Peter took her hand. "Dr. Kodaly," he said, "I am sorry. I was told a half-hour in Budapest always meant an hour."

Maria Kodaly looked at him with interest and amusement. "You were misinformed, Mr. Dowling. It really means an hour and a half. But I was hungry too."

"And thirsty?" Peter asked hopefully.

She smiled and nodded. "Let's go see your bar."

They walked around to the elevators. As the doors shut and they started up, Maria looked at him with curiosity. "You must be very important," she said. "This hotel has been full since the first night it opened."

"Impossible," said Peter, as the thought crossed his mind that she might be right for unpleasant reasons unknown to him. Still, the Hungarians had given him a visa without any trouble. "I'm a victim of an Arab guerrilla. Nothing more."

The doors opened and they stepped out. "An Arab?" She looked puzzled.

"As a matter of fact, he looked and sounded like a German to me," said Peter, "but he was shouting pro-Arab slogans."

He steered her into the bar and to a table by the window overlooking the river. "It still makes no sense," she said.

She studied the view for some time in silence. The Vár seemed closer than it had from Peter's room, almost as though the river didn't intervene. The waiter approached. "Whiskey?" asked Peter.

Maria nodded and smiled. "That will make it a foreign evening for me, too." She gazed out the window again. "It's a superb view," she said. "Thank you for showing it to me."

Peter smiled. "It's a pleasure. You must come and show me

149

New York some time." He caught her glancing with mild curiosity at the package he had set on a chair alongside him. He handed it to her.

"Very kind of you to have brought it all this way—even involuntarily," she smiled. "I know what it is, so I'll open it later," she added, putting the package next to her bag.

"It was only kind—and involuntary—so long as I had not seen you," Peter answered. She raised her eyebrows at his compliment, as though in surprise, then smiled her pleasure.

Peter looked at her with interest. "And how do you come by your perfect English?" he asked.

"Thank you." She smiled. "For Hungarians languages are a necessity, not just decoration or pleasure," she said. "I was taught English at home, as a child. And German. And French. It was characteristic"—she spoke softly, and with fine sarcasm—"of the bourgeoisie. The idea will spread, in time." Her mouth curved in a teasing smile. "And where did you learn the expression '*Szervusz*,' Mr. Dowling?"

Peter smiled and dodged the question. "Why, the Viennese use it too," he said innocently. He signaled the waiter for two more whiskies.

Maria Kodaly nodded and smiled. "Our sister city," she said reflectively. "From the days of the Monarchy. We're still trying to get together. Hungarians go to Vienna any chance they get, and the Viennese come here in carloads, from now until the end of autumn. Even without visas. Just a pass for a busload of so many Viennese visitors."

"And do you go to Vienna?" Peter asked.

A faint expression of longing crossed her face, and she shook her head. "No," she said. "*I* don't travel."

Peter wondered whether to pursue the subject. "How will you ever show me New York, in that case?" he asked with a smile.

She shrugged, her green eyes observing him. "We'd better begin with Budapest."

"That was my plot from the beginning," said Peter, not quite truthfully. "So what do you suggest for our dinner?

150

Surely you won't confine me to this hotel, agreeable as it is?"

"My plot is to release you, not confine you," she said. A mischievous smile crossed her lips, and then she was thoughtful for a moment. "We'll go to a restaurant in Buda. The Kis Royal." She pronounced it "Keesh." "It's what I think you call a 'tourist trap,' but the food and the wine are good, and there's music. And it is more Hungarian than this."

Peter signed the check, tossed off his drink, and rose. "Lead on, Doctor," he said.

As they waited for the elevator, the Swissair captain came out of the restaurant nearby and joined them. "There will be another plane here in the morning to take you to Munich," he said to Peter in German. "Departure is at eleven." Peter thanked him and they rode down together. As they parted in the lobby, the captain gestured to Peter's chin. "No pain?" he asked.

Peter smiled. "Obviously, none," he answered.

Maria Kodaly smiled at Peter and took his arm. "Now, where do we get a taxi?" Peter asked.

She dropped his arm and looked at him reproachfully. "You don't trust my driving?" she said, in a small voice.

"Why, but, of course," said Peter, momentarily confused. "I didn't know." She took him by the arm again and led him out to the street.

"All you have to do is to bend a little in the right places," she said as she opened the door of a bright red Fiat 850.

Peter helped her in, then went around, doubled up, and squeezed in beside her. "Dr. Kodaly," he said, observing her pleasure, "it's a dream car. Take us away!"

With a proud flourish, she started the engine. She tapped the dashboard. "He is called Ficko," she said, pronouncing it "Fitsko." She released the hand brake. "It means 'the guy,' " she said, and then thought better. "That's English. With you it's 'the kid.' "

"Don't worry," said Peter, "it's universal. With the Cubans it's 'Che.' "

She glanced at him and her eyes flashed. "Careful what

151

you say of my true love," she said, with a pat for the car and a smile for Peter. With a renewed flourish she drove to the end of the street, turned around the length of Roosevelt Square, and rolled onto the Chain Bridge.

She guided the car across the bridge, around Adam Clark Square, and headed the car into the tunnel under the Vár. Peter watched her driving—competently, a bit preoccupied, and happily. Suddenly he felt more expansive than two whiskies could possibly warrant. He was in a strange city, with no possibility of doing anything for the moment about any problem whatsoever, with a very attractive woman he didn't know, and no consequences to flow therefrom beyond eleven o'clock the next morning. It was, he realized, a definition of freedom.

WITH A SIGH Eva Kanday rose and turned off the television. She went to the living room window and looked out into the Aurorastrasse. Opposite, in the dimming light, the fairways of the Dolder golf course glowed a lighter green against the dark, wooded slopes of the Adlisberg behind. As she watched, a metallic blue Ferrari 365 GT pulled to the curb in front of the apartment building. Gunter Roessli stepped out and slammed the door. She turned from the window and put on her coat. She picked up the telephone and was about to call for a taxi when there was a slamming of doors and her husband strode into the room.

"You going somewhere?" His voice was rasping, charged with fury. His eyes were narrowed, the carefully fostered youthfulness of his features twisted with rage.

Eva watched him calmly. "To the St. Gotthard, as usual at this hour," she answered.

Roessli grasped her wrist brutally, pulled her across the

room, and threw her onto the couch. "You've plenty of time for that—and for other things, apparently," he shouted. "Right now you're going to answer some questions."

Eva rubbed her wrist and looked at him evenly. "If you wish," she said quietly.

"I damn well do," said Roessli. He sat down in a chair and leaned forward. "Where were you at two thirty this afternoon?"

Eva blinked, and then answered coolly, "I was at the Franziskaner Hotel, in Niederdorfstrasse. Why?"

"I'll ask the questions," snapped Roessli, but he appeared somewhat surprised by the forthrightness of her answer. "And what were you doing at the Franziskaner?"

"I was seeing a lawyer," said Eva.

"What the hell about?" Roessli shouted.

Eva shook her head. "Gunter, he wasn't a divorce lawyer. He wasn't even a Swiss lawyer. He was an American lawyer," she said. "I was seeing him about my appearing at a jazz festival in Bavaria."

Roessli leaned back in his chair, eyeing Eva with an expression of superiority. "Look, I know he's an American lawyer. Peter Dowling is his name." He snorted. "What the hell has he got to do with a jazz festival in Bavaria?"

Eva raised her eyebrows. "Why, he's Otto Miller's lawyer. You know, the publisher I was supposed to do a record for in Nice last week. He's also putting on the jazz festival."

"I thought you told me Miller was hurt in an automobile accident."

Eva nodded. "Exactly," she said. "That's why his lawyer came to see me to talk about the festival."

"What? In bed?" Roessli sneered.

Eva sighed. "If you know I saw him at the Franziskaner this afternoon, presumably you also know we were together hardly an hour. Not even. Not much of a tryst, particularly as I'd never seen the man before."

"Quite enough time for you," snapped Roessli. "Also, you

153

lie. You spoke to him last night at the St. Gotthard, after your performance, while I had my back turned and was talking with the Stoessels."

Eva bit her lip. "If you had your back turned how do you know I spoke to him?"

Roessli slapped the arm of his chair. "I'll ask the questions," he shouted. "Why was he in the St. Gotthard Bar last night?"

Eva gave him a patient look. "He only had a few hours in town and he hoped to talk to me there. I told him you and I were busy last night, as we were, and he made the appointment for this afternoon."

"I see," said Roessli. His expression was sardonic. "So what else did you talk about this afternoon? Besides your Bavarian Jazz Festival?"

Eva shrugged. "He said he might be going to Budapest so I gave him a package of cosmetics to take to Maria Kodaly."

Roessli started. Softly, he asked, "What did you tell him about Maria Kodaly?"

Eva looked mystified. "That she is my best friend, of course." Roessli chewed his lips for a moment, and then appeared to change his mind. "And this package of cosmetics for Maria," he went on, "you just happened to have it with you this afternoon?"

For a fraction of a second a look of surprise passed over Eva's face and then disappeared. "Of course not," she said. "Otto Miller had told me in Nice that his lawyer, this Peter Dowling, might be going to Budapest. I took the package along on the chance he would be kind enough to take it."

"Ah?" said Roessli. "You and Miller seem to cover a lot of ground in your recording sessions."

Eva snorted. "Don't let your fantasies run away with you," she said. "You saw Otto Miller at our wedding. He's old enough to be your father, let alone mine. I told him about our trip to Budapest. He is Hungarian, after all. And I asked him if he knew of anyone going there who might take a package for me."

Roessli leaned forward. "And what did you tell Mr. Dowling about me?" he asked.

Eva raised her eyebrows. "You? This was a business meeting. Your name wasn't even mentioned. Why should it be?"

Roessli thought for a moment, and then answered bitingly, "Normal between lovers to mention the husband, isn't it?"

Again Eva shrugged. "The fee for that festival will be a very good one, and you couldn't buy the publicity it will give."

Roessli appeared to reflect. "All the same, I forbid you to see this Dowling, or to have anything to do with him. Is that clear? Otto Miller can handle your affairs personally. You're important enough."

"But that's crazy," said Eva with a gesture of impatience. "How can Otto handle my affairs when he's staying in Italy with friends, recovering from his accident? For the time being he's confided all *his* affairs, which include mine, to his lawyer."

"You heard what I said," Roessli snapped. "If this Dowling isn't after you, he's after other game. I don't want him around." He spoke deliberately. "Do I make myself clear?"

Eva sighed and looked at her watch. "You're clear," she said, "but crazy. I can't choose Otto Miller's lawyer for him. And now I have to go." She rose, went to the telephone, and called for a taxi. Silently, she went to the door. Roessli followed her. He took her wrist roughly and twisted it so she couldn't move.

"You see, Eva," he said quietly, but with a harsh ring in his voice, "there's nothing crazy about it, because *you're* lying. I don't know whether this Dowling is Otto Miller's lawyer or not. I only have your word for it. And, as I say, you're lying. Just to give you one example. Dowling was staying at the Baur-au-Lac. But this morning he moved out and checked into the Franziskaner, where he met you. It was the only business he apparently had there. Wasn't the Baur-au-Lac good enough for you? Or were you afraid you might be seen going to his room in the Baur-au-Lac?"

Eva looked at him steadily. "You're hurting my wrist, if that's what you want. And I have no idea of Mr. Dowling's hotel problems. He gave me an appointment at the Franziskaner. I kept it, and we talked about my singing at Otto Miller's festival in Bavaria. And that's that."

Roessli dropped her wrist and Eva opened the door. He smiled at her, coldly. "If you're lying, as I'm sure you are, you've chosen the wrong occasion for it, Eva," he said ominously. "It will take me no more than twenty-four hours to find out."

Eva passed through the door. "I hope your apologies will be as forceful as your suspicions," she said.

"Right," said Roessli, still with his cold smile. "By the way, I won't be here for lunch tomorrow. I'm lunching out of town. But I'll be back in time to see you in the evening. You can count on that."

PETER HAD a profound sense of well-being; what a pleasure to eat and drink with a woman—a beautiful one at that —who plainly relished eating and drinking. The waiter brought the small copper pots of Turkish coffee. Maria leaned forward and gestured to Peter to wait. Intently, she poured from the pot into her cup and tasted. She made a brief remark in Hungarian to the waiter, who shrugged. "It's drinkable," she said to Peter. "Coffee is almost a sacred drink with us. It's also an accurate symptom of the state of the nation. At the moment, the hardest thing to get in this city is good coffee." She sipped hers with a look of resigned disappointment. "This will do. Until something better comes along."

Peter tasted his. He had asked for it only "half-sugared," as the local expression had it, but still it was quite sweet. That didn't disguise the fact that it was inferior, green coffee. "I'm told Viennese coffee is as good as it has ever been," he said.

A mischievous smile played about her lips. "The only way I'll ever taste it is if you bring me some."

"It's bringing the mountain to Mohammed," said Peter, "but if that's what you want, that's what you'll have." She laughed appreciatively.

There was a sudden wail in the doorway and Peter looked up. The musicians, who had been playing in the next room, had returned. Peter glanced about the room. The decor was a bit too consciously Hungarian—red and green curtains and table linen, minutely embroidered, combined with the white walls to make the national colors. He listened. The predominant language in the room was German. There was a sprinkling of Slavic types at various tables, and here and there islands of Hungarian being spoken—its even-metered intonation and Central Asian inflection cutting through the German gutturals and Slavic sibilants. Over all rose the glissandos and pizzicatos of the music, as the violinists moved from table to table, their playing and singing alternately lusty and obsequious. They had already visited Peter and Maria twice, and Peter hoped they wouldn't do so again. So far as he was concerned, they interjected an unnecessary obstacle between Maria and himself. He turned to her. "What will you show me now?"

She nodded her agreement with the suggestion that they leave and picked up her handbag from the bench. "We'll go look at the view from the Vár," she said. Peter signaled the waiter and paid the bill, handing him a quantity of forints that he knew represented at least a third of the average Hungarian worker's monthly wage.

As they made their way out through the other rooms Peter's eyes fell on a pageboy bob in a far corner of the last room. He started. There was no mistaking that short, knobby forehead, the sunken eyes, the wide, flat nose and protuberant jaws—although the latter were now ruptured by a toothy grin. Two men in civilian clothes sat at table with him, both obviously enjoying his joke.

Peter was seized by a surge of anger. His impulse was to

157

walk over, grab the boy by his fringed jacket, lift him up, and then knock him flat. He thought better of it. He turned his head as though he had seen nothing and followed Maria into the street.

Silently, he helped her into the car and then doubled himself up again to get in beside her. "I'll be damned," he said when he had shut the door. Maria looked at him in surprise. "The thug who hijacked the plane this afternoon was having dinner in that restaurant," said Peter in explanation.

"The pirate?" Maria's expression was one of incredulity.

"The pirate," nodded Peter. "Laughing and joking with two men in civilian clothes as though it was his birthday. Some custody they took him into."

Maria looked at him for a moment, and then shook her head. "It makes no sense at all," she said. No, thought Peter, it makes sense somewhere. It's just that it makes no sense to you and me, because we're on the outside. Watching Maria start the car, her pleasure in it so evident, Peter found his anger dissipated as abruptly as it had risen. That imbecile had rendered him a service after all; he had brought about this evening. Peter laughed to himself; the final victory was his own.

"Maria," he said, "the hell with him. I just realized he's done me a great service." He turned to her as though dismissing the subject. "Tell me," he said, "how long have you and Ficko been keeping up this mad affair?"

Maria's answering laugh held a note of gratitude for his perception. "He came into my life four months ago, in January," she said. "There hasn't been a harsh word between us since." She drove around the block and turned left on a broad boulevard.

"How long did you wait for him?" asked Peter, who knew that although Hungarians could buy private cars, the terms involved putting up the full purchase price and then waiting one's turn.

"Sixteen months," said Maria, "and that was quick."

Peter glanced at her with admiration; independent fore-

sight and the ability to carry through a plan were not quali-
ties he had found often in women beautiful enough to stir
him. "I hope he's not the jealous type," he said.

"He's choosy," Maria answered, "but he likes you. He took
you to dinner without a cough, and see how nicely he carries
you along now."

They rolled past the South Station. Maria drove on until
the Vár was almost behind them, and then turned right up a
steep hill. The street curved around to the right, climbing
ever more steeply, until they were right under the bastions.
A final leap and they passed beneath a fortified archway into
a cobblestoned square. A wide street leading off it was
fronted by palaces, their proportions and the smooth areas of
their facades testifying to the Hungarian simplification of baroque. The name of the square caught Peter's eye. "Bécsi-
kapu?" he asked Maria.

"Vienna Gate," she translated.

"We're going in the wrong direction," Peter observed.

She smiled and turned left into a street lined with ancient
houses. Again the street sign caught Peter's eye. "Fortuna
utca." Last night he had gone to Fortune Street in Zurich to
meet Eva Kanday, and tonight he was riding along Fortune
Street in Budapest with Maria Kodaly. Fortune was not only
with him, but improving with each step.

At the end of the street they emerged into a large square,
and Maria parked the car. On their left rose the great tower,
carved and spiky, and the spired and buttressed mass of the
Coronation Church. Maria led the way around the church to
the rear, where a proliferation of carved archways, squat
round towers, battlements, terraces, balustrades, and a stairway descending the bluff, formed the Fisherman's Bastion.
They went to the edge of the upper terrace and leaned
against the parapet in silence. The moon, a few days past the
full, was high enough in the eastern sky to bathe the scene in
silver light. Far beneath them the Danube cut its gently curv-
ing swath between the two parts of the city. On its far side
the lights of Pest spread eastward in a jumble almost to the

horizon. On its near side the streets and houses of Buda merged towards the north into a cap of lights set upon the inverted bowl called the Rose Hill. Far to the north dark masses indicated the foothills of the mountains of Slovakia. "It is very beautiful," said Peter.

Maria nodded. "It is," she said softly. The night air was warm, stirred only occasionally by a wispy breeze from the north. Peter became acutely aware of Maria beside him. At the moment he would have spoken she turned and looked up at him.

"Pay-tehr." It was the first time she had pronounced his name, and she did so as in Hungarian, the *t* light, but very clear, the *r* with just a hint of a single trill. It sounded marvelously intimate, pleasing Peter if only for that reason. He looked down at her. "Why did the Swiss captain ask if your chin gave you pain?" she asked.

Peter leaned back and laughed. "You're too observant, or maybe it's acute," he said. But he explained what had happened in the plane. She nodded. "I thought it was something like that," she said with a touch of concern. "And no one examined you?"

"I didn't need it," said Peter simply. "Besides, as I told you," he added, his voice beginning on a joking note, and then quickly losing it, "I've realized I'm grateful to that idiot. Without him we wouldn't be here together."

Maria smiled up at him. The moonlight bathed her face and surrounded her with an aura.

For the second time that evening her smile became mischievous. "That's all very well to say here," she said, "but you didn't like the dinner."

Peter looked at her in astonishment. "Ridiculous," he said, "you know better than that."

"I mean, you didn't like the musicians."

Peter smiled. "That's true. They got in my way. They came between us."

She looked steadily at him. "They need not come between us now," she said. "Come. We'll go to the gypsies."

In the northern suburb of Aquincum, by the Roman amphitheater, Maria turned right and drove to the edge of the Danube. There she turned left and they followed the river upstream. Through a screen of trees there was an occasional glimpse of the water and of an island opposite. They sped along a country road, Peter's cramped position in the little car relegated to oblivion by the physical nearness of Maria and the delight of their easy talk. They came to an open space. Maria pulled off the road and came to a stop. There were several other cars parked, and a bus with Austrian license plates. Maria nodded at it. "The Viennese," she said. Between the parking space and the river, surrounded by trees, was an old stone building, a sort of pavilion. Peter and Maria walked to the entrance and stepped into a plain vestibule. Beyond a closed door at the end came the wail of violins.

They passed through the door into a large room whose windows gave onto the river. Except for the tables and chairs, benches along the walls, and the shaded lamps fixed to the walls, the room was bare of decoration. Smaller rooms, similarly bare, extended beyond either side of the main room. Peter recognized the Viennese accents of the crowd filling the large room, drinking white wine, and alternately singing and volubly expressing their pleasure. In the middle of the room the cymbalum player sat enthroned before his instrument, his face set in an expression of diabolical glee as his long, thin, spoonlike hammers drew celestial sounds from the metal strings. The scattered violinists played with him in perfect harmony.

A ruddy-faced man, an almost classic Magyar type with his bushy, drooping mustaches, greeted Maria and Peter with a flourish. Without further to-do he led them into one of the side rooms, seated them alongside each other on a bench, and disappeared. The room was dimly lit; the few others present took no notice of Peter and Maria. The man returned in a moment with a bottle of white wine and glasses. He was followed by two violinists. Dark men, slight, almost emaciated, but intense, they bowed and addressed Maria in Hungarian. They nodded in vigorous agreement with her reply and began to play.

Peter had heard gypsy violins in restaurants, as at the Kis Royal tonight, where they got in the way of both the dinner and the conversation. What he now experienced was very different. The violinists began with a rapid, rhythmic song, smiling as they played, and watchfully observing the effect on Peter and Maria. Maria's hand in his, Peter felt her growing response to the music. Bit by bit he found himself caught up in it. Gradually, the rest of the room was obliterated from his consciousness, and the circle of his awareness narrowed to Maria and himself, the wine, and the musicians—a tight circle of complicity. After a time, even the faces of the violinists became indistinct, and Peter felt that he and Maria, their emotions bared, were alone with the whirling, penetrating music.

Occasionally the violinists would pause to drink some wine, and Peter and Maria would experience a momentary sense of loss. It was almost like a drug. Absently, automatically, Peter would place some forints on the table, and he and Maria would lean forward expectantly. The playing resumed, Peter's mind would be crowded with images. The next moment they would reduce themselves to a single phrase. When he spoke it to Maria she would nod with understanding, or he would find that a word or remark of Maria's would say exactly what he was thinking or feeling. At other times words were not necessary; they had only to look at each other to know that their thoughts and feelings were in unison.

Then the music became sad; the notes were long drawn out, and Peter felt they went to the very sources of his memory and feelings. Maria leaned her head on his shoulder and squeezed his hand tightly. Peter knew an exquisite melancholy. Maria's eyes were moist. Slowly, the music changed. The rhythm quickened and the tone mounted. Peter and

Maria left behind the valley of sweet despair, and were carried again to the heights.

Over several hours the cycle was repeated three or four times. After the final return to the heights, Peter felt an extraordinary inner clarity. It was as though he had been reborn with wisdom and without fear. He looked at Maria. She returned his gaze steadily, tenderly, her eyes shining, her lips parted. Peter leaned down to her and gently, softly, kissed her. A kiss of promise. The music came to an unobserved end.

Together, Peter and Maria rose. Silently, Peter lifted his glass to the violinists and drank the rest of his wine. They lifted their glasses in response, drank, and then bowed. Peter laid some more forints on the table, put his arm about Maria, and guided her out of the room. He scarcely heard or saw the Viennese. He paid the bill and he and Maria left.

In the clearing in front of the pavilion Maria looked up at the sky. The moon was past its zenith and descending towards the west. She took Peter by the hand and led him around the side of the pavilion, on a graveled path, through a clump of trees until, at some distance from the pavilion, they emerged onto a grassy knoll overlooking the Danube. The river sparkled in the moonlight, the swift current in the middle racing past the beam of reflected light, the stiller waters near shore turning in slow eddies. Around them rose walls of rushes. There was not a sound.

Peter could feel the throb of his own pulse and, through her hand, of Maria's. He looked at her. She turned to face him, her eyes bright in the moonlight, her breast rising and falling rapidly. Peter felt a sharp pang: desire, tenderness, the wonder of her beauty all in one. He drew her to him, enveloped her in his arms, and kissed her avidly. His world was reduced to the sweet taste of her mouth.

He pressed her to him. She answered, her breasts jutting against his chest, her thighs strained against his. Peter's hands moved over the warm roundness of her body. Her hands clasped his back. She began to breathe quickly, and little moans escaped her. Peter was no longer conscious of anything except the glory of the body beneath the dress, the soft caress of her hair, the rich warmth of her mouth.

Hastily he stripped off his jacket and laid it on the grass. She smiled at him. He kissed her and slowly lowered her into his jacket. She kept her hands clasped about his neck, her eyes, misty, fixed on his. Peter kissed her again. He ran his hand over her breasts, down her belly, and onto her thighs. He felt himself surrounded by her, blinded by the blissful warmth and softness. Their private darkness began to glow. Into it, from his core, he flooded her with lightning. Her cry of acceptance mingled with his of giving.

The Danube flowed on as they lay on its bank in the stillness. Desire rose in Peter again, it seemed to him almost instantly, more fiercely than before. He raised his head and looked into Maria's eyes. They spoke to him as he might have spoken to her. "Let's go home," she whispered. "I want you there."

They got to their feet and stood looking at the river for a moment, remembering. Then Peter put his arm around her and they walked to the car. "You want me to drive?" he asked.

"You don't know the way," she answered. They spoke softly, as if not to disturb the current flowing between them.

"We've found *our* way," said Peter. "A mere road should be easy. You guide me."

As he drove away from the pavilion Peter glanced in the mirror and saw a car's lights turn onto the road behind them. Time for even the gypsies to go home, he thought.

At a large grilled gate on a Buda hillside Maria told Peter to stop. She got out and opened the gates. Two or three other cars were parked in a broad driveway. Maria motioned to Peter to park the car on the left. She caught up with him as he got out, and put her finger to her lips. She led the way up stone steps to the front door. Inside she flicked on a light. The main staircase of what had obviously once been a luxurious private villa climbed up to a landing. On either side of the hallway were large double doors. Maria opened the one on the left with her key, took Peter's hand and led him inside. She led him through the darkness and sat him on the bed. She let go of his hand and lit a bedside lamp. It gave a warm golden light. Peter caught a glimpse of high ceilings, two heavily curtained windows, and of highly polished furniture. Then he turned and watched Maria as she went and closed the door and drew two heavy curtains across it, the movements of every part of her body registering on his brain with almost physical force. She came and stood before him, her green eyes studying him. He stood and embraced her. "*Te*," she whispered. "It's what English lacks. An intimate 'you.' "

"We'll find our way around that, too," said Peter.

Quickly they slipped out of their clothes and dropped onto the bed, pressed tightly together. Again Peter knew the bliss of her around him. Slowly, they emerged from the spell, only to fall under it again, exploring each other with a thirst renewed at each touch and taste.

In the darkness she put her mouth on his a last time; her kiss in the dark seemed to Peter to be filled with a light he had long known about but never actually seen until this night.

ALEXANDER SATORI glowered at the clock on his night table in the Bayerischer Hof. Eight fifteen. Thirty-six hours had passed, and those bumbling idiots had no word for him yet. What if Dowling got here to Munich today before Trumbull?

The telephone rang. He grabbed it. "Yes?" he barked.

"Pfalz here," said the slightly accented voice. "Sorry to take so long to call you back. But it's taken quite a while to check and re-check those figures."

"Yes?" Satori snapped.

"That second place was quite correct. As of the day before yesterday, of course." For speed of delivery the voice could have belonged to a snail. "As for that fourth, it seems to have slipped. It's in ninth place." Satori cursed.

"Not all bad news, by any means," the slow voice went on. "That's first category, instead of second."

"Ah," said Satori. Eleven this morning. It would be all right. "Thank you very much," he said. "Very kind of you to call."

THE CURTAINS at the windows glowed with the bright light of day. Peter reached for his watch on the night table. Eight fifteen. He could not have slept more than two hours, at the most, yet he felt marvelously refreshed. And clearheaded: on awaking he had known exactly, and gratefully, where he was. On the instant he had stroked Maria's hair, their night together flowing into the day with uninterrupted continuity. He replaced his watch on the night table.

Maria lay as she had when they slept. With the noise of his watch on the table she stirred. Her arm crept around his back and pressed him to her. Without moving her head she asked, "What time is it?"

"Eight fifteen," said Peter gently. "What time do you have to be at work?"

There was a pause as she hugged him. "I enter my laboratory at the moment your plane takes off," she answered. Peter turned on his side so that their bodies touched throughout their length. He closed his eyes and breathed deeply. The perfume of her body flowed up and over him.

Maria stirred against him, then raised her head and smiled down at him. Her tousled hair framed a face aglow, and graced by an ineffable tenderness. Peter looked into her eyes, their whites so startlingly clear. She kissed him softly and rose in one quick movement from the bed. "I must get you some breakfast," she announced. Peter sat up and gestured slowly to her to come back to bed. She drew the curtains at the windows and the sunlight flooded in. Peter still beckoned. "You do not leave my house hungry," she said.

Peter smiled. "There are different kinds of hunger," he said.

She blew him a kiss and disappeared through a door near the foot of the bed. Peter looked about the room. Except for their clothes tossed here and there it was in perfect order. It was large, probably once the living or dining room of the house. Several chests of drawers, a fine old desk in the far corner, a round table, were clearly pieces of value. The walls were covered with paintings and old prints, and there were flowers in the vases on the various tables and commodes. The effect was of calm, of care, and of taste.

Maria came out from the kitchenette wearing a light blue, transparent negligee. She set down a tray on which was toast, butter, fresh cheese, salt, pepper, and paprika, coffee and cream. Peter smiled. "I don't take back a word of what I said, but I will eat."

"Do eat, and don't take back anything," said Maria.

"Your apartment is a delight, Maria," said Peter as he sipped his coffee.

She looked pleased. "I'm lucky to have it. It's what the French call *petit bonheur*. The happiness that comes from small things." She looked out at the garden reflectively. "It is a good thing to learn," she said. "For a nation or a person. We have had to learn it. The happiness from small things, tended and cultivated, is as great as that from big things. And threatens no one."

Peter leaned forward and kissed her forehead. "It seems to suit me," he said. "I have never felt better in my life." He gazed into her eyes. "I tell you seriously."

She smiled and nodded her head. "I too," she said. "But now we're talking about the *grand bonheur*." It was Peter's turn to nod.

167

They finished breakfast and Peter rose. "How do I get back to our favorite river from here?" he asked reluctantly.

"Speak softly or you'll hurt Ficko's feelings," she said. "Obviously, we take you. And we must hurry."

Hastily, they washed and dressed. As they started out Maria stopped him. "Your jacket," she said. "It's covered with grass stains." Peter smiled. "And it will stay that way," he said.

At the door they kissed. "I'll be back," Peter said, "as soon as I can."

She smiled up at him, her green eyes calm. "That would be nice," she said.

As Maria turned off the Chain Bridge and into the street leading to the Intercontinental, she asked, "And just how do you plan to get to Ferihegy?"

"A taxi, I suppose," said Peter.

"I have a much better idea," she said with a triumphant smile. She pointed to Ficko.

"Won't you be late?" asked Peter.

She shook her head. "I won't be able to wait until you take off, but I'd prefer not to, anyway." She pulled up in front of the hotel. "I'll wait for you here."

Peter checked that the Swissair plane had arrived, carried his suitcase himself to the lobby, paid his bill, and rushed out to the little red car, jamming his suitcase into the tiny back seat. "Lead on, dammit," he said to Maria.

Maria worked their way through surprisingly heavy traffic and out onto the broad Üllöi ut leading to the airport. There they moved along with little difficulty. "How long have you known Eva?" asked Maria.

"Since yesterday afternoon," said Peter. Maria looked at him with surprise. "She's a friend of a friend," he explained. "A friend, and client, of mine, who wants her to appear in something he's staging next month. I went to see her about that."

Maria thought for a moment. "That would be Otto Miller?" she said. Peter looked at *her* in surprise. Maria laughed. "There are no secrets among Hungarians," she said. "At least not where the heart is concerned. Eva told me about him."

"Told you about him?" asked Peter.

"Why, yes, when she was here two weeks ago. With her husband."

"She was here two weeks ago? With her husband?"

"Yes," said Maria. "Didn't she tell you?"

"No," said Peter. He shrugged. "And no reason why she should have, either."

"That's when she brought me the dress I wore last night," said Maria happily. "Did you like it?"

Peter felt an odd twinge of jealousy. "I loved it," he said, "too." He scowled. "Henceforth I'll bring you your dresses." Maria touched his hand for a moment, and then put her own back on the wheel.

Peter looked out at the fields and occasional houses they were passing. The mention of Eva and her husband had started up a train of thought that had been absent from his consciousness for twelve hours. It resumed its place at the forefront of his brain. "Maria, did you ever know a man here in Budapest named Satori? He left in 1956." Peter gave him his Hungarian name and spoke it in the Hungarian style, last name first. "Satori Sandor?"

Maria shook her head. "No. Would it help if I did?"

"I don't know," said Peter. "I just wondered. He's Otto Miller's partner in the venture I spoke of, and I'd like to know if he's a crook. A purely legal interest, you might say."

Again Maria shook her head. "If you're interested in crooks, what did you think of Eva's husband?" she asked. As Üllöi ut became Red Army Street she turned off it and onto the special highway to the airport.

"I didn't meet him," said Peter. "I just caught a glimpse of him. It was enough. I gather Eva's unhappy with him. What makes you think he's a crook?"

Maria grimaced. "I can't stand him. And not just from what Eva told me about him."

169

"What else?" said Peter, curious.

"The next to last day they were here, he maneuvered things around somehow so as to take me to lunch alone, without Eva," said Maria. "You know, the husband making friends with the best friend, and all that. He took me to Gundel's, our most elegant restaurant. But the lunch had nothing to do with my friendship with Eva. In fact, he told me not to tell her what it was about—and then he succeeded in never letting us alone until they left. So I couldn't tell her. Not that it was important."

"What was it?" said Peter, his annoyance outstripping his curiosity.

"Oh, it was something to do with some inheritance I'm supposed to have." Maria drove into the circle before the curved facade of the airport building. She slowed down. "Can you imagine it? He said that, as a banker, he often came across such things, and that he had learned of an inheritance I could have. He didn't know how much; not a great sum, but comfortable to have, he told me. But then he said that there were considerable difficulties. He wanted me to sign a paper authorizing a lawyer in Munich—I've forgotten his name—to represent me, and giving half of the inheritance, whatever it was, to a company called VIGIL. That I do remember, because he explained that they were 'vigilant' in protecting people who might otherwise be victimized. Hah!" Her exclamation was vigorously scornful. "What does he want to hide all that from Eva for?"

Peter ignored the last question. "Maria, my love," he said, "the lawyer's name wasn't Pfeundner by any chance? Dr. Hans Pfeundner?"

"Yes!" said Maria. "That was his name." She stopped the car before the terminal. "Do you know him?"

"Not yet," said Peter. "So what did you tell Dr. Gunter Roessli?"

"I told him politely but firmly that I wasn't interested," she said. She shrugged. "And it was the truth. Even without him and his proposition. What could I do with an inherit-

170

ance here? I have my work"—she smiled at Peter—"and my
petit bonheur. The government would take most of anything
I received, and there's nothing I could buy with the rest that
interests me for all the trouble."

"Maybe you could spend it outside Hungary?" Peter suggested.

She shook her head. "They won't let me out. No, it's all
right as it is."

"And where is this inheritance?" Peter asked. "After all, I
am a lawyer, you know."

Again she shook her head. "It's somewhere in America. It
seems a cousin of my grandfather died. His name wouldn't
mean anything to you, but my grandfather was a very famous
physician here. He was at one time head of the Medical Fac-
ulty. I remember him well. It's really because of him that I
became a doctor. My mother was his only child, and she was
a doctor, married to a doctor, and I was an only child, so it
was only natural that he encouraged me to become one too."

Peter bit his lip. "What was his name?" he asked. "Maybe
I have heard of him."

"Forbath," said Maria. "Professor Geza Forbath. Have you
heard of him?"

Peter went hot and cold. Oh, no, he thought. Not that.
This can wreck everything. I need time. Time so that she
will know that last night came first. *Not* the Forbath inheritance. If she ever thinks it was the inheritance that came first,
everything will be ruined. And the last two minutes before I
run for an airplane is not the kind of time I need for this.
Not the time to explain to her that she has thirty million
dollars, that I'm legally obliged to tell her that she has it, and
I wish to hell she didn't. "I've heard of the name," he said.

He got out of the car, reached into the back, pulled out
the suitcase, and set it on the ground. He leaned back into
the car and kissed Maria, longingly. Her mouth tasted as
though she were still bathed in moonlight. "My darling
Maria, I'll be back just as soon as I can." This time her eyes
suddenly brimmed over. She nodded and smiled.

171

"*Szervusz*," he said.

"*Szervusz*, she whispered. She gestured to him to shut the door. She drove off immediately. Peter stood watching the little red car turn around the circle and leave the airport. He felt the invisible thread it was pulling unwind steadily from his heart.

ALTHOUGH Alexander Satori took his customary precautions en route to his Thursday morning rendezvous in Haydnstrasse, even arriving from the Goethe-Platz end of the street instead of, as the last time, the Kaiser-Ludwig-Platz end, he was more than habitually absorbed in his thoughts. He accordingly took no notice of the black Mercedes parked across the street and several houses up from number 2 nor of its two occupants apparently engaged in earnest conversation. At exactly eleven o'clock he rang the bell beside the card reading "Heinrich Pfalz," leaned against the door, and entered as the lock buzzed and gave.

Ross Trumbull, looking somehow tousled despite an alert manner, greeted him at the apartment door. "Damn, Sandy," Trumbull said as he closed the door behind Satori, "I wanted to be here earlier this week, but I got hung up in Paris, thanks to that old coot of an Ambassador we have there."

Satori shook his head commiseratingly. "I had hoped you could get here before." He smiled up at the taller man and shrugged. "But, as we know, it isn't the enemy that gives us trouble. It's always our own allies."

Trumbull snorted. "You can say that again. God knows the only way we get our work done is by end runs around our own people."

They passed into the bare living room, and Trumbull seated himself on the stained couch. Satori drew up a chair

172

and sat down. "I hope you had no more than the usual quota of troubles, Ross," he said.

Trumbull frowned. "It was more than the usual," he answered. "In fact, I've got to find another safe house. This won't do any longer." He took a cigar from his breast pocket and went through the ritual of cutting and lighting it. When at last the smoke billowed out of it, clouding the space between him and the attentive Satori, he spoke. "I kept our appointment here because I didn't have time to arrange anything else. I only got into town less than an hour ago."

Satori raised his eyebrows in inquiry, but Trumbull, continuing to puff out clouds of smoke, was unable to observe the gesture. Absorbed, he went on, "There's something fishy going on, but I haven't got it figured out yet. Anyway, we'll stop it before it gets started."

Satori kept his eyebrows raised. "Yesterday, the Ambassador ordered me to give him this address," Trumbull continued. "I don't know if he was being nosy for a purpose, or just got that way in a fit of temper. Whichever, this place is out as a safe house. I'm giving it up, as of today. I don't mean the Ambassador is going to send the K.G.B. around here, but a safe house that too many people know about, even on your own side, is no longer safe. I'll stay in Munich until I've worked something else out. In the meanwhile, if we have to meet, it can't be here."

Satori sighed as if in relief. "I appreciate your prudence, Ross," he said, "but apart from the inconvenience to you, the situation is not really serious. We can meet quite safely in a thousand places in this town. For that matter, with all the precautions we've taken, we could even meet now in public without danger."

"You think so?" asked Trumbull. He looked absent-mindedly at the window.

With a suggestion of dejection in his voice, Satori said, "I hope this has nothing to do with that Miller affair."

Trumbull came back to life. "I think it probably has

plenty to do with it. That mess gets more disturbing every day."

"Oh?" said Satori, leaning forward expectantly.

"Yes," said Trumbull. "And, I think, more dangerous. Listen to this. We've found out the man in the Jaguar wasn't Miller. It was a garageman from Cannes."

Satori, an expression of gratified amazement on his face, interrupted. "You mean Otto Miller's alive?"

Trumbull shook his head warily. "That's the assumption," he said, "but it's only an assumption. I'll come to that in a minute. Meanwhile, we've also found out the Nazi leaflets scattered around the scene of the accident were printed in East Germany."

Satori frowned and then shrugged, as the explanation of *this* development was beyond his powers of logic.

"Now I come to the assumption that Otto Miller is alive," Trumbull continued. "Ambassador Ballard, not to mention Roger Heston, take it for granted that he is. But they're basing their belief on only two things. One, the fact that he was not the person killed in the Jaguar crash. And two, on the fact that that bastard Peter Dowling is passing the word around that Miller has gone on a Mediterranean cruise." Satori studied Trumbull carefully as the latter continued to speak. "There are several things wrong with that last item. The most important is that we only have Dowling's word for it. The other is that when he showed up at Eze last Saturday he apparently came in the conviction that Miller was dead. Now he says he's alive, and well, and living on a yacht in the Mediterranean."

Satori looked thoughtfully at Trumbull, and then spoke modestly. "Yes," he said, "that's what Dowling told me on the telephone."

Trumbull, his little gambit having received a satisfactory reply, nodded vigorously and gestured with his cigar as he expelled smoke. "That's the worst of it!" he said explosively.

Satori looked at him inquiringly.

"Frankly," said Trumbull, "we had it from the French that he'd gotten in touch with you. That's what worries me the most in all this. For one thing, he's now got your name on the French rolls. For the moment that's not serious, but with the French doing their eternal dance on both sides of the fence, for the greater glory of *la France,* it could be one day. The serious thing now is the way Dowling is muscling his way in to see you, on the excuse that he speaks for Miller. What did he have to say when you saw him?"

Satori spread his hands in bewilderment. "I wasn't anxious to see him, but what could I do? If he says he has Miller's power-of-attorney and represents Miller, I have to see him. If only to keep my cover intact." Trumbull nodded approvingly. "So I politely invited him to dine with me last night," Satori went on, "and then he never showed up."

Now Trumbull looked mystified. Satori shook a finger to indicate that an explanation was forthcoming. "I only figured it out this morning," he said. "He told me he was coming from Zurich on the plane that left there yesterday afternoon at four. This morning I read the papers and find that that was the plane hijacked to Budapest."

Trumbull was startled. "What kind of a fancy cut-up is that?" he exclaimed. "Dowling already had a visa to go to Budapest. He didn't have to hijack a plane to get there."

Satori smiled. "You saw the papers. It was apparently a young pro-Arab German who did the job. Seemed to think the Swiss are pro-Israel. So presumably Dowling will show up here today."

Trumbull frowned again. "Sandy, you've got to be triply careful with that guy. Frankly, I think he may be a penetration attempt from the other side. Supposing he put Miller out of the way to get into position to reach you himself?" He smiled sourly. "Ambassador Ballard wants me to get Pegov to check on whether Dowling is working for the K.G.B. *That*'ll show you what the old jerk knows about this business. Imagine, Pegov passes along the query to the people

Dowling is probably working for. The next thing is that Pegov's throat is cut. Not to mention your own." His mouth curled in sarcasm. "First-class Ambassadorial nonsense!"

Again Trumbull drew on his cigar and exploded smoke. "Why, do you know what that sonofabitch Dowling did to my man tailing him in Nice?"

Satori listened with mouth agape. "He was found the next day, Sunday morning," said Trumbull, "stretched out on the sidewalk of a back street in Nice with a concussion." He sounded especially bitter. "A Yale man," he said. "We've had to notify the family he was robbed and beaten while drunk, to avoid any complications for my office." He looked at Satori and shrugged. "You understand it was an intricate cover situation. For everybody."

Trumbull thought for a minute and then resumed. "Anyway, Dowling disappeared from Nice for two days, and then surfaced Tuesday in Paris, with his story about Miller's cruise and his acting for Miller. Now if, as I think, he's working for the opposition, and he gets to you, that puts both you and Pegov in danger. You've got to be extremely careful when you see him, Sandy. Don't let him get beyond purely business discussions and contacts with you."

Satori nodded sagely. "I see it now, Ross. You're right, of course. Maybe I can even cut those out."

Trumbull nodded his approval. "When do you see Pegov again?" he asked.

"This afternoon," said Satori. "I'm keeping in close touch with him, Ross. He's very nervous these days. He says knives are being sharpened in the Politburo. As you know, when the heads begin to roll, no matter who is doing the chopping, Pegov may have no choice but to run for it."

Trumbull looked glum. "Well, let's hope it isn't too damn soon," he said. "If he were to come over tonight I wouldn't have a place to receive him." He rose from the couch with an air of weariness. "If you need to get in touch with me during this blank spot, I'm staying at the Regina. Best I can do for the moment."

176

Satori had risen with Trumbull. "Ross," he said warmly, "you work too hard. Have you ever relaxed in this town?"

Trumbull's small mouth widened in appreciation of the tribute. "Never," he said. The pride leaked through the simplicity.

"Look." Satori put his hand on Trumbull's arm. "I do a lot of entertaining in Munich. I know just about every place in town, who is there, and why. Nothing could be more normal than for us to be seen together on this town in the evening. You're another buyer or promoter I'm entertaining. Be my guest for dinner tonight. I'll get a girl to join us—you know, window dressing, pretty externals, nothing in the head —and we'll have a pleasant evening. It will do you good."

"I'd like to, Sandy," said Trumbull, "but I don't want some German creep getting the idea you're in touch with Americans."

"Americans?" cried Satori. "But, Ross! Thirty percent of my customers and contacts are Americans. Nothing more usual than to see me with an American. It's good business— and good cover. Furthermore, it could help establish a pretext for future meetings. I wouldn't like to need you urgently and be unable to get to you because you had no safe house and I couldn't be seen with an American. It won't violate the cover—it'll help build a new one." Satori wound up his argument with a bow. "Besides," he added, "it would be a very great, personal pleasure for me."

Trumbull looked absently out the window. "Thanks, Sandy," he said finally. He smiled a bit crookedly. "It might be fun at that."

"Good," said Satori. "I'll pick you up at the Regina at seven thirty."

When Satori emerged into the street he again took no notice of the parked black Mercedes. There must have been eight or ten identical cars parked in the Haydnstrasse. Nor did he notice the occupants of the car, for one was now walking vigorously around the Kaiser-Ludwig-Platz, while the other strolled aimlessly in the Goethe-Platz.

"WILL THIS BE satisfactory, sir?" The reception clerk of the Vier Jahreszeiten stepped back, the knifelike crease in his striped trousers breaking just below his black jacket as he bowed slightly. Peter looked at the vast room. Three towering windows let in light from the silent courtyard. At the far end, twin beds, diminished by perspective, seemed as remote as a Himalayan kingdom. The walls were covered in a pale green silk, a couch and chairs in gold brocade. On the whole, thought Peter, German luxury, if not as sure in its taste as French, is much more comfortable. It always has its little touch of the *gemütlich*.

"Yes," he said. "Everything except the weather. I was in summer not two hours ago, in Budapest, and here I am back in winter."

The clerk shook his head with the worried air of one who is burdened with the consequences of a grave mistake. "It is a very late spring," he said somberly.

Peter smiled at his gravity. "Well, no doubt it'll warm up in time for the Olympic Games in August," he said. "Perhaps while I'm here I'll reserve a room for then on the chance it will."

The clerk, stepping carefully backward to the door as though retiring from an audience, brightened. "I'm afraid it's already too late for that," he answered with a cheerful smile. "We're fully booked." He bowed, withdrew, and closed the door.

There'll be no revolution in a country where the fourth assistant reception clerk is gleeful over the hotel owner's good fortune, thought Peter. He walked the length of the room to the bedside telephone and asked for Lord Killitoe's room. He and Burroughs were both out. Peter left messages for them to call, and then asked for a city number.

"Melodie Verlag," a female voice answered.

"This is Mr. Dowling," said Peter. "Is Mr. Satori there?"

The answering voice was efficient. "No, Mr. Dowling, Herr von Satori has gone to lunch. Are you calling from Munich?"

"Yes, finally," said Peter.

She took no notice of his irony. "Herr von Satori left word that if you called from Munich he would be expecting you at three this afternoon at his office. Will that be convenient for you?"

"Yes, thank you very much," said Peter. "Please tell Herr von Satori I shall be there at three." He hung up and looked at his watch. Everybody in the London office would be out to lunch too. Better wait an hour. He rose, took off his jacket and threw it down on the bed. It lay with the back up—the grass stains evoking a thoughtful smile from Peter, then a worried frown. He tried to visualize Maria at work in her laboratory, but couldn't; instead he saw her tawny head and parted lips in the moonlight, her golden body moving about in the early morning sunlight, and then her green eyes swimming with tears as he leaned inside the car to kiss her good-bye. He shook his head, undid his shirt, and went into the bathroom.

He had finished shaving and was putting on a clean shirt when there was a knock at the door. "Come in!" he called, expecting the maid. The knock was repeated. He went to the door and opened it.

David Killitoe, dressed with the severity Englishmen of his class and generation feel is called for whenever the population exceeds a thousand, his round face topped by his permanently unruly black hair, grinned at Peter. Behind Killitoe was the slight figure, faintly malicious smile, and balding, wispy head of Caxton Burroughs. "We're looking for a chap named Dowling," said Killitoe. "Tried to get away from us by hijacking his plane to Budapest."

Peter opened the door wide to let them enter. "I'm your man," he said. "You'll notice the trick worked. I had peace and quiet." Sourly, he added, "For less than twenty hours."

179

Burroughs strolled to the center of the room and gazed about. "We got your message this morning," he said, "but the news was on television last night. However, David, who doesn't watch television or listen to the radio, at least not outside England, was calling Jake in Paris frantically during the night. He thought you'd come to a bad end." Burroughs continued strolling the length of the room and pressed the buzzer on Peter's night table. "May as well order some lunch," he said to no one in particular.

The waiter entered with the menu and they ordered. "I'll have some sherry right now," said Killitoe. The other two nodded their agreement.

When the sherry had been brought, Peter tasted his, and then looked at Burroughs. "Where are we now?" he asked.

Burroughs looked at him inquiringly. "Do you yet know where Otto is?"

Peter nodded.

"Is he safe?" Burroughs asked.

"He is as long as no one else knows where he is," Peter answered firmly.

Burroughs smiled. "Don't worry. We won't ask you where he is."

"So where are *we?*" Peter repeated.

Killitoe laughed. "While you were enjoying peace and quiet in Hungary, we were hard at work. Caxton here was peering through knotholes."

Burroughs grinned and recounted Whitney Ballard's conversation with Trumbull and Heston. "Then," Burroughs went on, "I had a stroke of luck this morning. I came to Munich on the same plane with Trumbull. David met me at the airport, with a splendidly inconspicuous Mercedes, so we trailed Trumbull into town. About fifteen minutes after checking into the Regina Hotel, in the Maximiliansplatz, he went to the Haydnstrasse address. We waited awhile, to see if anything developed, and sure enough, in another quarter of an hour a little, dark man, sharply dressed—you know, the kind who wears Cardin suits—came along. He answered to Helen Goodman's description of Satori."

The waiter entered with a tray. Killitoe gave his schoolboy giggle, and spoke up, exactly as though he were responding to Burroughs. "I've got a better one about this blasted language, which as you know I don't understand," he said. "An Englishman, a Frenchman, and a Spaniard are having a drink in a bar. At the next table is a German, alone. 'Wonderful thing, language,' says the Englishman. 'So expressive. Take *butterfly*, for example. What could be more delicate, more evocative?' The German frowns. The Frenchman, with just a trace of superiority, says, 'In French we call it *papillon*. What could be more graceful?' The German stirs. The Spaniard expands his chest, smiles condescendingly, and says, 'In Spanish, my friends, we call it *mariposa*. What could be more poetic?' At this the German explodes. He rises from his chair and, shaking a fist at his neighbors, he shouts, 'And what's wrong with *Schmetterling*?' "

Peter and Burroughs burst into laughter. The waiter, stony-faced, glanced sideways at Killitoe, then finished setting out the lunch and headed for the door. As he opened it he looked back at Killitoe with a sly grin. *"Farfalla,"* he said. The door clicked shut behind him.

Burroughs's eyebrows shot up. He looked at Peter and then at Killitoe. The latter's face expressed utter astonishment, which suddenly gave way to a shout of laughter. It was some time before Peter and Burroughs could get Killitoe to speak. When he did, he was still laughing. *"Farfalla!"* he said. "It's Italian for *butterfly!*"

While Peter laughed, Burroughs frowned, then finally conceded a weak smile. "To return to my story," he said somewhat impatiently, "the street is only one block long, so David patrolled one end and I the other. The man we thought was Satori left by David's end, and he followed him. He went, by a roundabout route, to the Melodie Verlag offices in the Briennerstrasse, just off the Maximiliansplatz, so it must

181

have been Satori. Trumbull left about twenty minutes later, and went back to the Regina. It's not much to go on so far, but at least we've had a look at Satori." Burroughs grimaced his distaste.

"I'm getting a closer look at three o'clock," Peter said. "I called his office when I arrived and was told 'Herr von Satori' would expect me then."

"What time did you call?" asked Killitoe.

"Quarter to one."

Killitoe nodded. "He'd just gone out to lunch. He left his office with another man. They went to eat at Humplmayr's, further down the Maximiliansplatz."

"I'd like to go with you at three o'clock," Burroughs said abruptly to Peter.

Peter looked askance at him. "How? And why?"

"Pass me off as a type from your London office. Use someone's name from there," said Burroughs. "That's for the how. The why is that I want to see the place. I think we should pay another visit there. Tonight, when we have the place to ourselves. I'll see if it's possible."

Peter shrugged and looked at Killitoe. The latter nodded. "It always pays to let him have his way," he said.

"Okay," said Peter. He pushed back his chair and rose from the table. "Excuse me a second," he said. "I have a call to make." He went to the night table and asked for the number of his London office. The connection was quick. "Mr. Griffith," he said. The operator put him through. "Bill? This is Peter Dowling. I need some more information." He paused. "Yes. The Vier Jahreszeiten in Munich. Will you find out whatever you can about a Dr. Hans Pfeundner." He repeated the name slowly. "A lawyer here in Munich, apparently specializing in Jewish claims. He's the one who handled the Kaplan case with the Swiss. Also, I'd like whatever you can turn up on a company called VIGIL. I have no idea what it is, or even where it's located. You should start with Switzerland, though." He listened. "Right. Along with whatever you have on the Kaplan papers. Ring me here. Thanks very much."

Peter put down the telephone and rejoined Killitoe and Burroughs. "Sorry," he said. "I've got some problems on a couple of inheritance cases. They're the original reason for my coming over here this trip, so I can't ignore them completely."

"I gather everyone has to moonlight to make a living these days," Burroughs observed condescendingly.

AT THREE O'CLOCK Peter Dowling and Caxton Burroughs entered an archway in the Briennerstrasse leading to a large courtyard. At the far end stood a warehouse with a sign, "Melodie Verlag." On the left rose a compact concrete office building of six stories. The directory in the vestibule showed that Melodie Verlag occupied the first and second floors, European-style, with the reception on the second. In the small elevator Burroughs nodded thoughtfully. "So far so good. Let's hope the rest is as easy. What's my name, by the way?"

"Henley. William Ernest Henley," said Peter.

"The late poet?" inquired Burroughs.

"Important man in our London office," said Peter. "A molder of men. You'll fit perfectly."

On the second floor there was a solid oak double door, marked "Melodie Verlag." "You go first," said Burroughs.

Peter opened the door and entered. Burroughs trailed behind, his hand holding the door as though he were uncertain they were at the right address and expected to be ejected immediately. "Herr von Satori?" Peter said to the young receptionist. She looked at him inquiringly. "Mr. Dowling and Mr. Henley," Peter added.

The girl nodded, rose, and went into the next office. In a

few minutes she emerged. "This way, please." She led the way down a corridor with a window at the far end. Offices gave off both sides, and in the middle a transversal corridor led off to the right to a stairway descending to the first floor. The girl knocked at the last door on the left side of the corridor.

It was opened by a middle-aged woman of severe expression who invited Peter and Burroughs to enter. "Please be seated," she said, indicating two chairs before a large desk. Behind the desk a window with venetian blinds overlooked the warehouse and courtyard behind. The wall opposite the entrance to the room was covered with built-in recording and sound equipment, compartments for storing records, tapes, and cartridges, and, behind the desk, several built-in filing cabinets. Besides the door through which Peter and Burroughs had entered, there were two others, at the opposite end of the wall facing the window. "One minute, please," said the woman. She disappeared through the door on the left side of the back wall.

She had no sooner left than Burroughs quickly rose and stepped noiselessly on the thick carpet to the window and glanced out. In a moment he was back in his chair, looking at the ceiling. "Soundproofed," he said, as though impressed.

The door through which the secretary had disappeared opened. A tall, heavy man, solidly built, his expression resembling that of a mastiff nursing a grudge, entered. Peter and Burroughs rose. Peter stepped forward and extended his hand. "Dowling," he said, in the European fashion. The man bowed and shook his hand. "This is Mr. Henley," Peter said, indicating Burroughs. The man raised his eyebrows slightly, but shook Burroughs's proffered hand. "Mr. Satori?" said Peter.

"I am very sorry," said the tall man. He spoke courteously, even pleasantly, despite his expression. "This is Mr. Satori's office, but he was called out urgently. It was too late to notify you. I am Horst Krieger, the vice president of Melodie Verlag. Mr. Satori extends his apologies. He asked me to receive you on his behalf." He spread his hands. "I am at your service." He drew up a chair and sat down with Peter and Burroughs.

"Very kind of you," said Peter. "I'm sorry Mr. Satori was called away. I had hoped to wind up several questions concerning the jazz festival with him. Actually, I'm running a bit short of time on this trip, which is why I brought along Mr. Henley from our firm's London office." He nodded at Burroughs. "If I am called away urgently, Mr. Henley will be able to represent Mr. Miller's interests."

Krieger stared at Burroughs, made a gesture of acquiescence, and turned to Peter. "Of course, Mr. Satori had planned to have dinner with you last night," he said. Then, as though the reminder was sufficient, he added, "I understand you had a very unpleasant experience."

"It could have been worse," Peter observed. "Now, the main problem I wanted to take up with Mr. Satori was the filling of the final empty spot in the festival program. Mr. Miller urges Eva Kanday for that spot."

Krieger frowned and looked out the window. "Eva Kanday?" He shook his head. "I don't think we know her." Peter noticed that Burroughs began to fidget in his chair.

"She's originally Hungarian," said Peter. "Perhaps Mr. Satori has heard of her. She's singing in the St. Gotthard Bar in Zurich at present. Very well, too," he added.

Burroughs twisted his body about and crossed and uncrossed his legs. Krieger shot a quick glance at Peter and then looked at the ceiling. Finally he nodded his head. "Yes, that says something to me. But if I'm correct, doesn't she specialize in Hungarian and Viennese songs? Schmalz? Hardly the thing for a jazz festival with several hundred thousand kids gathered in a field."

Burroughs strained at his chair, his knuckles white as he grasped the arms. "True," said Peter, "but she is preparing new and more suitable material. Mr. Miller has great confidence in her."

Again Krieger shot Peter a glance, but before he could say

anything Burroughs leaned forward. He spoke to Krieger in an agonized voice. "I'm terribly sorry," he said, "but I wonder if I could use your, ah, facilities."

Krieger looked at him in surprise. "Oh," he said. "Of course." He pointed to the door on the right side of the back wall. "There." Burroughs nodded with a grateful smile and made his way hastily across the room. The door shut behind him.

"Well, I imagine it will be all right," Krieger said to Peter, "if Mr. Miller has that much confidence in her. I'll have to check with Mr. Satori, of course."

"Meanwhile," said Peter, "in order to save time, I'd appreciate it if you'd have a contract drawn up for her. If Mr. Satori agrees, he can sign it immediately, and I'll sign for Mr. Miller."

Krieger nodded. "I'll have it prepared, but in the meantime I wonder if you'd be good enough to present your authority to sign for Mr. Miller to our legal counsel for verification." The sound of running water came from the bathroom. "A pure formality, of course," added Krieger, "but as you know German law is very strict in these matters."

"Of course," said Peter. "Perhaps you would call him in?"

Krieger shook his head. "I'm afraid you'll have to go to his office. It's at Pacellistrasse number 7." Peter took out his notebook and jotted down the address. He looked inquiringly at Krieger. "Pfeundner," said Krieger. "Dr. Hans Pfeundner."

The bathroom door opened and Burroughs emerged, looking greatly relieved. Peter rose. Krieger rose with him and said, "I'll tell him you're coming."

"Thank you," Peter answered. "I don't know that I can make it today, but I'll be there tomorrow in any case. And I'll hope to get together with Mr. Satori tomorrow too."

Krieger walked to the door by which they had entered and opened it. Burroughs, smiling affably, passed through first. He turned and shook hands with Krieger. Having done so he suddenly put the back of his hand to his mouth. His slight

186

frame was immediately wracked by a coughing fit. As he coughed and choked, Krieger stepped back and let go of the door. With his left hand, Burroughs grasped the door for support. Finally, his coughing spell subsided. He looked at Krieger with watery eyes and an apologetic smile. "Sorry," he said. "And thank you so much."

Peter shook hands with Krieger, nodded politely, and followed Burroughs down the corridor. Behind them the door of Satori's office clicked shut.

As they came out through the archway and into the Briennerstrasse Peter shook his head in puzzlement. "You didn't hear it," he said to Burroughs. "You were in the bathroom. But their lawyer is the same one I was just asking London about in connection with those inheritance cases of mine."

"Oh, I heard it," said Burroughs. "You can hear everything in that office from the bathroom, soundproofing or no. That was a fringe benefit, of course, and probably of no great value. The real point was to see what was behind that door. So it's a bathroom. I couldn't have been less interested. Or more relieved."

"OF COURSE, you were right, Lazar Matveyich," said Satori. He looked beyond the Russian's shoulder to the curtained window overlooking the Liebigstrasse, a trace of almost boyish embarrassment on his features. Pegov nodded sagely, a smile on his thin lips. Otherwise, his expression was one of paternal benevolence.

"Trumbull's second attempt on Miller failed," Satori explained, "because Begovic fell into a trap set by the C.I.A. We don't have the entire story yet, but our evidence is that the C.I.A. man Dowling, as you suggested, is running the operation. However, we are several steps ahead of them."

Pegov lifted his eyebrows and interrupted. "I would hope so," he said coldly.

Satori nodded reassuringly. "Trumbull's man is still on Miller's trail. Miller is in Italy. We will have the exact address tonight. I am certain the operation will be carried out successfully by Saturday."

Pegov's right eye, with its cast, seemed to jump nervously. "You are certain?"

"Certain," said Satori positively.

"And who is carrying out the operation?"

Satori smiled as though preparing to tell a good joke. "Trumbull was seriously considering doing it himself. He has become very impatient with these slip-ups. He's a realist, of course, but with a strong streak of perfectionism. However, the realism prevailed. He has not yet told me who his man is, but he guarantees him."

Pegov thought for a moment, then shrugged. "It is high time. There has been some dissatisfaction expressed."

"There need be none now," said Satori. "And in the meantime, you *did* suggest proceeding with alternative targets?"

Pegov frowned. "I did. But you know how it is. They follow their own reasoning. Correctly, of course," he added, with a barely perceptible sigh.

"Of course, Lazar Matveyich."

"However," Pegov continued, "they have at least specified the operation which is to follow Miller."

"Ah?" Satori started to lean forward, then resumed his relaxed position.

"Yes," said Pegov. "It will be the man known as Laszlo Forbath."

Satori drew a deep breath. Almost imperceptibly, he exhaled. He coughed, and crossed his legs. "And where do we find him?" he asked, skepticism tinging the dutiful tone of his question.

Pegov shook his head. "One thing at a time, Aleksandr Pavlovich. He is to *follow* the Miller case. I am to give you your instructions concerning Forbath when the Miller case is completed."

188

"Well, the sooner we start the better. As they can see, these things take time."

Pegov nodded. "In the meantime I have been queried about the hijacking of the Swissair plane to Budapest yesterday. This sort of thing can have serious repercussions. The Hungarians tell us it was done on your orders. Is this so?"

Satori raised his eyebrows in surprise. "But of course it was done on my orders. That is to say, my people handled it —quite successfully, I think you'll agree—and I explained to Budapest that it was done because the C.I.A. agent Dowling was on that plane."

"Oh?" said Pegov, showing surprise in turn. "I was not informed of that."

"But of course, Lazar Matveyich," said Satori. "Obviously, I do not undertake an action of that sort for amusement. Dowling was coming here to Munich, ostensibly to see me as Miller's lawyer and representative. Trumbull sent me a message that I must postpone his arrival here until he, Trumbull, could get here to brief me before I saw Dowling."

"And why couldn't Trumbull get here in time himself, and thus avoid risking an international incident with that Swiss plane?" Pegov interjected with evident irritation.

"Because his Ambassador held him in Paris," answered Satori quickly. "And that is the point I was coming to," he added forcefully. "Trumbull is extremely nervous these days. I judge with good reason."

Pegov leaned forward attentively. "And what is the trouble?"

"He was apparently held in Paris by his Ambassador, deliberately, to allow Dowling to get here first. As it is, even diverting the Swiss plane, I only just managed to see Trumbull today before I would have had to see Dowling."

"Would have had to see Dowling?" Pegov regarded Satori studiously.

Satori nodded vigorously. "Dowling is in my office at this minute. After I heard what Trumbull had to say I contacted

Helga to see you this afternoon, and passed Dowling off on my vice president. First, to give you Trumbull's information. But secondly, to avoid seeing Dowling myself. Trumbull suspects strongly that Dowling's protection of Miller is only incidental to his real mission, which is to penetrate Trumbull's relationship with me." He nodded deferentially. "Or, to put it more precisely, Trumbull's relationship with you."

Pegov's studious look turned into a glare. "But this Dowling doesn't know about me!"

"Not yet," said Satori. "But Trumbull thinks the C.I.A. may suspect something. Hence Dowling. That is why I warn you that Trumbull is nervous, and with cause. He may be obliged to come over to us any day now if his suspicions are confirmed."

Pegov swiveled in his chair and looked out the window for a moment. When he turned back his face was bland. "You had better make clear to him that he cannot come before the Miller operation is completed. I have made that clear to you before."

"Of course, Lazar Matveyich." Satori rose. "In the circumstances, do you still think it advisable that I bring Helga together with Trumbull?"

Pegov had risen and was standing with his hands clasped behind his back. His eyes twitched, but there was a faint smile on his lips as he regarded Satori. "Of course, Aleksandr Pavlovich," he said. "Now it is more important than ever."

"Very good," rejoined Satori briskly. "It's arranged for tonight."

"I KNEW something was wrong when I saw him come out of Humplmayr's from lunch," said David Killitoe. "The chap with him went back to the Melodie Verlag office, but he climbed into a disreputable looking Karmann Ghia, and was whisked away by a frizzy-haired popsie. She seemed to like

190

him. The amazing thing about sex is the way people one wouldn't personally associate with it seem to be associated with it anyway." Killitoe took a bite of his smoked trout, down the middle of which ran two thin stripes of creamed horseradish and, between them, a black line of caviar. "Delicious," he said. "By the way, I noticed the chap who'd lunched with our friend looked apoplectic as they left Humplmayr's. Maybe the food is bad. What did you say this place is called?"

"Walterspiel," Peter answered. "Certainly one of the half-dozen best restaurants in Germany."

"Very convenient having it right here in the hotel," Killitoe commented. "A trifle austere, though, don't you think?" There was indeed a hush in the room; everyone spoke in low voices, as though in a temple.

"What do you expect? An Irish jig with the caviar?" snapped Burroughs.

Killitoe eyed him coldly and addressed himself to Peter. "As I understand it, you were saying Caxton behaved badly this afternoon?"

Peter smiled and shook his head. "Not badly. He just fell to pieces in that office."

"Actually, he's sturdier than he looks," said Killitoe thoughtfully. "He only falls to pieces with a purpose. I only hope it worked as well this time as I've seen it do before."

"We'll see," said Burroughs noncommittally.

When they had finished dinner they went into the lobby of the Vier Jahreszeiten. Burroughs gave directions. "I'll be waiting for you both in the Briennerstrasse entrance. Eleven fifteen sharp. Separate now, fill in the time in a crowded place, and come there from different directions." They parted with polite good-nights.

Peter crossed the Maximilianstrasse. He paused for a moment, then headed into a side street. In London, hearing he was going to Munich, they'd asked in the office for postcards from the Hofbräuhaus—from the place where Hitler had got his start. It was sacrilege after a succulent meal, but he might as well do it now. Also, it was the sort of thing an American tourist with an evening to kill might do. That would do no harm if someone had an eye on him. Slowly he ambled the two short blocks to the Hofbraühaus. The small square in front was jammed, as usual, with people milling in and out of the great beer hall and the music hall opposite. Peter turned into the Hofbraühaus, made his way upstairs to the main hall, and took a seat at one of the long tables halfway down the room. Nine or ten Germans seated farther down the same table greeted him with noisy cheers. Peter signaled the waitress for a stein, then shouted to her to bring him some postcards as well.

The din of singing and shouting was deafening. It was the only place Peter knew where, literally, "the rafters echoed." A broad and beaming waitress brought him his stein—an entire liter of beer—and dropped a half-dozen postcards alongside him. I must remember not to bring Maria here, Peter thought; not her cup of tea. Or stein of beer. He took a swallow from the stone mug and masked his distaste; later, perhaps—but not right on top of dinner at the Walterspiel. He began writing quickly on the postcards. A hand dropped firmly on his left shoulder. Peter forced himself to turn his head slowly and casually to his right. The hand was slowly withdrawn, and its owner clambered over the bench and sat down on Peter's right. He was about Peter's age, his blond hair smoothly brushed; the face was handsome in a solid German way, marked by deep-set gray eyes and a strong chin. He smiled broadly at Peter, a habitual tinge of irony in his expression.

"Herr Peter Dowling," the man said. "*Guten abend*. It's been a long time."

Peter regarded his new companion with pleasure. He laughed. "Sixteen years by my count," he said. "*Guten abend*, Ahmed. I would have expected to find you in a place with prettier girls, if I may say so."

Ernst Seger's childhood in Turkey, where his German Socialist father and mother had taken refuge during the Nazi and war years, had contributed only partly to his nickname; it was an early German girl friend, in despair at breaking him to monogamy, who had bestowed it on him. He laughed in response to Peter's greeting. "I was shocked to find *you* here," he retorted.

Seger signaled a waitress, then took out a pipe, filled and lit it. Peter gestured to the pipe. "I gather you're still in the business. You've even adopted the trademark."

Seger regarded Peter blandly. "I'm the head of the Bavarian State Section," he said.

Peter bowed from the waist. Head of the Bavarian branch of the Federal Office for the Protection of the Constitution, the West German domestic security service, was not a sinecure. "Congratulations," he said. He meant it.

Seger shook his head. "Not all merit," he said. "After all, the chancellor now is a Social Democrat." He smiled. "And it's definitely not as diverting as the days when we worked together." Peter bowed again and raised his stein. The two men drank.

"And you?" Seger asked.

Peter shook his head. "I quit. Not long after I left here. I practice law in New York now. My work brings me over here fairly often. One of the compensations." He looked at Seger and saw something more in his expression than the habitual irony. By God, he doesn't believe me, Peter thought. Well, that's customary. He laughed. "I'll get you a letter from the senior partner to prove it," he said.

"I'd rather you didn't," said Seger enigmatically.

Peter glanced at his watch. Dammit! He had to leave. That was going to make Seger even more sure he was being fed a cover story. With a stab of annoyance Peter realized that whatever excuse he now gave for leaving would in fact be a cover story. He had thought himself well out of all this, long ago; Otto Miller had indeed dragged him back into it, and deeply. "Ahmed," said Peter, "I'm terribly sorry, but I just dropped by here for a minute on my way to an appointment. I do want to see you while I'm here in Munich, though. Come and lunch with me tomorrow. The Vier Jahreszeiten. One o'clock?"

Seger looked at him with open amusement. "Gladly, Peter." He rose and shook hands, apparently not at all affronted. "A happy coincidence I stumbled onto you. We'll talk more tomorrow." Peter shook hands warmly and turned to leave. "Good luck," Seger said after him. Peter stopped and turned back, but Seger had already sat down. It was only when he was out in the street that Peter remembered, with a start, that he had left the postcards on the table.

As Peter crossed over from the north side of Brienner-strasse he recognized Killitoe's figure turning into the street from the Maximiliansplatz. They entered the archway at the same time. Burroughs stood in the shadows. He spoke softly. "The charwomen have already gone. There's a watch-man, but he's in back, at the warehouse. It's locked off at night by a grille, but the office building is open. There's someone working late up on the fifth floor. So much the better. We don't look unique. Just unusual. Let's go."

They walked across to the entrance to the building and stepped inside. Killitoe headed for the elevator but Bur-roughs stopped him. "It should be either on the ground or on an upper floor if someone happens to pay a visit while we're here. We'll take the stairs." He led the way around the elevator shaft to the fireproof door opening onto the stair-way. In darkness they made their way up two flights and emerged in the hallway outside the Melodie Verlag offices.

Burroughs tried the door. It was locked. "You would have thought someone would have had the decency to forget to do that," he muttered. He handed Peter a flashlight. "Give me some light on the lock, will you?" Peter obliged. "These are child's play," said Burroughs. "The old-fashioned, very con-venient kind with two buttons underneath the tongue," he explained. He pulled a small steel tool, resembling a den-tist's mirror-holder without the mirror, from an inside pocket. It had an engine-turned handle, and then a forty-five-degree angle of smooth, thin, specially hardened steel; at the tip was a right-angled point, no more than a millimeter long. "These locks are always unlocked from the inside," said Burroughs, "and you lock and unlock the outside by pressing one of the buttons. Which we will now do." He inserted the angled end of the jimmy and felt about with the tiny probe. The steel scraped against the lock, then clicked as Burroughs explored the buttons. With a quick movement he pushed the handle of the jimmy towards the door opposite the lock. There was a crunch of wood as the steel handle pressed against the facing door, and a click inside the lock. Burroughs pocketed the jimmy and opened the door.

"The only trouble," he said, "is that it leaves visible damage to the wood. We'll fix that now. Keep the light on that gash, Peter." Again Peter obliged. Burroughs extracted from his pockets a small can of putty and filled the deep cut in the edge of the facing door. He replaced the can and came up with a small bottle. He unscrewed the top, which had a small dauber attached. With it he stained the filler in the gash. The result would have been immediately apparent to a practiced eye looking for signs of forced entry, but was adequate for the ordinary, casual eye. Burroughs dropped the bottle back in his pocket. "Bootblack's dye," he said. "Makes an evening."

He followed Peter and Killitoe through the door, snapping the lock back to its original position as he did so. He took two more flashlights from his pockets and gave one to Killitoe. "Don't use them yet," he said. The night flow of the city, reflected from the overcast sky, turned the window at the end of the corridor into a faint beacon. Burroughs led the way down the corridor to the last door on the left. "Where we spent a pleasant interlude this afternoon," he said. "Same kind of lock as the main door, but I unlocked it during my coughing fit this afternoon. Just to make it simpler. We can probably go around through the secretary's office, but better not to get mixed up in a maze of offices. Satori's is the only one that interests us. For the moment, anyway." He tried the handle and the door opened.

They entered. Burroughs walked swiftly to the window and looked out through the open slats of the venetian blinds at the courtyard below. "Good," he whispered. "The watchman is inside the warehouse." He reached over and closed the blinds. "Now we can use the flashlights," he said, "but don't shine them on the ceiling. Keep them directed as low as possible."

Peter went to the desk. The drawers were unlocked. Rapidly, he went through them. It was all seemingly innocuous correspondence relating to Melodie Verlag. A file labeled "Otto Miller" had nothing but papers relating to the Bavarian Jazz Festival, a number of which Peter had already seen in his own or Otto's office. He turned to the address book on top of the desk. Page by page he went through it: there were no Haydnstrasse or Liebigstrasse addresses; the only name that meant anything to Peter, apart from Otto's, was that of Dr. Hans Pfeundner. The file cabinets, likewise open, contained Melodie Verlag accounts. "A clean, open society," said Peter, disgustedly.

He looked over at Burroughs and Killitoe. They were staring at the wall of sound equipment. "He definitely has one too many tuners," said Killitoe. Burroughs stepped forward and shone his flashlight on one tuner. He flipped the switch. The panel lit up, and a hum came from it. He switched it off and turned to the other tuner. He switched it on. Nothing happened. "Ah," said Killitoe in the manner of an old-fashioned schoolmaster who had caught a boy cheating.

Burroughs turned the finder dial. The station indicator moved. He reached for the volume dial. It spun freely, with no block at what would normally have been maximum and minimum sound. "Aha," said Burroughs. "Put your flashlight here, David."

Burroughs put his own flashlight in his pocket and rubbed his hands together vigorously. Then he rubbed the tips of the fingers of his right hand against his trousers. Finally, he tested his right fingertips with his thumbnail. Then he took

196

the volume dial and moved it very slowly to the right and to the left, settling at last on the right. He held his ear to the dial as he moved it, from time to time rubbing his fingers briskly on his overcoat. "One," he said at last, and began moving the dial to the left. After a long pause he murmured, "Two," and began turning again to the right. There was a faint click and Burroughs stepped back. Grasping a switch on the left side of the tuner panel he pulled. The panel swung open.

Quickly Peter came around from behind the desk and looked where Killitoe was shining his flashlight into the recess behind the panel. "Dammit!" said Burroughs. A foot behind the panel was the steel door of a safe. On it was a handle, a combination lock, and two locks requiring keys. Burroughs reached in and tugged at the handle. The safe was firmly locked. "I can't do it," Burroughs said. "I might be able to manage the combination one, but I need either dynamite or much fancier tools than I have for those key locks." Peter cursed. Killitoe groaned.

They stood for some minutes looking at the safe. Suddenly, Burroughs whispered, "Hold it!" On tiptoe he raced to the door by which they had entered. Silently, he opened it. From the corridor came the distant rattle of a key in the front door, and the muffled sound of men's voices.

Burroughs pressed the door shut, turned, and crossed swiftly to the other two. He closed the panel of the false tuner and spun the dial. There was the sound of footfalls approaching in the corridor. There was laughter, and a voice said "Glad to have this chance to see it."

"Quick!" whispered Burroughs. "Into the bathroom. There's a curtained shower. It'll hold all three of us." They had just closed the door of the bathroom when a key turned in the door of Satori's office. The door swung open and the light was switched on. Satori and Ross Trumbull stood in the doorway.

SATORI WITHDREW HIS KEY from the lock of his office with a look of puzzlement. He tried the outside handle. "That's odd," he said. "This door is always kept locked from the outside."

Trumbull, his face slightly flushed, expelled cigar smoke, leaned down, and peered at the lock. "You have night charwomen?" he asked. Satori nodded. "So they unlocked it," said Trumbull, and turned to look at the office. He nodded his head gravely. "Sandy, you do very well by yourself."

Satori looked pleased, but spoke diffidently. "It's good for the business," he said. "I wanted you to see it, but also I'm unfortunately expecting this call. Since we're wandering about town this seems the easiest place to take it. It's a Swiss deal that could be important to the business." He glanced at his watch. "Helga said she'd join us here after her art class. She's late as usual." He laughed lubriciously. "Probably hasn't got her clothes back on yet."

Trumbull grinned and dropped into a chair. "Let's hope she forgets to put them on," he smirked. He studied the sound equipment as he puffed on his cigar. "Great dinner, Sandy. Now how about some music?"

"Specialty of the house," said Satori. He switched on the tape recorder, adjusted the tone, and took a chair next to Trumbull. "Glad you could see my place, Ross," he said.

Trumbull suddenly became severe. "You don't keep anything to do with our business here, I hope," he said warningly.

Satori shook his head. "Of course not." A blare of music filled the room, the rhythmic chantings and deliberate discords of a Dutch pop group. Satori shook his head and rose from his chair. "It sells," he shouted above the din to Trumbull.

"I sort of like it," Trumbull shouted back, his feet tapping with the rhythm.

Satori reached to turn down the volume. Just as he did so a voice cut in over the sound of the Dutch group. "No immigration papers on Forbath," intoned the voice, "but invoice Cunard liner Caronia September 22, 1908."

His back to Trumbull, Satori flushed. He snapped off the machine. Glowering, he rewound the tape and removed it. Trumbull laughed. "My God, they'll use any damn thing for a lyric these days," he said.

Satori thought for a split second, then turned and faced Trumbull, his expression one of long-suffering. "True," he said, "but that group's gone too far. That's the kind of nonsense I have to listen to all day. No reason to do it at night too." He put the rewound tape into a drawer. A distant banging broke into the ringing silence.

Satori hastened to the door, opened it, and disappeared into the corridor. There was the sound of a girl's voice. In a moment Satori returned, followed by Helga. She was enveloped in a coat, reaching almost to the floor, of patchwork. It would have resembled an American quilt except that the patches were of different furs—orange fur, brown, white, yellow, mustard, black, and spotted furs, all scruffy. It was a masterpiece of atrocious taste, and Helga wore it with an air that would have done justice to sables. Her black hair, usually frizzy, was almost spiky. Beneath it the heavy green makeup on her eyelids made two gashes of color in her pale face.

Trumbull glanced up and appeared to wrestle with a decision. After some hesitation he rose awkwardly from his chair. "Ross, this is Helga," said Satori. "Helga, this is Ross Trumbull, from Chicago. He's here to buy a fortune's worth of my releases. If you can sell him on the idea, that is."

Helga went up to Trumbull and took his arm. "I'm on the buyer's side," she said to Satori. "What exactly are you offering?"

"Crazy lyrics," Trumbull answered for Satori. Satori smiled faintly. Trumbull looked down at Helga. "Say, that's, uh, that's quite a coat," he remarked, his eyes large and blurry behind his thick glasses.

"You like it?" said Helga enthusiastically. She pirouetted before Trumbull and ended facing him. "It's so cold tonight I had to wear it. I've got so little on underneath." She opened her coat. She was wearing a flesh-colored tunic which reached only to the tops of her thighs. It appeared to be crocheted of very fine threads, the design resembling chain-mail, but with much wider apertures. The only other thing she wore, besides gold sandals bound with thongs, was flesh-colored bikini panties. Helga moved her torso slightly, so that her nipples emerged through the blank spaces in the tunic. Trumbull's eyes widened behind his glasses, which suddenly gave the impression of having fogged over.

Satori glanced quickly at Trumbull, and then said jovially to Helga, "You're right. It's definitely a summer dress." As he spoke the telephone rang. "Excuse me," he said, and went to his desk.

He spoke into the telephone in German. The talking seemed all from the other end after the first exchange of greetings, and Satori only grunted rapidly from time to time. Finally, he tore a piece of paper from a pad and began to scribble on it. *"In Mailand?"* he asked, then grunted and scribbled again. He put down his pen with an air of satisfaction. He nodded and then spoke gravely. "Fully within your rights," he said. "Horst gave you the throwaways?" he asked. He nodded again. "Good. Just remember, it's essential to the next step." Again he nodded, this time vigorously. "Good, I'll be expecting your call," he said, and hung up.

Satori rose from his desk with an air of satisfied decision. "Sorry to have dragged you here, but that's the way this business is," he said to both Helga and Trumbull. His tone of weary complaint contrasted oddly with his air. He clapped his hands. "Well, let's go on and enjoy ourselves. Helga, if you'll cover yourself up against the cold, we can go along to

Der Nackte Ritter. There we'll be happy to have you uncover again."

"'The Naked Knight,'" said Trumbull with a short
laugh. "I like that."

"No, *I* like that," said Helga, with a glance upward at him
and a teasing smile on her face. She turned to Satori. "But I
can't wait until we get there," she said to Satori. "Do you
have a bathroom or do I have to flood your office?"

Satori grinned. "Please don't. The bathroom's there." He
pointed to the corner door. Helga walked across the room,
opened the door, and disappeared inside.

She switched on the light and shut the door. She took off
her coat, hung it on the hook on the door, and set her bag on
the washstand. Then she reached down into the lining of the
coat, near the back hem, and undid some snaps. She slid a
zipper back and pulled out a small black plastic box with several buttons and a dial on it. Then she sat down on the
toilet, the box in her hand.

Behind the shower curtain Peter, Killitoe, and Burroughs
stood transfixed. To avoid the sound of inhaling and exhal-
ing, they were all three breathing shallowly through their
open mouths. Peter's chest was pounding, and he was sure
the girl could hear his heartbeat. From time to time Killitoe
shook slightly with the effort not to tremble, and Burroughs
was covered with sweat.

After a time Helga stood up, reached behind her, and
flushed the toilet. Covered by the sound of rushing water, she
swiftly and deftly pulled out a long aerial from the black box,
and inserted the aerial into the air vent at the top of the wall
behind the toilet. Then she pressed a button on the box,
making a click which was barely audible over the sound of
the toilet. She pressed another button, held it down for three
seconds, then clicked the first button, and pushed the aerial
back into the box. As the sound of flushing died away, Helga
restored the box to its pocket in the lining of the coat, zipped
it shut, and closed the fasteners.

She went to the washstand, washed and dried her hands,

and then coolly regarded her image in the mirror. She moved her shoulders several times, so that the flimsy tunic slipped about, revealing different views of her breasts, and nodded with satisfaction at her reflection. She turned, put on the coat, looked in the mirror, and did some last-minute primping. Gradually her expression became thoughtful. Taking her handbag, she stepped over to the shower curtain. Silently, she pulled it part way open and looked in.

Peter and Killitoe, in front, froze. From the rear of the shower Burroughs whispered, "Grab her!" Helga stepped quickly back before Peter and Killitoe could reach her. Holding an edge of the curtain at arm's length, she smiled and shook her head. Then she lifted a finger to her mouth in a warning gesture of silence. The curtain fell back into place.

Helga turned, switched off the light, and stepped back into Satori's office. "Come on," she said petulantly to Satori and Trumbull as she closed the bathroom door. "I'm hungry and I'm thirsty." She walked determinedly across the office, opened the door to the corridor, and stepped out. With an exchange of amused glances the two men followed her. Satori pressed the button to lock the door from the outside, and it swung shut automatically behind them.

CONSIDERING that it was the fourth night of his self-chosen Milanese purdah, Otto Miller was feeling only mildly uncomfortable. He stretched to his full length in Cristina's voluptuous bed and sighed. Why didn't Peter send him some word? Assuming he had gotten in touch with Eva. If Peter was fearful of telephones—and rightly he should be—he could always send him a letter inside an envelope addressed to Cristina. What was he waiting for? The newspapers were no help: today's had reported terror and deaths in Northern Ireland, a Swissair plane hijacked to Budapest by some Arab sympathizer, the vicissitudes of the dollar—nothing that was of the slightest relation to himself and his present predicament.

From the bathroom, at the other end of the hall, came the characteristic, faintly muffled sound of splashing in the bidet. Otto frowned.

To be only fair, he corrected himself mentally, if it were not for Cristina his spirits would be much worse. For three nights and days, refusing her numerous calls, she had pampered and spoiled him and, he confessed to himself, he had enjoyed it. She had brought him things from outside, whatever he asked for, and catered to all his appetites. Ay, there was the problem. Could he go on fulfilling *her* appetites?

Otto sighed. The splashings from the bathroom were ominous. But perhaps she would forgo it tonight. He turned on his side and closed his eyes. In the morning. With the force provided him by a night's tranquil sleep. And tonight's splendid dinner. He opened his eyes.

The dinner had been her idea, too. She knew a trattoria in the neighborhood. No one would see him. And the food was marvelous. And it would do him good to get out for a bit. She had been right on all counts. *And* she had paid for the dinner.

After coffee and cognac Otto had called for the check. But when it came Cristina reached across the table with a smile and picked it up. Otto had regarded her thoughtfully. When rich women pay for men, he observed to himself, they attach either too much or too little importance to the gesture. With a whore it is different. Although money runs through her fingers at the same high speed it formerly did through those of Polish cavalry officers, if she pays for a man's drinks and dinner it is because it is the nicest gesture she can think of. Otto had leaned back and let her pay.

"My thanks," he had said, and meant it.

"My excursion," she had said, her smile one of genuine pleasure.

There was the patter of bare feet in the hallway, and Cristina came into the room. Otto rolled onto his back and looked up at her. She was wearing only a short, pale blue satin slip, the shoulder straps no more than thin strands. The rich curves of her body were smooth and shimmering in the satin. Keeping her eyes on Otto's, she lowered the straps of her slip from each shoulder and then dropped slowly onto the bed beside him. She rested with her knees drawn up, her long thighs invitingly bare. Idly, slowly, she moved her legs from side to side, her mouth slightly open, her breath audible in the stillness of the room.

Later, Otto still did not understand how it had come to pass. She was unhurried. Easily, gently, she caressed him. She said not a word. The stillness began to hum in Otto's brain. Gradually, his lassitude left him. Cristina's hair began to sweep his belly and thighs in long rhythmic motions. The focus of his mind narrowed, then concentrated. The warmth in his loins gradually became more insistent, then demanding.

Suddenly a jarring ring shattered the heavy silence. He started violently.

The telephone. Cristina exploded. "Macché!" she spat out. "Not now!" Cursing, she dived across the bed, reached down to the wall, and unplugged the telephone. It fell abruptly silent.

"IF THAT WAS a lyric, it was one of the damnedest coincidences I've come across," said Peter, sprawled on his bed. He sat up. "That name, Forbath, is one of those inheritance cases of mine I mentioned earlier today." He rubbed his forehead. Burroughs and Killitoe exchanged a swift glance.

Killitoe shook his head, rose from his chair, and walked to the door of Peter's room. "All I know," he said, his hand on the doorhandle, "is that that girl was the same one who picked Satori up in the Karmann Ghia after lunch today and drove off with him. Beyond that I'm baffled." He stared reflectively at the floor and frowned. "Frightening hair she has," he said. Then he brightened and smiled at Burroughs and Peter. "But a lovely bottom."

Burroughs snorted and joined Killitoe at the door. "David," he said acidly, "you're the only man I know who, in the circumstances we were in tonight, could have managed to be a Peeping Tom." Burroughs smiled sardonically. "The hell with *her* bottom, I say. What I want to see is the backside of that hidden safe. Goodnight." Taking Killitoe by the arm Burroughs led him out.

Exhausted, Peter undressed and fell into bed. His sleep was fitful in spite, or perhaps because, of his fatigue. Several times he drifted into a half-asleep, half-awake state, in which he tossed as he relived the anxiety of those minutes in Satori's office. About five o'clock he fell into a deep sleep dominated by the sense of Maria's presence. When the ringing of the bedside telephone finally penetrated to his brain, his thought continued in the private logic of his sleep. "It's Maria," he said to himself. He came out of his sleep and grabbed the telephone.

"Peter?" Her voice sounded very far away, almost tired. Odd way for her to sound, thought Peter. But of course, the connection with Budapest would not be very good.

"This is Eva. Eva Kanday."

Peter shook his head, noticed the morning light coming through the windows, and glanced at his watch. Six fifteen.

"I'm sorry, Eva. I was asleep." Stupidly, he added, "I delivered your package."

Eva ignored his last remark. "Are you awake now?" Her voice was weak, but urgent. "If not, wake up. Otto is in danger."

Peter awoke. "What do you mean, Otto's in danger?"

"Listen carefully," said Eva. "I'm very tired. And weak."

"Go ahead, Eva," said Peter in a calm voice, pushing aside the questions that rushed into his mind.

"Gunter knew I saw you Wednesday," she began. "He questioned me that night about it. He knew all your move-

205

ments, from the time you arrived in Zurich until you left. I explained you were Otto's lawyer and I was seeing you about singing in the festival. When he asked why I was talking with you and not Otto, I told him only that Otto was with friends in Italy recuperating from an automobile accident. I'd already told him Otto had had an accident, to explain my returning early last week, when Otto had to leave Eze so suddenly." She paused. Although her voice was distant when she spoke, Peter could hear her breathing when she paused, and it sounded labored.

"Eva, are you all right?"

She didn't answer, but resumed her story. "He didn't believe me. He said he could check what I told him in twenty-four hours. I don't know how." Again she paused. Peter could hear her effort.

"He left Zurich yesterday morning. I don't know where he went. But he was back in the evening. At home, when I returned from work. I've never seen him in such a state. He was berserk." Again there was a pause.

"Yes, Eva. Go on," Peter urged her.

"He had found out all about me and Otto. He knew I'd been with Otto at Eze. Or he said he did. He beat me until I was unconscious. When I came to he was just finishing a telephone call in the living room. I don't know who it was to. He came back in the bedroom, and for the rest of the night he sat there drinking, or raging about the apartment, or beating me.

"Twenty minutes ago he took his army pistol and left here in his car." Eva began to sob, made another effort, and went on. "I don't know where he was going at six in the morning, but if he knows so much about Otto I was afraid he might somehow have found out the address. So I started to call Otto. I didn't remember the number—it was in my little address book, one that Gunter didn't know about. It was then that I discovered he had rifled my things while I was unconscious. He had taken my book, with Otto's address in it."

206

Peter sat up in bed with a start. Eva was sobbing into the telephone. "Eva!" he said sharply. "Listen to me. Quickly! What is the make and license number of Gunter's car?"

Slowly, she brought herself under control. "It's a Ferrari." It would be, thought Peter. "The license number is ZH forty-five, one sixty-five."

"Do you know the model and color?" Peter asked.

"It's blue," she said. She made an effort. "I don't know the model. It's a number and ends in GT."

"365 GT?"

"Yes, that's it."

Peter spoke slowly and forcefully. "Eva, are you able to call a doctor?"

"Yes."

"Call him. Right now. Get him to admit you to a hospital, and to not list you. Tell him on no account to let your husband know where you are. If you can manage, call here and leave a message where you are. If not, have the doctor or a nurse call. I'll call you later today. I've got to move fast now. Okay?"

"Yes." She sounded exhausted.

"Good girl." Peter hung up. Immediately he called Caxton Burroughs and told him to get Killitoe and come to his room. Then, urgently, he asked for 647-033 in Milan. The connection clicked, paused, buzzed, paused, squeaked, and at last was made. The number rang.

Peter was still holding the telephone waiting for Otto's number to answer when Burroughs and Killitoe knocked on the door. He laid the receiver on the bed, opened the door, and raced back. The Milan number was still ringing.

Holding his hand over the telephone Peter told Burroughs and Killitoe, looking like caricatures of themselves in their bathrobes, who Eva Kanday was, and of her call. "I didn't know she'd been with Otto at Eze when Jake asked me whether Otto had been alone that night," he added. "I only found it out when I saw her in Zurich to get Otto's address and telephone number from her. And now Otto doesn't answer."

Burroughs waved at the telephone. "Either he's not there, so he's in no danger, or something's wrong with the telephone —and he is. What time did this Roessli leave?"

"Six," said Peter.

"And how far to Milan from here?"

"An hour's flight."

"When are the planes?"

Peter rang the airport. A plane for Milan was scheduled for ten twenty.

"Well, that's out," said Burroughs. He snapped his fingers as he concentrated. He turned to Killitoe. "You'll have to call your Italian friends," he said. "Either to head him off, if Milan's where he's going, or to guard Otto."

Peter leaned forward and spoke quickly. "No," he said. "The Italians can't 'head off' a Swiss citizen traveling to Italy. All they can do is follow him, and grab him if he does something wrong. And if you put a guard around Otto that might scare him off so that he won't do something wrong. We've got to let him make his move, and catch him in the act. I think there's more to this than just a jealous husband. And the only way we'll find out is to catch this Roessli."

"What would you suggest?" asked Burroughs coldly. "That we let him kill Otto and then question him?"

Peter ignored the sarcasm. "Let David ask his Italian friends to send a plane or a helicopter here. Now. We'll go back with them, and trail this Roessli to Otto's hideout, if that's where he's headed, and grab him then—when his intentions are clear. And before he can carry them out, of course."

Killitoe shook his head. In the morning he was a bleary, tousled sight, but his brain seemed unaffected. "Impossible," he said. "Difficulties about an Italian official craft crossing Austrian territory. The Austrians would be very official about it. They're polite, but they're still boiling about the Alto Adige. Or the South Tyrol, as they call it. We'd still be waiting for word this afternoon. The best my friends could do right now is to send a helicopter to the Brenner Pass."

Peter calculated for a moment. "That'll do it, David. It'll be close, but we can make it."

Burroughs snapped, "How far by car from here to the Brenner?"

"About a hundred and thirty miles," Peter said. "Most of it's Autobahn. We can do it in two hours, or less."

"And how far by helicopter from the Brenner to Milan?" Burroughs asked Killitoe.

"A bit more," said Killitoe. "Say, a hundred sixty-five miles. Following the valleys down from the Pass. Those machines can't make good time going over the higher ranges."

"And how long will it take this Roessli in his car from Zurich to Milan?" Burroughs asked.

"That's about a hundred sixty-five miles all told," said Peter. "But it's not fast going, until near the end. It'll take Roessli about five hours, I think, even in a Ferrari. I did it two years ago in a BMW and it took me nearer six."

"Still, it's his one hundred sixty-five miles against your three hundred," said Burroughs reflectively.

"I'm for trying it," said Killitoe.

"Unless he takes a plane," said Burroughs. "Peter, check the flights from Zurich to Milan," he ordered.

Again Peter rang the airport. The first flight was at eleven o'clock. Peter relayed the word to Burroughs and put down the telephone. "We have to try it," he said. "If he's gone by car it's our only chance."

"All right," said Burroughs. He looked at his watch. "Six forty now. You might just make it. Then again, you might not. It would probably be interesting to catch Dr. Roessli, as Peter says. But our job is to protect Otto Miller. A caught Roessli against a dead Otto is not the bargain we're here to make. So we'll try it both ways. David, call your friends. Ask them for a helicopter at the Brenner. If you see that you and Peter aren't going to make it in time, radio the police from the helicopter to put a guard on that apartment. *And* have

209

them watch the airport for the arrival of that eleven o'clock plane from Zurich."

Killitoe grabbed the telephone and asked for the number of the Prefettura in Milan. Under the torrent of Killitoe's Italian, Burroughs said to Peter, "I'll stay here and mind the shop. I'll notify Jake and I'll keep trying Otto's number. You'd better let me have it, by the way," he added with a smile. Peter wrote down the number and the address and began flinging on his clothes.

Killitoe hung up. "It's set. Nine o'clock at the Brenner," he said, and made for the door.

"Take two of the pistols from my room," said Burroughs, almost absent-mindedly. He returned to studying the address Peter had given him. "Any idea who C. Laggi is?" he asked with a sniff.

"No idea at all," Peter answered as he knotted his tie. "Eva Kanday thinks it's a woman."

"Yes," said Burroughs. "It occurred to me that she might have thought so."

Peter turned his head sharply and looked at Burroughs. "What does that mean?"

Burroughs shrugged. "Who else besides Eva could have filled her husband in on the fact that she was Otto's mistress?"

PETER BROUGHT the Mercedes to a stop in front of the Austrian customs post, and looked at his watch. Seven fifty. "Fifty minutes," he said. "We're doing all right."

Seated beside him, Killitoe handed his passport to Peter to give to the Austrian guard. "We're doing all right for ourselves. The trouble is we're in a race, and we have no idea how the other chap is doing." He glared at the mountains lowering over Kufstein. "And what now?" he asked.

"The valley opens out," Peter answered. "Then twenty-five miles of ordinary road. Then about fifty miles of Autobahn again up to the Pass. We don't have to go into Innsbruck." He took the passports from the guard, and drove on past the raised barrier. The Autobahn, following the Inn River, made a wide curve to the right. Two miles further on it ended abruptly, and Peter jogged left onto the old road. Six miles further on, in the town of Wörgl, they were on Austrian Highway Number 1, the former imperial highroad that runs the length of Austria from Bregenz on Lake Constance to Vienna.

Except in the towns and villages the traffic was not heavy, but for the first fifteen miles beyond Worgl the road wound over and around the hillocks and hummocks of the valley of the Inn. Twenty minutes of this, with Killitoe swaying and bouncing stolidly alongside Peter, and then the road straightened. To the south the Zillertal reached up into the mountains, dividing the Kitzbühler Alps from a soaring range to the west—the Tuxer Gebirge, on whose western flanks lies the Brenner Pass. Peter pressed on the accelerator.

Twenty minutes more and Peter swung the Mercedes to the right and back onto the Autobahn. To the northwest appeared the towers and spires of Innsbruck, behind it the steep slopes of the Karwendel Mountains. The Autobahn turned south, away from the city, and began the climb to the Pass, now thirty miles distant.

The car climbed steadily, snaking around the long curves. Ahead, the summits of the mountains were hidden in the gray clouds that had covered the sky ever since Munich. The road was clear, but in the forest snow still lay on the ground. Killitoe leaned forward in his seat, his eyes on the approaching summit, for all the world like an Italian rushing to leave behind him the cold and alien Teutonic north.

At last they came out on top of the Pass. Peter and Killitoe's eyes no longer strained upward, but now looked down into Italy. Above them, the clouds began to scatter in wisps, and a cold but brilliant blue sky was visible.

"We may be all right," said Killitoe under his breath.

A quick wave of their passports and they left Austria behind. At the Italian control Killitoe leaped out and shouted to the guard. The colonel who had been with them at Portofino emerged from the customs office on the run, and waved to the guard. Killitoe and the colonel got swiftly into the car.

The colonel spoke rapidly to Killitoe, and pointed across the vast concrete parking area to the waiting helicopter. Peter looked at his watch. "I was ten minutes off," he observed. "On the wrong side." It was nine ten.

Thirty-five minutes earlier and a hundred and forty miles to the west, an electric locomotive had emerged from what appeared at a distance, in proportion to the vast face of the mountain surrounding it, as a ridiculously small opening. It was the southern side of the St. Gotthard Tunnel. Behind the locomotive, rattling and swaying slightly, was a string of flatcars, carrying eight or ten automobiles. A blue Ferrari 365 GT was the first.

The sun was shining brightly. The air, now only cool, held the hint of blossoms and the promise of softness further down the Ticino. The driver of the Ferrari grimaced at the sunlight. As the guard dropped the low barrier at the side of the flatcar with a metallic clang on the loading platform, the driver of the Ferrari pulled sharply on his steering wheel, and drove off with the powerful engine roaring. He descended the ramp, raced along the tracks, turned right and up onto the overpass, right again and down the other side into the village of Airolo. The Swiss railroad guard watched disapprovingly. What was the rush?

Milan was only a hundred miles away.

Peter watched the great wall of cliffs that forms the western shore of Lake Garda slide by. Next to him Killitoe studied a map. The colonel sat with earphones and a microphone clamped to his head. A break appeared in the wall of cliffs on the right, and a town nestled at the edge of the Lake. Killitoe pointed at the miniscule houses in the warm sunlight. "Gardone Riviera," he said.

The helicopter swung to the right and headed towards shore and the low mountains behind the town. The colonel suddenly lifted his head. *"E bène,"* he said with a look of relief.

Killitoe listened to his explanation and translated to Peter. "They're watching at the border stations both in Chiasso itself and outside, on the Autostrada. Roessli has just passed through the Swiss station on the Autostrada." Peter looked at his watch: Ten eighteen. The pilot had followed the safest course down the valley of the Adige River, but then, pressed by Killitoe, he had climbed west over the mountains outside Trento so as to follow Lake Garda down to the Po Valley. But they still had ninety miles to go to the far side of Milan, where Roessli would presumably enter the city. He, at Chiasso, had only another twenty-seven miles to go to the city, in an automobile that could cruise at a hundred and twenty-five miles an hour.

Brescia came into view beneath them, a round citadel at the edge of the mountains. The colonel spoke up. Killitoe looked puzzled, but translated: "He says that Roessli has arrived at the Italian controls." He looked questioningly at the colonel. The Italian spoke briefly, but forcefully. Killitoe's momentarily puzzled look vanished. "The colonel's orders are to delay him as much as possible without arousing his suspicions," he said to Peter.

Alongside the new gray building inserted into the middle of the Autostrada five border guards in the gray-green of the Italian armed forces, with yellow collar tabs, and the peaked caps resembling a blini on a pedestal which are their trademark, stared stonily across to Switzerland. They glanced only cursorily at the license plate of the blue Ferrari 365 GT as it slowed to a stop, and then continued to stare stonily across at Switzerland. One of the guards leaned negligently against the side of the building, and a bell rang twice in the row of offices behind him. Three Carabinieri in black uniforms with red trim and white belts hovered around the door of one of the offices. They chose that moment to turn their backs, easily, casually, to the roadway.

The driver of the Ferrari waited a moment, an irritated frown on his forehead. Then he stepped out of his car and approached the huddle of Carabinieri. They ignored him. The driver shoved his papers at one of them. The Italian looked over his shoulder in surprise at the interruption, then gestured impatiently to the next office. The driver strode to it and entered. The room was occupied by two Carabinieri officers. Papers in hand, the driver waited as they carried on a loud, interminable argument about some fine point of the regulations which weigh even more heavily on the Italian bureaucracy than the bureaucracy weighs on the populace.

At last, by dint of shouting louder than the two arguing Italians, he attracted their attention. One, in a fine rage, turned to him, took his passport and car insurance certificate, and began to study them.

The officer's rage was too much, however. Holding the driver's papers in his hands, he turned back to his adversary. He exploded with repressed logic and invective. He piled his arguments one on top of the other, and then pushed them over onto his awed adversary in an avalanche of rhetoric.

Finally, the driver banged on the counter. The Italian turned and regarded him with cold, malevolent disdain. The driver expostulated. "My papers!"

The Italian looked at them again and suddenly smiled. A great, broad smile, redolent with civilized charm. *"Scusi, signore,"* he said. He appeared to study the papers, then handed them back to their owner. The latter dashed for his car.

"Signor Roessli!" cried the Italian, hot on his heels. The driver paused and turned. "Your tourist gasoline coupons. Next office."

Roessli looked at him coldly. "I don't want any," he said, as he climbed into his car.

214

The Italian frowned. "Why not?" he asked suspiciously.

"Because I am in transit," Roessli snapped. As an afterthought, he added carefully, "To St. Moritz."

The Italian made a gesture of immense regret. Solicitously, he continued to hold the door of the Ferrari open. Roessli reached out his arm to shut it. The Italian clapped his hand to his mouth. "But what am I saying, *signore?*" he cried. He leaned around the door, pouring forth a torrent of apologies, ending finally with the smiling explanation, "We no longer give tourist gasoline coupons!" Roessli glared at him, slammed the door, and gunned his car out of the Chiasso border station and onto Italian Autostrada A9, which leads to Milan. The time was ten thirty-five.

The helicopter whirred steadily along to the west, over the flat fields of the Po Valley. They were approaching Treviglio when the colonel spoke again. Killitoe looked at his watch, then smiled at Peter. "We've got him. He's just pulled out of Chiasso." Peter looked at his watch. Ten thirty-five. He checked Killitoe's map. It was too close for comfort.

Killitoe pointed to the map. "There," he said. Milan looked like a great heart on the map. A broad artery branched out to the northwest, splitting in three just outside the walls of the heart. The middle branch continued northwest, dividing again a bit beyond into two. Killitoe pointed to the northern sub-branch. "That's the one he's on," he said. "A9. It joins A8 just west of Lainate, here." He moved his finger back towards Milan and stabbed a spot south of the artery labelled Rho. "We'll pick him up about here."

Otto Miller had been awake for some time, but he lay quietly, his eyes closed, so as not to disturb Cristina. Finally, he opened his eyes and turned his head slightly to the left. She was lying on her back, staring at the ceiling. She glanced sideways at him and smiled.

Otto sat up abruptly. "What are we being polite for?" he boomed. "We're awake. Up! I'm hungry."

"Andiamo!" Cristina cried. *"La prima colazione per il principe!"*

"If this is the way princes live, I shall immediately apply for a title," said Otto as Cristina stretched and then scrambled from bed. Naked, she disappeared towards the bathroom.

There were sounds of splashing, and occasional snatches of song, from the bathroom. Then there was the slap of bare feet in the hall and Cristina, still naked, appeared in the doorway. Her face was shining and fresh, the color heightened by a dab of lipstick. She went to the closet, bent over, and pulled out a pair of mules. She slipped her feet into them, and thus attired for breakfast, went off to the kitchen. "No breakfast in bed, even for a prince," she called over her shoulder as her round bottom disappeared from the bedroom.

Otto climbed out of bed and padded down the hall to the bathroom. As he washed he noted once again the evidences of female occupancy: the colorful jars and boxes, the bits of soft and intimate apparel hanging or drying here and there. "Damn," he said to himself. "Not even Schattenwald had all these conveniences. I must see that my bathroom at home is decorated this way."

After washing he swept a yellow terrycloth bathrobe from its hook, put it on, knotted the belt loosely, and pattered into the living room. The morning sun poured through the windows. "A day worthy of the night that preceded it," he said to Cristina in the kitchen.

She stood before the stove, the curves of her long legs enhanced by the mules, her naked body glowing in the sunlight. She turned and smiled at him. "Sit down," she said. "It'll be a few minutes."

Otto sat down on the couch. Automatically, he glanced out into the hallway, at the double-locked front door. Then he leaned back against the couch and watched the preparations in the kitchen. Cristina, intent on her work, was in full song. "A magpie," Otto said.

Cristina, artless in her nakedness, came into the living room and set some plates and cutlery on the coffee table. "A nightingale, you mean," she corrected him.

"Not at this hour of the morning," said Otto. "What time is it?"

"Eleven o'clock," Cristina answered as she swept back to the kitchen.

Peter looked down at the ground. They were passing over the industrial suburbs on the north side of Milan. To the south he could make out, hazily in the sunshine, the dark outline of the Duomo, soaring above the center of the city, and to the left, near the Central Station, a string of sky-scrapers soaring even higher. They crossed an Autostrada and left it to the south. Then, abruptly, they were above another one. The helicopter dropped down and moved slowly towards the northwest, just off the edge of the Autostrada. Everyone's eyes were glued to the three lanes of oncoming traffic.

The pilot spoke first. *"Eccolo!"* he said. He swung the machine to the right and then back to the left in a slow circling maneuver over the Autostrada. As he crossed the southbound lanes a dark blue Ferrari with the distinctive white Swiss license plates flashed beneath them in the outside lane. The pilot swung left and followed down the Autostrada.

The colonel lowered the binoculars he had had trained on the car as it emerged from beneath the helicopter. He spoke to Killitoe. "ZH forty-five, one sixty-five?"

Killitoe asked Peter. Peter nodded. "That's him," said Killitoe.

Peter looked in alarm at Killitoe. The helicopter was chugging along at a modest speed, falling gradually farther and farther behind the Ferrari. "No matter," said Killitoe in answer to his look. "We don't want to scare him off. Also, there's a traffic circle at the edge of town that he has to go through. We can't follow him through the city. The streets are too short and narrow in the center. The colonel has men at the circle who will tail him. He's talking to them now."

The helicopter approached the traffic circle. Peter looked down and saw a dizzying whirl of cars; from the air it seemed like some activity purely of machines, with no visible connection with the human race. The colonel barked to Killitoe. "They're behind him now," said Killitoe. "He's heading towards the Corso Sempione and the center. But, as the colonel points out, so does every traveler arriving in Milan from the north."

Lazily, the helicopter circled and weaved back and forth above the bustling city. Peter watched the colonel anxiously. He spoke again. "He's heading into the Piazza del Duomo," said Killitoe. "That could take him out towards the Via San Gregorio. Or not."

The colonel gave an order and the helicopter, now west of the Duomo, banked over slightly and began to head towards the Duomo, towards the east and the Public Gardens. Suddenly the colonel cursed and looked at Killitoe in alarm.

Killitoe jerked forward in his seat. "They've lost him," he snapped to Peter.

TRAFFIC MOVED quickly in the Via San Gregorio. As the dark blue Ferrari approached number 81, a delivery truck pulled out of a parking space in front of a bronze-colored Porsche. Gunter Roessli signaled his turn, went just beyond the newly liberated space, and with two quick twists of the wheel was into it. At the next corner a policeman was whistling to traffic on the Via San Gregorio to speed up, while he held back a line of cars waiting in the intersecting Via Lecco. Roessli shrugged. It had only taken him two seconds to park. Nothing conspicuous. A helicopter, coming from the direction of the Public Gardens and the Via Lecco, crossed above the Via San Gregorio at the intersection. Disdainfully, Roessli turned his head to look at the entrance to number 81.

For a few moments he watched the doorway. The *portiere's* lodge was empty. He walked to the elevator. It was resting on the ground floor. He opened it, stepped in, and pressed the button for the third floor.

Quietly, Roessli stepped from the elevator. He pressed the button to light the hallway, and went to apartment 39. He peered intently at the nameplate on the door: "C. Laggi." He listened for a moment. There was the sound of a woman's voice. He frowned. Then a man spoke. Roessli flushed, and nodded to himself. From a pocket in his jacket he took a nylon stocking and pulled it over his head. The stocking was Eva's; he had felt an eerie pleasure, in the long hours of the night before, as he had cut holes in it for his eyes and mouth. He pulled it over his head. It brought to him the faint perfume of Eva; through the slits he had cut, his eyes glinted with a quick rush of anger. With his right hand, he took his army pistol from his pocket. With his left hand, he pressed the doorbell.

"Coffee for the prince?" called Cristina from the kitchen.

"The prince will have coffee," replied Otto from the couch, sententiously.

Cristina emerged from the kitchen carrying a half-full bottle of wine by the neck in her left hand. "I shall have wine," she announced haughtily. "It adds tone to the day."

"It will end your days," Otto retorted.

The doorbell rang.

Cristina gestured to Otto to step to the kitchen, out of sight. "It's the *portiere* with the papers and the mail," she said.

Otto rose and started for the kitchen. Cristina walked across the living room, negligently carrying her bottle of wine. Otto, as he headed for the kitchen, regarded her splendid nakedness. How would she hide it from the *portiere*? The door opened from the left side. Her only recourse was to hide behind the door, and take the mail with her left hand. But her left hand held the bottle. Quickly, Otto slipped across the living room and stood by the doorway, hidden from sight of the front door, to watch Cristina's performance. Slowly, his head leaned forward, past the doorway, as Cristina arrived at the front door.

She stood to the right of it, so that when open it would cover her nakedness. Then she switched the bottle to her right hand. With her left hand Cristina opened the door wide.

The helicopter came in high over the Via Lecco, but the pilot, aiming for the far, wider side, had already begun to settle it down as it crossed over the intersection with the Via San Gregorio. Even so, the descent took some minutes.

Before a quickly assembled crowd, with police holding back the automobiles, and with most of the housed population of the street hanging from their windows to watch, the helicopter plumped down into the street itself. Peter and Killitoe, followed by the colonel, dropped out of the machine. They crouched to avoid the whistling blades, then straightened and dashed for the corner of the Via San Gregorio.

They rounded the corner and ran at full speed to number 81. As they reached the entrance Peter saw the blue Ferrari with white license plates parked a few paces away. "Quick, for God's sake! It *was* his car that was parking as we came down," he flung at Killitoe, just behind him.

They ran to the elevator. The door was firmly shut. In response to their pressing the button they heard the cabin begin a leisurely descent from an upper floor. Peter whirled his head and saw the stairway, behind glass doors, on the opposite side of the vestibule. He, Killitoe, and the colonel headed up the stairs, three at a time.

As they reached the doors opening onto the third floor they heard a shot, a scream, the thud of a heavy weight, and the tinkle of falling glass.

Peter raced to the open doorway. Pistol in hand, he burst in just as a man's figure slumped to the floor directly at his feet. A heavy pistol rattled onto the floor as he fell. Peter plunged to the floor and grabbed it. Then he looked at the fallen figure. The head was covered with a nylon stocking. It was spattered and soaked with a dark, red liquid—too dark, and too thin, for blood.

Peter glanced up. Otto Miller's head was just appearing around one side of the doorway leading into the living room. His expression was one of utter astonishment. "Are you all right?" Peter asked sharply.

Otto swallowed, then spoke, his voice hoarse. "He caught a glimpse of me," he said. "I ducked back just as he fired. He missed." His eyes shifted to Cristina. "And then she laid him out," he said wonderingly.

Peter glanced to his left as he started to rise. His eyes fell on a pair of mules, traveled quickly up the bare legs, and then the naked body of a speechless, wide-eyed woman. Her blond hair was freshly brushed. In her right hand she held the broken neck of a wine bottle.

Peter looked at Otto, his own expression in turn one of utter astonishment. Behind him, Killitoe and the colonel pushed into the flat. The colonel looked at the body on the floor, then brushed past Killitoe demanding of Otto, "*Telefono?*" Otto gestured to the bedroom. The colonel's eyebrows shot up as he glimpsed Cristina, but he went on to the bedroom.

Killitoe shut the door. Cristina still stood in the doorway like a statue. He put his hand on her bare shoulder. "It's nothing," he said in Italian. "It's all over. Put on some clothes now." She remained motionless. Gently he led her to the bathroom. "Put something on," he said in a kindly tone.

In the bedroom the colonel sat down on the unmade bed and dialed. Nothing happened. Mystified, he yanked on the cord. It flipped onto the floor in front of him. He cursed, re-plugged the telephone in its socket, and dialed again.

Killitoe came back from the bathroom and knelt beside the prone figure in the hallway. He went through the pockets. "No more arms," he growled. He pulled out a sheaf of papers, glanced at them, and threw them to Peter in the living room. "I suppose we might have expected these," he said.

Peter unfolded them. They were the same crude sheets that had been scattered at the site of the accident near Eze. He handed one to Otto. Otto looked at it and handed it back to Peter. For the first time Peter saw him look deeply frightened. Peter shook his head. "This man's no Nazi," he said. "He's Gunter Roessli."

Otto's eyes widened. Then he scowled ferociously. "You mean Eva gave him this address?"

"No," said Peter. He told Otto of Eva's telephone call. "If she hadn't called, we wouldn't be here. The question is, of course, what the hell Roessli's doing with these leaflets," he concluded.

The colonel hung up the telephone and walked to the living room. Expressionlessly, he said to Otto, "The signora's telephone was unplugged."

From the doorway Killitoe cursed softly. Otto looked coolly at all three men. "The signora," he said with dignity, "has been very insistent that my rest here not be disturbed."

The colonel nodded and chewed his lip. "Thanks to her insistence," said Killitoe in English, "you damn near had a permanent, undisturbed rest."

The colonel turned and went to where Killitoe was kneeling beside Roessli. "We may as well see how much the signora dented his skull," he said.

Killitoe leaned forward and pulled the stocking from Roessli's head. He and the colonel rolled him over on his back.

"My God, Peter!" Killitoe almost shouted.

Peter stepped quickly into the hallway and looked down at Roessli. He recognized the vulpine features of the man he had glimpsed in the St. Gotthard Bar in Zurich with Eva.

Killitoe looked up at Peter in astonishment. "This is the man who lunched yesterday in Munich with Satori," he said.

Peter looked at Roessli in disbelief, and then at Killitoe. "No question of a doubt?" he asked Killitoe.

222

"No question of a doubt," Killitoe answered firmly.

Phrases resounded in Peter's head. "He left Zurich yesterday morning. I don't know where he went. But he was back in the evening," Eva had said. "He had found out all about me and Otto." And then she had said, "When I came to he was just finishing a telephone call in the living room. I don't know who it was to."

Now Peter knew. *"In Mailand?"* Satori had asked his unnamed caller over the telephone while Peter, Killitoe, and Burroughs trembled in the shower. And, "Fully within your rights. Horst gave you the throwaways?" Satori had also said. The "throwaways" were here; Peter had them in his pocket. He should have put Satori and Roessli together earlier; he had known they were both interested in the Forbath inheritance, or at least the name Forbath.

Most ominous of all, Satori had concluded his mysterious telephone conversation with, "Just remember, it's essential to the next step." What would be "the next step"?

"David," Peter said, "can the colonel get me a priority for a telephone call to London?"

Killitoe stood up. "I expect so." He spoke rapidly to the colonel, who nodded, went into the bedroom, and dialed a number on the telephone. He spoke inquiringly to Killitoe. "What number do you want?" Killitoe asked Peter. Peter gave him the number of his firm's London office. Killitoe translated and the colonel barked into the mouthpiece. After a moment's delay he handed the telephone to Peter.

Peter heard the characteristic London ring—two rings in rapid sequence, sounding as though made by two buzzers in an echo chamber. "Hammer, Rutledge, and Barry," said a female voice, making the familiar New York name sound for all the world like an ancient firm of London solicitors.

"Mr. Griffith, please," said Peter. "This is Mr. Dowling."

In a second Bill Griffith's voice came on. "That was quick," he said. "When I called a quarter of an hour ago I was told you were out."

"I was, and am," said Peter. "I had to come to Milan for,

223

uh, some quick business. I'll be back in Munich later today. You have any news for me?"

"It's not much," said Griffith, and then began to pour out a rapid sequence of information. With his singing Welsh accent, he sounded like a voiced computer out of control. Digging out information was Bill Griffith's specialty—and passion; he should have been a professor, Peter thought as he clocked in the flow. The Kaplan papers were a forgery. Done in East Germany. "I was able to check with some of my friends," said Griffith. "If you have the same kind of friends they'll probably tell you the same thing. Seems there's a center in the East Berlin that does this kind of thing. For a variety of purposes. You can imagine under whose sponsorship. It's somewhere on Dimitroff Strasse."

"Dr. Hans Pfeundner," said Griffith in response to the second of Peter's queries, "is extremely well regarded. We suggest you can have full confidence in him. We've worked with him on several cases, and we know for a fact that he handles Jewish claims on a strictly cost basis. No fee for himself. He's rather exceptional."

"Too bad," said Peter. Griffith's voice broke as it soared upward in surprise. "What?"

"If he was a crook," said Peter, "I might have been able to dig something out of him about one of his clients I'm interested in. If he's as honest as you imply, he's hopeless. Anything on VIGIL?"

"I'm afraid we failed you there, Peter," said Griffith. "All we know is that it's a Liechtenstein corporation. Apparently an investment holding company. Impossible to find out who the principals are. All its operations are handled behind a screen of Zurich lawyers and banks."

The doorbell rang. The colonel stepped to the door and snapped a query. The answer, though muffled, came through the door in the same military tone. The colonel opened the door. "Many thanks, Bill," said Peter. "I'll be in touch with you."

He hung up and went into the hallway as a doctor and

two stretcher-bearers came through the door. Outside, in the corridor, three Carabinieri held back a murmuring, gawking group of people. The Colonel pointed to Roessli on the floor. The doctor bent down to examine him, taking his pulse, feeling his skull, and raising his eyelids to peer into his pupils. While he was doing this, watched by Peter and the colonel, Otto went over to Killitoe by the window. "David," he said, "my curiosity is almost as great as my gratitude. I figure all this panoply of Italian power is your doing. What I can't figure out is how *you* were dragged into this."

Killitoe smiled his schoolboy smile. "*That* was Whitney's doing," he answered. "And Caxton's." He glanced quickly at Peter, then took Otto by the arm and led him to the window, talking earnestly. For a moment Otto looked perplexed, he glanced at Peter, then, understanding, smiled and nodded. The two turned back to watch the examination of Roessli.

The doctor stood up. "I don't think there's a fracture," he said. "Certainly there's a severe concussion. He'll have to be hospitalized immediately." The bearers began to lift Roessli onto the stretcher.

Cristina emerged from the bathroom, wearing a blouse and skirt. She looked at Roessli being lifted onto the stretcher and paled. Then she looked at the colonel. She was trembling, and her eyes were frightened. The colonel put his arm on her shoulder. "You were very brave signora," he said. He smiled gently at her. "You were also very effective." He gestured to Otto. "You saved the life of the signore." He waved a hand at Roessli. "You need not worry about him. He will recover. So that he can enjoy his spell in prison." Cristina looked at the colonel skeptically, then she smiled. She went over and sat down by Otto.

The stretcher-bearers prepared to leave with their burden. Peter turned to Killitoe, and shook his finger negatively. "No," he said. "Not yet."

Killitoe looked at him in surprise, but asked the colonel to stop the departure. "How long," Peter asked Killitoe, "can the colonel hold Roessli without charging him?" Killitoe translated, and the colonel thought for a moment. Then, with gestures indicating his impotence in the face of larger forces, he answered. "The colonel notes Roessli's condition," Killitoe translated. "He finds it worrying. Obviously, it can stretch out for a considerable period of time. Several months, perhaps. How can he charge a man who is unconscious? Or not in his right mind? He adds that in the end it will all be deducted from Roessli's prison sentence, of course."

"No matter," said Peter. "If my guess is right the Swiss will clap him in prison when the Italians are through with him. I just don't want him charged for the next few days." Otto looked at Peter questioningly.

"At San Fruttuoso," Peter said to Otto, "our problem was that you were dead for the right people and alive for the wrong ones. This time we're going to reverse it. You're going to be dead for everyone except those who need to know."

GRADUALLY, the scrapings of spoons and forks against the dessert plates diminished. Lillian Ballard's trained ear remarked that the human voice, now undisturbed by cutlery, had regained its supremacy. Assuring herself by a quick glance down the table that there was not a hidden dawdler, she rose and led the way into the main salon. In the flat gray light coming through the great windows the butler circulated with coffee and liqueurs.

The butler approached Whitney Ballard, bowed, and spoke to him in an undertone. The Ambassador excused himself and went into the library off the main salon. The butler shut the door behind him and disappeared into the hallway. In a few minutes the butler reappeared. Spotting the young American Second Secretary, he went to him, bowed—this time less deeply—and spoke to him in an undertone. The Second Secretary excused himself and disappeared into the library.

Whitney Ballard was sitting by the telephone. "You

wanted to see me, Mr. Ambassador?" asked the young man. The Ambassador looked at him, his expression one of private amusement. "Thank you, Ulmer, yes." He lowered his voice and spoke conspiratorially. "It is now two ten. You have twenty minutes to sweep them all out. All of them."

Ulmer swallowed, then rose to the challenge. "Yes, sir," he said. He started to leave, then turned back. "Perhaps I could suggest that you have been summoned to the Elysées Palace?"

Whitney Ballard shook his head. "No. It would cause a local flap. And the man from the Quai d'Orsay would find out it wasn't true. Good lying, Ulmer, should be as near to the truth as possible. And the distance between it and the truth should not be subject to verification." He thought for a minute. "I suggest you imply, without actually saying it, that the President is telephoning me at two thirty. The President in Washington, that is." Ulmer nodded smartly. "Just the implication, you understand?" said the Ambassador.

"Right, sir." Ulmer disappeared into the main salon. After a minute Whitney Ballard followed. Affable, courteous, interested, he returned to his guests and took up the thread of conversation as though he had not been absent at all.

Ulmer circulated from group to group, a word here, a word there, a brief aside to one, a joke and a whispered confidence to another. At two twenty the Moroccan Ambassador and his wife, after profuse thanks, expressed their regret that they had to leave, and said farewell to the Ballards. They were followed at two twenty-three by the Englishman, and at two twenty-five by the Frenchman and his wife. Several other guests had left by two twenty-seven and at two twenty-eight the Dane and his wife took their leave. They were followed at two thirty exactly by Ulmer and his wife.

Lillian Ballard looked about the large room in surprise. "Can you tell me what happened to our luncheon guests, Whitney? They've never left in a stampede like that before."

"No doubt they all wanted a bit of fresh air," said the Ambassador. "Very bracing outside these days."

His wife suddenly turned pale. He shook his head. "You see, my timing was right. Go on upstairs and lie down," he said with an affectionate pat.

"But, darling," she protested, "you can't sweep everyone out just because I have an upset stomach."

Her husband kissed her on the cheek and propelled her gently towards the door. "That isn't why I did it," he said. "I have a caller coming in a few minutes. Someone I didn't want seen by any of those people. I'll be in the library."

"Brought up in this rarefied atmosphere," she observed, "our children will all be knaves and pickpockets." She smiled, a trifle wanly, and headed for the stairway.

Five minutes later the butler introduced Jake Forman into the library. He was still deeply tanned, but it was evident that he had not been much outdoors for the past few days. His features were as square-set and strong as ever; he nonetheless looked tired. Still, there was something more relaxed about him; he seemed to smile more readily.

Whitney Ballard rose and put out his hand. "That was one hell of a morning they gave us, Jake. I could barely abide this damned luncheon waiting for your second call. Sit down and give me all the details. Coffee? Cognac?"

Forman smiled. "Thanks, Whitney. I'll take both, by way of celebration." The Ambassador poured Forman's coffee and cognac, took a cognac for himself, and sat down with his guest on the couch.

Forman described the Carabinieri's loss of Roessli in mid-Milan, the helicopter's landing, the race up the stairs, and the scene which had greeted Peter's and Killitoe's eyes—omitting only to mention that the woman who had laid Roessli out with the bottle had been naked—and recounted Peter's recognition of Roessli in the apartment as Eva's husband and the fact that Killitoe recognized him as the man who had lunched the day before with Satori in Munich. "That closed the circle there," Forman said. "It seems they have other evidence of the connection between Satori and

Roessli, but Caxton didn't want to go into it over the telephone."

"So it is Satori, then," Whitney Ballard ruminated.

"Definitely," said Forman. "Caxton didn't tell me how, but they also know he provided Roessli with the Nazi leaflets that he was to leave in the apartment in Milan after killing Otto. Those leaflets are identical with the ones found at Eze. In other words, they must be of East German fabrication."

"And in short, it's a Russian operation," the Ambassador observed.

"It looks that way as of now," said Forman.

"Which suggests that my man Trumbull has been turned by Satori for the Russian account," the Ambassador said thoughtfully.

"It suggests it, but it doesn't prove it," Forman commented. "Trumbull is in Munich, and seeing Satori, but there's no evidence he saw Roessli. Trumbull might be merely a dupe."

"Or he's trying to make me into one," said Whitney Ballard grimly. "In response to a query I made yesterday of Heston as to how Trumbull was making out with my suggestion that he use Satori to check on Peter Dowling through the Russians, I got word from Trumbull today that the moment 'isn't opportune.' He expects Pegov to be defecting to our side at any moment, he says."

"I'll pass that on to Caxton, if it's all right with you," said Forman.

"Please do," said the Ambassador. "I hope Peter and David aren't loitering in Milan. Munich is the place for them to be now."

"They're on their way there," Forman replied. "The Italians are flying them back up to the Brenner. They should be back in Munich later today."

"And Otto?" Whitney Ballard asked. "How are we going to find a safe place for him?"

"That's been done," answered Forman. "We hope you

won't take it amiss, but at Peter Dowling's insistence, we've reversed your ploy of a week ago."

"How's that?"

"This time we're announcing that Otto's dead. The Italian police have handed out a statement to the press that he was killed by an unknown assailant, who escaped, and that Nazi leaflets were found at the scene of the crime. They've also said that the woman present in the apartment with Otto was wounded."

Whitney Ballard reflected for a moment, then smiled. "I arranged for Otto to be alive because I thought he was dead. Now that we know he's alive, it makes sense that everyone else think he's dead," he said. "Good thinking by Peter. It protects Otto—if he's holed up somewhere safe. But it also brings the rest of you into danger. You yourself could be the next one, Jake."

It was Forman's turn to smile. "Perhaps. But you know as well as I do they won't be looking for me here. And I won't be back where I should be until we solve this business. As for the others, Caxton and David go along with Peter on this. Peter insists that the next move, whatever it is, will bring the whole thing out into the open. Better than waiting around for another attempt on Otto."

Whitney Ballard nodded. "If you all go along with it, I certainly do," he said. "But it depends on Otto being well hidden. What's been done about that?"

"The Italian police told the press that the body on the stretcher, which was all covered, was Otto's corpse," Forman answered. "Roessli himself is now in a maximum-security wing of the Milan prison hospital—unnamed, and with no charges filed against him yet. Otto actually went out of the apartment disguised in a Carabinieri uniform. David went out babbling Italian like a plainclothesman, and Peter trailed along, keeping quiet as a proper subordinate. The woman was also taken out on a stretcher to avoid having her talk to the press. She and Otto were put in the helicopter taking David and Peter to the Brenner, but the two of them are being left off near Lake Garda. They'll be taken to a government villa somewhere on the Lake—under constant guard by the Carabinieri—none of whom will know who they are. No one, except the Italian colonel in charge knows both where the villa is and who's in it. Any messages for Otto have to go through the colonel."

The Ambassador nodded approvingly. "That's sound enough. Send the first message from me, congratulating Otto on still being with us—in spite of jealous husbands—and thanking the colonel for his help. Thank the, ah, lady with him as well."

"I'll pass that to Caxton this afternoon, Whitney," said Forman stolidly.

The Ambassador leaned back. "And you, Jake? How is the situation, as you see it?"

Forman looked suddenly grim. "Two things will save us, in the end," he said. "Ourselves, and you. I can vouch for us. But the time will come, and it's getting closer and closer, when there will be a great big crunch. It will matter then as much what you do as what we do."

The Ambassador nodded. "I agree. And that's the sense of my advice to Washington. For whatever that's worth," he added with a sigh. "And you? How are you bearing up?"

Forman smiled. "No problem there," he said. "It's a hell of a life, but it's worth it." He reflected for a moment. "You know, I lost my wife several years ago," he said somewhat diffidently. "That's the only real void." A slow smile spread across his features. "The idea has recently come to me of marrying again," he said quietly.

"*That* is good news," said Whitney Ballard heartily. "Congratulations."

"Thanks, Whitney," said Forman. "I also want to thank you for calling me in on this case. My people very much appreciate it."

The Ambassador rose and accompanied Forman to the door of the library. "The thanks are from me to you, Jake," he said. "Let's hope there won't be any more such cases."

Forman shrugged. "If it *is* the Russians, I doubt cases like this will stop just because you're talking disarmament with them."

THE BLACK MERCEDES, dusty and streaked, pulled to the curb in the Maximilianstrasse. Peter and Killitoe climbed out and shivered in the cold, blustery Munich air. "What a difference a few Alps make," Killitoe observed with a scowl. Stiffly, they mounted the front steps and entered the Vier Jahreszeiten.

The concierge handed them their keys and a message for Peter. It was from Eva Kanday, asking him to call her at a clinic in Baden. "Good she took the precaution," Peter said to Killitoe. "Baden's fifteen miles from Zurich—and in another canton. Fortunately, the precaution's no longer necessary." He showed the message to Killitoe. "Why don't you take the telephone number and pass it to the colonel now, so that Otto can call her? He was pretty anxious about her. I'll give her a ring and tell her the news. Or as much of it as she needs to know."

From his chair in the lobby Caxton Burroughs watched them amusedly, then rose and joined them at the elevator. "I hope you gentlemen had a profitable day," he said casually.

Peter, his eyes ringed with fatigue, looked up at the sound of Burroughs's voice and smiled. "A little untidy in spots," he said.

Killitoe turned and looked calmly at Burroughs, as though returning from an inspection of a cheese factory in the environs of Munich. "But very impressive on the whole," he said, with the air of someone trying to be fair, even generous, to the natives.

"Why don't we meet in Peter's room in fifteen minutes and you can tell me all about it?" said Burroughs as they entered the elevator. "Meanwhile, I have a message from Whitney you might pass on, David." The doors closed behind them. In the lobby a portly gentleman who had dropped his copy of the *Suddeutsche Zeitung* on his lap when Burroughs had left his chair, and stared absent-mindedly after him, put his paper aside, rose, and walked rapidly to the cloakroom and telephones.

In his room Peter strode its length, sat down on the bed, and asked the hotel operator for the number of Eva's clinic at Baden. While he waited he stretched out full length and reflected on how eminently desirable sleep was. When the call came through Eva recognized his voice. "Peter! Is everything all right?"

"Absolutely," Peter answered. "How are you?"

"I'm beat up. But the doctor says I should be visible in a week or so. Tell me what happened."

Peter was hard put to fend off her curiosity, but Eva finally settled for the simple statement that she was no longer in danger, which was made more acceptable by Peter's news that Otto would call her that evening. At the end Peter added, "And thanks on my private account."

"Oh?" said Eva.

"For Maria," Peter said.

There was a pause. "Ah! You saw her," Eva said. "You liked her?"

"I was conquered," Peter answered.

Eva laughed. "Well, just remember, if I hadn't liked you, I wouldn't have sent you to her."

Peter felt attached to this girl, who even from a hospital bed showed spirit. "Long live the Hotel Franziskaner," he said. He hung up as there was a knock at the door.

He opened it to admit Burroughs and Killitoe. "I have taken the precaution of ordering a bottle of whiskey," said Burroughs as he eased into the room, his eyes automatically glancing about, a faint smile on his lips.

"Charged to Whitney, of course," added Killitoe, with his schoolboy giggle.

Peter smiled. "I'd gladly pay for it myself at this point," he said.

As they sat down Peter looked at Burroughs. "What's new on the home front?" he asked.

Burroughs smiled maliciously. "Love has struck again," he said. Peter looked at him inquiringly, as Killitoe grinned.

Burroughs laughed gleefully in recollection. "I woke Miss Helen Goodman with my call to Jake this morning at six forty-five. I expected it would be some time before I would hear from Jake. You know, she'd have to call him at his hotel, then he rushes over to use her telephone, and so on. Not at all. In about the time it takes someone to roll over in bed, Jake was on the phone. He tried to sound awake, but he wasn't."

Killitoe chose to be skeptical. "Doesn't mean anything. Probably standing watch," he said. "Good soldier, Jake." Peter turned his head at a slight sound at the door. Burroughs shot Killitoe a quick glance of warning. "Good for Jake," Killitoe rephrased himself. Peter turned back to them and smiled. Good for Helen, he thought.

Burroughs waved his hand. "But for the moment, there are more important things. Our major problem is where we go from here. Frankly, I don't have an idea, myself. Except that somehow, we've got to get onto Trumbull and Satori again, and now Pegov too." He frowned. "Jake saw Whitney this afternoon, and called me afterwards. Whitney had asked Heston how Trumbull was doing with his suggestion that he check through Satori and Pegov on Peter. In reply he got the word from Trumbull that the moment was not opportune. Trumbull claimed he expects Pegov to defect at any moment now."

There was a knock at the door. "No doubt it will all look a bit clearer seen through some whiskey," said Killitoe.

"Come in," Peter shouted.

The door remained shut. Irritated, Peter went to the door and opened it. The waiter bowed and entered. "Feel free to use your passkey," Peter said shortly to him. As the tray went past Peter he noted the ice, a siphon, a pitcher of water, the bottle of whiskey, and four glasses. Peter shrugged.

He let the door go. It remained ajar. Peter leaned against it, to shut it. It stopped against something. Peter leaned around to look. There, his foot inside the doorway, his hand against the door, and a cordial smile on his face, stood Ernst Seger.

Involuntarily, Peter flushed. "Ahmed!" he said. Seger stepped forward, grinning broadly. "It wasn't much of a lunch, Peter," he said, "but I gather you must have been detained somewhere."

The waiter had set down the tray and now headed for the door. Peter stepped back to let him pass. Seger took advantage of the movement to step all the way into the room. The waiter went past him and out, and shut the door. Seger bowed to Burroughs and Killitoe, his expression a study in politeness. The two men rose.

Peter spoke up rapidly. "This is Mr. Seger," he said. Before he could say anything further, Seger walked over to Killitoe and bowed again. "A very great pleasure, Mr. Minister," he said, and shook Killitoe's hand. Peter raised his eyebrows in surprise to Killitoe behind Seger's back. Killitoe mumbled something inaudible, and smiled awkwardly. Seger shook Burroughs's hand. "Mr. Burroughs," he said. Burroughs, his face impassive, inclined his head slightly.

Seger sat down, looked pointedly for a moment at the tray, and then up at Peter. "I hope I'm not disturbing you," he said, tentatively. "Have a whiskey, Ahmed," Peter said warily. He stepped forward, opened the bottle, and poured. Seger took his with ice and soda. Peter passed the bottle to Burroughs and Killitoe. Burroughs took his with a bit of ice and lots of soda. Killitoe poured a large amount of whiskey, spurned the ice, and tipped the water pitcher over his glass so that it splashed but once, and briefly. Peter added ice and water to his whiskey.

Seger sipped his drink. In the silence he smiled at the three men. "If you don't mind my saying so, I've had a hell of a day," Seger said affably.

"I'm really sorry about that lunch, Ahmed," said Peter. "I

was called away very early today, and in the confusion I forgot to let you know."

"Mmm," said Seger. "I quite understand, Peter. That wasn't the worst part of my day, by any means."

Silence settled again on the room. Peter glanced from Seger to Burroughs and Killitoe. Seger knows who everybody is, he reflected. How much else does he know? Peter waited.

Seger leaned forward. "No doubt Peter has had time to tell you about my work," he said, glancing alternately at each of the three men. He looked at his watch. "At least I hope I allowed sufficient time," he said. Nobody stirred.

Seger sighed and went on. "I see I didn't. I am Ernst Seger. Peter and I are old friends. And colleagues. I now head the Bavarian L.f.V.—our Office for the Protection of the Constitution." There was no reaction from his listeners. "The security service in these parts," Seger added.

He smiled pleasantly. "It was my hope that you gentlemen could help me with a problem I have. It isn't often that I can turn to men as distinguished and as experienced as Lord Killitoe"—he nodded respectfully to Killitoe, who froze—"and Mr. Burroughs." He looked squarely at Burroughs, who made a slight gesture of impatience. Seger looked at Peter. "I've had the benefit of your counsel in the past, Peter. I hope I can have it again."

"I can give you legal counsel, Ahmed," said Peter pointedly.

Seger shook his head. "Not what I need. I have lawyers all over the place." He looked steadily at Peter. "What I need at this moment is some cooperation from the C.I.A."

Killitoe snorted. Burroughs fluttered his eyelids in boredom. Peter shook his head. "I certainly can't help you there, Ahmed. I'm out of it." He gestured to the others. "And neither of these gentlemen has ever been in it."

Seger nodded. His face took on a dogged expression. "Let me put it this way," he said. "I could pick up Pegov today. And Satori. But there are complications. Satori also works for the C.I.A."

236

Burroughs sipped his drink. Killitoe tossed his off and poured himself another, without looking at Seger. Peter shrugged. "I don't know what you're talking about, but you've got plenty of C.I.A. men here you can talk to, certainly."

Seger shook his head. "Not that many I can trust. The situation's very delicate, indeed. Satori's American case officer, as you know, is a C.I.A. man named Trumbull. Trumbull, as you also know, operates out of Paris. He's completely independent of the C.I.A. here." He paused. "Not very polite, but understandable," he commented, then went on. "Going to the C.I.A. here involves two risks. One is that someone, a friend, a confederate, of Trumbull will tip him off. The other is that, even if this didn't happen, any approach to the C.I.A. here is going to be long and roundabout. I don't have time for that. Trumbull is liable to defect at any moment to Pegov."

Killitoe didn't budge. Burroughs blinked. Peter was tempted to say, It's the other way around—but held his tongue.

Seger spread his hands before him. "Since you're already working on the case I thought I could avoid both risks by coming to you."

Peter glanced at Burroughs. Imperceptibly, Burroughs signaled a negative with his eyes. How much does Ahmed know? Peter asked himself. He decided to chance it. "The case we're working on," he said to Seger, "is a legal one. It has nothing to do with whatever it is you're talking about, Ahmed."

Seger shook his head sadly. "I don't understand it," he said. "Here you are working with the Italians, but you won't work with us."

Warning lights flashed in Peter's head, but Killitoe fell into the trap.

"We were working with the Italians on Italian territory," he said firmly. He took a swallow of his drink, and smacked his lips.

Seger nodded, and smiled. A friendly smile. Softly, he said, "Exactly. And here you're working on German territory."

Burroughs attempted to recoup. He shook his head and leaned forward, as though mediating between two disputants. "Lord Killitoe's point is correct," he said. "We have been seeking to solve an attempted murder. One of Mr. Dowling's clients. The attempt took place in Italy. Lord Killitoe's connections in Italy have been most useful. The trail of the suspected murderer merely happened to lead here."

"Of course," said Seger, placatingly. "We have had an inquiry from the Italians about Begovic's supposed employer, Trumbull. It wasn't Trumbull. It was Satori's assistant, Horst Krieger, who hired Begovic under the name of Trumbull. Gave him Trumbull's Munich address."

Burroughs retired into silence. Seger continued. "I suspect you gentlemen may have been misled. You are investigating Trumbull only because of his supposed implication in the attempted murder in Italy. Trailing him here in Munich, you came across Satori. In the Haydnstrasse." He paused, and corrected himself. "You of course knew about Satori from Trumbull's reports to Washington. What you didn't know, and apparently still don't, is that your man Trumbull is working for the Russians. It is not Trumbull who is Satori's American case officer. It is Satori who is Trumbull's Russian case officer. The whole thing is directed by the Russian Resident here, Pegov. And time is now short."

Peter looked again at Burroughs. How was he going to get out of this one? He certainly couldn't reveal that they were working for Whitney Ballard. Sooner or later that would get around and backfire badly on the Ambassador.

Seger made a final attempt. "Peter, I beg of you. Consider this carefully. You're using up a lot of my men. We had to cover the Briennerstrasse last night, in case the three of you got in trouble inside Satori's office. Luckily, you didn't. In other words, you could save me a lot of time and trouble and expense. If that doesn't interest you, look at it the other way.

238

I can save you a lot of trouble. I could have put you on top of the Brenner Pass this morning, by helicopter, for your Italian rendezvous, for example."

There was a heavy silence. Seger broke it at last. A look of polite puzzlement on his face, he addressed himself to Killitoe. "What *is* wrong with Schmetterling, Mr. Minister?" Peter laughed to himself. Seger certainly had them well staked out: surveillance, taps, bugs, the whole business. He looked at Killitoe. The Englishman's black hair was more unruly than ever, his round face flushed. He was on the verge of either rage or laughter, no telling which. Peter glanced at Burroughs; his sharp nose was shiny, and a faint smile had reappeared around his lips, otherwise he was perfectly composed.

"You saved Mr. Miller today," Seger continued quietly. "You owe it to him to see that no other attempts are made. On him or on anyone else," he added significantly. Burroughs stirred slightly, and for the first time Killitoe looked squarely at Seger. "I can help you there, too," Seger said.

"Why would Satori want to kill Otto Miller?" Burroughs asked Seger abruptly.

"The question doesn't present itself exactly in that way," Seger answered. "You know as well as I do that our chancellor's efforts to establish better relations in the East have not met with unanimous approval in the Kremlin. Not to mention East Germany. What it comes down to is what, for the sake of argument, we might call Easterners against Westerners in the Kremlin. The Easterners, who think they can handle the Chinese, are against the improvement that is taking place in relations with the West. This operation is their answer to the Westerners. The murder of Otto Miller—and perhaps of others to come—ostensibly by vengeful Nazis, was intended to show that the Federal Republic is still seething with revenge-seekers, and is thus an immediate danger."

Seger paused delicately. "It is nothing against Mr. Miller personally. Or even you, Mr. Burroughs." He turned to Killitoe and spoke respectfully. "Or even you, Mr. Minister. Mr.

Miller was chosen because he was the chief of your wartime Unit 37. Your wartime operations simply happen to make you all ideal targets." Peter nodded to himself. So Burroughs and Killitoe *would* be next. "If only for that reason, sir," Seger went on, speaking directly to Killitoe, "it is my duty and my pleasure to protect you. And your former colleagues." He turned back to Burroughs. "So the Russian faction picks the targets and executes the operations. The East German contribution is the forgery factory on Dimitroff Strasse in East Berlin." Peter hummed to himself. "Satori gets the false Nazi leaflets from them."

"Forgive me, Mr. Seger," said Burroughs. His voice was silky. "How do you know all this?"

Seger smiled openly and spread his hands. "Because I have penetrated Pegov's operation, Mr. Burroughs."

Burroughs reached forward and took Seger's empty glass. "More whiskey, Mr. Seger?" he asked. Without waiting for an answer, he poured, added ice and soda, and passed Seger's glass to him. He finished his own glass and refilled it. Then he sat back and looked at Peter.

"Peter, I'm sorry to have put you in such an awkward position," he said. "Particularly with an old friend of Mr. Seger's standing." He nodded at Seger. "And insight." He took a sip of his drink, and continued speaking to Seger. "You understand the situation, I'm sure. Peter has spoken very highly of you indeed. But I am in charge of this operation. Peter's instructions did not allow him to present himself to you otherwise than he did, Mr. Seger."

Burroughs took another sip of his drink, and went on, "I am, however, authorized to modify those instructions, if I see fit, and if the circumstances warrant. In my estimation, they obviously do warrant it. We *are* from the C.I.A., Mr. Seger."

Burroughs gestured to Killitoe, whose normally small eyes suggested an advance case of strangulation. "Lord Killitoe, of course, is not from the C.I.A. He does, however, represent the British service's obvious interest in this matter." Killitoe rolled his eyes to the ceiling. "We shall naturally be very

240

happy to cooperate with you in this operation," Burroughs concluded. He raised his glass to Seger.

Peter choked. What was Burroughs thinking of? "Goddammit!" Peter said.

Seger put his hand on Peter's arm, and gave him his familiar, ironical smile. "Don't take it so hard, Peter," he said. "Now you won't have to forge that letter from the senior partner." Peter glared at Burroughs, who looked blandly back at him. Seger raised his glass. "I hope you gentlemen had a profitable day," he said.

"A little untidy in spots," Peter scowled.

Killitoe beamed at Seger. "But very impressive on the whole," he said.

"Of course," Burroughs said amiably to Seger, "you can now take the bugs out of our rooms."

Seger nodded his agreement to Burroughs. After a pause, he reached into the pocket of his jacket and extracted a half-dozen postcards. He handed them to Peter. "You forgot your cover in the Hofbraühaus," he said.

IN THE LIVING ROOM of an apartment in the Bayerischer Hof a waiter set down a breakfast tray, a pile of newspapers, and departed. After a few minutes Alexander Satori strode in from the bedroom. He was immaculately turned out, his dark hair sleekly brushed, his singularly smooth skin devoid of even the intimation of having had to shave. But his expression was one of watchful nervousness. Abruptly he sat down and poured some coffee and cream. He took a sip, and then, with a gesture of impatience, set the cup aside and reached for the papers. He flipped through them searching for the *Corriere della Sera* he had ordered the evening before. Finding it, he turned the pages rapidly, scanning each column. At last his eyes came to rest. He read, nodding to himself as he did so. When he had finished he set aside the paper, raised his head, and stared directly in front of him. The expression on his face was of neither triumph nor relief; it was coldly pensive, and determined.

He drank his coffee, glancing through the other papers, occasionally nodding his approval, then rose, went to the telephone, and dialed. The female voice that answered was unintelligible.

"Wake up, *liebchen*," Satori said drily, "I'll be there in half an hour."

"No," Helga answered.

"Yes," said Satori firmly. "I have made special plans for our weekend."

"*Einen moment*," she said. There was a long silence. Finally, she came back on the telephone. "One hour," she said. "I'm not presentable."

"I didn't say I was bringing you presents," said Satori. "See you in an hour."

He went to the bathroom for a final glance and pat at his hair, then returned to the living room. Scooping up the newspapers, he took the elevator to the basement, emerging from the hotel by the garage entrance in the rear, and walked rapidly to his office. There he buzzed Horst Krieger. The mastiff-faced giant entered Satori's office with what passed, for him, as an expression of high good humor, his mouth, forming a straight line instead of its customary near-pout.

Satori nodded at the papers. "You've seen them?"

Krieger nodded in turn. "Looks very good. Any word from Gunter?"

Satori shook his head. "No. He's probably taking a long way back. Or, having seen the papers himself, he'll wait until Monday to call from his office. By then, Horst, we will have taken the next step."

Krieger arched his massive eyebrows. "Already?"

Satori pursed his lips. "If everything goes as it should today," he said. "We'll know by this afternoon. Meanwhile" —his voice assumed a note of command—"I must have the Berlin tickets and reservations within a half-hour. I'll need the Paris tickets and reservations by the end of the morning.

And"—he looked at Krieger calmly—"the dispatch case at the same time."

Krieger looked at Satori thoughtfully. "And the girl?" he asked.

"If the rest works out as planned, it will have to be tonight," said Satori coldly. "We'll talk about it later. Let me have those tickets now."

"Right away," said Krieger, and left. A half-hour later he returned and laid two sets of tickets on Satori's desk. "The top two are Berlin," he said. "Air France, eight thirty this evening, reservations confirmed. The other two are Paris, Lufthansa, eight forty-five, also confirmed."

"Good," said Satori. He put the Berlin tickets in his pocket and left the Paris tickets on his desk. He took the newspaper under his arm and went to the door of his office. "Now we'll see," he said to Krieger.

In the Briennerstrasse Satori caught a passing taxi and told the driver to take him to the National Museum. In the Prinzregentenstrasse the cab driver hesitated, as though about to attempt a U-turn to deposit Satori directly in front of the heavy Wilhelmian tower of the Museum. "Don't bother," said Satori, "I'll make my way across." He paid the driver and waited until the taxi disappeared. As though dismayed by the traffic, he went to the next corner where, instead of crossing Prinzregentenstrasse he turned right, went one block, and came out in the Liebigstrasse. A bit further up the street he entered the drab, fortresslike building. On the fourth floor he knocked at Helga's door.

She opened it immediately. Satori winced. Her black hair was in curlers. She was wearing a transparent white bra, with black hands outlined on the cups, and blue jeans. The latter, sopping wet, clung to her hips and thighs; below the knees, where they flared, water ran down the material and dripped over her bare feet. "But, my dear," Satori said, entering and closing the door behind him, "you're still not presentable."

"Shrinking my jeans," said Helga with a preoccupied air. "One must pay constant attention to one's cover," she added, as though reciting from a manual. She marched across the room, picking her way over discarded clothing, to the bedside table. She turned the radio on, then off, then on again. As she bent over, Satori regarded her blue, wet behind.

The orange light in the radio flashed twice.

Helga walked to the farthermost closet, unlocked it, and reached in to the button. Noiselessly, the trapdoor rose and the ladder dropped down.

In the room below, Lazar Matveyevich Pegov, his back to the descending Satori, was peering intently at his bookshelves. He ignored Satori's "Good morning, Lazar Matveyich," until the very last moment, when, as Satori began to repeat his greeting, Pegov turned and said, "Ah, Aleksandr Pavlovich. Good morning." He spoke absently, professorially. His bulbous nose was flushed.

Satori smiled to himself. He recognized the Russian's heavy-handed technique, intended to intimidate, or possibly to amuse himself, and probably both. Satori bowed gravely. "And what is so important early on a Saturday morning?" Pegov asked reprovingly. "You are aware that you have interrupted my schedule. I have a patient waiting even now." He waved at Satori and the desk. "Press the button for the ladder," he commanded.

Satori pressed the button and the ladder slid silently into the ceiling. "Tardiness is perfectly in keeping with your adopted profession—if not with ours, Lazar Matveyich," Satori said sourly. "I understand all Western psychiatrists keep their patients waiting. If the patient is late it is a Freudian sign that he is resisting the treatment. When the doctor is late it is a useful reminder to the patient of how much he needs the doctor."

Pegov took quick advantage. "Perhaps I should have kept you waiting," he said drily.

Satori stepped around from behind the desk and approached Pegov. "Surely not when I bring important news, Lazar Matveyich?"

Pegov leaned his head back and laughed. He put his hand

on Satori's shoulder. "Don't mind my little joke, Aleksandr Pavlovich. I am very glad to see you, of course. Had you not called I would have summoned you. I too have seen this morning's papers." He put both hands on Satori's shoulders. "Well done, Aleksandr Pavlovich. Well done, indeed. You know the service you have rendered. You will also know our gratitude." The cast in Pegov's right eye lent his beaming expression a sinister aspect. Yet his good humor seemed genuine. "I wouldn't be surprised to see a new colonel on my staff," he said heartily.

Satori looked bewildered. "But, Lazar Matveyich," he said. "I thank you, of course, but the conclusion of the Miller affair is merely a routine report. You gave me my orders. They were fulfilled. That is not the important news I bring."

"Ah?" Pegov's eyes shifted hastily in an effort to anticipate whatever Satori had to announce. "Sit down, Aleksandr Pavlovich," he said. He indicated his continuing good humor by remaining in front of his desk and taking the chair next to Satori. His expression as he waited for Satori to speak combined a fatherly interest with professional watchfulness.

"Your congratulations, of course, should go to Trumbull," said Satori. "And now you'll be able to deliver them in person," he added.

Pegov frowned and stiffened. "How is that?" he asked.

Satori shook his head wearily. "We have done our best, Lazar Matveyich. We've held this off as long as possible, according to your instructions, but Trumbull must come over to us today. No later. He routed me out at midnight last night to tell me."

"Why so suddenly? What has happened?" Pegov snapped.

"Two things," Satori answered quickly. "Dowling is one. He spent all day yesterday with the C.I.A. people here. They are tracing documents. No doubt there has been a leak somewhere from our own people."

Pegov nodded. "That could be. The last imbecile who went over to them knew what we had been receiving from Trumbull."

"Trumbull is convinced they will strike tonight," Satori went on. "And even without that, the death of Otto Miller will raise a new ruckus. Trumbull is certain he is well-covered on that—but he says the combination of risks is now just too great." Satori spoke solemnly. "He reminds you of your promise to take care of him in the event of danger."

Pegov looked at the ceiling thoughtfully. When he lowered his head he had apparently made his decision. "And we *keep* our promises to our people, Aleksandr Pavlovich," he said forcefully. He added, "This is rather short notice, of course."

Satori shrugged. "These things are always on short notice," he said.

Pegov appeared to be musing. "Comrade Helga told me she was very impressed by Trumbull," he said. He was obviously sparring for time. "She found him exceptionally clear-headed and cultivated for an American, she said." Satori blinked. Pegov laughed shortly. "But she suspects him of sexual impotence."

"You will forgive me, Lazar Matveyich," said Satori. "While I don't know about Trumbull's case, I think Comrade Helga suspects all men of sexual impotence. Her stock in trade, so to speak."

Pegov lowered his eyelids and stared sullenly at Satori for a minute. Then he opened his eyes, and stared at the window. "A very useful comrade," he said absently. After a short time he appeared to have reached his decision. "Trumbull can only come after dark," he said. "And he cannot come here."

"Of course, Lazar Matveyich." Satori appeared to study the problem. After a time he spoke, as though he had at last hit on the solution. "It seems to me the answer is for you to receive him in Helga's room."

Pegov looked skeptical. "But he does not know that Helga is a comrade."

Satori nodded. "No, and it's probably better security that he doesn't." He reflected for a moment. "Thanks to their

246

meeting the other night, though, he does associate her with me. I will simply tell him that in fact I pay for Helga's room. As I have arranged for her to be absent, I have also arranged, without her knowledge, for your meeting to take place there. I will tell Trumbull you have approved meeting this way on the grounds that his coming to her room will appear a normal sequel to his meeting with her Thursday night."

Pegov paused. "Yes, that's all right," he decided. "Helga, then, can come to me at, say, seven o'clock," Satori continued, "and Trumbull can come to her room at seven forty-five. It will be dark then."

Pegov took out an American cigarette, lit it, and immediately began to cough. He stamped out the cigarette, gasped for air, then scowled. "The only good thing about this at this moment," he said, his eyes watering, "is that I shall see Moscow again—and have civilized cigarettes." He cleared his throat at last, and spoke quickly. "It is too late to arrange special transport. And I do not want Trumbull hanging about Munich. Our facilities do not permit it. One must move very quickly with these things. I will have to take him on to Berlin tonight, by commercial flight."

"Of course, Lazar Matveyich."

"Your office will get the tickets, Aleksandr Pavlovich," Pegov ordered. "And I shall need false papers for Trumbull."

Satori reached into his inside pocket, withdrew the two tickets for Berlin, and handed them to Pegov. "I will give Trumbull his false papers made out for the name on that ticket. Yours is as usual."

Pegov took the tickets, glanced at them in surprise, then waved them at Satori. "Aleksandr Pavlovich, if you have one fault, it is too hasty initiative." He frowned. "As with that Swissair plane." He relaxed and smiled. "But in this case you have done well. Again." He pocketed the tickets. "One more thing, however. Just to be sure. He is to come without baggage, of course."

"Of course, Lazar Matveyich," Satori said. After a pause he

added. "Except for a dispatch case. It will be full of photocopies of documents he is bringing to us." Pegov looked uncomfortable. "I'm certain there is no question about our wanting to accept this last consignment," Satori commented. "Also, he will look much less conspicuous getting on the Berlin plane with a dispatch case than without one. What respectable man in the West travels today without his brief case or dispatch case?"

Pegov sighed. "We invented it. You did not know Moscow, all of Russia, in the thirties. We went to bed with those damn cases." He nodded his agreement to Trumbull's dispatch case. "Just so that he doesn't look like a man fleeing." Pegov rose and went to his desk. He pressed the button for the ladder. As it dropped down he observed, "You will have a quiet period, Aleksandr Pavlovich. This may take me some time in Moscow." He smiled affably, paternally. "Probably you can use a little rest."

Satori stood up and moved towards the ladder. "Perhaps I could," he said, "but I fear events will not permit it. You saw how long this Miller affair took. I should be getting started on the Forbath case. You have his whereabouts and particulars?"

Pegov looked vague, then frowned. "Of course, Aleksandr Pavlovich. But not in this office at the moment." He thought for a minute, then waved his hand reassuringly. "I will send it with Helga to you this evening."

Satori bit his lip, then reached for the ladder. "Very well, Lazar Matveyich. Do not forget. It would be regrettable to lose this precious time, now that things are under way at last."

Pegov looked down his bulbous nose. "I do not forget things, Aleksandr Pavlovich," he said frostily.

"Of course, Lazar Matveyich." Satori shook hands formally. "A good trip to you."

"Thank you, Aleksandr Pavlovich," Pegov replied enigmatically. As Satori started up the ladder, he added, "But *you* have forgotten one thing."

Satori turned and looked at him questioningly. "This is my first meeting with Trumbull," said Pegov. "What are the recognition signals? What is the password?"

Seeing Pegov relishing his little triumph Satori assumed an expression of embarrassment. He smiled diffidently. "The dispatch case he carries will be the recognition signal," Satori said. He thought for a moment. "And if that is not enough," he said, "his first words after stepping into the room will be 'Congratulations, my friend,' to which I suggest you reply, 'Not at all. The congratulations are due to you.'"

Pegov noted the phrases in his memory and signaled his approval. "Apt enough," he said.

Satori continued up the ladder. As he stepped out into Helga's room she reached behind him, pressed the button to raise the ladder, and shut the closet door. Her curlers were still in place, as well as her suggestive bra. Her jeans were now only damp, rather than sopping wet. Satori turned to her and frowned. "You will come to my place at the Bay-erischer Hof at seven this evening. We'll dine afterwards. You will be bringing me a message from Lazar Matveyich. Do not, on any account, forget to bring it," he said ominously. He stepped past her unmade bed, noticing the wet spot where she had been sitting, and the total disarray of the room. "Charming," he added coldly. "Have the room—and yourself—cleaned up by this evening."

ROSS TRUMBULL shuffled back and forth in his room at the Regina-Palast Hotel. Wearing only his undershorts, he definitely showed more flesh on his bones than appeared to be the case when he was clothed. But it was stringy flesh, except around the waist, where it seemed of a more rubbery texture. The general effect was of gracelessness, and his movements contributed to it. Nervously, he peered left and right, sat again on the unmade bed as he re-read the newspaper, cursed, jerkily swallowed some cold coffee, grimaced, and then went to the window, pulling and sucking on his cigar in an effort to calm himself.

The telephone rang. He regarded it suspiciously for a moment, then warily answered. His "Hello" was distant and noncommittal.

A hearty voice greeted him. "Mr. Trumbull, this is Alexander Satori, at Melodie Verlag."

Trumbull brightened. His voice still distant, he nonetheless spoke with a taut smile. "Ah, yes," he said, "how are you today, Mr. Satori?"

Satori, all business, passed over the politesse. "Mr. Trumbull," he said, "I've got those tapes we spoke about the other evening. The full collection. Perhaps you'd like to come over here and listen to them, and then you can take them with you?"

Trumbull sucked on his cigar. "I don't think that will be possible, Mr. Satori. I'm in a hurry to leave. However, I would like those tapes. Could you bring them over here to my hotel?"

There was a slight pause, and then Satori spoke accommodatingly, if hurriedly. "But of course, Mr. Trumbull. Ten minutes from now convenient?"

"Right," said Trumbull. He hung up. Deliberately, he put on a shirt, drew on some trousers, and brushed his hair. He grimaced at himself in the mirror and then reached for a new cigar. He barely had it lit when there was a knock at the door. Satori had only had to cross the Maximiliansplatz from his office.

Puffing vigorously on his cigar, Trumbull opened the door. Small, neat, with his permanent air of worry, Satori slipped in. "Hi, Sandy," Trumbull said when he was safely inside. "Have you seen the goddamn papers this morning?"

"Not yet," said Satori with an air of baffled surprise. "I've been too busy."

Trumbull led the way into the room. He grabbed the *Herald Tribune* and shoved the third page under Satori's eyes. "Look at that, for God's sake!" he exclaimed.

Satori was carrying a dark brown dispatch case. It was virtually new, and had both combination and key locks, and a burnished metal handle. He leaned over and set the dispatch case down by a chair, then straightened and looked at the paper in Trumbull's hands. For the second time that morning he read the *Herald Tribune*'s account of Otto Miller's murder in Milan. He looked stunned. "Ross, how can that be?" he asked.

"I know," Trumbull said sarcastically. "You thought he was on a cruise. Just because Dowling said so. I *knew* that was a phony. He used that story while they tracked him down again."

Satori shook his head. "Can't it be a mistake, like the last time?" he said, almost pleadingly.

Trumbull shook *his* head. "I did a little checking on friend Dowling yesterday. I found out he left his hotel at seven in the morning. With some thug. He didn't get back until seven last night. That would have given him the time to get to Milan, do the job, and get back here. Ambassador Ballard's going to be all tied up in knots about this. That's why I have to get back to Paris. Maybe he'll listen to me now."

Satori sat down in the chair next to the dispatch case. "Ross," he said gravely, "you can't leave until this evening. Whatever you do. You know how much Otto Miller meant to me. But there's nothing we can do about that now. And there is something you can do—have to do—that is much more important. It will not only finish off your Ambassador's suspicions, whatever they are, it will cap your months of work. Your career, even."

Trumbull's eyes strained behind his thick glasses. He sat down on the bed. "What do you mean?" he asked, a trace of suspicion in his voice.

"I've just come from Pegov," said Satori. Trumbull stopped chewing on his cigar. "And?" he said tensely.

"He's on the run, Ross," said Satori. "He got a message last night to return to Moscow today. He knows it's the end for him. He routed me out first thing this morning. I met him in the Englischer Garten. He asks me to remind you of your promise to him."

Trumbull's face took on a look of intense satisfaction, almost glee. He nodded his head thoughtfully. "Yes, by God, that'll show Ballard. And the rest of them, too," he said, as though to himself. He looked at Satori and wagged his cigar at him. "Sandy," he said with great solemnity, "we keep our promises to our people."

He leaned back against the headboard. "It sure comes at a hell of a time, though," he said thoughtfully. "Can't he put this off for a few days?"

Satori shook his head. "You know as well as I do, if you're ordered to go to Moscow today, you go today. Just to keep up appearances, he's bought his ticket to Berlin. He won't use it, of course, but we can't risk his falling into the hands of the Germans. It has to be today."

"Hell," said Trumbull angrily. "I don't even have a place to receive him. And I can't let our people here in on this, because then the Germans will get in on the act. Probably even insist the interrogation take place here. Not after all my months of work. No, thank you."

Satori looked pensive. Finally, he said, "I think I've got the answer, Ross." Trumbull looked at him skeptically.

Satori leaned forward. He spoke with a combination of modesty and persuasiveness. "No, it'll work. You'll see. You remember Helga from the other night? She has a one-room flat in the Liebigstrasse. I'll hide Pegov there today, and then, after dark, you go there and pick him up. From there you can go straight to the airport, and fly to Paris with Pegov in your hands."

Trumbull pulled on his cigar. "There're two things wrong with that, Sandy. What about Helga? How do we get her out of the way? The other is, how am I going to buy a ticket to Paris for Pegov? And if he does it himself his own people will probably find out about it, and that's the end of him."

Satori smiled. "It's not as bad as that, Ross." His smile became diffident. "So far as Helga's concerned, I pay the rent on her apartment. I can assure you she will be out of there long before Pegov arrives, she won't be back until after the two of you have gone, and she'll never know who used her flat for a few hours." He looked at the floor, then raised his eyes to Trumbull, and laughed modestly. "My little contribution to the cause," he said.

Trumbull laughed salaciously. "Now you tell me, Sandy! I almost made a pass at her the other night."

Satori smiled in some embarrassment. "Oh, my relations with her are not that serious, Ross," he said deprecatingly. "You can try it next time you're here." His tone became that of the helpful subordinate. "As for the tickets, in view of the shortness of time, I have arranged that." He took the two tickets for Paris from his pocket and handed them to Trumbull. "One is in your name. The other is in the name of Dr. Egon Treplitz. That's a cover name for Pegov. He has the documents to go with it. The plane leaves at eight forty-five."

"By God, Sandy," Trumbull exclaimed, "we really trained you right. That's what I call first-rate staff work!" He took the tickets, puffed on his cigar, and gave Satori a broad smile. "If we keep on like this, we'll beat the bastards yet, Sandy."

Trumbull looked out the window of his room, his thin mouth gradually drawing back from its smile. He frowned slightly. "All right. Where is her apartment, and what time shall we make it?"

"Apartment 42 at 29 Liebigstrasse," Satori said. He appeared to calculate. "Let's say seven forty-five. It'll be dark then. And it gives you time to get to the airport easily."

Trumbull nodded, then frowned again. "Look, he better not give the appearance of being on the lam. No baggage, okay?"

Satori nodded gravely. "None except this dispatch case," he said. He pointed to the dispatch case beside him on the floor. "This represents a good part of your labor, Ross. Pegov gave me this this morning, for safekeeping. It contains photocopies of a mass of documents he's bringing over with him.

All stuff you haven't seen yet. He's sent it to you to bring along with you tonight. It will be his only baggage. And better this than none at all."

Trumbull eyed the dispatch case narrowly. "Damn," he said. "If I was on home ground we could open that now and have the stuff all sorted and distributed by the time I see him tonight."

"Don't do it, Ross," Satori said seriously. "He's sent this to you for safekeeping. He'll feel tricked if you try to open it before he does. And he'll know it. You see the kind of security he's had put on it." Satori gestured to the case. "He sent it for another reason, too. That's how he'll know you when you show up this evening."

Trumbull looked for a moment at the ceiling. "That's how he'll know *me*. How will I know *him?*"

Satori thought for several moments. "Use a password," he said at last. "After you've walked into the room, say to him, 'Congratulations, my friend.' He'll reply, 'Not at all. The congratulations are due to you.'"

Trumbull twirled his cigar in his mouth, then smiled. "Apt enough," he said.

Krieger looked across the desk at Satori. "So what's wrong?" he asked. "They've both fallen into line. We do the rest."

Satori tapped nervously on his blotter with his fingertips. His small face was tense, and his eyes restless. "It's in motion now, Horst. We can't stop it. And you know what's at stake. Trumbull won't mess it up, he's too stupid. But we still don't have that damned address." He tapped ever more rapidly on his blotter. "And for that we have to depend on that drunken, egomaniacal Russian. Assuming he's not playing games, we then have to depend on that idiot girl."

Krieger, his long heavy form stretched out in the chair before Satori's desk, was impassive. "And what's the solution for her?"

"I've told you," Satori answered nervously. "And this is

going to take perfect timing. When you see me leave the Bayerischer Hof entrance with her, you take your car immediately and wait for me at the entrance to the Salzburg
Autobahn. I'll pass by the Liebigstrasse, then meet you there.
You know the place by the Chiem See. She'll be finished, or
at least unconscious, by the time we get there. When I push
her out, you know what to do. There'll be no autopsy on a
body in that condition."

Krieger stared at the ceiling. "And if she forgets to bring
the message? Or neglects to?"

Satori murmured, "Don't worry, she won't. I've put her in
her place. Today, for the first time, I had no backtalk from
her when I left."

"NOT A VERY profitable Saturday," Burroughs observed
moodily. He plodded along the damp path behind Peter,
with Killitoe bringing up the rear. Around them the trees,
still without leaves, rose in lifeless shapes against the gray
sky, like so much barren underbrush.

"It's only three-quarters over," said Peter.

"Quite," retorted Burroughs. "And when it was only half
over he told us to stand by. Since then six hours have slipped
through our fingers." His face flushed from walking, Burroughs chewed thoughtfully at his lower lip. "You don't fore-
see the possibility of complications?" he asked Peter.

"None you haven't already created yourself," Peter rejoined. They came to a clearing with two benches. "This is
it," he said.

"What do you think is on his mind?" Burroughs asked
Peter.

Peter remained standing. He shrugged. "Maybe he got the
same word you got from Jake this afternoon."

"I hope not," said Burroughs with a quick sardonic smile.
"That will really complicate things."

Peter strolled out of the clearing and onto the path. Along the path, from the direction opposite to that by which they had come, a man approached. He walked at an even, unhurried pace, apparently deep in thought. He saw Peter and nodded. From the humorless brevity of his greeting and the preoccupied look in his gray eyes, Peter could see that Ernst Seger was worried.

They turned into the clearing. Seger bowed to Burroughs and Killitoe, and sat down on the bench across from them. Peter joined them. There was silence while Seger filled and lit his pipe. Finally, Peter spoke up. "Why so glum, Ahmed?"

Seger drew on his pipe. "You know how it is," he said. "The moment just before a possible victory is the most treacherous."

"I didn't know we'd come that far," Burroughs observed blandly.

Seger lifted his eyes and glanced at Burroughs for a moment. "Sorry to have kept you waiting," he said. "I had word at noon that I would have important news this afternoon. That's when I asked you to stand by. I didn't get the news until five o'clock. Then I had a few arrangements to make before we could meet." He paused. Burroughs made no visible effort to hurry him.

"The fact of the matter is," Seger continued, looking in turn at all three men, "at seven forty-five this evening—an hour and a half from now—your man Trumbull is defecting to the Russians. To Pegov, that is, who will take him on to Berlin tonight." He shook his head. "The only trouble is there are a couple of things that don't fit."

"I agree," said Burroughs, glancing at Killitoe and Peter. "What do you see that doesn't fit?"

"I don't understand the rush, for one thing," said Seger. "The reason given for all this is your investigation of Trumbull. That makes sense, of course. Except that it was specifically said that Peter spent all day yesterday with the local C.I.A. office checking documents. We know that's not true." He frowned in puzzlement.

"And the other thing?" Burroughs asked softly.

"The other thing," Seger said with a sigh, "is that Pegov, using his cover name of Dr. Egon Treplitz, has a ticket for Berlin on the eight thirty flight. Another ticket for Berlin was purchased at the same time in a cover name which we assume is Trumbull." Again he sighed. "However, Trumbull has a ticket for the Paris flight, leaving at eight forty-five. That ticket was purchased at the same time as another one for the same flight to Paris, for Dr. Egon Treplitz."

"The old shell game," Peter said.

Burroughs leaned forward. "I'll give you another thing that doesn't fit, Mr. Seger."

Seger looked inquiringly over his pipe at Burroughs. "We are informed," Burroughs said deliberately, "that Pegov is defecting to Trumbull this evening, and that Trumbull will bring him to Paris on the flight that leaves Munich at eight forty-five."

Seger raised his eyebrows. He thought for several moments. "You know," he said at last to Burroughs, "in this business rules sometimes have to be violated. I'll violate one and ask you who your source is."

Burroughs smiled. "In that case, we'll exchange violations," he said. "Our source is Trumbull. Who is *your* source?"

Seger nodded. "Fair enough. Pegov."

"It's Satori," Peter said to Seger. "Somehow he's fed one story to you through Pegov, and another one to us through Trumbull."

Seger looked at Peter skeptically. "For what purpose?" he asked. He thought a moment, then shook his head. "No, that doesn't fit, either. It doesn't serve either Russian or American interests, and Satori is working for one or the other. As far as I'm concerned, he's working for the Russians."

All the same, thought Peter, it does fit the facts. The only thing it doesn't fit is the assumption that espionage is the end-all for everyone engaged in it. What if Satori has some other motive? Something that to him appears bigger than either the Russians or the Americans? And why not? Before he could pursue the thought further, Seger shook his head again and spoke, this time decisively. "I can't risk it," he said. "Whatever you feel about Trumbull, I can't let Pegov get on that Berlin plane. I can't even let him get on the Paris plane, if that's the one he ends up taking. Supposing your information is wrong, Paris is just a dodge, and they go from there to Prague?"

"And if our information is right," Burroughs said with a weary air, as though repeating a lesson, "you would lose your chance to interrogate Pegov, once we had him in Paris. Unless we decide to bring him back here," he added.

"Mmm," said Seger. He looked at the ground, then looked up again. Peter recognized his ironical smile. "As I say, Mr. Burroughs, I can't risk it," he said. "I've already made all the necessary preparations. Once Trumbull gets together with Pegov this evening, I'm picking them both up." He corrected himself. "That is to say, the state prosecutor and the police will make the actual arrests." He nodded at Burroughs. "It's the same position here for us as for you in the C.I.A., or for the F.B.I., for that matter. I can't make arrests." Burroughs nodded perfunctorily. "But I'll be directing the operation," Seger added, his tone leaving no doubt as to who would be in command. He turned to Peter. "And to satisfy you, I'll be picking up Satori, too." He turned back to Burroughs and spoke with patently sincere courtesy. "Naturally, I hope you and Lord Killitoe and Peter will join me in making the arrests."

Peter leaned back and watched Burroughs. Now what, he asked himself. Burroughs nodded gravely, and cleared his throat. He's searching for time, Peter thought. Why? What in God's name are three private citizens going to be doing joining in the arrest of Russian and American secret agents?

"And what if our information turns out to be correct?" Burroughs asked.

Seger leaned forward. "Then obviously Trumbull is a free man. But we will have to retain Pegov. After all, he's been working on our territory, against us as well as you. We will, however, share the interrogation here with you."

"And if your information turns out to be correct?" Burroughs asked evenly.

"We'll keep Pegov, of course," Seger answered. "Under the same conditions. You will participate in the interrogation. As for Trumbull, you can take him. We don't want the scandal that will go along with arresting one of your people here. Neither do you, I imagine. Naturally, we would appreciate the results of your interrogation of Trumbull, as they affect us."

Burroughs smiled broadly. "Very fair. Very satisfactory, Mr. Seger," he said.

Seger stood up. "In that case, gentlemen, I suggest we move along. The wheels will start turning any minute now."

IN THE MAIN SALON just off the lobby of the Bayerischer Hof, Horst Krieger sat impassively, a brandy and soda before him, his eyes on the entrance to the hotel. From his vantage point he saw Helga pass through the doorway and turn left to the elevators. Krieger looked at his watch, shrugged, and ordered another brandy and soda.

Four floors above, Satori came to a stop in his pacing and stood for a moment regarding his telephone. He reached down to take the receiver off the cradle. As he did so, the buzzer of his door sounded. He whirled, went to the door, and opened it. Helga stood in the doorway, her old black coat drawn around her, her black hair spiky.

"It's seven twenty," Satori barked. He motioned her into the room and slammed the door. He turned and glared at Helga.

She opened her coat and began slowly to remove it, keeping her handbag in her hands. Underneath she was wearing her purple satin shirtwaist dress, open to below the navel. Rows of chains swung between her breasts. As she removed her coat she moved her shoulders so that her breasts jiggled and the chains swayed between them. "Not my fault," she said. "He forgot your message."

"What?" Satori cried. He took a step towards her.

Helga inhaled deeply and blinked her green eyelids. "But I didn't," she smiled. "I had to remind him, then he had to go back down to get it, then come back up to give it to me. All that took time."

Satori looked mollified. Not to lose his advantage, he said coldly, "I trust you cleaned up your room."

Helga nodded disdainfully. "Spotless," she sniffed. "I left out a pair of my panties, though. So they'd have a conversation piece. I washed them first," she added.

Satori looked at her with distaste. He put out his hand. "Let me have the message."

Helga started to open her purse. "Don't I even get a drink first?" she said plaintively.

Satori glanced at his watch. "But, of course," he said. He went to the bar and picked up a glass of whiskey and soda, already poured. He handed it to Helga.

"Just a second," she said. She dug in her purse and came out with a small folded paper. She handed it to Satori and took the glass in exchange. Rapidly she took a large swallow of the drink.

Satori went to the table on which his drink was set, drank the rest of it, and sat down in the chair alongside. He unfolded the paper and began to read. Helga took another swallow of her drink and walked over to where Satori was sitting. She stood in front of him and set her drink down alongside Satori's. The clasp of her handbag snapped open.

Satori paid her no attention. As he read his features expressed surprise, then disbelief. He read, re-read, then, scowling, slipped the paper into his pocket. For a moment he rested his head in his hand, while he appeared to reflect. Unseeing, he stared at Helga's legs beneath her brief skirt. Finally, he looked up—into the muzzle of the pistol Helga had pointed at him.

Satori started violently. He made to lunge forward, but Helga stepped back out of reach of his arms.

"Don't move," she said, "and don't cry out. If you do it will all end up with the police, and that you surely don't want."

Her handbag still on her left arm, her right hand holding the pistol pointed at Satori, she stepped sideways to the bar. There she slid the bag off her arm, and reached into it with her left hand. She withdrew a thick roll of nylon fishing line and tossed it to Satori. "Tie your ankles together," she commanded, "and do a good job. I'll be checking any loose knots, you may be sure."

Satori began to do as she ordered. When his ankles were securely bound, she said, "Now, stand up, holding the rest of the line in your left hand, and turn and face the chair."

Satori stood. With difficulty he turned himself about. Helga approached him from behind and took the roll of line from his hand. "One move and I'll kill you," she said. Satori remained motionless.

Still holding the pistol in her right hand, Helga drew the line up from his ankles. Without cutting it, she rapidly and expertly bound Satori's wrists behind his back. Then she passed the line up and around his neck, formed a slip knot at the back, and ran the line down again to his wrists.

"Squat," she ordered. Satori bent his knees, she ran the line down to his ankles, and secured it. She tested the knots. Then, still with the pistol in her hand, she turned Satori, held in his bent-over position by the fishing tackle, around so that he faced her, his head on a level just below her breasts. Abruptly, she pushed him. He fell over backwards into the chair.

"The technique should be familiar to you," Helga said drily. "It's a cousin to the way they hang people in your country. If you twist around enough, that's what you'll do—garrote yourself." She picked up a towel and went over to Satori. Quickly she gagged him, and knotted the towel behind his head. She looked at her watch, grabbed her coat from the chair where it lay, and put it on. She slipped her pistol into her handbag and started for the door. She paused and looked at Satori. "Don't worry," she said. "There'll be someone along for you shortly. Meanwhile, if you have to go to the bathroom . . ." She interrupted herself. "Perhaps if you'd gone to the bathroom in your office Thursday night, where the American, Dowling, and his friends were hiding, you wouldn't be here now." She sighed. "Maybe you'd already be in jail."

She turned to the door and paused again. She thought for a moment, then quickly reached up and grabbed at her hair. With a quick motion she tore it off. A black spiky wig rested in her hand, and a heavy mass of straight blond hair fell down below her shoulders. She shook her hair free, and walked over to Satori. She jammed the wig onto his head. "A pleasure to be rid of you both," she said.

She returned to the door, opened it, and stepped out into the hall. The door closed behind her with a brief, almost ladylike, click.

In the darkened room the light from the street rested on the walls like patterns askew. The heavy, drab furniture seemed shapeless. In the rear of the room a man wearing a headset was seated before a table on which rested a field telephone. He nodded as Seger entered. At the other end of the room a large window overlooked the street. Another man was seated before it, at the point where the glass curtains were divided. On a chair beside him were a pair of binoculars and a camera with a telescopic lens. He glanced up at Seger. "The girl left at seven twelve," he said.

Seger nodded, turned to the three with him, and gestured to the building across the street. "That's it," he said. "Number 29. Pegov's set-up is on the third floor, street side. He has another room on the fourth floor, directly above. It's not a bad arrangement at all," he added judiciously.

"I might say your own arrangement is not bad at all," Burroughs commented.

"A stroke of luck," said Seger. "When we started on the case we discovered that one of our secretaries lived in this apartment, right opposite. We moved her and her mother into another one while this one is being 'redone.' "

The shadows in the room turned in a dizzying circle as a car's headlights passed. The street shone black and oily in the rain.

On the opposite side of the street a tall thin figure appeared to the left of number 29. In one hand he carried a dispatch case. The lookout lifted his binoculars to his eyes. He muttered something in German. Seger answered with an order. Burroughs leaned forward and squinted. He looked at Killitoe, who nodded. "You're right," said Burroughs to Seger. "It's Trumbull."

"Trumbull," confirmed the lookout.

The tall figure disappeared into the entrance of 29 Liebigstrasse.

"Nothing proved yet, of course," said Burroughs.

Seger looked at his watch in the light from the street. He smiled confidently. "He's right on time, though." He turned to the back of the room. "No one in or out of the building," he ordered. The signalman repeated the order into the headset.

No more than three minutes passed. Peter saw that there was a sudden increase in the pedestrians in the street. A half a dozen plainclothesmen entered 29 Liebigstrasse and disappeared inside. They were followed within instants by four uniformed policemen, who took up posts just inside the doorway. He saw Killitoe blink involuntarily at the sight of the characteristically high-peaked German caps. "The uniformed ones will do the arresting," explained Seger. He turned to the signalman. "Have the prosecutor's office get their man over here. *Schnell!*"

The battered elevator rose in the shaft, swaying and creaking. Ross Trumbull examined the cabin's scarred walls with interest. His small mouth was set in a smile. Almost imper-

263

ceptibly, he hummed to himself. As he left the elevator on the fourth floor, his stride was alert, yet sure; the drab, grimy hallway could just as well have been one of the gray corridors, marked by bright-colored doors, in the vast building at Langley, Virginia, whose upper reaches danced before Trumbull's eyes.

Oblivious to the dim lighting, squinting through his thick glasses, Trumbull peered at the numbers on the apartment doors. In front of number 42 he hesitated a moment, patted his jacket pocket, shook his head in reassurance to himself, and pressed the bell. There was silence. Then heavy footsteps sounded behind the door. It was opened by Lazar Matveyevich Pegov.

Pegov's expression was one of cold suspicion. He glanced quickly at the dispatch case in Trumbull's left hand, and broke into a smile. He stepped back, with a small courteous bow, to allow Trumbull to enter. Even his right eye beamed.

Trumbull stepped inside. He too beamed. "Congratulations, my friend," he said.

Pegov shut the door, took Trumbull's right hand, and pumped it vigorously. "Not at all," he said. "The congratulations are due to you."

Still holding the dispatch case, Trumbull energetically reciprocated Pegov's handshake. For some minutes the two men, hands clasped, regarded each other closely. The Russian was bulkier, but shorter. Nevertheless, in looking up at Trumbull, he managed, still with a smile, to look down his bulbous nose at him. The American responded by leaning closer to Pegov. This made his greater height more evident, and gradually forced the Russian's head farther and farther back. From this vantage point, a toothy smile fixed on his face, Trumbull looked down *his* nose at the Russian.

"Well, at last," Pegov finally said.

Trumbull nodded in agreement. "Finally," he said.

Pegov gave Trumbull's hand a terminal shake and turned him towards the room. "Come in, come in," he said. Trumbull glanced about. A bed, a bedside table with lamp and radio and telephone, a couple of chairs, a row of closets along one side—all scrupulously neat. "Come," said Pegov, "we will have a drink. Just a short celebration, for the moment."

"Good idea," said Trumbull. He glanced at his watch. "But it better be quick."

Pegov gestured to him not to worry, and opened a cupboard. He took out a bottle of Bourbon whiskey. "Especially for you," he said to Trumbull. The American looked askance at the bottle. "You know," he said, "I really can't stand that stuff. These days all I drink is vodka. She got any?"

Pegov looked at him in mystification. "Does *she* have any . . . ?" Then he threw his head back in understanding. "Of course, of course," he said. "Yes, *she* has some vodka." He reached into the cupboard and withdrew a bottle of Stolichnaya.

Trumbull looked at it approvingly. "The best," he said.

Pegov looked at *him* approvingly. "I agree," he said heartily as he poured. A bit ruefully, he added, "But it's not always so easy to get there."

"I can imagine," said Trumbull.

Pegov handed Trumbull his glass. Trumbull bent over, set the dispatch case on the floor, and took it. Pegov looked pridefully at the dispatch case. "Ah, yes," he said, "the papers."

Trumbull waiting for Pegov to pick up his own glass, nodded. "Yes, the papers," he said appreciatively. "Intact."

Pegov took his glass from the cupboard. He looked at Trumbull in solicitous surprise. "But, sit down, my friend, sit down," he urged. He pointed to one of the chairs, and pulled up the other one. Trumbull stepped to his chair, and was about to sit down, when he suddenly paused. He leaned over and peered at the chair through his thick glasses. A woman's panties were lying on the chair.

Trumbull gestured to them and looked inquiringly at Pegov. The Russian leaned over and peered. "Hah!" he roared. He swept the panties off the chair and threw them on

265

the bed. He gestured to Trumbull to sit down, then, pointing alternately at the panties on the bed and Trumbull's chair, he cried, "The seat of love!" He laughed uproariously.

Trumbull, laughing with him, sat down, and Pegov seated himself opposite. The dispatch case rested on the floor between them. The Russian raised his glass. "To a good voyage!" he said.

Trumbull raised his glass. "To a good voyage!" he repeated.

Both men downed their glasses. Pegov wiped his hand across his mouth, and beamed at Trumbull. "We'll outwit them," he said.

Trumbull, his lips still wet from his drink, grinned back at Pegov. "That's what we're here for," he said.

Looking neither right nor left, her blond hair streaming behind her, Helga walked rapidly from the elevator to the door of the Bayerischer Hof. Horst Krieger, about to take a sip of his brandy and soda, watched her pass. His arm paused in mid-air and he frowned. After a moment's hesitation, he set down his drink, got up, and strode quickly to the entrance of the hotel.

Outside, Helga turned right and went to the Karmann Ghia. She unlocked it, and reached in to the seat. She drew out a small black box. Deftly she extended the aerial, turned on the switch, pressed a button, and held it for three seconds. Then she switched the box off, tossed it into the car, and got in herself. She started the engine, and with a quick jerk on the wheel to leave the parking space, she drove off.

From the entrance Krieger watched her. When he saw the battered Karmann Ghia pull away, he turned and raced back into the hotel. He paused at the desk. "Let me have a key to Herr von Satori's apartment," he said.

The concierge looked at the row of keys behind him. "I believe he's there now, Herr Krieger."

"I know he's there now," Krieger snapped. "Give me a

266

key. He just telephoned down to me to come up. He's in his bath."

The concierge nodded. "Of course, Herr Krieger."

At the fourth floor Krieger stepped out of the elevator on the run. He jammed the key into Satori's door and pushed it open. He stared for a second at Satori, bound and gagged in his chair, then slammed the door and rushed to him. He untied the gag. Satori's eyes were murderous, but he spoke with full control. "Well done, Horst," he said. "Quick! Cut the cords."

Krieger took out a pocket knife and began to slice. "Since when is she a blond?" he asked. He slid the noose from Satori's neck.

"She's always been," Satori said, twisting his neck from side to side. "I caught her out on it the first time I saw her, but she managed to sidetrack and fool me on that, as she did on everything else. She's working for Dowling."

Krieger freed Satori's hands. "And who's *he* working for?"

Satori rubbed his wrists. "Himself, I suspect. I didn't tell you, but Gunter told me Dowling had been to see Maria Kodaly in Budapest. It was my mistake to think it was just a coincidence." Krieger freed Satori's ankles, and he stood up. "But we can't take the time to figure that out," he said. "Someone will be here any minute now. Or so the girl promised."

"Did she drink?" Krieger asked, replacing his knife in his pocket.

"Yes," said Satori, "but that doesn't save us. Everything's changed, Horst. Everything except the need for speed. Let's go."

Satori headed for the door, snapping out his orders as he went. "Take your car," he said to Krieger. "Instead of following me, go to the office and empty my safe. We're on the run, now. Bring the necessary documents for us both. Take the Salzburg Autobahn, and turn off to Kufstein. I'll be waiting for you in the last rest area before the Austrian frontier. We'll get rid of my car there, change the plates on yours, and

267

cross over in that. Meanwhile, I'll go by the Liebigstrasse in mine. Come on. Move fast."

On the sidewalk in front of the hotel Krieger looked down at the smaller man. "Did you get the address at least?" he asked.

"Yes," Satori answered curtly. His jaw tightened. "For whatever it's worth."

Without looking back, Satori hurried to a dark blue Mercedes 250 SEL coupe parked just ahead of the space that had been occupied by Helga's car. He got in, started the motor, then leaned forward and down as he checked something beneath the dashboard. Apparently satisfied, he straightened up, pressed a button to raise the car's aerial, and headed the car around the Promenadeplatz, in the direction of the Liebigstrasse.

"Orange signal," said the man in the rear of the room loudly.

"Dispatch the squad for the Bayerischer Hof," Seger answered. He turned to Peter. "Let's go," he said, and led the way out. The four men, followed by a sallow, worried-looking assistant prosecutor who had joined the group without benefit of introduction from Seger, crossed the street. Except for the building enclosing Pegov and Trumbull, which stood grim and sodden gray, the street and buildings were swept a shiny black by the fine drizzle.

They entered number 29. In the grimy hallway were two uniformed policemen, and two of Seger's plainclothesmen. The policemen saluted. A plainclothesman approached Seger. "Three men each on the third and fourth floors," he reported. "The cars are around the corner, on call."

"Good," Seger nodded. He looked anxiously at the doorway.

Minutes passed. Then there was a rush of heels in the entrance. Peter turned his head quickly. A girl in a plain black coat, her long blond hair glistening from the rain, burst into

268

the hallway. She went directly to Seger, who grasped her by the shoulders and beamed at her. They spoke rapidly in low voices, and the girl nodded. Then the girl looked at Peter and his companions. She smiled at all three.

Killitoe looked in puzzlement at her face, the eyelids smeared a bright green. Burroughs studied her with a slight frown. Peter watched her for a moment, then, with a smile, he bowed. Killitoe nudged Peter. "She's wearing a wig," he said.

She smiled briefly at Killitoe. "No, I was wearing a wig *then*," she said in clear English.

Peter looked at the expression of triumph on Seger's face. "Well done, Ahmed," he said.

"You can congratulate Helga later," Seger answered. "Let's get moving." He took her by the arm and started up the stairway. Peter, Killitoe, and Burroughs followed. Looking more worried than ever, the assistant prosecutor brought up the rear.

Seger signaled for quiet. At the third floor a plainclothesman stood on the landing. He shook his head at Seger's unspoken inquiry, and the group passed into the corridor.

Helga took off her shoes. On tiptoe she headed towards the front of the building. The men followed, Seger and a policeman with their pistols drawn. At the end of the corridor Helga turned left and stopped in front of a door. From her pocket she produced a ring of keys, chose one, and handed it to Seger.

Seger inserted the key in the lock. He pulled the door towards him, and then slowly turned the key. Gently, he pushed the door open. There was only darkness.

Seger beckoned to the plainclothesman, who stepped forward and shone a flashlight on the inner door across the corridor. Helga reached forward and inserted a key in it. Carefully, she turned it and opened the door. Again, there was darkness. Seger took the flashlight and turned it on the room. Pegov's office. The heavy curtains at the window were drawn. Seger whispered to the plainclothesman to alert the men on the fourth floor. He left, and the others filed silently into the office.

On tiptoe Helga crossed the room and went to the desk. She leaned over and pressed something behind it. Seger switched off the flashlight. Peter became aware of the muffled sound of men's voices. Seger switched the light on again. A flash of metal caught Peter's eye. From the far left corner of the ceiling a metal ladder was suspended against the wall. It led into a black cavity in the ceiling. The muffled voices came from the cavity.

The dark blue Mercedes 250 SEL left the Hofgarten behind, passed through a narrow one-way street, crossed the Herzog Rudolf Strasse, and entered the far end of the Liebigstrasse. Satori pressed his foot down on the accelerator.

Lazar Matveyevich Pegov leaned forward and handed Ross Trumbull an envelope. "Your ticket," he said.

Trumbull looked at the envelope in surprise. "Oh, I have the tickets," he said. He reached into his inside jacket pocket and took them out. He glanced at them and handed the one in the name of Dr. Egon Treplitz to Pegov. The Russian scowled, took the ticket, and pressed his on Trumbull. Trumbull took it, looking puzzled. The two men opened their tickets at the same time.

Trumbull looked at his and paled.

Pegov glared at his.

Slowly, Trumbull put his right hand into the outside pocket of his jacket.

Below, Seger reached for the ladder. His pistol, still held in his right hand, struck against a rung of the ladder. It rang loudly and clearly in the stillness.

Pegov snapped his head up. *"Chort!"* he cursed. "A trap, eh?" His right hand slipped into the pocket of his jacket and emerged in a second holding a pistol, aimed at Trumbull.

Pegov's eyes narrowed. Trumbull's right hand held a pistol aimed at him.

Their eyes fixed on each other, the Russian and the American each inched his left hand forward, reaching for the dispatch case on the floor between them.

Seger grasped the ladder and swung himself up.

In the street below, the dark blue Mercedes rolled past. As it did so, Satori leaned down and flicked a switch under his dashboard. He turned a knob full to the right. A green light glowed.

For a fraction of a second Peter thought he was dancing. Then he was flat on the floor, the noise of the explosion echoing in his ears. The dull, ringing echo was broken by the far-off sound of masonry falling on cars parked in the street below, and by the unmistakable tinkle of a shower of broken glass. Then there was stunned silence. The darkness was broken only by a shaft of light coming through the shattered door at the top of the ladder.

They were all of them covered by a grayish-white plaster dust. Seger, who had picked himself up from the floor and scrambled up the ladder as the noise of the explosion died away, dropped back down the ladder as everyone in the lower room regained his feet. Helga, in the light from the flashlight held by Peter, went to the wall and switched on the room light. Miraculously, it worked. Seger looked at Burroughs. "We will not be able to carry out our agreement," he said. He grimaced. "There is nothing left either to arrest or to interrogate."

"As for you," Seger said to Helga, "we'll have to get you a new wardrobe."

"It's almost worth it," she said drily, but a bit shakily.

One of Seger's men came into the room. His face was grim. "From across the street they report that Satori's car drove by here just at the time of the explosion," he said. Seger looked at him in astonishment. He turned to Helga.

She looked at Seger's aide in disbelief. "But he was all trussed up when I left," she protested.

271

The plainclothesman shrugged. "When the squad got there the cords were there. Cut. Satori was gone."

Helga leaned against the desk and looked pleadingly at Seger. "I don't understand," she said. "There was no one there but the two of us. He gave me a drink and I delivered Pegov's message to him. While he was busy reading it, I pulled the gun on him." She seemed to be having trouble speaking. "I checked the bindings. They were all secure." She was breathing heavily, and her eyes had taken on a peculiar, flat look. "He was gagged. The door locked automatically when I left."

"Helga," Peter said, "what was the message you gave Satori?"

"It was written," she said. She spoke thickly. "But I read it." Killitoe had been studying Helga. As Peter and the others waited for the rest of her answer he quickly stepped forward. He was just in time to catch Helga as she turned deathly pale and sank to the floor.

PETER STROLLED to the departure gate and glanced back down the long hall of Riem airport. A modest Bavarian version of the Baths of Caracalla. Across the hall Peter glimpsed Killitoe's unruly hair and square-set face approaching. The Englishman broke into his warm, oddly diffident grin when he saw Peter.

"Is she better this morning?" Peter asked as Killitoe came up to him.

"Remarkable girl," said Killitoe. "Seger won't tell me her name. Seems she's a baroness. Balt family, from Latvia. Yes, she's out of danger. Luckily, she didn't drink all the knock-out dose Satori fixed for her. But she's in no condition to talk yet. Are you sure the message is so important, Peter?"

"It's my guess it is," said Peter. "Satori didn't blow up

both Pegov and Trumbull because Helga pulled a gun on him. He had to prepare all that before. As well as Helga's knockout dose. He'd decided for some reason to get rid of everybody who knew him in his double-agent role. At one blow. Wipe the slate clean. My guess is that the message will tell us why."

Killitoe's eyes creased in a smile. "I understand Caxton ducking out this morning on the pretext he has to talk to Whitney," he said. "It'll save him excruciating embarrassment over the C.I.A. story he gave Seger. What I don't understand, if you think that message is so important, is why *you're* in such a hurry to leave."

"David," Peter answered wearily, "I've already explained. I'm not leaving. I'll be back here in forty-eight hours. I hope less. But we're not equipped to track down Satori, certainly not when Ahmed Seger's got a police alert on murder and attempted murder charges out for him all over Europe. So we can't do anything at the moment. It may be another day, two days, before Helga can talk. I'll be back by then. Meanwhile, I have my own affairs to take care of." He ignored the skeptical expression on Killitoe's face. "What did the Italians say this morning?" he asked.

Killitoe shrugged. "They'll guard Otto until Whitney decides whether he can be released or not. Meanwhile, they questioned Roessli about Satori. They got nothing out of him. He sticks to his story that so far as Otto's concerned he's the offended party: a husband who was within his rights. But the colonel says Roessli had one strange reaction. When they told him Satori had disappeared, and was being sought by the police on murder charges, he was silent for a time. Then he smiled. 'Be sure you catch him,' he said. After that he went back to his story about being a wronged husband." Killitoe sighed. "In Italy, it may well get him off with a very light sentence."

A female voice came huskily through the loudspeakers, in the airport elocution intended to be both informative and soothing, but in which only the alert ear can pluck the announcement from the hypnosis. "My plane," said Peter. He turned toward the gate.

"One other item," Killitoe said. "Seger told me this morning that Satori's man Krieger, the one you and Caxton saw, apparently has also disapeared."

Peter paused. Finally he said, "David, get the Italians to ask the Swiss to search Roessli's apartment. His office. His safe deposit box. Anywhere he might hide valuable papers."

Killitoe raised his eyebrows. "What are they supposed to look for?"

"I'm not sure," said Peter. "Possibly an agreement of some kind with Satori's name on it. Possibly just stock certificates." He raised his arm to Killitoe as he turned to the gate. "I'll ring you when I'm out," he said.

"Stock certificates?" Killitoe called after him. "In what?" But Peter had gone.

The great river stretched to the south, the sunlight turning its even, muddy brown into a broad silver stripe at the horizon. Peter looked down on it with affection, as on a friend, an accomplice. He squinted in the bright light. The airplane banked to the left and swooped in to land.

With the other passengers Peter filed into the terminal. He took his place in line, heedless of the others, his mind already on the other side of the customs gate. Mechanically, he stepped to the police desk and handed over his passport. The officer flipped its pages back and forth. Then he frowned. He looked up at Peter and waved him to one side. He rose from his seat and disappeared into an office behind, Peter's passport in his hand. A minute later he reappeared without the passport, resumed his seat without a word, and took the passport of the person in line behind Peter. The other passengers looked at Peter with a mixture of incomprehension and fright, then studiously turned away from him.

A man in civilian clothes emerged from the office, and came to the barrier. Peter noticed first his mustache; it spread wide and full below a long, straight nose, tending to droop, but neatly trimmed, a fine mouth visible beneath it. Then Peter saw his eyes; they were lively and had a look of intelligence and authority. Peter had a momentary sensation of knowing the man. He carried Peter's passport negligently in his right hand. He spoke with complete assurance. "You do not have a visa for Hungary, Mr. Dowling," he said. His English was English, and his statement was equable—devoid of polemics, reproach, or hostility.

Peter responded in the same tenor. "I was given one in New York," he said. He smiled slightly. "It should still be in my passport."

The other man smiled slightly in turn. "It's there, all right," he said, "but meanwhile you've been here. In Hungary, that is. And your visa was given for only one trip." Again the equable tone, almost as though urging Peter to provide a satisfactory response.

"True," Peter said, "but that other visit was last Wednesday, if you'll notice the date. I was on the Swissair plane that was hijacked here. I didn't think a forced visit would cancel my visa."

The Hungarian evidenced no surprise. "I don't think it does," he agreed. He smiled more warmly. "We hope you enjoyed your visit, in spite of the circumstances."

"Very much indeed," said Peter. His eyes fixed squarely on Peter's, the man nodded. After a moment he asked, "And where do you plan to stay this time, Mr. Dowling?"

"The Intercontinental."

"You have a reservation?"

"No."

"An unfortunate lack of foresight." With a slight bow and a smile, the Hungarian turned and went back into his office, still carrying Peter's passport. Peter was now the last passenger from the Munich plane. He looked towards the customs gate, impatience beginning to get the better of him. At last the mustachioed man appeared. Without haste, but without dawdling, he came to Peter and handed him his passport. "I

275

have given you another visa," he said, "for the sake of bureaucratic order."

"Thank you," Peter said. He smiled, bowed, and started for the customs. The even, smooth voice stopped him. "You also have your reservation at the Intercontinental," it said. Peter looked at him in surprise. "They claimed they were full," the man said. His eyelids blinked slowly, and there was a faint smile beneath the mustache. "But you have your reservation."

"Why, thank you very much," said Peter. "Very kind of you."

Still looking him squarely in the eyes the man bowed. "Not at all. Do enjoy your stay in Budapest, Mr. Dowling."

Peter made his way to the customs. Either I have been mistaken for an important person, he thought, or the Hungarian shortage of foreign exchange has become really critical. The performance of the customs convinced him it was the latter. He paid duty in German marks on a package in his suitcase, and then carried the suitcase himself out into the hall, followed by the porters' glares.

Maria Kodaly, wearing a thin white blouse and a simple navy blue skirt, was standing a little bit back from the customs gate. Her tawny hair was haloed in the bright light streaming into the hall, but she looked deliciously cool and fresh. Peter's senses responded to the familiar silhouette and intimate curves of her body. Her smile was alive with anticipation. Peter went straight to her, looked for a moment into her shining green eyes, and then bent and kissed her. Her lips were moist and warm, and he lingered over the taste. *"Szervusz,"* he said.

"Szervusz," she breathed. She regarded him for a moment, steadily, then flushed. "You mustn't look too closely," she said. "I didn't sleep a wink after you telephoned last night."

Peter took her by the arm and they walked to the entrance. "I haven't really slept since last Thursday morning," he said, and knew it would have been also true had he spent the three intervening days in bed instead of alternately racing

276

and slinking about Munich, Milan, and the countryside between.

Maria led the way to the car. Peter looked at the little red Fiat with affection. "No trouble with Ficko?" he asked as he threw his suitcase in the back.

"He developed a cough when you left," Maria answered. She climbed in behind the wheel and started the engine. "A sympathetic reaction. It disappeared when I told him why we were coming to the airport this morning." She pulled out of the parking space, drove around the circle, and headed for the center of the city.

"My own symptoms took a turn for the better with the same news," said Peter, "but I'm sorely in need of attention, Doctor. Let's just stop by the Intercontinental first, and I'll check in and leave the bag."

Maria's whispered "Me too," crossed his last sentence in mid-air.

At the hotel Peter pulled his suitcase out from the back. "It's wiser," he said, "but it's a goddamn nuisance." He looked at his watch. With mock surprise, he expostulated, "But—it's one thirty! Don't you think we ought to have some lunch?"

A small frown knit her eyebrows. "What would you do if I accepted?"

"I'd suffer tortures," Peter said quickly.

She laughed at him. "And you'd deserve them. Hurry!"

In less than three minutes Peter was back in the car, a package in his hand. Maria glanced at it as she drove off. "Another package?" she asked.

"I've brought you four things," Peter answered. They crossed the Chain Bridge and slipped into the darkness of the tunnel under the Vár.

In the stifled hum of the tunnel her voice came to him clearly. "What are they?"

Peter rested his hand on the smooth nape of her neck, and Maria pressed her head back against his fingers. "You'll see," said Peter.

277

The shaft of light from the southern window overlooking the garden had moved a good two feet to the east when Maria looked up from the bed.

"The first thing I brought you is my love," said Peter, "but that's only a preface."

Her eyes stared up at him. "You have mine," she answered softly. Peter leaned down and kissed her gently. "You can't have brought me anything else that matters," she said.

Peter smiled teasingly at her. "Not even Viennese coffee?" She laughed. "Not even Viennese coffee," she said. "And besides, you weren't even in Vienna."

Peter brought over the package. She tore it open and stared in surprise at the two pounds of coffee from a Viennese store in the Graben. She laughed gleefully and hugged the two bags to her. "How did you manage that?" she cried.

"I telephoned Thursday afternoon," Peter explained. "Lucky I did, too, because it only came in the mail yesterday."

Maria leaped up from the bed, pulled on her bathrobe, and disappeared into the kitchenette. Peter turned and looked thoughtfully at the ray of light at the window. He was still deep in thought when she came back with the coffee. She pulled back the curtains and sat down beside Peter on the bed. The thick, strong flavor was a marvel of freshness. "Ah," they said in unison, and nodded at each other. Maria kissed Peter's shoulder, and then leaned against him. "Now we really need nothing more," she said.

Peter looked down at her. He put his cup on the table nearest him, and took Maria's from her. "There's the third thing," he said quietly.

She leaned her head against his shoulder. "I don't think I can manage it," she said.

"That's what I was afraid of," said Peter. "I've brought you news about your inheritance in America. It amounts to thirty million dollars."

"IT'S RIDICULOUS!" Maria exclaimed for the tenth time. "Why"—her hands turned in circles as she again sought some expression to convey the enormity of it—"why, it's preposterous!" She lapsed into Hungarian. *"Nevetséges! Abszurdum!"* After a moment's thought she suddenly looked puzzled. "It's sweet of you, darling, to bring me this news," she said, "but how did you find it out in just three days?"

"Nothing sweet about it," said Peter. "I'm charged with finding the heir to the Forbath estate by the lawyers handling it in Los Angeles. It's one of the reasons I came to Europe this time." He sighed. "I wasn't even thinking about it last Thursday morning. Then you dropped your bombshell on me on the way to the airport. I realized it was you." He shook his head. "But I couldn't tell you about it then, two seconds before catching a plane. And by then I had my own, very personal interest in you."

She took his hand and brought it up to her breasts. "Tell them to give it to someone else," she said. "I can't do anything with it. I can't think of anything more useless to me than thirty million dollars."

"The law won't allow it to be given to someone else," said Peter. "You can give it away if you want, but you have to accept it first." He laughed. "It's just one of those crosses you'll have to bear." Then his face became serious. "Which brings us to the fourth thing."

Maria lay back on the bed. She reached up and drew him down on top of her. Her lips still swollen with kissing, her eyes now tinged with a sudden sadness, she looked up at him. "Let's go back to the preface," she said.

Peter leaned down and kissed her lightly. "In a manner of speaking, it *is* a preface," he said.

She shook her head. "I can't solve riddles now."

279

"I want you to come with me," Peter said flatly. "To leave here with me."

Maria blanched. She looked at him gravely, in silence, for a long minute. "I've thought about it too, these three days," she said, "but I can't, Peter. I've told you that. I've tried to get a passport. Everyone else has one, or practically everyone else. But not me. I don't even get a refusal. I just don't get a passport."

"Is it your work?" Peter asked.

Maria shrugged. "Who knows? I can't believe it is. My work is neurological research, but it's nothing secret."

"So much the better," said Peter. "Come with me. With that money you can build a dozen laboratories, just the way you want them. If you don't want the money, I'll build you a laboratory." He smiled. "Small at first."

Maria looked at him sadly. "Why do you keep on when you know I can't get out?" she asked. "It hurt when you left last time, and I don't want to think about it this time."

"Don't," Peter answered. "I'm not prepared to accept that hurt any more than you are. That's why I want to take you out with me. Without your passport."

Maria sat up abruptly. "*Pay*-tehr!" Her tawny hair shook in a vigorous negative. "The frontier is too well guarded. We can't do it. They've taken down some of the barriers, but enough are left. And they shoot at anyone who tries to escape."

"I don't plan for us to sneak through. I plan for us to ride through. If I can convince you it's possible, will you come with me?"

Maria got up and went to the window. She looked out over the valley of Buda. Peter looked at the grace of her body and felt a sharp pang. She must say yes. He watched her face, troubled, thoughtful. At last she turned from the window. She came and knelt before him, resting her head on his knees. Then she raised her head and looked into his eyes. "What if you are wrong, Peter? What if the Forbath inheritance belongs to someone else?"

He took her face in his hands. "That would be splendid," he said. "I loved you before I knew you had an inheritance of any kind."

She lowered her head and rubbed her lips against his knees. "Yes," she said, "I'll come with you. Not for thirty million dollars. To be with you." She raised her eyes to his. "When?"

"Tonight," said Peter firmly.

Maria shivered. She raised herself onto the bed and pressed herself against him. "I'm frightened," she said. "Oh, Peter, how?"

Peter took her hands. "Something you said last time gave me an idea," he began.

AT THE PAVILION on the banks of the Danube, the cymbalum player, leaning over a rush of sound like a marionette master staging *Götterdämmerung,* shot a quick diabolical glance at Peter and Maria as they entered. The violinists, dropping not a note, bowed deeply. The room resounded with singing, drinking, boisterous Viennese. Seated at long tables, they were toasting each other, the room in general, the host, the wine, and days of long ago. As before, Peter and Maria were greeted by their ruddy-faced host, looking like the "Magyar" illustration from a book of ethnic types. A broad smile beneath his drooping mustache, he gestured to the small room they had occupied before.

A cheer from the Austrians greeted the new arrivals. "No," said Peter softly to Maria. "Tell him we want to stay here." He turned and responded in German to the greetings of the Viennese as though hailing long lost friends. *"Nem. Itt akarunk maradni,"* Maria said to their host. He looked surprised, but hastened to seat them and bring a bottle of wine.

Peter quickly fell into conversation with his neighbor, a small, round, stolid man whose teeth clacked as he talked, and whose shapeless wife sat beside him in her cups, beaming

281

wordlessly. Wine, he had come to Budapest for wine, the man said to Peter. *"Ich bin ein Apotheker,"* he added in his soft Viennese accent, and went on to explain that he sold Hungarian wine at his pharmacy as a tonic.

"Tut, tut," said Peter, grinning in what he hoped the man would take for complicity. "That's against the law, isn't it?"

The little man looked shocked. Indignation suffused his face. "I never break the law," he said finally, coldly.

Peter, continuing to grin, nodded. Then he turned to Maria. In an undertone he said to her in English, "He's a pharmacist. Law-abiding. Very proud of it."

A fat moon-faced man across the table who had been staring at Maria rose at his place. Glass in hand, he leaned toward Maria. *"Gnädige frau,"* he began. Everyone leaned forward to hear what he would say. He paused, then began a slow progression backward. Working his lips with the effort of speech, he continued backward. He passed the vertical, went on, then abruptly, without a word, disappeared from sight. The thunder as he hit the floor brought forth cheers from the company.

They took advantage of the fat man's fall to move down the table. Two men slid sideways to make room for them. Maria quickly fell into conversation with the man on her right, whose somewhat supercilious smile when his face was in repose turned into a marked leer under the impulsion of gaiety. Peter turned to the man on his left. He had a peaked face, and, while appearing to keep his own amusement within bounds—dictated by some inner sense of propriety, or perhaps by his wife, who sat on his far side in regal calm— nonetheless seemed to enjoy the boisterousness of the others. The two conversations went on, animatedly enough, until suddenly behind them there was a wild scream of violins. Peter glanced behind him. Their friends the violinists had come to do them honors.

He swung round to Maria. She leaned to him and said, beneath the din of the music, "No. I think he's more interested in you than in me. Anyway, he's traveling alone."

Peter grimaced. "Also no," he said. "Government statistician. Gets his pension next year."

Maria shrugged. The music got wilder. She rose. "Let's see what this will bring," she said. With that she stepped away from the table and began to dance. The Austrians cheered again, leaning forward or turning around to watch her. Peter watched Maria's hips move in the restrained but steady gyrations intended to set a peasant girl's heavy skirt and anywhere from eight to eighteen petticoats aswing, and any peasant boy's lust afire. She swung about and into the arms of a dark-haired, compact, muscular young man, smiling broadly above a neatly trimmed black beard, who suddenly appeared at her side. The Austrians cried their approval and encouragement. The young man took Maria's hand. He was an expert dancer. The violinists played more and more wildly, Maria wove the complex pattern of the dance, and the young man faltered not once. In a final cry of violins, the dance came to an end, accompanied by torrents of applause.

Maria, breathless, thanked her companion. He bowed deeply and kissed her hand, speaking the ritual phrase— "*Kezit csokolom*"—as he did so. A Hungarian, Peter said to himself: the French and Italians kiss the hand and say nothing about it; Germans and Austrians say they will kiss it, and then don't; only the Hungarians say, "I kiss your hand," *and* kiss it. The young man straightened and stepped up to Peter. "Thank you, sir," he said pleasantly, in faltering English. "Your wife is a wonderful dancer. She is certainly Hungarian."

"Almost inevitable in Hungary," Peter answered with a smile.

The young man laughed. "Come and have some wine with us," he said, switching to German. He pointed to where a young girl sat at an adjoining table. "My fiancée," the young man said.

"With pleasure," Peter answered. With an air of mixed triumph and hopefulness Maria took Peter's arm.

"Klari." The young man presented his fiancée in the prevailing fashion of discounting the family name. She was pretty, with the dark, delicate features sometimes found in Austrian girls. Peter and Maria introduced themselves in the same manner. "And I am Johann," said the young man. He poured them wine. Maria spoke to him rapidly in Hungarian. He laughed and answered her in Hungarian. Then he translated into German for the benefit of Klari and Peter. "She is right. It was Janos. I was born here in Hungary. But my parents took me out in 1956. Now I am an Austrian citizen," he said proudly. He smiled at Maria. "And you are now an American citizen," he said, with a deferential gesture to Peter. Maria allowed her face to become pensive. "Not yet," she said.

Klari plied Maria with questions about Hungary. "Jancsi," she confided to Maria, using the Hungarian diminutive of his name, was not interested in coming to Hungary; it was she who had insisted on this weekend trip.

Jancsi interrupted to observe acidly, "The country's behind the times." Then he smiled teasingly at Klari, and knowingly at Peter. "But how could I refuse? After the baby comes, there won't be much traveling."

Klari blushed. But not overly. Maria regarded her sympathetically. "When is it due?" she asked.

"September," said Klari, half-delightedly, half-worriedly. "I hope we'll be married by then," she murmured to Maria. Jancsi waved a hand expansively, and went on talking to Peter. Klari, he said, was a salesgirl in a small town; he was a skiing instructor nearby.

"Ah?" said Peter. "Where can I get in some good spring skiing in Austria?"

"We have some of the best," answered Jancsi.

"Where's that?"

"The Gräfinstal."

Peter shook his head. "And where's that?"

"An hour or so from Salzburg," Jancsi said. "South, and then up into the mountains."

Maria, who had been deep in conversation with Klari, suddenly swung her head around to look at the cymbalum player. She leaned her head against Peter's, and whispered in English into his ear, "They do want to get married. The obstacle is a shortage of money. Twenty thousand schillings for an apartment." Peter calculated rapidly. Not quite a thousand dollars. He had a little over five thousand German marks with him—about sixteen hundred dollars.

Peter raised his hand to their host. "More wine," he called.

A half-hour passed before Peter judged Jancsi was ripe for the proposition he wanted to put to him. It was only minutes after that, as the two men stood on the terrace outside the pavilion, overlooking the Danube and the rising moon, that Jancsi perceived its merits. "It'll be easy," he agreed with Peter. "You take our Austrian passports and go in the tour bus. All we have to do tomorrow is show our papers to the Austrian Embassy and say we lost our passports. They'll give us new ones, and then we take the regular bus." He shrugged, then spoke sympathetically to Peter. "You're right. You can't leave Maria here. She's too good a person for these bastards," he said with the superiority of a connoisseur. "Klari likes her," he added in final justification.

Peter reached into his pocket and handed three thousand marks to Jancsi. The young man looked at them for a moment, hesitated, then pocketed them. "Klari likes her a lot," he observed. He thought for a moment. "But the driver's got to be in on this," he said reflectively. "He holds the passports once you're on the road. He knows who his passengers are. The others don't matter. They have nothing to do with the formalities." He gestured to Peter. "Wait here. I'll go talk to him."

The music from inside the pavilion scarcely penetrated Peter's ears as he paced up and down on the terrace. He bit his lip as he looked out over the river. The door of the pavilion opened, then shut. Jancsi came up to him, accompanied by a small wiry insect of a man. His jaw was permanently askew, and his eyes glinted in the moonlight. His right hand enclosed the glowing stub of a cigarette. The man nodded to

Peter, spat, and then shook his head. "Very risky business," he said.

Peter nodded in agreement. The man watched Peter for a moment. "I'd have to be compensated for the risk, you understand."

"Of course," said Peter. "Only reasonable. How much?"

The little man shuffled as he calculated. In a low voice, he said, "Twenty-five thousand schillings." Over eleven hundred dollars. Peter saw Jancsi's eyes bulge out.

"I only have German marks," Peter answered.

The little man shuffled again. Again the low voice. "Four thousand marks." Upped it to more than twelve hundred dollars to get a round figure, thought Peter. "Two now, two in Vienna," Peter said.

"Four now," the voice said, stronger.

"Your logic's wrong," Peter said. "If we're caught you'll lose everything. The other way around you'd at least have your two thousand compensation."

Eyes glinting, the little man stared flatly at Peter. He threw away his cigarette. "Four thousand now," he repeated.

At least he's optimistic; the risk must be nil, Peter thought. He withdrew two thousand marks from his pocket. "It's all I have with me," he said. "We'll be together. You can come with me to the bank in Vienna."

The driver spat, and started to turn away. Jancsi frowned. "Wait a minute," he said to the driver. "Where are you going from Vienna?" he asked Peter.

"Munich," Peter answered.

Jancsi reached into his pocket. "You can come by Gräfin-stal? The Hotel Waldstein?"

Peter sighed inwardly with relief. "First place I'll go from Vienna," he said. "Tomorrow night. Tuesday at the latest." Jancsi studied him for a minute. Then he pulled two thousand marks out of his pocket and handed them to the driver. Peter handed the driver the other two thousand marks.

"Eight o'clock," the driver said, pocketing the money. "The Emke coffeehouse."

"The son of a bitch," said Jancsi in broken English as the driver disappeared into the pavilion.

Peter laughed. "A skiing term?" he said in German. He put his arm on Jancsi's. "Thanks, Jancsi. That could be the best investment you ever made." Or the worst, he added to himself as they went inside.

In the car Peter kissed Maria. "Luck," he said. "Blessed luck. For which we have you to thank."

At their table in the pavilion Jancsi kissed Klari. "Luck. Blessed luck," he said. He shook his head in wonderment. "I never expected it here, on this trip," he said. "But like I told you, I knew if we could somehow get onto a rich American— hell, any American, they're all rich—we'd get the money. It was clever of you to have figured out they were in trouble," he added admiringly.

"I CAN'T SLEEP my last night here," Maria said. "I'm too keyed up. Let's walk through the city." Peter nodded. He watched her rise from the bed. She disappeared into the bathroom. When she emerged Peter was dressed. Maria stepped into the Italian print dress, and drew it up over her shoulders. Peter zipped it up. "This dress at least I won't leave behind," she said. Maria looked about her thoughtfully, then she turned and picked up her handbag. "Let's go now," she said quickly.

"You have all your papers?" Peter asked. "Birth certificate? Family papers?" Maria nodded and pointed to her handbag. Silently they passed through the door into the hallway, and out into the morning.

Maria stopped in the driveway in front of her red car. She patted the hood and murmured something in Magyar. Her face clouded. "It's the only thing I really regret leaving," she said to Peter. Not entirely unsentimental himself, he took her arm and waited until she was ready. Then they went out the gate and down the hill.

At the bottom they turned towards the river. Only halfway down the western sky, the moon was already pale, dimmed by the curtain of clear blue, its bottom edged with pale yellow, then gold, then a fiery red, rising out of the east. The city was still.

Slowly, inexorably, as they made their way through Buda and across to Pest the city awakened. A tramway overtook them, a bus passed in the opposite direction. The occasional truck became three, the single pedestrian became a hurrying file, and the traffic piped, and clanged, and hummed in crescendo. Finally, at a large intersection the National Theater loomed before them, its nocturnal promise stale and worn in the daylight. To their right was the Emke Kavehaz. They entered and ordered espressos. Maria grimaced when she tasted hers. "It'll get better as we go along," said Peter confidently.

At five minutes to eight they stepped out into the street. The bus stood a little beyond the Emke, where the Lenin Ring widens. They made their way to it through a scurrying crowd. They were the first arrivals. Peter handed the driver their tickets and the two Austrian passports. "Sit where you like," the driver said affably. Amazing what a thousand dollars can do, Peter thought. He helped Maria in. "All the way to the back," he said to her. It would be less conspicuous, and less likely to provoke one of the legitimate passengers who wanted a more favored seat.

The other passengers arrived *en bloc*—and paid them no attention. The fat man who had fallen over was obviously suffering; he didn't recognize them. The single man ignored them. The statistician, trailing behind his queenly *frau,* wore a smile as though in a reverie. The pharmacist, somewhat pinched, was unobservant. At times, Peter thought, freedom consists of nothing more than being ignored by one's neighbors. The door swung shut, the motor started up, and the bus swung out into the traffic. Maria said nothing, but squeezed Peter's arm. A sudden surge of optimism swept over Peter. He leaned back in his seat. It was an adventure that would end well.

Peter figured they should do the hundred and fifteen miles to the border by ten thirty. The bus retraced their morning walk along the inner ring to the river, crossed the Margit Bridge, and turned right. A mile further on Peter glimpsed a street sign: Becsi ut—they were on Vienna Street. As they came out into open country Peter felt Maria relax; sleep overtook her and her head dropped onto his shoulder.

By nine o'clock they had left the hills to the northwest of Buda, with their coal-mining towns no less depressing than their Western counterparts, behind, and were rolling along the flat of the Danube valley. They skirted a good-sized town, and left it behind. Komarom, Peter guessed. At nine thirty Maria awoke. Her green eyes opened, and for a moment she was silent. Then she said, "For a minute I didn't know where I was." She squeezed Peter's arm. "Now I know."

"If you do, where are we?" Peter asked.

She sat up and looked ahead. "We're coming into Györ," she said. Fifteen minutes later they passed through the metropolis of western Hungary; to Peter it didn't seem vastly different from a large Iowa town. The road turned northwest, with thirty-odd miles to go to the frontier. At Mosonmagyarovar Maria whispered, "There was a terrible massacre here in 1956." The bus rolled on, keeping to the left at a fork in the road. Peter turned to catch the sign. "Bratislava," said the sign to the right; their own read "Hegyeshalom." They were near. A mile further on the bus suddenly slowed; the driver shifted down and brought it to a halt.

Peter peered forward. A knot of fear jabbed into his stomach. A small detachment of frontier guards blocked the road. One strolled to the door and signaled to the driver to open it. The driver obeyed. There was a short palaver, and then the guard, his tommy gun slung across his chest, pointed to the left. The driver started up and swung the bus to the left, onto a dirt country road. He shut the door and spoke over his shoulder to the passengers directly behind him. Peter glanced anxiously into the fields on either side of him. Then the word drifted back with the passengers, and he sighed in relief. "Road closed. Accident up ahead. Detour."

The bus rolled and bounced along the small road, making its way through broad fields. They passed through a wood and back into open fields. The adrenalin had drained from Peter's system and his heartbeat had dropped back to normal when, abruptly, the bus came to a stop. Peter peered forward. There was a simple wooden guardhouse, and a log barrier. Two Hungarian guards stood in the road. Peter saw the driver hand the passports out the window. The guards counted them, then walked up and down the sides of the bus counting the passengers. They handed the passports back to the driver, and one of them raised the barrier. The bus ground ahead. Wide-eyed, Maria clutched Peter's arm. "Was that it?" she whispered.

"Could be," Peter whispered back, astounded at how simple it had been. "If it was, the Austrians will be next."

The driver shifted and the bus moved forward rapidly across a broad field and a ditch. At the far side, just short of some woods, a red-and-white barrier stretched across the road. From a distance Peter recognized the Austrian uniforms. "That was it," he whispered. "One more and we're through."

The Austrian guards went through the passports curiously, handed them back to the driver, and waved him on. The barrier went up. As they passed underneath Peter gripped Maria's hand. "We're through," he said. He glanced at her; she was smiling gleefully, and wiping a tear away at the same time.

"It was so simple," she said.

A burst of elation revealed to Peter how tense he had been; in his relief he waved his hand, and as it passed through a beam of sunlight coming through the bus window he noticed for the first time that morning that the sun was warm.

Not even a mile further on, they bounced onto the cobblestones of a small Austrian village. The freshly whitewashed houses clustered sturdily and respectfully around the baroque onion-dome steeple of the church. In the village square the bus once again ground to a halt. The driver addressed the passengers. "Fifteen minutes' stop," he said. "Engine's heating up. You can get something to eat or drink in the Gasthaus." He gestured over his shoulder, opened the door, and stepped out of the bus. Peter looked about the square. A sign said "Bäckerei-Konditorei"; another advertised "Eisenwaren." Painted in black scroll lettering across the facade of a house somewhat more solid and imposing than the rest were the words, "Burgenlander Gasthaus." The Viennese passengers, somnolent, looked with indifference at the village.

"Come on," Peter said to Maria. "It won't be Viennese coffee yet, but at least it's on the right side of the border."

There were two tables on the sidewalk in front of the Gasthaus. The proprietor, standing in the doorway, bowed them to one. "*Zwei Kaffee,*" said Peter. As an afterthought he asked, "*Mit Schlagobers?*" The proprietor nodded and went inside. "For now we'll celebrate with whipped cream in our coffee," Peter said to Maria. "For lunch it'll be champagne." The proprietor set their coffees on the table. Eagerly Maria tasted hers. Her eyebrows shot up in surprise and pleasure.

"We don't need champagne if we can have this," she said. Peter tasted his. She was right. It was quite the best coffee he had had in years; rich without being oily, strong without being bitter, thick without the sensation of sediment.

"*Austria felix,*" said Peter.

"At last I know what the phrase means," said Maria.

Peter smiled in contentment and looked across the square. The driver was at the rear of the bus, the door of the engine open, but he appeared to be reflecting more than repairing. When he saw Peter looking at him he buried his head in the engine. Behind him a man appeared at the corner of the square. Peter watched him make his way across. He seemed oddly out of place. He was dressed in a well-cut gray suit, and carried himself with elegance, but also with an air of quiet authority. The local landowner, Peter guessed. He came closer. A wide, drooping mustache, neatly trimmed, beneath a long, straight nose; intelligent eyes, a fine mouth. "Man looks just like one I saw in the airport at Budapest yesterday," Peter remarked casually to Maria. "The one who helped me about my visa."

Maria looked up. The man came straight to their table. Courteously, cheerfully, he bowed to Maria, then to Peter. "Good morning, Dr. Kodaly," he said. "Good morning, Mr. Dowling. Would you mind if I joined you?" Maria's eyes widened. The man reached over to the next table and took a chair, then stood awaiting Peter's response. Peter, speechless, stared at him. The man sat down. "I would have preferred an invitation," he said. He smiled at Peter. "After all, I was able to do you a service yesterday."

"Sorry," said Peter. "I didn't recognize you." The man was politely skeptical.

"Really?" he said. "I was counting on the fact that you would."

Maria froze in her chair. Peter bristled defensively. "Is the coffee good?" the man asked.

"Excellent," said Peter coldly.

"I'm glad," the man said, Peter thought irrelevantly. Peter looked across the square at the bus driver. He was still standing by the engine. Summoning up his reserves of politeness Peter asked their self-invited guest if he would like some coffee. "Thank you," he said, and signaled to the proprietor. "Pleasant little village, isn't it?" he commented, glancing about the square.

"Very," said Peter.

The proprietor brought the man's coffee. He tasted it and nodded his agreement to Peter. "You're right. It's excellent."

"You are on holiday?" Peter asked politely.

"No," the man answered. There was a long silence. Then he looked from Peter to Maria and back. "Do forgive me," he said, with a pleasant smile. "I didn't introduce myself. I am Colonel Haris." He pronounced it "Harish." He took a sip of his coffee. "Of State Security," he said. Out of the corner of his eye Peter saw Maria start. "Hungarian State Security," the polite, English-accented voice added.

Peter glanced quickly at Maria. She had gone pale. Colonel Haris looked directly at Peter, his eyes exhibiting amusement. When he spoke his tone was polite, conversational. "As usual, you need help, Mr. Dowling," he said. "Obviously, that's why I'm here." He reached into his pocket and took out a booklet, which he handed to Maria. "Dr. Kodaly, for example, forgot her passport. And you, Mr. Dowling, forgot to pay your bill at the Intercontinental. Very embarrassing for me, having made your reservation for you."

Peter leaned towards Maria. "No oversight at all," he said over his shoulder to Haris. "It will be paid from Vienna."

Maria had the booklet in her hands and was staring at it incredulously. "It's a Hungarian passport," she said. "In my name. It even has my photo."

Haris smiled, reached over, and lifted it out of her hands. He put it back in his pocket. "I'm sure you meant to pay your bill, Mr. Dowling," he said. "Excuse me."

He turned his back to Peter, and Peter saw him signal to the bus driver. The driver slammed the door of the engine shut, went to the front, and climbed into the bus. The other passengers were all in their places. Hastily he started the engine, and the bus began to move away. Peter rose and shouted. He reached over and grabbed Maria's hand, to pull her with him.

"Don't, Mr. Dowling," said Haris reproachfully from his seat, as though asking Peter not to make a social *faux pas*. From the corner of the square from which Haris had come, Peter saw three Hungarian frontier guards, tommy guns at the ready, march into the square. Three more came from around the corner behind which the bus was just disappearing. Peter whirled about. From the other two corners of the square came a half-dozen more Hungarian uniforms.

Peter looked down at Haris. "What the hell have you

done?" he blurted. "Invaded Austria? Your men have no right to be here!"

"Sit down, Mr. Dowling," Haris shot back at Peter, his voice suddenly authoritative. "This is Hungary. Austria is three kilometers down the road. We have taken over this 'Austrian' village, as you think it is, including the false frontier posts, from one of our film companies for the morning," he said. His tone became slightly ironical. "We wanted to receive you suitably."

"I WON'T APOLOGIZE for the deception, Mr. Dowling." Haris's voice had once again become polite, but his smile was not a little bit ironic. "After all, you made your little effort to deceive us."

"With just cause," Peter retorted. He felt Maria's hand in his, icy.

Haris sighed. "A view characteristic of the citizens of the superpowers," he said. "Superpowers, you will agree, always do everything for just causes." His tone was only mildly sarcastic.

"I'm not talking about superpowers," said Peter. "I'm talking about your own laws. Your presidential council decree of March 3, 1970, said that 'every Hungarian citizen has the right to obtain a passport and travel abroad,'" Peter recited. "So why no passport for Dr. Kodaly?"

Haris laughed, not unpleasantly. "Spoken like a true New York lawyer, Mr. Dowling," he said. "Well-briefed. And selective. You chose to omit the clause which reads, 'provided that he complies with the conditions stated in the rules of law.' No doubt it was awkward."

Maria's eyes flashed. "And just what conditions have I not complied with?" she asked heatedly.

Haris regarded her in friendly fashion. "Surely you can't believe, Dr. Kodaly, that your own government knows nothing about your thirty million dollars in America?"

Maria started, then flushed. "That is not why I am leaving Hungary," she said. She looked at Peter in desperation.

Haris waved a hand before Peter could speak. "We know that," he said. "We are aware that you turned down Roessli's proposition, and that Mr. Dowling is more to you than—shall we say, more than merely a legal adviser? Fortunately. It makes it easier to help you."

Peter studied Haris. So they were wired into Maria's lunch conversation with Roessli at Gundel's, and into her room in Buda. That's easy, he thought. But it hardly comes under the heading of helpful. "That's the second time you've mentioned being of help to us," Peter said. "I don't see it."

Haris looked at him reproachfully. "I have been more helpful than you know," he protested. "Let us dismiss those small services yesterday." He waved a hand. "Professional courtesies for a colleague from a superpower." He laughed shortly, then looked closely at Peter. "Are you sure, Mr. Dowling, that yesterday was the first time you ever saw me?"

His fleeting impression when Haris first approached him the day before came to Peter's mind. "I had a feeling yesterday I'd seen you before," he admitted, "but I couldn't recall where. I still can't."

Haris nodded. "You're right. I should have made the occasion more memorable for you. I thought so at the time. But then you were not as observant, perhaps, as you should have been." He inclined his head towards Maria. "I quite understand why. You were, after all, dining with Dr. Kodaly for the first time. At the Kis Royal. Last Wednesday night. When I learned you were there I hurried there myself. In the company of a young man. A German. The one who hijacked your plane from Zurich."

Peter raised his eyebrows. "Of course!" he said. "I saw him on the way out. And you were with him. But what's helpful about that? If I'd obeyed my instincts I'd have come over and punched him in the nose. *That* would have been helpful."

"Pity you didn't," Haris sighed. "You're right, it was too

subtle," he went on in his normal, pleasant tone. "But when we got Satori's message that he was diverting the plane because you were on it, I knew something was wrong. Satori's explanation was that you were a dangerous C.I.A. man who had to be delayed in reaching Munich for the success of a high-level operation. Now, we make a practice, Mr. Dowling, of following the work of those who have followed our own. We Hungarians, that is. We know you are no longer a C.I.A. man. To me this meant that you were somehow interfering with one of Satori's private operations. As he had already sent Roessli here to contact Dr. Kodaly, unsuccessfully, our guess was that you might be working against Satori—or even possibly with him, we didn't know—in fleecing her of her inheritance. We found out later, of course, that you weren't. Just trying to exclude us," added with a touch of censure. "In the meantime, I thought it would be useful to give you a sign that your hijacking was, as you might say, phony." He looked regretful. "But you didn't get the sign."

"No, I didn't," Peter said. "How could I?" He leaned forward. "But do you mean Satori and Roessli work together on fleecings? And together they've been after Maria's inheritance?"

"You see, I'm still being helpful to you," Haris smiled. "Satori's real business, at least up till now—Dr. Kodaly's inheritance seems to represent a new departure, affecting us directly, you understand—has been providing false claimants for unclaimed Jewish assets in Switzerland," Haris went on unsmilingly. "Roessli tells him what funds are available, and what papers to present. Satori and his man Krieger dig up stooges, provide them with the necessary documents from the East German false document center, to which Satori, as a Russian K.G.B. officer, has access. They split the proceeds with the stooges for whatever the market will bear. Anywhere from 50 to 80 percent for Satori and company. The funds go into a Liechtenstein company controlled by Satori, with Roessli and Krieger as minority stockholders."

Peter nodded. "VIGIL," he said.

"Very good, Mr. Dowling," Haris smiled. Maria looked in mystification at the two men.

Peter shook his head. "But Satori is a Russian agent, Colonel," he said. "Surely the Russians are in on this?"

Haris looked pityingly at Peter. "VIGIL owns Melodie Verlag, among other things," he said patiently. "Melodie Verlag is Satori's cover for both his Russian and American operations. You will recall that he's an American agent, too, Mr. Dowling? But Melodie Verlag is really a three-cornered cover. It is also Satori's cover for his real interest, which is VIGIL, about which neither the Russians nor the Americans know anything. A Liechtenstein company." He smiled ironically. "Swiss protection for the secrecy of Liechtenstein companies is never more iron-clad, or fanatic, than when Russians and Americans are concerned. We smaller nations get around more easily, of course." He shrugged. "You will notice Satori has now simplified his operations. Declared his independence, so to speak. He blew up both his American and Russian chiefs in Munich Saturday night. True?"

Peter smiled. "You're very well-informed indeed." To himself he reflected that intelligence services know only what their own interests dictate. Haris knew what the Germans, Russians, and Americans didn't know about Satori. But he apparently didn't know about the K.G.B. plan to kill Otto Miller. And somehow it was that plan that dictated the timing of Satori's "declaration of independence" of Saturday night.

Haris shook his head. "We've known about Satori for a long time. But he's a lieutenant-colonel in the K.G.B. and an officer in the C.I.A. Who are we to criticize the personnel of the superpowers? The Americans don't talk to us, and the Russians don't listen to us. Our best policy—when possible —is to keep quiet and mind our own business. It gives us quite enough to do." He looked at the table reflectively for a moment, then called for the proprietor. "Drei Kaffee, bitte," he ordered. "Which brings us back to our business here," he said gently.

The coffees were brought, and Haris sipped his appreciatively. Maria ignored hers and watched the two men. The Hungarians have decided to scratch Satori by exposing him to the Americans—via me, Peter thought. So much for Haris's "help" there. But he does have Maria's passport in his pocket. "What are the conditions that Maria has to comply with?" Peter asked.

Haris took another sip of coffee. "Two-thirds," he said.

Peter stared at him. "Twenty million dollars for a passport!" Inadvertently, he blurted out, "What in God's name will you do with it?"

Haris eyed him coldly. "That *is* a corrupting atmosphere you live in, Mr. Dowling," he said mildly. "We are not discussing a bribe. What we are discussing is, if you like, a tax, arrived at by mutual agreement." He leaned forward. "You suffer from superpower myopia. You do not understand our situation. We are a very small nation. We will not benefit from your largesse, no matter what happens. The Russians do not give largesse; they take it. But the Russians will not be here forever. One day, I don't know when, they will be gone. Near, of course, but gone. Against that day our job is to keep the country intact. Develop it. Quietly. Very quietly. Tend our orchard. Twenty million dollars buys a lot of trees."

Maria took a sip of her coffee. Peter frowned. "Two-thirds?"

Haris sighed. "Ten million is more than adequate for Dr. Kodaly. As of now, you are in a very difficult situation, Mr. Dowling. Both of you. Dr. Kodaly has tried to escape the country. A very serious offense. You have abetted that escape. With your C.I.A. background the consequences could be incalculable. I remind you that being found in a frontier zone —which is what you are in now—without the required special papers is interpreted by our courts as conclusive proof of an attempt to leave the country illegally."

"In other words, you have us," Peter said.

"Exactly," Haris agreed.

Then why not take us? Peter asked himself. If they put us in jail they can take the whole of Maria's fortune, confiscate it for the State, and that's that. What are we bargaining about? Or are we bargaining? He looked around the square. The guards were still posted at the corners. "And what do you think, Colonel, is the value of an agreement made under duress?" he asked.

"Duress?" Haris regarded him with surprise. "Surely you can't call sitting at a café table drinking excellent coffee duress? What will happen is that we will return to Budapest in my car. At your convenience we will to go the American Embassy where Dr. Kodaly will sign a document voluntarily assigning two-thirds of her interest in the Forbath estate to the Hungarian government in full payment of all claims and taxes by the government. No duress there. You will also sign the document as her legal counsel. Dr. Kodaly will leave the American Embassy with her passport. You can leave Hungary today if you wish."

"But why two-thirds?" Peter asked.

He thought he detected just a flicker of doubt in Haris's eyes. The Hungarian lowered them as he took a sip of his coffee. When he raised them he was smiling at Peter. "If you consider the circumstances, Mr. Dowling, I think you will agree that we are being eminently fair." He paused. "These are perilous times," he went on smoothly. "Financially, as well as every other way. The situation of your dollar has surely not escaped your notice." He shrugged. "We offer a simple, clean arrangement. And prompt. With things the way they are, Dr. Kodaly's ten million dollars might be worth only six tomorrow."

Peter saw it. Haris was stressing the value of time to Maria, when it was his own real concern. If the Hungarians jailed Maria and Peter, the American government, in the ensuing flap over Peter's arrest, might well freeze the Forbath funds. In that case the Hungarian government would touch nothing for years. And if they arrested only Maria and expelled Peter, they no doubt figured that if Peter told the story in the right places the funds might well be frozen anyway. "And in a sense we have you," Peter said.

Haris nodded. "In a sense." He smiled. "A sound basis on both sides for an agreement, Mr. Dowling."

Peter nodded. "In that case, everyone should give a little something to make agreement possible," he said. He calculated quickly; surely the rules of the bazaar indicated an even split. He decided to play the first hand high. "Forty per cent for the Hungarian government would be a more equitable agreement," he said.

Haris broke into a short laugh. Then he sighed and shook his head. "What you really think is that fifty-fifty would be a more equitable agreement," he said. "I don't blame you for trying, Mr. Dowling. You have some strength in your position, as I acknowledged." His face became hard. "But not enough to bargain. Think for a minute. Two-thirds for the government is a more accurate reflection of the true situation." As Peter watched him, Haris slowly moved his gaze to Maria, and then back to Peter.

Peter grimaced inwardly. Damn him, he's right, he conceded to himself. If we were just talking money, I would be right. The difference is my feeling for Maria. Even if I went free eventually, it would be cold comfort to me that the funds were frozen if Maria was still in prison. He nodded amicably to Haris. "The decision, of course, is Dr. Kodaly's," he said.

Maria stood up. "You men complicate things so," she said. "What are we waiting for?"

Haris signaled to the guards. A black Mercedes, its windows curtained in the fashion dear to the Spanish bourgeoisie and Hungarian bigwigs, drew up at the foot of the square. Maria smiled at Peter. "I'm so happy," she said.

He looked at her in astonishment. "At what?" he growled. "Giving away twenty million dollars?"

She gestured impatiently, then took his arm and squeezed it. "Now we can take Ficko," she said, her eyes shining.

Peter laughed and reached automatically into his pocket to pay for the coffee. Haris frowned. "Please, Mr. Dowling. You are my guests."

Peter nodded. "Fair enough," he said. "Tell me, how did you get that marvelous coffee?"

Haris shook his head. "That was the hardest part," he said. "You notice I spoke to the man in German. Had to bring him, with his coffee, from Vienna. Very expensive." He brightened and looked at Peter cheerfully. "A good investment though, don't you think?"

Peter grimaced in agreement. Then he remembered. "My own didn't turn out so well," he said to Haris, irritation edging his tone. "Which reminds me. How much did you pay that bus driver?"

Haris again shook his head. This time he added a sigh. "Still the superpower myopia," he said. "That's not our way in these small countries, Mr. Dowling. We just let him keep what *you* paid him."

SOUNDING not unlike the paddlewheel of a river boat approaching shore, the clack and singsong of spoken Hungarian slowed to a stop amid sibilants, and Maria put down the telephone. "She couldn't believe I was in Vienna," she laughed, "or that I was here with you." She sat up in the broad bed and put their breakfast tray to one side.

Peter, seated on the edge of the bed, took in the picture of tousled hair, shining eyes, and naked, glowing shoulders with delight. "How is she?" he asked.

"She's all right now," said Maria. "She's going back to Zurich today. To the Franziskaner Hotel for the time being." Peter smiled to himself; Eva Kanday in the Franziskaner seemed a long time ago. "And I thought life in the West was peaceful," she said.

"A little crime now and then, a few riots here and there," Peter observed. He put his arm around her. "But you'll find *me* a haven of repose."

Maria shook her head. "From what I've seen and heard," she said, "I won't so long as Satori isn't caught."

"He's on the run," Peter demurred. The telephone rang and he reached for it. "Probably this is the good news now." He picked up the telephone.

"Your call to Munich," said the hotel operator.

"Hello, David?" said Peter.

"You're a model of punctuality," came Killitoe's voice in reply. "Sunday morning at eleven you said 'Forty-eight hours, maybe less.' Forty-six hours later you're there. Wherever you are. Where are you?"

"Sacher's, in Vienna," Peter answered.

"Successful trip?" Killitoe asked.

Peter thought for a minute. "Let's put it this way," he said. "There was a little something in it for everyone. But I came off with the first prize." He stroked Maria's shoulder.

"Mmm," Killitoe sounded more vague than enthusiastic.

"Have they found Satori yet?" Peter asked.

"Not yet. They found his car. It was equipped with a radio impulse sender. That's what set off the bomb. Oddly enough, Helga used somewhat the same device to signal Seger."

"I stumbled onto some useful news about Satori," said Peter. "I'll tell you when I see you. How is Helga?"

"Fine now," Killitoe said. "Up and around. Remarkable girl."

"What about the message?"

There was a silence. At last Killitoe spoke, as though just coming back onto the line. "Uh, we have that, Peter," he said, a trifle hurriedly, "but it better wait until we're together. When are you coming to Munich?"

"Well, we have some things to do here in Vienna—bank, shopping, and so on," Peter said in leisurely fashion. "Then we have to stop off at a place called Gräfinstal on the way. I might try a little skiing. Say, tomorrow afternoon."

302

"We?" said Killitoe, his voice rising.

"Me and the first prize," Peter answered smugly.

"Mmm," said Killitoe. Again there was a silence. Again Peter had the impression that Killitoe was just coming back onto the line. "Ah, Peter," Killitoe said. "I have a message for you from Otto." Killitoe's tone became tentative, almost apologetic. "Otto said to ask you if you've made any progress in finding the Forbath heir."

"That's the we," Peter said triumphantly. "She's with me."

"Ah?"

Again there was the silence. It stretched out until at last Peter said, "David, are you there?"

"Yes, yes, of course," Killitoe answered hurriedly. "Just thinking. Tell me, where is this Gräfinstal? And when will you be there?"

Peter told him where it was, adding, "We'll be there this afternoon."

After a slight pause Killitoe said, "Where will you be staying?"

"The Hotel Waldstein."

Again there was a pause. "Good," said Killitoe. "We'll meet you there this afternoon."

"We?" Peter asked.

"Just a small group," Killitoe said vaguely. "See you this afternoon in Gräfinstal." He rang off abruptly.

Peter looked at the receiver in surprise, then frowned as he put it back in its cradle. "He sounded very strange," he said to Maria. "And I'd swear he wasn't alone."

DRIVING SOUTH out of Salzburg, there was no sky, only a low flat line of steely clouds. Wet and black, a pine forest spilled from them and sloped silently down to the meadow abutting the road. To one side the Salzach, ice green, raced past. A flurry of snow dashed against the windshield. The flakes were large and soggy; touching the glass they turned gray, and in a second had dissolved into a surprised spatter of round, glaucous raindrops. Maria shivered. "It was a short spring," Peter observed.

At Golling the turnoff to the southwest, to Gräfinstal, was well marked. The road crossed the Salzach, followed it upstream for a short distance, then turned abruptly into a narrow canyon and began to climb. Peter could see nothing. The road twisted and turned around sharp corners, cutting off his vision. Above, the treetops merged into the gray mist. Somewhere below was the sound of rushing water. In the cold and damp the inside of the Fiat fogged up; Maria's efforts to wipe off the windshield only transformed the gray condensation into rivulets of water. "An Italian car," said Peter. "It dislikes cold fog as much as I do."

The Fiat leaped over a hump and the road flattened out. Peter imagined they were in a mountain meadow—but he could only imagine it; they were no longer running beneath the clouds, they were in them. "I think this is going to be one of those skiing trips spent entirely in front of a roaring fire," he said.

"Not being a skier myself, that was all I had planned," Maria said.

The road suddenly turned steeply upward. Peter groaned, and shifted down. "If we didn't owe Jancsi money, and a lot more, I'd change our planning right now and head for the Vier Jahreszeiten in Munich," he grumbled.

They crept upward in an eerie silence. The edge of the road no longer showed a strip of dark grass, but slabs of rock and, on and between them, tongues of snow, streaked beneath, fresh on top. Peter negotiated a series of hairpin turns at a crawl, Ficko growling. He glanced upward. For a second he saw a patch of blue race by. "The sky," he said to Maria. "It still exists." The light became whiter. With a final growl the car rolled over a steep summit and left the clouds below and behind. Peter blinked in the bright sunlight.

"Peter!" Maria cried. "It's beautiful!" He stopped the car.

Spread before them was a great bowl. At its far, western edge it was rimmed by jagged peaks, their vertical faces powdered with snow, their rounded flanks smooth white. Domes and ridges sloped and tumbled to the bottom of the bowl, the clear blue shadows of ravines alternating with sunlit promontories. On the north side of the valley a great pine forest, like a dark and immutable shadow on the snow, lay across the mountainside. At its lower edge, stretched lengthwise along the floor of the valley, was the village. Smoke drifted up softly from chimneys, bespeaking warmth, and wafted around the green, bulbous steeple in a blue haze.

"You're right," said Peter. "And no more than we deserve."

They coasted down to the village—one long street that meandered along the bottom of the valley, edged by hotels, inns, shops, apartment houses, and, on the slopes behind, chalets. They found the Hotel Waldstein without difficulty. With terraces and a restaurant on the street, the hotel itself was set back against the edge of the forest. It was clearly the senior establishment in Gräfinstal. Peter asked for a corner room. "And a double bed," he added as he registered.

"We only have twin beds," the clerk murmured sympathetically, "but they are arranged alongside, so that in effect it's a double bed."

Civilization in decline, Peter sighed to himself. To the clerk he said, "In effect." He put down the pen. "Has Lord Killitoe arrived yet?"

"No sir. His Lordship called from Munich this morning, but he and his party haven't yet arrived."

In Austria it *would* be "His Lordship," Peter reflected. "Tell him we're here when he comes, will you?" he said. "And another question. Where can I find Johann, the ski instructor?"

"Just ask in the ski shop," the clerk said. "Downstairs, in the far back corner of the hotel."

In the room Maria, after a brief inspection, a look out one window over the village and then out the other up to the high peaks in the west, turned to Peter and put her arms around him. "Right now I'm going to take a bath. A very hot one."

Peter kissed her. "I'll go down and give this roll of money to Johann. I told him he'd made a good investment; now I have to deliver."

Peter went outside and around the hotel to the ski shop. It gave onto a little square with a fountain. Just opposite was the terminal for a funicular which went straight up the mountain behind, in a swath cut through the forest. Peter glanced up and saw the red double-decker car sliding down from high up. He entered the ski shop. The young man who greeted him answered Peter's inquiry about Johann. "He's up on the Angstjoch this afternoon."

Peter smiled. The Anxiety Saddle. "Is that a place or a state of mind?" he asked.

The young man laughed with Peter. "If you're a good skier, it's just a place. If you're not, it's both," he answered.

Peter looked out at the sunlight. "Can I get up and ski down in what's left of the day?" he asked.

"Twice if you're a good skier," was the answer.

"I only want to do it once," Peter said. "Can you let me have what I need?" The young man nodded, and began to reach into the shelves. Peter changed and called Maria on the telephone. "Jancsi's up on the mountain," he said, when she finally answered. He decided against telling her the name of the mountain. "I'll go up and see him and then ski down."

"Have a good time, don't break anything, and excuse me, I'm dripping wet," said Maria.

"Stay that way until I get back and I'll join you," Peter retorted. He hung up and turned to the clerk. "Now, how do I get up to the Angstjoch?"

"Take the funicular right there." The young man pointed across the square. "At the top there's a chair lift. They'll sell you a ticket for both here at the funicular. At the top of the chair lift is the Angstjoch. Johann should be there. He's on stretcher patrol this afternoon."

His skis on his shoulder, Peter strolled across the square to the funicular and bought his ticket for the ascent to the Angstjoch. He regarded the contraption with admiration before boarding; surely, he thought, the only thing in the village that can vie with the church for age. The angle of the track was some 45 degrees: the double-decker car was arranged so that the two passenger cabins were horizontal, one partly overlapping the other. There was only one loading platform. When the lower cabin had discharged its passengers it sank into a hole in the ground, bringing the upper cabin alongside the platform. Loading also took place in two stages. Peter entered the upper cabin. It resounded with his footsteps. Gräfinstal on a Tuesday at the end of April was not crowded; he was the sole passenger.

A whistle blew. As the door to the cabin was closing a man raced up and slipped inside. Peter smiled politely and the man nodded. He was short and slight, but carried his skis and himself with a distinct air of superiority. A salt-and-pepper beard, scraggly, and obviously in its early stages, proclaimed his youthful, or fashionable, sympathies. His head was covered in a heavy woolen cap. The tip of his beard pointed forward and slightly up; a small rucksack on his chest, and a certain dapper quality, added to the impression of a pouter pigeon.

The cabin moved forward and up. It had gone only a few feet when there was another whistle and it stopped abruptly. Hasty footsteps and the rattle of the door in the lower cabin signaled last-minute loading at the lower level. The funicular resumed its upward progress. Peter looked out into the pine forest. The sun barely penetrated to its interior. The little snow which lay between the trees was old and crusty. A good refuge in a blizzard, Peter thought. "Beautiful trails in there," his companion commented in German, *"Das ist der Schattenwald."*

Peter turned and looked at him in surprise. The small man was looking steadily at him, his expression of superiority unchanged, an awkward—or was it ironic?—smile about his mouth. "Ah, but you are American," he said to Peter in

English. "I said there are beautiful trails in that forest. It is called Shadow Wood." His smile became more pronounced. "You can see why." He spoke in an oddly determined manner.

"I understand you," Peter said. "I happen to have heard a great deal about an Austrian resort called Shadow Wood. The name surprised me."

"But this is it," the man said. He gestured out the window. "Named for that forest." Peter smiled. "But I'm supposed to be in Gräfinstal," he said.

The man smiled tightly. "Same thing," he said. "Years ago when it was just a small summer resort it was known as Schattenwald. But then when it became a big winter resort, stretching all over the countryside, they took the name of the whole valley. Gräfinstal. Maybe it sounded less gloomy." He nodded with some undefined satisfaction. "But the forest is still there." The funicular jerked to a stop, the door of the upper cabin level with the single loading platform. I wonder if Otto Miller knows all that, Peter said to himself.

The door opened and Peter motioned to his companion to go ahead. The man shook his head and stepped back. He gestured to the door. "Please. After you. You are our guest." Peter stepped out and up the steps, the voice echoing in his ears. It had an unusual ring, as though there was always something left unsaid. Also, Peter had the vague impression he was hearing a speech he had heard before, but with new words. Luckily, one could always ski down alone, he reflected.

The summit of the funicular was at the edge of a great half-moon of the forest. There was a large flat area, lightly covered with snow, from which the chair lift began. The chair lift crossed a deep gully and went up diagonally across a high ridge on which rested the right tip of the half-moon. In the ridge, deep in snow, Peter could see a cleft where the chair lift ended. The Angstjoch.

He seated himself in the chair lift, leaving his seat belt unfastened. His companion from the funicular took the seat beside him. As the chair swung forward and out over the gully, Peter heard the funicular grind upward once more, to discharge passengers from its lower cabin. Not a bad system, he thought; keeps down crowding around the chair lift.

Peter looked down the gully and out over the valley. Far below the village was printed on the snow. The chair moved upward across the void. Peter's gaze rose to the trails down the mountainside from the Angstjoch. His companion reached into the rucksack on his chest for something. Peter thought of asking him about the best descent, then changed his mind; Jancsi would give him the best advice. He stared up at the saddle on the ridge. "Since we'll be going on farther together," said the voice next to him, "it really is time we met, Mr. Dowling."

Peter jerked his head to the right. The man's expression was unchanged. Cool. Determined. Superior. The smile was clearly ironical. But his right hand held a pistol aimed at Peter. A pistol fitted with a silencer.

Peter stared at him. His heart pounded violently, and he cursed himself; I should have known; that wasn't a speech with new words I heard, it was the voice I've heard twice before, once on the telephone, once hidden in the bathroom. "I am Alexander Satori," the voice said.

The chair rose gently as it approached a pylon. There was a click as it passed it, and then the chair eased downward on the long loop to the next tower. "Congratulations," said Peter. He watched Satori closely. The cool exterior is only a millimeter deep, he decided. This man is in a rage. Whatever he has in mind nothing is going to stop him.

"I'll explain our program," Satori said. "So that you'll make no slips. When we get to the top we won't put on our skis. We'll not be going down by the usual route. You'll find a path there that leads along the far side of the ridge. To the forest. You and I will go for a walk in Shadow Wood, Mr. Dowling." He watched Peter calmly. "Don't think of trying anything at the Angstjoch. I will not hesitate to kill anyone there you might try to summon to your rescue." He would, too, Peter recognized. The blackmail of the self-pitying. "I will be well away from here long before the discovery of any bodies," Satori added. "Officially, I have already left the village."

"There doesn't seem to be much choice," said Peter.

Satori laughed harshly. "You didn't leave *me* much, Dowling." The chair rose, clicked, and subsided as it passed another pylon. "I leaned to the theory that you were a C.I.A. man for a while. It was my error. I should have known you were after the Forbath inheritance. You made the mistake of trying to ease me out. You tried to destroy me. You and your friend Helga. I am merely reciprocating. It's very simple." He laughed again, still harshly. "I gather from the Budapest license plates on your car that you're traveling with Maria Kodaly."

Peter saw the picture. Satori and Krieger hiding out in the village under false identities. I arrive with Maria. Krieger identifies me to Satori. Probably Roessli had told Satori that Eva gave me a package for Maria. And then the Budapest license plates. Satori follows me up here while Krieger checks out of their hotel for them both, and drives out of the village. He'll be waiting now for Satori at the far side of the forest, down in the fog somewhere. Satori disposes of me in Shadow Wood and, knowing the trails through it from childhood, will not be seen in the village again. If questioned, he can say he left with Krieger; once his beard is shaved and he's rid of that woolen cap the ticket-taker on the funicular would never recognize him. My only chance is the Angstjoch. And expose Jancsi and anyone else there to the risk?

Satori laughed again. "That's another one of your mistakes, Dowling. Maria Kodaly. A natural-enough one. I confess I made it myself at the start." A chill struck Peter to the marrow. The Americans and the Russians don't know about VIGIL, Haris had said. Apparently no one did. Even his London office had been unable to find out anything about it. It was Satori's reserve treasure—even if he didn't touch the

Forbath inheritance. But Maria knew about VIGIL. And Satori knew she knew. From her conversation with Roessli. And Krieger was down below. "Although I must admit," Satori went on, "she's not at all hard on the eyes." His smile became malicious.

Peter glanced ahead out of the corner of his eye. Two more pylons before the top. They were on the steep slopes of the ridge. The chair moved steadily forward beneath the long sagging cables. They were at the low point before the next pylon; after that the ridge loomed up, with its sharp outcroppings of rock. In one motion Peter ducked his head and dived forward.

He heard the pop of the silencer as the thin air whistled past his ears. He remembered to push his legs forward. Sky and snow whirled about him. Then he landed on his knees. There was a sensation of plunging through snow and then sudden, hard resistance that knocked the breath from his lungs. His face was buried in wet and cold, and there was a kind of quivering blackness before his eyes. In the distance he heard two distinct shots.

Frantically, he began to burrow in the snow. He heard a thud. He stopped. Satori's pistol had a silencer, but those shots had been audible. And they came from behind him. So did the thud. Cautiously, he raised his head from his burrow and looked up at the chair lift. Far ahead his own chair glided forward, empty. Overhead the next chair, also empty, followed in parade. He looked forward across the slope. Thirty yards away there was a small black patch on the snow.

Peter raised himself higher and turned behind him. A figure was thrashing through the snow towards him, carrying a pistol. Beardless and bareheaded.

Peter recognized Jake Forman.

"You all right?" Jake shouted.

Peter nodded and whirled to look at the black patch ahead of him on the snow. It moved slightly. Forman reached Peter. "Look out, for God's sake, he's armed," Peter said.

"Not now he isn't," Forman answered. "I got him in both

shoulders. He dropped the pistol when he fell out of the chair."

Peter climbed out of his hole and stood up. "Quick!" he said. "We've got to get down to the village. Krieger may still be there."

Forman nodded, calmly. "He's there, but he's in David and Helga's custody. As he drew up to the hotel Helga recognized Satori following you onto the funicular. I took you and Satori. David and Helga took Krieger."

Peter exhaled. "Then he didn't get to Maria."

"Who's Maria?" Forman asked innocently.

HORST KRIEGER had fallen relatively easily. Killitoe entered the lobby of the Hotel Waldstein first, with Helga trailing behind. Krieger was at the reception desk, checking himself and Satori out under false names. Killitoe, whom Krieger would not have known by sight anyway, merely walked up to him and stuck a gun in his back. Helga, also armed, came to reinforce Killitoe while he frisked and disarmed Krieger.

The only difficulty came from the clerk. Thinking he was confronted by a holdup, he dropped to the floor, slamming the cash drawer shut and pressing various alarms on the way. Then he started to crawl on his belly to the back office. Various porters and kitchen help answered the alarms. Some ducked back into the kitchen; others took refuge behind the furniture. Krieger swung at Killitoe, but Helga, waving her gun, backed him into a corner where he subsided. The bedlam, however, threatened to continue indefinitely. It was brought to an end by Helen Goodman, who had meanwhile come in from the car. After a quick study of the situation, she grabbed a nearby vase and emptied the contents on the other side of the reception desk, then leaned over and bellowed to the clerk, "Calm down and call the police, stupid!"

By the time Jancsi and the stretcher patrol had brought Satori down, accompanied by Peter and Jake, the latter equipped with a pair of boots and skis by Jancsi, the Austrian police had come up from Golling, Helga had Ahmed Seger on the telephone, and Killitoe was trying to get Whitney Ballard on another line. Peter, entering the lobby with Jake on his heels, stopped in surprise when he saw Helen Goodman. At the noise she turned to the door. Her eyes lit up. She opened her arms with a little cry and rushed towards him. Oh, no, thought Peter, frozen where he stood. Helen swept past him and threw her arms around Jake. "I was frantic," she said.

Peter heaved a sigh of relief and strode to the reception desk. Helga, her long blond hair hanging over her shoulders, was behind it, talking to Seger. She winked at Peter. Killitoe, another telephone to his ear and an expression of agonized patience on his face, broke into a triumphant smile when he saw Peter, then scowled at the telephone and said, "No, I want the Ambassador personally."

The clerk, his hair and shirt soaked, leaned over the desk, swallowed, and spoke to Peter in an undertone. "Lord Killitoe and his party have arrived, sir."

Peter picked up the house telephone and called Maria. "Wonderful bath," she said, "but I didn't wait for you. I'm dressed. I was about to go out and look at the village. Was it fun?"

"At the end," said Peter. "Come down and we'll tell you about it."

"We?" Maria asked.

"Our friends are here," Peter answered. He put down the telephone as the Austrian police marched Krieger, looking more like a mournful Great Dane than ever, out of the lobby to the street. Hastily, Peter spoke to the officer in charge. He turned and looked questioningly at Helga, as she put down the telephone. She nodded. The Austrian gave an order, and a policeman went out and returned with the bags from Krieger's car.

Peter bent down and went through them rapidly, as Helga looked over his shoulder. In one suitcase he unearthed two thick packets of hundred-dollar bills and five-hundred-franc Swiss banknotes, together with sixty certificates of a hundred shares each in the company called VIGIL. Peter's eyes popped. They were bearer shares. The other bag had lesser amounts of cash, and only twenty one-hundred-share certificates in VIGIL. Krieger's share. Peter looked over to Killitoe. "Whitney can tell Caxton we got to the bottom of Satori's safe," he said.

Killitoe repeated the message, and then put down the telephone. As he did so, Maria stepped from the elevator. Killitoe paused and looked at her admiringly. Peter rose and performed the introductions, slightly at a loss for not knowing Helga's name. Killitoe beamed; "Baroness von Uxkull," he murmured in a polite, but pleased, tone.

When it came to Forman, Peter said, "*This* is Maria." Forman smiled gravely, and bowed.

Killitoe addressed Peter and Forman. "Otto's leaving tonight," he said. "He'll stop off in Zurich and then come along here tomorrow."

"He has a surprise in store," said Peter. "The real name of this place is Schattenwald. Shadow Wood. It's that favorite childhood haunt of his that he's always talking about." Peter recounted Satori's remarks in the funicular.

Maria's eyes grew large and she stared at Peter. "You mean Satori is here?"

Peter gestured to Forman. "You tell it," he said. Forman's version implied that Peter had not really been in danger, but Maria was not taken in.

She looked at Peter with mixed tenderness and chagrin. "A haven of repose?" she said bitingly.

Peter took her arm. "Now that it's all over, yes," he said reassuringly, his smile nonetheless faintly chastened.

Killitoe intervened, and took Maria's other arm. "The only haven of repose at a moment like this is the bar, dear lady. I'm standing drinks all around. Come."

They moved into the bar, and when all were seated and

had ordered, Killitoe said, "Now, what was it you picked up in Hungary about the loathsome Satori, Peter?"

Peter recounted the story of his and Maria's escape and capture, and Haris's remarks about Satori, finishing up by way of explanation with the final arrangement which had allowed them to leave. As he did so he felt a rising sense of awkwardness at the table. Helga kept her eyes downcast, Killitoe squirmed, and Helen's expression, when she looked at Maria, was a mixture of defiance and pity. Forman seemed preoccupied. Politely, Peter cut the story short. When he had finished there was a long silence. Glad to change the subject, he turned to Helga. "And the message you delivered to Satori," he said. "What was it?"

Helga looked at Peter and then at Killitoe. Killitoe looked at Forman. The latter's tanned face was set in a determined expression. From his pocket Forman took a piece of paper and handed it to Peter. "This is it," he said. "As Helga remembers it."

Peter opened the paper. "Jacob Bekhor," he read. "Colonel, Israeli Army Intelligence. Presently on duty in the Sinai. Born 1921, Veszprem, Hungary, as Laszlo Bakony. Father's name originally Forbath, but changed to Bakony in 1920 to avoid confusion with People's Commissar, 1919 Hungarian Soviet Republic, of same name. Emigrated to U.S. 1938. Served American O.S.S. 1942–1945, Unit 37, under original family name of Forbath. Emigrated to Palestine 1946. Terrorist. On establishment Israeli State entered Army, taking as Israeli name Jacob Bekhor."

Peter looked up at Forman. "He was the next victim marked out by the K.G.B. for Satori to have murdered," said Helga in a small voice.

So *that* was the reason for the timing of Satori's "declaration of independence," thought Peter. This was Otto's "Forbath," that Satori had tried to find out about in Paris. Then Satori's words in the ski lift rang in his ears: "That's another one of your mistakes, Dowling. Maria Kodaly." He turned to Maria with a frown.

At the same moment Forman began to speak to Maria. His tone was courteous, friendly. Peter saw Maria's surprised smile, heard her say *"Igen,"* animatedly, and realized they were speaking Hungarian. Forman went on talking, his tone becoming apologetic, then explanatory, and finally, with a smile and a shrug of his shoulders, he finished. Maria had been watching him with her lips slightly parted. Now she burst into laughter and turned to Peter. "We're cousins," she said. "That is to say, our grandfathers were first cousins. His real name is Forbath."

Forman looked steadily at Peter. "I am Jacob Bekhor," he said. "Bekhor means first-born. My paternal grandfather and Maria's maternal grandfather were cousins," he said. "My father's father was a brother of Imre Forbath. The Emery Forbath who recently died in California," he added firmly.

Peter stared at Forman.

Killitoe coughed. "I'm dreadfully sorry about this, Peter," he said. "We knew about it ever since last Wednesday night, in Satori's office, when the name Forbath came up and you said it was a case you were working on. I checked with Otto when we were in Milan Friday and he told me what it was about. Naturally, we had to inform Jake. I'm sorry we couldn't tell you, but Jake was sent here to help us by the Israeli government on condition that his real name and his official rank not be known. That's why Otto couldn't tell you, either. I had to swear him to secrecy until Jake could get permission from Jerusalem to tell you. He got it yesterday, and came immediately to Munich."

"Well, I'll be damned," said Peter. Satori was on the right track after all.

He looked at Maria. She was looking back and forth from Forman to Peter, an amused smile on her face. Peter remembered their first night in Budapest, then their second visit to the inn, the strain of their attempt to escape, and the fear that had gripped them in Haris's movie-set village. He felt his temper rising. He glared at Killitoe and Forman, then turned to the latter. Holding himself in check, he said flatly,

"Do I understand that you propose to take all of the Forbath inheritance?"

Maria's brows knit together; under the table she laid her hand on Peter's knee. Forman looked at Peter thoughtfully and stolidly, for a good minute. "I don't want that money for myself," he said at last, quietly. "When I have it it will all go into our aircraft production. It will make an enormous difference in our budget. You're aware that we have to buy our aircraft, even from you."

Peter gestured impatiently, as though to say, "My interest is Maria, not the Israeli government." Forman looked at Maria, then at Peter. "In answer to your question," he said evenly, "I don't intend to see twenty million dollars that we need so desperately go to the Hungarian government. Maria —and you—have an obligation to them, if she touches the money first. I have no such obligation." Killitoe stirred in his seat and frowned. "I shall therefore take the full inheritance," said Forman.

Peter leaned forward, but Forman raised his hand. "Maria is, of course, my cousin. Among Hungarians we take these things seriously." Peter could not contain himself. "Thirty million dollars worth of seriously?" he interjected. Maria's hand under the table squeezed his knee in remonstrance.

"No," said Forman. "Not thirty million dollars worth. But since without me Maria will be obliged to surrender two-thirds of the estate to the Hungarians, I will take the full estate, thus eliminating the Hungarian government. I will then keep twenty million," he said. He glanced at Killitoe, who appeared to breathe a sigh of relief. "Maria thus will have her same one-third share," Forman concluded. "I will take what you have already given the Hungarians. Only *they* lose."

Helen Goodman broke into a broad, proud smile and beamed alternately at Maria and Jake. Helga looked amusedly at Killitoe. The Englishman looked questioningly at Peter. "I don't give a damn about the Hungarian government," Peter said to Forman, "but I care very much about

317

Maria and her interests. I think in the circumstances, considering all she's had to go through for this, and the fact that you wouldn't know anything about it otherwise, that fifty-fifty is a more equitable arrangement."

Forman looked at him steadily. "You've just told us you tried that on Haris, and it didn't work," he said. "Since by consanguinity I'm entitled to the entire estate, and since to contest that would be a lengthy, expensive affair, and would result at the best in Maria getting no more, in view of her commitment to the Hungarians, why do you think it's going to work on me?"

Peter started to bridle, then leaned back. He looked at Maria. She was looking at him reproachfully. Not only that, Peter thought to himself, but Forman just happens to be right. He shook his head, as though to clear it. He lifted his glass to Forman. "I just don't seem to be able to win that point," he said with a grin. "I should have gone to that Hungarian school you and Haris obviously both attended." He turned to Maria. She nodded approvingly. "It's a deal," said Peter.

Killitoe broke into a wide grin. "Splendid, ladies and gentlemen," he said. He held his glass high. "Is everyone satisfied?"

"No," said Maria.

With a sigh Killitoe put his glass back on the table. Maria turned to Forman. "You have your obligation to your country," she said to him. "I have mine to mine." She looked steadily at Peter. "Two-thirds of my share goes to Hungary, as we agreed."

Peter looked at her in astonishment. "But it's not necessary now," he said.

"For me it is," she replied. "They need the trees."

Peter groaned and put his head in his hands. "You liked Colonel Haris's speech," he said to her accusingly.

"Yes."

"That leaves you just over 10 percent from an original inheritance of thirty million," he exclaimed.

"That's the way I want it," said Maria firmly. "It's quite enough."

Peter sighed, then shrugged. "And is that agreeable to you?" he asked Jake.

The Israeli colonel spread his hands. "It's her money," he said.

Peter looked about the table, then shook his head. "I've never seen such universal magnanimity in money matters," he commented to Killitoe, a hint of irony tinging his air of resignation.

Killitoe smiled and lifted his glass again. "Oh," he said deprecatingly, "it's not as though anyone really worked for the money." As Peter glared at him and leaned forward to demur, Killitoe raised his hand. "And after all," he added, his smile at its broadest and most infectious, "we are among friends."

Peter leaned back as an echo rang in his mind. "The pleasant, comforting stench of comrades," he recited softly.

Killitoe leaned forward. "I know that quotation," he said brightly, then shook his head. "I've always thought a good man could have both."

319

International
Herald Tribune

Published with *The New York Times* and *The Washington Post*

Paris, Tuesday, May 16, 1972

Bavaria—and All That Jazz

By HENRY PLEASANTS

MUNICH, May 15—With 150,000 other persons, all apparently over five years old, I attended the Bavarian Jazz Festival in a field near here last Saturday night. Any further comment on the audience would be venturing into sociology, and I shall limit myself to the music. The volume was more than adequate: country-and-western, rock, blues—the subtle nuances of each all reached perfectly to the farthest ear. I found no need for the various hearing aids, such as rather loosely rolled, strange-smelling cigarettes, hypodermic needles, and the small lozenges and powders favored by my fellow members of the audience, and politely declined their generous offers. Even they seemed to dispense with them during the rousing, moving, catching, and all-too-brief hour offered by the unquestioned star of the Festival, Eva Kanday. Miss Kanday has everything. . . .

Society Greets the Spring

By PHOEBE HORSEY

PARIS, May 15—Spring finally condescended to come to Paris this year, and the *tout-Paris* promptly sallied forth to

greet it. Among the more striking outdoor
entertainments of this Pentecost weekend
was the dinner given by Whitney and Lillian Ballard yesterday evening on the garden terrace of Laurent. The distinguished
American Ambassador and his chic and
lovely wife had a small circle of friends in
celebration of the success of the American-
backed Bavarian Jazz Festival a day—and
night—earlier. The guest of honor was, of
course, the American impresario Otto
Miller, whose success the festival was. He
was accompanied by the ravishing singer,
Eva Kanday—whose success the festival
also was. Others present were Peter Dowling, a handsome New York lawyer who
was in the company of a green-eyed Hungarian beauty, Maria Kodaly, whose
charm makes the large fortune she recently inherited superfluous; Viscount
Killitoe, from London, squired a striking
German blonde, Baroness Helga von Uxkull; Colonel Jacob Bekhor, the Israeli
industrialist and his fiancée, Miss Helen
Goodman; and the kindly, affable secretary of the Voyagers' Club, Caxton Burroughs. I very nearly mistook a tall Italian
Colonel of Carabinieri in a gorgeous uniform for Vittoria di Sica; he was escorting
the Italian Countess Cristina Laggi, whose
classic Byzantine beauty had a visibly dev-
astating effect on a distinguished German
guest, Ernst Seger. A place was reserved
throughout the evening for a Colonel
Haris, who was apparently detained, and
never showed up. . . .

Music Firm, Rumored
Shaky, To Expand

PARIS, May 15 (NYT)—The rumored
collapse of Miller Enterprises, the American music-publishing firm based in Paris,
as a result of losses incurred at the Bavarian Jazz Festival due to monumental

medical expenses for which the State of Bavaria insists on being reimbursed, and to thousands of gate-crashers who overwhelmed the entrances, was denied here today. Peter Dowling, New York lawyer and a director of the company, said that Miller Enterprises had now taken over the prosperous German concern, Melodie Verlag, under an arrangement with the Swiss government, which is the legal owner through its possession of all the shares of the Liechtenstein investment trust VIGIL. "Otto Miller," Mr. Dowling stated, without revealing the source of the funds, "has recently attracted considerable international capital." . . .
